PENGUIN ACADEMICS

# FICTION
## A Pocket Anthology

SECOND CANADIAN EDITION

Edited by **R. S. GWYNN** *Lamar University*

**WANDA CAMPBELL** *Acadia University*

PEARSON
Longman

Toronto

**Library and Archives Canada Cataloguing in Publication**

Fiction: a pocket anthology / edited by R. S. Gwynn, Wanda Campbell. — 2nd Canadian ed.
(Penguin academics)

Includes index.
Also issued as part of *Literature: a pocket anthology*. 2nd Canadian ed.
ISBN 978-0-321-42797-7

1. Short stories. 2. Fiction—Technique. I. Gwynn, R. S. II. Campbell, Wanda, 1963–III.
Series.

PN6120.2.F53 2008     808.83`1     C2006-906970-0

ISBN-13: 978-0-321-42797-7
ISBN-10: 0-321-42797-1

Editor-in-Chief, Vice-President of Sales: Kelly Shaw
Acquisitions Editor: Chris Helsby
Marketing Manager: Leigh-Anne Graham
Developmental Editor: Charlotte Morrison-Reed
Production Editor: Richard di Santo
Copy Editor: Sharon Kirsch
Proofreaders: Barbara Czarnecki, Nancy Carroll
Production Coordinator: Sharlene Ross
Composition: Integra
Art Director: Julia Hall
Interior and Cover Design: Susanna Brusikiewicz
Cover Image: Getty Images / Michael Boyny

1 2 3 4 5     12 11 10 09 08

Printed and bound in Canada.

PENGUIN
ACADEMICS

PEARSON
Longman

# Contents

# *Alphabetical List by Author*

# Preface

When the *Pocket Anthology* series first appeared a decade ago, the chief aim was to offer a clear alternative to the anthologies of fiction, poetry, and drama that were available at the time. We are very pleased to offer new Canadian editions of the *Pocket Anthology* series, including this second Canadian edition of *Fiction: A Pocket Anthology*.

*Fiction* addresses the four wishes and concerns most commonly expressed by both instructors and students. First, of course, is the **variety** of selections it contains. Admittedly, a pocket anthology has to be very selective in its contents, so we are especially proud that the 40 stories in this book include both established canonical writers from the 19th century to the present, as well as many new voices which reflect the diversity of gender, ethnic background, and national origin that is essential to any study of contemporary literature. We are also pleased that nearly one half of the selections in *Fiction* are by women, and that Canadian, international, and minority writers are well represented. More important, the contents of *Fiction* have been shaped by the advice of experienced instructors who have cited the stories that are most often taught and that possess proven appeal to students. The editors have also made a strong effort to include a number of works that reflect contemporary social questions and thus will easily stimulate classroom discussion and writing assignments. We strongly believe that the works in *Fiction* will provide a reading experience that is not only educational but thought-provoking and enjoyable as well.

Our second aim is **flexibility**—a book that can be used as either a primary or supplemental text in a variety of courses, ranging from an introduction to fiction to advanced literary analysis to creative writing. When combined with one of its companion volumes, *Poetry* or *Drama*, or with novels, collections of short stories or poems by individual authors, or plays available from Penguin, *Fiction* may also be used in introductory literature courses. *Fiction* contains, in addition to its generous selection of short stories, biographical headnotes for authors, an introduction that covers the techniques and terminology of the genres, and a concise section on writing about fiction and on research procedures. A *Question Book* for the Canadian edition, available to instructors on request, offers ideas for discussion questions and writing topics, as well as some additional background information.

The third goal is **affordability.** The second Canadian edition of *Fiction* reflects the original claims of the *Pocket Anthology* series, that these books represent "a new standard of value." Because of its affordability, *Fiction* may be easily supplemented in individual courses with handbooks of grammar and usage, manuals of style, introductions to critical theory, textbooks on research methods, or instructional texts in creative writing.

Finally, we stress **portability.** Many instructors express concern for students who must carry large literature books, many of which now approach 2000 pages, across large campuses in backpacks already laden with books and materials for other courses. A semester is a short time, and few courses can cover more than a fraction of the material that many bulkier collections contain. Because most instructors focus on a single genre at a time, *Fiction* and its companion volumes, *Poetry* and *Drama*, remain compact yet self-contained editions that, if a snug fit in most pockets, we trust that instructors and their students will be grateful for a book that is a more manageable size.

In its second edition, the *Pocket Anthology* series offers increased Canadian content, an updated critical framework, and enhanced audio/visual pedagogy with the addition of **MyLiteratureLab** at no extra charge. This extensive website provides a number of resources that will be of interest to users of this new edition. It contains interactive readings and lectures on a variety of well-known works, biographical information about authors, a glossary of literary and critical terms, and many other useful multimedia resources for your course.

In closing, we would like to express our gratitude to the instructors who reviewed all or part of the Canadian *Pocket Anthology* series and offered invaluable recommendations for improvements:

Julia Denholm, Langara College
Cecily Devereux, University of Alberta
Fraser Easton, University of Waterloo

Thomas Ezzy, Dawson College
Melanie Fahlman Reid, Capilano College
Gordon Fulton, University of Victoria
James Gifford, University of Lethbridge
Christopher E. Gittings, University of Alberta
Kathleen Irwin, University of Regina
Tobi Kazakewich, University of Ottawa
Christine Kerr, Champlain Regional College
Ric Knowles, University of Guelph
Jean-François Leroux, University of Ottawa
Kathy McConnell, Dalhousie University
Ninian Mellamphy, University of Western Ontario
Paul Milton, Okanagan University College
Paul Matthew St. Pierre, Simon Fraser University
Dawn Neill, University of Victoria
Catherine Nelson-McDermott, University of British Columbia
Miriam Pirbhai, Wilfred Laurier University
Nicole C. Rosevere, University of Winnipeg
Mary Silcox, McMaster University
Anna Smol, Mt. St. Vincent University
Cheryl Suzack, University of Alberta
Eleanor Ty, Wilfred Laurier University
Paul Tyndall, University of British Columbia
Lynn Wells, University of Regina
Patricia Whiting, University of Ottawa
Lorraine York, McMaster University

*R. S. Gwynn*
*Lamar University*

*Wanda Campbell*
*Acadia University*

**Wanda Campbell** has edited several other books, including *The Poetry of John Strachan* and *Hidden Rooms: Early Canadian Women Poets*. She has authored two collections of poetry, *Sky Fishing* and *Haw [Thorn]* and has published academic articles, fiction, and poetry in journals across Canada. She teaches Literature and Creative Writing at Acadia University in Wolfville, Nova Scotia.

**R. S. Gwynn** has edited several other books, including *Literature: A Pocket Anthology*, *Drama: A Pocket Anthology*, *Fiction: A Pocket Anthology*, *The Longman Anthology of Short Fiction* (with Dana Gioia), and *Contemporary American Poetry: A Pocket Anthology* (with April Lindner). He has also authored five collections of poetry, including *No Word of Farewell: Selected Poems, 1970–2000*. In 2004 he was awarded the Michael Braude Award for verse from the American Academy of Arts and Letters.

Professor Gwynn teaches at Lamar University in Beaumont, Texas.

# Introduction

## The Telling of the Tale

Alice Munro writes that "a story is more like a house [than a road]. Everybody knows what a house does, how it encloses space and makes connections between one enclosed space and another and presents what is outside in a new way." Stories are dwellings we love to build, to visit, and to inhabit. To respond to the simple magic of the storyteller's art is to enact one of the human race's oldest rituals, but before we can begin to examine the elements of literary fiction we must bear in mind that literature in its written form is historically a recent innovation; indeed, its two most common modern forms, the short story and the novel, have been in existence for little more than two centuries. Yet long before the invention of writing, for thousands of years ancient peoples developed complex **oral traditions** of literature; these stories, dealing with the creation of the cosmos and the origins of gods and goddesses, formed a body of **myths,** supernatural narratives widely believed to be true by the people of a given culture, and **legends,** popular stories about characters and events that may contain trace elements of historical truth. Even in modern societies, elements of this primitive folklore survive in regional or ethnic tales passed on through the generations, most often taking the written form of **folk tales** collected by literary scholars; **fairy tales,** like Charles Perrault's "Beauty and the Beast" or Hans Christian Andersen's "The Little Mermaid"; **beast fables** with animal characters; or **parables** like those found in the Gospels. Many of these, especially the fables and parables, are to some degree **didactic,** with the narrative events illustrating a **moral** that is either stated or implied. A fable is a short, non-realistic narrative that is told to illustrate a universal moral concept. A parable is similar but generally contains realistic characters and events. Thus, Aesop's fable of the tortoise and the hare, instead of telling us something about animal behaviour, illustrates the virtue of persistence against seemingly unbeatable competition. The parable of the Good Samaritan tells the story of a man who is robbed and beaten and eventually rescued by a stranger of another ethnicity in order to define the concept of "neighbour" for a questioning lawyer.

Even in modern societies, other ancient forms of oral literature still enjoy a good state of health. These include **anecdotes,** accounts of single incidents usually involving a well-known person, and **riddles** and **jokes** of all types, which often seem to spring into circulation overnight and often unwittingly mirror the basic situations and coarse humour of venerable **fabliaux**—short, realistic tales from the Middle Ages that often turn on a bawdy situation. Recently, much attention has been given to **urban legends,** so named by folklorist Jan Brunvand, which are short narratives involving grotesque incidents that are widely accepted as true. When myths and legends are assembled around the exploits of a great hero, the result is the **folk epic,** a long narrative in elevated style that is generally considered a starting point for any culture's literary history. Like most types of oral folk literature, epics were originally composed in verse for the sake of memorization, but they otherwise contain the same elements as modern literary forms like the short story and novel. For example, the individual **episodes** of Homer's *Odyssey*—such as Odysseus outwitting the Cyclops or his adventures with the sorceress Circe—can stand alone as exciting tales and also can fit into the larger structure of the epic, like chapters in a novel. Later authors, living in societies that had invented writing, consciously imitated the style of folk epics in composing **literary epics;** the *Aeneid* by Virgil (70–19 B.C.) and *The Divine Comedy* by Dante (1265–1321) are two famous examples. In the Middle Ages, **romances,** written in both verse and prose, gained great popularity among all social classes. These tales of chivalry involving a knightly hero and a series of exciting, if improbable, adventures were ridiculed by Miguel de Cervantes (1547–1616) in *Don Quixote*, a realistic account of an impoverished Spanish gentleman driven mad by reading too many romances. The eventual form that Cervantes gave Don Quixote's adventures was perhaps influenced by **picaresque novels** like the anonymous *Lazarillo of Tormes* (c. 1450), which involved a young orphan (or *pícaro*, Spanish for "rascal") in a series of loosely connected adventures. These picaresque tales are rightly considered the ancestors of modern realistic fiction. Many novels, from Mark Twain's *The Adventures of Huckleberry Finn* to J. D. Salinger's *The Catcher in the Rye* and Aritha Van Herk's *No Fixed Address*, borrow their structure from the picaresque novel, and the modern short story is indebted to its often stark level of realism.

## The Short Story

There is no agreement on the precise origins of the modern short story. One important influence in its development was the Italian **novella** of the late Middle Ages and Renaissance. The most famous collection of these realistic prose narratives is *The Decameron* by Giovanni Boccaccio (1313–1375). *The Decameron*, in which the individual stories are narrated by young men and women who have taken to the country to escape a plague, is an example of a **frame tale,** in which the stories are "framed" by a larger narrative. The famous Arabian collection *A Thousand and One Nights* is one of the earliest examples of this genre (a structure that is ressurrected in films like *Pulp Fiction* and *Magnolia*). In translation, these tales were popular in other countries and widely imitated. In writing his plays, William Shakespeare frequently borrowed from Italian writers; his tragedy *Othello* takes its plot from a sensational novella by Giraldi Cinthio. We still use the term novella for short stories that are long enough (usually over 15 000 words) to be published separately in book form. Count Leo Tolstoy's *The Death of Ivan Ilyich* is a classic Russian example, and Ernest Hemingway's *The Old Man and the Sea* is one of the best-known novellas in American literature.

The first half of the nineteenth century is the great period of the growth of the short story as a distinct **literary genre,** or type, and its rise takes place in many countries at roughly the same time. Many reasons for this rapid development could be put forth, but perhaps the most important was the literary market established by newspapers and magazines aimed at middle-class audiences. The United States, with its increasingly high rate of literacy and expanding middle class, led the way in this period; Washington Irving's tales, like "Rip Van Winkle" and "The Legend of Sleepy Hollow," were among the first American writings to attain international popularity. Edgar Allan Poe, the first great theorist of the short story and one of its notable practitioners in this period, supported himself primarily (although not very prosperously) as a magazine editor and contributor, and thus had a large personal stake in promoting short fiction. Poe's influential review of Nathaniel Hawthorne's *Twice-Told Tales* in 1842 first stated the theory that a short story ought to be a unified artistic creation, as carefully shaped as a sonnet.

> *A skillful literary artist has constructed a tale. If wise, he has not fashioned his thoughts to accommodate his incidents; but having conceived, with deliberate care, a certain unique or single effect to be wrought out, he then invents such incidents—he then combines such events as may best aid him in establishing this preconceived effect. If his very initial sentence tend not to the outbringing of this effect, then he has failed in his first step. In the whole composition there should be no word written, of which the tendency, direct or indirect, is not to the one pre-established design. And by such means, with such care and skill, a picture is at length painted which leaves in the mind of him who contemplates it with a kindred art, a sense of the fullest satisfaction.*

This idea of the *single effect* is perhaps Poe's most important contribution to the development of the short story as a serious literary genre. Most of Hawthorne's and Poe's stories are perhaps more properly termed **tales,** narratives that contain elements that are exotic or supernatural and that depart from the level of ordinary experience. Poe himself established many of the conventions of the horror, science fiction, and detective tales still being written and read today. **Formula fiction,** which rigidly follows the clichés and conventions of a particular genre, is sometimes half-affectionately called **pulp fiction** (the source of the title for Quentin Tarantino's film), a reminder of the low-grade paper once used in inexpensive magazines. Still, the tale remains a lively tradition among serious artists as well. Among the contemporary stories collected in this volume, selections by Borges, Barthelme, Carrier, Walker, King, Shields, and others show their debt to the tradition of the tale.

The short story continued to develop in the nineteenth century, and its evolution was part of the larger literary movement of **realism,** which profoundly influenced the arts in the middle years of the nineteenth century. Defined as the "truthful treatment of material" by William Dean Howells, realism focused on unidealized explorations of common everyday life expressed in clear and direct prose. It has been rightly noted that realism represents the effect of democracy on literary history. Celebrating its appearance as early as 1837, Ralph Waldo Emerson noted, "The literature of the poor, the feelings of the child, the philosophy of the street, the meaning of household life, are the topics of the time." **Naturalism,** an outgrowth of realism that emerged in the second half of the nineteenth century, also proved influential because it joined realistic treatments of everyday life with understandings of human behaviour drawn from the new sciences of psychology and sociology. Both realism and naturalism remain vital currents in contemporary short fiction, as stories here by Alistair MacLeod and Jhumpa Lahiri will attest.

The twentieth century saw the short story rise to its highest level of popularity and just as rapidly decline in its influence as a literary form. In the second half of the century, many of the established magazines that regularly ran serious fiction ceased publication. Reading tastes have changed, and there is increased competition from movies, television, and the Internet. Still, the pages of so-called little magazines and literary quarterlies continue to provide outlets for publication, and new writers seem undeterred by the prospect of being paid with little more than what one disgruntled writer has called "two free copies of what I've already got." Almost every writer of short fiction prominent today first appeared in small-circulation periodicals of this type, and many have continued to publish in magazines that can offer, instead of money, prestige and a discriminating readership numbering in the hundreds. Indeed, the little magazines traditionally have been hospitable to many kinds of **experimental fiction** that editors of commercial magazines would never have considered. If the quantity of contemporary short fiction being published has shrunk from what it was in prior decades, the quality, one might argue, has remained the same or even improved. When we look at lists of recent winners of the Governor General's Award and the Man Booker, Pulitzer, and Nobel prizes, we discover many writers who have counted the short story as their first genre.

## Reading and Analyzing Short Fiction

We read for many reasons. In our daily lives most of our reading is strictly utilitarian—it is part of our jobs or education—or informational, as we scan the headlines of a daily newspaper for current events, business trends, or sports scores. We read short stories and other types of fiction for differing reasons. Sometimes our motive is simply to be entertained and to pass the time. Reading matter of this type is usually termed **escapist literature** and includes such popular categories as romance and detective novels, science fiction tales, westerns, and gothic novels. But literary fiction offers more than entertainment, making us think while engaging our imaginations. A short story that we can treat as a serious work of art will not yield all of its subtlety at first glance; in order to understand and appreciate its author's achievement fully we may have to examine its components—its plot, characterization, point of view, theme, setting, style, and symbolism—noting how each part contributes to the story's overall effect. Flannery O'Connor has warned that discussing story writing in terms of plot, character, and theme is like trying to describe the expression on a face by saying where the eyes, nose, and mouth are, and yet it is one way to explore the layered complexity of a story. The following exploration of aspects of the short story draws examples from "Reunion," a brief story by a modern American master of the genre, John Cheever (p. 162).

## *Plot*

In his discussion of tragedy in the *Poetics*, Aristotle (384–322 B.C.) gives first importance to plot as an element of a play, and most readers would agree that it holds a similar position in a work of fiction. Indeed, if we tell a friend about a short story we have enjoyed, we will probably give a **synopsis,** or brief summary, of its incidents. In the case of a very brief story like "Reunion," this synopsis is only a few sentences long:

> *In "Reunion" the narrator, a teenaged boy travelling by train, meets his estranged father during a stop for lunch in New York City. Over the course of an hour and a half, the father's alcoholism and potentially abusive personality are revealed. The story ends with the narrator boarding his train, indicating that this was the last time he saw his father, possibly by choice.*

Plot, according to Raymond Bradbury, "is no more than footprints left in the snow *after* your characters have run by on their way to incredible destinations." More simply, **plot** may be defined as a story's sequence of incidents, arranged in dramatic order. One is tempted to insert the word "chronological," but doing so would exclude many stories that depart from this strict ordering of events. Although its use is more characteristic in longer works like novels, many stories employ the **flashback** to narrate incidents in the past. Michael Winter's "Archibald the Arctic" begins with the policemen arriving at Gabriel English's door and then goes back in time to relate events that led up to that moment. Margaret Atwood's "Happy Endings" dispenses with a single plot line entirely, offering numerous possibilities for the fates of her characters. Conversely, writers sometimes use **foreshadowing** to provide hints of future actions in the story; an effective use of foreshadowing prevents a story's outcome from seeming haphazard or contrived. Of course, the manner in which stories handle time is largely illusory. During scenes with dialogue and action, time is slowed down by descriptive and explanatory phrases. At other times, stories cover gaps in chronology or leap over uneventful periods with transitional phrases and passages; the opening sentence of the second paragraph of "Reunion" ("We went out of the station and up a side street to a restaurant") compresses into a second or two an action that in reality would have taken at least several minutes. Even though "Reunion" does not take serious liberties with chronological time as we experience it, the ninety minutes of action in the story are compressed into about ten minutes of the reader's time. A plot like this, in which the action is more or less continuous within a single day, is called a **unified plot;** one that stretches over weeks or even longer periods and thus consists of isolated scenes connected by a thin tissue of transitional devices is called an **episodic plot.**

When we speak of the **dramatic structure** of a story, we refer to the exact way in which our emotional involvement in its plot is increased and relaxed. As Janet Burroway observes of the short story in *Writing Fiction,* *"Only* trouble is interesting." If we are not quickly engaged by the situation of a story and caught up in its plot, then we pronounce the cruellest of all critical verdicts on it by closing the book. The first part of this dramatic structure is the **exposition,** which provides the reader with essential information—who, what, when, where—he or she needs to know before continuing. Although writers of sophisticated fiction may try to disguise the fact, they often begin their stories with a version of the "Once upon a time" opening common to fairy tales. A variation on this type of beginning, called the **in medias res** ("in the middle of things") opening after the conventions of the old epic poems, may actually open with a "blind" bit of action before supplying its context.

The exposition of "Reunion" is fairly straightforward; in the first paragraph we learn who (Charlie and his father), what (a lunchtime meeting between trains), when (noon to 1:30 P.M.), and where (in and near Grand Central Station in Manhattan). Cheever might have begun the story with a slightly more "dramatic" sentence ("At twelve o'clock sharp I saw him coming through the crowd"), but he would have had to provide the essential contextual information in short order to avoid unnecessarily confusing the reader.

Exposition in a story usually describes a stable situation, even if it is not an entirely happy one. Charlie tells us that his parents' divorce is three years old and that he has not seen his father in that time. If he had not taken the step of writing the letter arranging the "reunion," that state of affairs might have gone on indefinitely. The appearance of "trouble" constitutes the second part of a plot, the **complication,** which is the appearance of some circumstance or event that shakes up the stable situation and begins the **rising action** of the story. Complication in a story may be either external or internal, or a combination of the two. A stroke of fortune that affects a character, such as illness or accident, is a typical example of an external complication, a problem that the character cannot ignore. An internal complication, in contrast, may not be immediately apparent, for it may result from a character's deep-seated uncertainties, dissatisfactions, and fears. The external complication in "Reunion" is the father's series of confrontations with waiters; the internal complication is Charlie's growing sense of pity and revulsion. Typically, the complication of a plot is heightened by **conflict** between two characters who have different personalities and goals. Charlie is overjoyed to see his father at the beginning of the story but, despite his knowledge that he will grow up to "be something like him," Charlie is more than eager to escape his father's company at the end, perhaps in an unconscious effort to run away from his own "future and [his] doom."

The body of a story is called the rising action and usually contains a number of scenes, involving action and dialogue, that build to **moments of crisis**—points in the story where a resolution of the complication momentarily seems at hand but quickly disappears. Aristotle used the term **peripety** for these moments of reversal, as the hopes of the characters rise and fall. Thus, in "Reunion" all that needs to be resolved, at least on the surface, is for the characters to order lunch, eat, and return in time for the departing train. The father's increasingly obnoxious behaviour, however, keeps postponing this resolution until the reunion has turned from a happy occasion into something very different. Unlike most stories, "Reunion" has a rising action as rigidly structured as a joke, with its four similar restaurant scenes that gradually escalate in absurdity as the father's senseless rage increases.

The central moment of crisis in a plot is the **climax,** or moment of greatest tension, which inaugurates the **falling action** of the story, in which the built-up tension is finally released. Some stories, particularly those involving a heavy use of suspense, have a steep "dramatic curve" and the writer uses all of his or her skills to impel the reader toward the final confrontation. Among writers included in this anthology, Edgar Allan Poe is the master of this kind of plot construction. Often one encounters the **trick ending** (also called the **O. Henry ending** after the pen name of William Sidney Porter, a popular writer of the late nineteenth century). A climax such as this depends on a quick reversal of the situation from an unexpected source; its success is always relative to the degree to which the reader is surprised when it occurs. The ending of Kate Chopin's "The Story of an Hour" hits both its protagonist and its reader with the same surprise. More typically, modern short stories instead rely on climactic devices that are somewhat subtler than unexpected plot twists. Many modern writers have followed James Joyce's lead in building not to a climactic event but to a moment of spiritual insight or revelation, what Joyce termed an **epiphany.** Epiphanies can take many forms, from an overheard chance remark that seems significant in the context of the story to a character's unpitying gaze at himself in a mirror. In the hands of a melodramatic writer insistent on sentimental happy endings, "Reunion" might have concluded with Charlie delivering a "tough love" sermon to his father, who would then fall to his knees and beg his son's forgiveness, having seen the error of his ways. Cheever's more realistic method of climax is, in this case, to avoid the confrontation altogether as Charlie escapes to his train.

The final part of a plot is the **dénouement,** or **resolution.** The French term literally refers to the untying of a knot, and we might compare the emotional release of a story's ending to a piece of cloth that has been twisted tighter and tighter and is then untwisted as the action winds down. The dénouement returns the characters to another stable situation. Just as fairy tales traditionally end with "And they lived happily ever after," many stories conclude with an indication of what the future holds for the characters. In the case of "Reunion," we return to the estrangement between Charlie and his father that existed at the beginning of the story, although this time all indications are that it will be a permanent one. A story's dénouement may be termed either closed or open. A **closed dénouement** ties up everything neatly and explains all unanswered questions the reader might have; a typical example is the "Elementary, my dear Watson" explanation of any remaining loose ends, which is provided by the sleuth Sherlock Holmes in the final paragraphs of Arthur Conan Doyle's famous tales. An **open dénouement** leaves us with a few tantalizing questions; the last phrase of "Reunion," which consciously mirrors the story's opening sentence, does not explicitly state *why* Charlie never sees his father again. Was it strictly his own choice? Did the father die soon after their meeting? Were other factors involved? We do not know, of course, and such an ending invites us to speculate.

One final word about plots: The fledgling writer attempting to invent a totally original plot is doomed to failure, and it is no exaggeration to say that there is nothing (or at least not much) new under the sun where plots of short stories are concerned. As Willa Cather maintains, "There are only two or three human stories and they go on repeating themselves as fiercely as if they had never happened before." Plots may be refurbished with new characters and settings, but they still draw on what psychologist Carl Jung called **archetypes,** universal types of characters and situations that all human beings carry in their unconscious mind. Plots deriving from these archetypes may be found in ancient mythologies, in fairy tales, and even in contemporary fiction. Among the most familiar are the triangle plot, a love story involving three people; the quest plot, which is unified around a group of characters on a journey; and the transformation plot, in which a weak or physically unattractive character changes radically in the course of the story. "Reunion" is an example of one of the most widely used of all archetypal plots, the **initiation story.** In a plot of this type, the main character, usually a child or adolescent, undergoes an experience (or **rite of passage**) that prepares him or her for adulthood. In this book, such stories as James Joyce's "Araby," Alice Munro's "Boys and Girls," Michael Winter's "Archibald the Arctic," and Madeleine Thien's

"Simple Recipes" share the same archetype, although they differ in many other respects.

## *Characterization*

Every story hinges on the actions undertaken by its main character, or **protagonist,** a term drawn from ancient Greek tragedy (literally "first debater") that is more useful in discussions of fiction than such misleading terms as hero or heroine. Additionally, stories may contain an opposing character, or **antagonist,** with whom the protagonist is drawn into conflict. In many modern stories, there is little, in any traditional sense, that is heroic about the protagonists; it may be more accurate to use a negative term, **anti-hero,** to designate one who occupies centre stage but otherwise seems incapable of fitting the traditional heroic mould. Indeed, writers of the last century have often been so reluctant to seem didactic in presenting characters that are "moral beacons" that they go to the opposite extreme in presenting protagonists whom we regard with pity or even disgust, rather than with admiration.

A character in a short story may be termed either a **flat character** or a **round character,** depending on the depth of detail the writer supplies. In "Reunion," the father is essentially a flat character, rendered with a few quick strokes of the pen and reduced to a single personality trait, his alcoholic rudeness. Minor flat characters in stories are often **stock characters,** stereotypes who may be necessary to advance the plot but otherwise are not deserving of more than the barest outlines of description. Round characters are given more than one trait, some of which may even seem contradictory, and are explored in depth as the author delves into the character's past and even into his or her unconscious mind. Characters of this type, usually a story's protagonist, begin to approach the level of complexity that we associate with real human beings.

**Development** and **motivation** are also important in any consideration of a story's characters. Characters can be either **static** or **dynamic,** depending on the degree to which they change in the course of the story. In "Reunion," the father is a static character. His personality was fixed long before the story opens, and there seems no likelihood that he will ever alter his course. But Charlie does attain some understanding in the course of the story, even if it is at the cost of his own disillusionment

goes far beyond a simple statement like "The last time I saw my father was a week ago in Grand Central Station." In general, first-person stories may seem more immediate than third-person stories, but they are limited by the simple fact that the narrator must be present at all times and must also have some knowledge of what is going on. If, for example, an attempt had been made to tell "Reunion" from the point of view of one of the restaurant waiters, the narrator might have had to resort to eavesdropping on Charlie and his father in order to report their circumstances. The ability of the narrator to tell the story accurately is also important. An **unreliable narrator,** either through naïveté, ignorance, or impaired mental processes, relates events in such a distorted manner that the reader, who has come to recognize the narrator's unreliability, literally has to turn the character's reporting on its head to make sense. Imagine how we would read "Reunion" if it had been told from the boozy, self-deluding point of view of Charlie's father.

**Third-person narration,** by definition, employs a **non-participant** narrator, a voice of authority that never reveals its source and is capable of moving from place to place to describe action and report dialogue. In third-person stories, the question of reliability is rarely an issue, but the matter of **omniscience,** the degree to which the "all-knowing" narrator can reveal the thoughts of characters, is. **Total omniscience** means that the narrator knows everything about the characters' lives—their pasts, presents, and futures—and may reveal the thoughts of anyone in the story. An **editorial point of view** goes even farther, allowing the godlike author to comment directly on the action (also called **authorial intrusion**). Most contemporary authors avoid total omniscience in short fiction, perhaps sensing that a story's strength is dissipated if more than one perspective is used. Instead, they employ **limited omniscience,** also called **selective omniscience** or the **method of central intelligence,** thereby limiting themselves to the thoughts and perceptions of a single character. This point of view is perhaps the most flexible of all because it allows the writer to compromise between the immediacy of first-person narration and the mobility of third-person narration. A further departure from omniscience is the **dramatic point of view** (also called the **objective point of view**). Here the narrator simply reports dialogue and action with minimal interpretation and does not delve into characters' minds. As the name implies, the dramatic point of view approximates the experience of reading a play; readers are provided only with set descriptions, stage directions, and dialogue, and thus must supply motivations that are based solely on this external evidence.

Technically, other points of view are possible, although they are rarely used. Stories have been told in the second person using "you" but they are rare. A plural point of view also may be employed, but such points of view are difficult to sustain and may quickly prove distracting to readers. Also, there is an unwritten rule that point of view should be consistent throughout a story, although occasionally a writer may utilize multiple perspectives to illustrate how the "truth" of any incident is always relative to the way in which it is witnessed.

## *Theme*

We have already discussed the manner in which fables and other types of didactic literature make their purpose clear by explicitly stating a moral or interpretation at the end of the story. Literary fiction, however, is usually much more subtle in revealing its **theme,** the overall meaning the reader derives from the story. Most of the early reading we did as children probably fell into two distinct categories—sheer entertainment or overt didacticism—with very little middle ground. Thus, many readers, coming to serious fiction for the first time, want either to avoid the tedious search for a "message" or to complain, "If the author was trying to say that, then why didn't she just come right out and *say* it!" To complicate matters further, the theoretical manner in which we analyze stories and the preconceptions we bring to bear on them may result in multiple interpretations of meaning. No single statement of theme is likely to be the "correct" one, although it is fair to say that some seem more likely than others. In fact, according to Flannery O'Connor, "When anybody asks what a story is about, the only proper thing is to tell him to read the story. The meaning of fiction is not abstract meaning but experienced meaning, and the purpose of making statements about the meaning is only to help you to experience that meaning more fully."

What, then, is the theme of "Reunion"? A reader insistent on a moral might denounce Charlie's father, commenting on alcohol's destructive effects. Another reader, slightly more charitable, might recognize alcoholism as a disease and feel some amount of sympathy for the father. Yet another, perhaps entirely too self-righteous, might fault Charlie for running away from his father, interpreting the older man's actions as a subconscious cry for help. If we investigate Cheever's own troubled biography and note his own serious problems with both parenthood and alcoholism, we may read the story as a psychological confession, with Cheever himself simultaneously playing the roles of father and son. With so many possibilities before us, it is perhaps best to summarize a story's theme broadly:

> *"Reunion," like most initiation stories, is about growth through loss of innocence. Children have to learn, often through painful experience, that they are not responsible for their parents' well-being, and sometimes they must distance themselves from their parents in order to survive.*

Such a statement does not encompass every possible nuance of the story's theme, but it does at least provide us with a starting point for arguing about the finer points of Cheever's meaning.

Still, many modern authors are not always reticent about revealing their themes. Alistair MacLeod says that he begins all his work with ideas, and that his story "The Boat" is about choice. Alice Walker's commitment to rendering African-American experience and Margaret Atwood's feminism are rarely hidden in these authors' stories and poems. Many modern stories are in fact **allegorical tales,** in which the literal events point to a parallel sequence of symbolic ideas. In many stories the literal setting of the story is a **microcosm,** a "small world" that reflects the tensions of the larger world outside. Thus, despite their outward sophistication, many of the stories included here reveal their debt to the ancient ethical functions of fables and parables.

## *Setting*

Novelists can lavish pages of prose on details of setting, just as they can describe characters down to such minutiae as the contents of their pockets. But short-story writers, hemmed in by limitations of space, rarely have such luxury and must ordinarily limit themselves to very selective descriptions of time and place. When a writer goes into great detail in his or her descriptions (for example, as Guy de Maupassant does in the opening sentences of "The Piece of String") it is likely that **atmosphere,** the emotional aura surrounding a certain setting, is more important to him or her than the actual physical locale.

**Setting** is simply the time and place of a story, and in most cases the details of description are given to the reader directly by the narrator.

A story may employ multiple locations in its different scenes, and its time frame may encompass a few hours or many years. "Reunion" is a story with relatively few details of setting. Because Cheever wrote his stories almost exclusively for *The New Yorker*, it is not necessary for him to describe the interior of Grand Central Station to an audience doubtless familiar with it; excessive details here would probably be irrelevant. Similarly, he spends no more than a sentence or two describing each of the restaurants: One has "a lot of horse tack on the walls," one is "Italian," and the other two are not described at all. The time setting is also relatively unimportant here. We know that the action is taking place during the lunch hour on a weekday, probably in the summer, but as far as a more specific time is concerned, we know little or nothing. "Reunion" could be taking place today or fifty years ago or, for that matter, twenty years from now.

Some stories, however, depend on their **locale** or time setting much more heavily and thus demand fuller exposition of setting. **Historical fiction** usually pays great attention to the altered landscapes and customs of bygone eras. A writer who carelessly lets an alarm clock go off in a story set in the early 1800s has committed an anachronism that may be only slightly more obvious than another writer's use of contemporary slang in the same setting. **Local colour fiction** depends heavily on the unique characteristics of a particular area, usually a rural one that is off the beaten path. Such places have become increasingly rare in contemporary writing, but locales such as Guy Vanderhaeghe's prairie or Ama Ata Aidoo's rural Ghana still possess intrinsic interest. Some writers first established their reputations as practitioners of **regionalism,** setting most of their work in a particular area or part of the country. Alistair MacLeod shows, in virtually every one of his stories, his deep connections to Cape Breton. Gabriel García Márquez continually draws us into the strange world of Colombian villages cut off from the contemporary world—places where past and present, history and folklore, natural and supernatural, seamlessly join in what has been labelled **magic realism.**

Stories contain both specific and general settings. The specific setting is the precise time(s) and place(s) where the action takes place. The general setting of a story, what is called its **enveloping action,** is its sense of the "times" and how its characters interact with events and social currents in the larger world. We have already mentioned how the specific setting of a story often is a microcosm that reflects the doings of society at large. It is impossible to read stories by Alice Walker and not be made aware of the social changes that have transformed the rural American South in the last thirty years. Stories sometimes depend on readers' ability to bring their knowledge of history and culture to bear on the events taking place. In reading Timothy Findley's "Stones," younger readers may be unaware of the widespread impact of the two world wars that older readers can painfully recall.

## Style and Symbol

**Style** in fiction refers equally to the characteristics of language in a particular story and to the same characteristics in a writer's complete works. The more individual a writer's style is, the easier it is to write a **parody,** or satirical imitation, of it, as the well-publicized annual "Faux Faulkner" and "International Imitation Hemingway" contests attest. A detailed analysis of the style in an individual story might include attention to such matters as diction, sentence structure, punctuation (or the lack thereof), and use of figurative language. In English we usually make a distinction between the differing qualities of words—standard versus slang usage, Latinate versus Germanic vocabulary, abstract versus concrete diction, and so on. While such matters are most meaningful in the context of an individual story or an author's work in general, we can clearly see the difference between one character who says, "I have profited to a great degree from the educational benefits of the realm of experience," and another who says, "I graduated from the school of hard knocks." However, in analyzing style we must be sensitive to the literary fashions of periods other than our own; it is senseless to fault Poe for "flowery diction" when we compare his use of language with that of his contemporaries. The prevailing fashion in fiction today is for the unadorned starkness of writers like Raymond Carver, a type of literature that has been disparagingly called "K-Mart realism" by one critic. Still, one should not be surprised if, as we move forward in a new century, fashions shift and writers compete to outdo Faulkner at his most ornate.

The style of "Reunion" is for the most part straightforward, with few flourishes of vocabulary (if we except the foreign phrases) or sentence structure. About the only significant departure from this plain style is in the opening paragraph, where Charlie momentarily rises to a slightly elevated rhetorical plateau: "as soon as I saw him I felt that he was my father, my flesh and blood, my future and my doom." The **tone** of the story, or what we can indirectly determine about the author's own feelings about its events from his choice of words, is also carefully controlled. Cheever avoids the twin pitfalls of sentimentality on the one hand and cynicism on the other by deftly walking an emotional tightrope. After the opening paragraph, at no point does Charlie tell us how he feels; instead he lets his father's actions speak for themselves. There are points in "Reunion" where we may laugh, but it is an uncomfortable laugh at which we probably feel a little guilty. The possible tones available for use in any given story may run through the whole range of human emotions, from outright comedy or satirical contempt to pathos of the most wrenching sort. It is possible for an unwary reader to fail to appreciate the keen edge of Guy de Maupassant's irony or the profound skepticism of Jorge Luis Borges, but this failure should not be laid at the feet of the writers. Appreciation of a writer's tone of voice can often be slow to develop, coming only after the experience of reading a wide range of stories and comparing how irony may or may not be present in them.

Like tone of voice, symbolism in stories is often a troublesome affair for beginning readers, as is indicated by the oft-heard phrase "hidden meanings." Are authors doing their best to conceal, rather than reveal, the significance of actions and things in their works? Usually they are not, but a superficial reading of a story may barely scratch the surface of its full complexity. **Symbolism,** by which we mean the use of one thing (usually a concrete object) to suggest another (usually an abstract idea), may occur in any of the elements discussed above: A plot or character or setting may have some symbolic value. There is little heavy symbolism in "Reunion," but if we think about the title, with its suggestions of emotional warmth, and the opening setting, a busy train station, we can see that Cheever has chosen his title carefully, and it has both ironic and symbolic overtones.

If the details of a plot seem consistently symbolic, with each detail clearly pointing the way to some obvious larger meaning, then we are reading **allegory.** Hawthorne's "The Birthmark" invites an allegorical reading because of the many abstract ideas suggested by Georgiana's birthmark, said to resemble "a crimson stain" and a tiny "human hand."

Or, using another approach to symbolism, in a given story, an author may employ a **traditional symbol,** a thing that most members of a culture instantly recognize as possessing a shared symbolic meaning. We may recognize a white gown or a red rose symbolizing, on the one hand, innocence and, on the other, romantic love without having to think very deeply about either. Familiarity with an individual author's works may also help us to recognize a **private symbol,** a symbol that the author has made his or her own by repeated usage. Other writers may use certain colours, situations, and actions repeatedly; it is hard to read much of Poe's fiction without becoming aware of the personal horror that small, confined spaces represent for the author. Finally, we may identify an **incidental symbol** in a story. This may be a thing or action that ordinarily would not have deeper meaning but acquires one in a particular story. How can we learn to spot these symbols? Paying close attention to the way an author repeats certain details or otherwise points to their significance perhaps in the title or in the conclusion is the key. Understanding what a symbol *means* is often less important than merely realizing that it *exists.* The exact meaning of an incidental symbol is usually open to interpretation and multiple interpretations of its implications do not necessarily contradict one another.

The variety of short stories in this collection is testimony to the versatility of the form. The short story has been called "a fierce pleasure" by Raymond Carver, "a musical composition" by Katherine Mansfield, and "an art of snapshots" by Alice Munro. That there are as many definitions of the form as there are practitioners can perhaps be explained by the fact that the short story is a dynamic hybrid. According to V. S. Pritchett, "It owes much to the quickness, the objectivity and cutting of the cinema; it owes much to the poet on the one hand and the newspaper reporter on the other; something also to the dramatic compression of the theatre, and everything to the restlessness, the alert nerve, the scientific eye and the short breath of contemporary life."

# *Writing About Short Fiction*

Writing assignments differ greatly, and your instructor's directions may range from general ("Discuss characterization in two of the short stories we have read.") to very specific ("Contrast, in 500–1000 words, the major differences in the plot, characterization, and setting between Alice Munro's short story 'Boys and Girls' and the 1983 film version of the story directed by Don McBrearty."). Such practices as choosing, limiting, and developing a topic; "brainstorming" by taking notes on random ideas and refining those ideas further through group discussion or conferences with your instructor; using the library and the Internet, if required, to locate supporting critical materials; and revising a first draft in light of critical remarks are undoubtedly techniques you have used in other composition classes. Basic types of organizational schemes learned in "theme-writing" courses can also be applied to writing about fiction. Formal assignments of these types should avoid contractions and jargon, and should be written in a clear, straightforward style. Most literary essays are not of the personal experience type, and you should follow common sense in avoiding the first person and slang. It goes without saying that you should carefully proofread your rough and final drafts to eliminate errors in spelling, punctuation, usage, and grammar.

Typical writing assignments on short stories fall into three main categories: explication or close reading, analysis, and comparison-contrast. An explication assignment is perhaps the most demanding of the three because it requires the closest attention to the precise nuances of a writer's language. Typically, an explication (literally an "unfolding") might ask you to focus carefully on a key passage of a story, perhaps even on a single paragraph, explaining how it contains some key element upon which the whole story hinges and without which the story could not succeed. Suppose, for example, that you are asked to explicate the opening paragraph of "Reunion" and are explicitly requested to focus on what the paragraph conveys beyond obvious expository information. After reading the paragraph carefully several times, you might decide it contains ample foreshadowing of the disastrous events that are about to occur. In particular, you might cite such telltale phrases as "His secretary wrote to say" or "my mother divorced him" as John Cheever's way of dropping subtle hints about the father's unsavoury personality. Then you might go on to mention Charlie's forebodings of his own "doom," all leading up to the aroma of pre-lunch cocktails that Charlie notices when he and his father embrace. Any explication demands that you quote extensively from the text, explaining why certain choices of words and details are important and speculating about why the writer made these choices. Your first step would be to examine the meanings, both denotations and connotations, of the words that the author uses. A standard college dictionary, of course, is useful, but if you are interested in finding other meanings of words, especially those that appear in stories written in earlier eras, you should consult the *Oxford English Dictionary*, a multivolume reference book that contains citations of words as they have been used in literature through the ages.

Analysis assignments typically turn on definition and illustration, focusing on only one or two of the main elements of the story, such as plot or theme. For example, you might be asked to explain what a "rite of passage" story is and to demonstrate that "Reunion" has most of the characteristics of that genre. Here you might first want to define the initiation story, using your lecture notes and your familiarity with other stories from popular sources like fairy tales or motion pictures. After demonstrating that this type of story is indeed well-established and describing its attributes, you might then focus on such details of "Reunion" as Charlie's age, his naïve expectations, his disillusioning experience, and his eventual "passage" out of his father's life at the end of the story.

Comparison-contrast assignments are also popular, especially for longer writing projects. Generally, comparison seeks out common ground between two subjects whereas contrast finds differences; most papers of this type will do both, first pointing out the similarities before going on to demonstrate how each story represents a variation on the theme. Comparison-contrast may focus on a single story, asking you to examine two characters' approaches to a similar situation or even a single character's "before and after" view of another character or event. If you are examining a single author in depth, you might be required to find other stories by him or her that deal with similar themes. Because Cheever writes extensively about alcoholism, family tensions, and divorce, you might locate several of his stories that reflect the same the basic themes that are present in "Reunion." Even more demanding might be a topic asking you to find stories (or even poems or plays) by other authors to compare or contrast. Among the stories in this book, there are several examples of initiation stories and others that deal with tensions between parents and children. Comparison-contrast assignments require careful selection and planning, and it is essential to point out significant examples of both similarities and differences to support your thesis. It would make little sense, for example, to attempt to write a comparison-contrast paper based on "Reunion" and Guy de Maupassant's "The Piece of String." The stories are separated by a century, the Atlantic Ocean, and the relationships of the characters to one another. They have little or no common ground and, thus, no basis for comparison.

It is always necessary to support the statements you make about a story, either by quoting directly from the story or, if you are required, by using secondary sources for additional critical opinion. If you are asked to support your paper with information gleaned from research, a logical first step would be to check reference books such as *Short Story Criticism* or an index such as *Twentieth Century Short Story Explication* for entries on the story you have chosen to write about. A subject search of the library's online catalogue may reveal several individual books about an author's short stories, or it may give the titles of general books on the analysis of fiction to provide you with a critical vocabulary. One of the best sources for secondary materials is the *MLA* (Modern Language Association) *Index*, which now exists in CD-ROM and online versions with computerized search tools. The *MLA Index* will direct you to essays in periodicals, which you will have to locate in your library or, in the case of smaller libraries, request on loan from another

one was being referred to by adding a shortened form of the book's title: (Stories 518). The reader finds the following entry among the sources:

> Cheever, John. <u>The Stories of John Cheever</u>. New
> York: Knopf, 1978.

Similarly, quotes and paraphrases from secondary critical sources should follow the same rules of common sense.

> Cheever's daughter Susan, in her candid memoir of
> her father, remarks that the author's alcoholism followed
> a familiar pattern. She notes that "there were bottles
> hidden all over the house, and even outside in the privet
> hedge and the garden shed. Drink was his crucible, his
> personal hell" (43).

Note how another writer might paraphrase the same material:

> Cheever's daughter Susan, in her candid memoir of
> her father, remarks that the author's alcoholism followed
> a familiar pattern. She reports how Cheever hid bottles
> all around the house, outside in the shrubbery, and even
> in the tool shed. Alcohol was his constant companion and
> personal torment (43).

In both these cases, the author of the quote is identified, so only the page number is included in the parenthetical citation. The reader knows where to look among the sources:

> Cheever, Susan. <u>Home Before Dark</u>. Boston: Houghton,
> 1984.

To simplify the whole matter of parenthetical citation, it is recommended that quotes from secondary sources be introduced, whenever possible, in a manner that identifies the author, so that only the page number of the quote is needed inside of the parentheses.

Of course, different types of sources—reference book entries, articles in periodicals, newspaper reviews of books, material collected from the Internet—require different bibliographical information, so be sure to check the *MLA Handbook* if you have questions. Here are a few more of the most commonly used bibliographical formats:

## A BOOK WITH AUTHOR AND EDITOR

Cheever, John. <u>The Letters of John Cheever</u>. Ed. Benjamin Cheever. New York: Simon, 1988.

## A CASEBOOK OR COLLECTION OF CRITICAL ESSAYS

Collins, R. G., ed. <u>Critical Essays on John Cheever</u>. Boston: Hall, 1982.

## A STORY REPRINTED IN AN ANTHOLOGY OR TEXTBOOK

Cheever, John. "The Five-Forty-Eight." <u>The Longman Anthology of Short Fiction: Stories and Authors in Context</u>. Ed. Dana Gioia and R. S. Gwynn. New York: Longman, 2001. 380-90.

## AN ARTICLE IN A REFERENCE BOOK

Seymour-Smith, Martin. "Cheever, John." <u>Who's Who in Twentieth Century Literature</u>. New York: McGraw, 1976.

## AN ARTICLE IN A SCHOLARLY JOURNAL

Kendle, Burton. "Cheever's Use of Mythology in 'The Enormous Radio.'" <u>Studies in Short Fiction</u> 4 (1968): 262-64.

## A BOOK REVIEW IN A PERIODICAL

Oberbeck, S. K. "Curdled Camelot." Rev. of <u>The World of Apples</u>, by John Cheever. Newsweek 21 May 1973: 97, 99.

## AN INTERVIEW

Cheever, John. Interview. "John Cheever: The Art of Fiction LXII." By Annette Grant. <u>Paris Review</u> 17 (1976): 39-66.

## AN INTERNET WEB SITE

"Literature Online: John Cheever." 18 Feb. 2001
    <http://longman.awl.com/kennedy/cheever/
    biography.html>.

## AN ONLINE REFERENCE BOOK

"Cheever, John." <u>Encyclopedia Britannica Online</u>. 12 Dec.
    2000 <http://www.britannica.com/bcom/eb/
    article/1/0,5716,23111+1+22745,00.html?query=
    john%20cheever>.

# Fiction

*Nathaniel Hawthorne (1804–1864) was born in Salem, Massachusetts, tracing his heritage back to the earliest settlers. One of his Puritan ancestors, John Hathorne, was a magistrate who assisted the prosecution during the infamous Salem witch trials that appear in Hawthorne's novel* The Scarlet Letter *(1850). His collection of short stories* Twice-Told Tales *(1837) was the subject of an enthusiastic review by Edgar Allan Poe. A dedicated craftsman, Hawthorne was a moralist who did not shrink from depicting the dark side of human nature, and his often painful examinations of American history and conscience have set the tone for many subsequent generations of writers. "The Birthmark," written in 1843 and published in* Mosses from an Old Manse *(1846), explores the perils of attempting to improve upon nature.*

## Nathaniel Hawthorne
# The Birthmark

In the latter part of the last century there lived a man of science, an eminent proficient in every branch of natural philosophy, who not long before our story opens had made experience of a spiritual affinity more attractive than any chemical one. He had left his laboratory to the care of an assistant, cleared his fine countenance from the furnace smoke, washed the stain of acids from his fingers, and persuaded a beautiful woman to become his wife. In those days when the comparatively recent discovery of electricity and other kindred mysteries of Nature seemed to open paths into the region of miracle, it was not unusual for the love of science to rival the love of woman in its depth and absorbing energy. The higher intellect, the imagination, the spirit, and even the heart might all find their congenial aliment in pursuits which, as some of their ardent votaries believed, would ascend from one step of powerful intelligence to another, until the philosopher should lay his hand on the secret of creative force and perhaps make new worlds for himself. We know not whether Aylmer possessed this degree of faith in man's ultimate control over Nature. He had devoted himself, however, too unreservedly to scientific studies ever to be weaned from them by any second passion. His love for his young wife might prove the stronger of the two; but it could only be by intertwining itself with his love of science, and uniting the strength of the latter to his own.

Such a union accordingly took place, and was attended with truly remarkable consequences and a deeply impressive moral. One day, very soon after their marriage, Aylmer sat gazing at his wife with a trouble in his countenance that grew stronger until he spoke.

"Georgiana," said he, "has it never occurred to you that the mark upon your cheek might be removed?"

"No, indeed," said she, smiling; but perceiving the seriousness of his manner, she blushed deeply. "To tell you the truth it has been so often called a charm that I was simple enough to imagine it might be so."

"Ah, upon another face perhaps it might," replied her husband; "but never on yours. No, dearest Georgiana, you came so nearly perfect from the hand of Nature that this slightest possible defect, which we hesitate whether to term a defect or a beauty, shocks me, as being the visible mark of earthly imperfection."

"Shocks you, my husband!" cried Georgiana, deeply hurt; at first reddening with momentary anger, but then bursting into tears. "Then why did you take me from my mother's side? You cannot love what shocks you!"

To explain this conversation it must be mentioned that in the centre of Georgiana's left cheek there was a singular mark, deeply interwoven, as it were, with the texture and substance of her face. In the usual state of her complexion—a healthy though delicate bloom—the mark wore a tint of deeper crimson, which imperfectly defined its shape amid the surrounding rosiness. When she blushed it gradually became more indistinct, and finally vanished amid the triumphant rush of blood that bathed the whole cheek with its brilliant glow. But if any shifting motion caused her to turn pale there was the mark again, a crimson stain upon the snow, in what Aylmer sometimes deemed an almost fearful distinctness. Its shape bore not a little similarity to the human hand, though of the smallest pygmy size. Georgiana's lovers were wont to say that some fairy at her birth hour had laid her tiny hand upon the infant's cheek, and left this impress there in token of the magic endowments that were to give her such sway over all hearts. Many a desperate swain would have risked life for the privilege of pressing his lips to the mysterious hand. It must not be concealed, however, that the impression wrought by this fairy sign manual varied exceedingly, according to the difference of temperament in the beholders. Some fastidious persons—but they were exclusively of her own sex—affirmed that the bloody hand, as they chose to call it, quite destroyed the effect of Georgiana's beauty, and rendered her countenance even hideous. But it would be as reasonable to say that one of those small blue stains which sometimes occur in the purest statuary marble would convert the Eve of Powers[1] to a monster. Masculine observers, if the birthmark did not heighten their admiration, contented themselves with wishing it away, that the world might possess one living specimen of ideal loveliness without the semblance of a flaw. After his marriage,—for he thought little or nothing of the matter before,—Aylmer discovered that this was the case with himself.

Had she been less beautiful,—if Envy's self could have found aught else to sneer at,—he might have felt his affection heightened by the prettiness of this mimic hand, now vaguely portrayed, now lost, now stealing forth again and glimmering to and fro with every pulse of emotion that throbbed within her heart; but seeing her otherwise so perfect, he found this one defect grow more and more intolerable with every moment of their united lives. It was the fatal flaw of humanity which Nature, in one shape or another, stamps ineffaceably on all her productions, either to imply that they are temporary and finite, or that their perfection must be wrought by toil and pain. The crimson hand expressed the ineludible gripe in which mortality clutches the highest and purest of earthly mould, degrading them into kindred with the lowest, and even with the very brutes, like whom their visible frames return to dust. In this manner, selecting it as the symbol of his wife's liability to sin, sorrow, decay, and death, Aylmer's sombre imagination was not long in rendering the birthmark a frightful object, causing him more trouble and horror than ever Georgiana's beauty, whether of soul or sense, had given him delight.

At all the seasons which should have been their happiest, he invariably and without intending it, nay, in spite of a purpose to the contrary, reverted to this one disastrous topic. Trifling as it at first appeared, it so connected itself with innumerable trains of thought and modes of feeling that it became the central point of all. With the morning twilight Aylmer opened his eyes upon his wife's face and recognized the symbol of imperfection; and when they sat together at the evening hearth his eyes wandered stealthily to her cheek, and beheld, flickering with the blaze of the wood fire, the spectral hand that wrote mortality where he would fain have worshipped. Georgiana soon learned to shudder at his gaze. It needed but a glance with the peculiar expression that his face often

---

[1]*Eve of Powers:* Hiram Powers (1805–1873), American sculptor, was famous for his white marble sculpture of Eve entitled *Eve Before the Fall.*

wore to change the roses of her cheek into a deathlike paleness, amid which the crimson hand was brought strongly out, like a bass-relief of ruby on the whitest marble.

Late one night when the lights were growing dim, so as hardly to betray the stain on the poor wife's cheek, she herself, for the first time, voluntarily took up the subject.

"Do you remember, my dear Aylmer," said she, with a feeble attempt at a smile, "have you any recollection of a dream last night about this odious hand?"

"None! none whatever!" replied Aylmer, starting; but then he added, in a dry, cold tone, affected for the sake of concealing the real depth of his emotion, "I might well dream of it; for before I fell asleep it had taken a pretty firm hold of my fancy."

"And you did dream of it?" continued Georgiana, hastily; for she dreaded lest a gush of tears should interrupt what she had to say. "A terrible dream! I wonder that you can forget it. Is it possible to forget this one expression?—'It is in her heart now; we must have it out!' Reflect, my husband; for by all means I would have you recall that dream."

The mind is in a sad state when Sleep, the all-involving, cannot confine her spectres within the dim region of her sway, but suffers them to break forth, affrighting this actual life with secrets that perchance belong to a deeper one. Aylmer now remembered his dream. He had fancied himself with his servant Aminadab, attempting an operation for the removal of the birthmark; but the deeper went the knife, the deeper sank the hand, until at length its tiny grasp appeared to have caught hold of Georgiana's heart; whence, her husband was inexorably resolved to cut or wrench it away.

When the dream had shaped itself perfectly in his memory, Aylmer sat in his wife's presence with a guilty feeling. Truth often finds its way to the mind close muffled in robes of sleep, and then speaks with uncompromising directness of matters in regard to which we practise an unconscious self-deception during our waking moments. Until now he had not been aware of the tyrannizing influence acquired by one idea over his mind, and of the lengths which he might find in his heart to go for the sake of giving himself peace.

"Aylmer," resumed Georgiana, solemnly, "I know not what may be the cost to both of us to rid me of this fatal birthmark. Perhaps its removal may cause cureless deformity; or it may be the stain goes as deep as life itself. Again: do we know that there is a possibility, on any terms, of unclasping the firm gripe of this little hand which was laid upon me before I came into the world?"

"Dearest Georgiana, I have spent much thought upon the subject," hastily interrupted Aylmer. "I am convinced of the perfect practicability of its removal."

"If there be the remotest possibility of it," continued Georgiana, "let the attempt be made at whatever risk. Danger is nothing to me; for life, while this hateful mark makes me the object of your horror and disgust,—life is a burden which I would fling down with joy. Either remove this dreadful hand, or take my wretched life! You have deep science. All the world bears witness of it. You have achieved great wonders. Cannot you remove this little, little mark, which I cover with the tips of two small fingers? Is this beyond your power, for the sake of your own peace, and to save your poor wife from madness?"

"Noblest, dearest, tenderest wife," cried Aylmer, rapturously, "doubt not my power. I have already given this matter the deepest thought—thought which might almost have enlightened me to create a being less perfect than yourself. Georgiana, you have led me deeper than ever into the heart of science. I feel myself fully competent to render this dear cheek as faultless as its fellow; and then, most beloved, what will be my triumph when I shall have corrected what Nature left imperfect in her fairest work! Even Pygmalion,[2] when his sculptured woman assumed life, felt not greater ecstasy than mine will be."

"It is resolved, then," said Georgiana, faintly smiling. "And, Aylmer, spare me not, though you should find the birthmark take refuge in my heart at last."

Her husband tenderly kissed her cheek—her right cheek—not that which bore the impress of the crimson hand.

The next day Aylmer apprised his wife of a plan that he had formed whereby he might have opportunity for the intense thought and constant watchfulness which the proposed operation would require; while Georgiana, likewise, would enjoy the perfect repose essential to its success. They were to seclude themselves in the extensive apartments

---

[2]*Pygmalion:* In Greek mythology, Pygmalion was a skilled sculptor who fell in love with his own creation of a perfect maiden carved in ivory, and prayed to Aphrodite for a wife like her. Aphrodite caused his sculpture to come alive, and creator and creation were married.

occupied by Aylmer as a laboratory, and where, during his toilsome youth, he had made discoveries in the elemental powers of Nature that had roused the admiration of all the learned societies in Europe. Seated calmly in this laboratory, the pale philosopher had investigated the secrets of the highest cloud region and of the profoundest mines; he had satisfied himself of the causes that kindled and kept alive the fires of the volcano; and had explained the mystery of fountains, and how it is that they gush forth, some so bright and pure, and others with such rich medicinal virtues, from the dark bosom of the earth. Here, too, at an earlier period, he had studied the wonders of the human frame, and attempted to fathom the very process by which Nature assimilates all her precious influences from earth and air, and from the spiritual world, to create and foster man, her masterpiece. The latter pursuit, however, Aylmer had long laid aside in unwilling recognition of the truth—against which all seekers sooner or later stumble—that our great creative Mother, while she amuses us with apparently working in the broadest sunshine, is yet severely careful to keep her own secrets, and, in spite of her pretended openness, shows us nothing but results. She permits us, indeed, to mar, but seldom to mend, and, like a jealous patentee, on no account to make. Now, however, Aylmer resumed these half-forgotten investigations; not, of course, with such hopes or wishes as first suggested them; but because they involved much physiological truth and lay in the path of his proposed scheme for the treatment of Georgiana.

As he led her over the threshold of the laboratory, Georgiana was cold and tremulous. Aylmer looked cheerfully into her face, with intent to reassure her, but was so startled with the intense glow of the birthmark upon the whiteness of her cheek that he could not restrain a strong convulsive shudder. His wife fainted.

"Aminadab! Aminadab!" shouted Aylmer, stamping violently on the floor.

Forthwith there issued from an inner apartment a man of low stature, but bulky frame, with shaggy hair hanging about his visage, which was grimed with the vapors of the furnace. This personage had been Aylmer's underworker during his whole scientific career, and was admirably fitted for that office by his great mechanical readiness, and the skill with which, while incapable of comprehending a single principle, he executed all the details of his master's experiments. With his vast strength, his shaggy hair, his smoky aspect, and the indescribable earthiness that incrusted him, he seemed to represent man's physical nature; while Aylmer's slender figure, and pale, intellectual face, were no less apt a type of the spiritual element.

"Throw open the door of the boudoir, Aminadab," said Aylmer, "and burn a pastil."

"Yes, master," answered Aminadab, looking intently at the lifeless form of Georgiana; and then he muttered to himself, "If she were my wife, I'd never part with that birthmark."

When Georgiana recovered consciousness she found herself breathing an atmosphere of penetrating fragrance, the gentle potency of which had recalled her from her deathlike faintness. The scene around her looked like enchantment. Aylmer had converted those smoky, dingy, sombre rooms, where he had spent his brightest years in recondite pursuits, into a series of beautiful apartments not unfit to be the secluded abode of a lovely woman. The walls were hung with gorgeous curtains, which imparted the combination of grandeur and grace that no other species of adornment can achieve; and as they fell from the ceiling to the floor, their rich and ponderous folds, concealing all angles and straight lines, appeared to shut in the scene from infinite space. For aught Georgiana knew, it might be a pavilion among the clouds. And Aylmer, excluding the sunshine, which would have interfered with his chemical processes, had supplied its place with perfumed lamps, emitting flames of various hue, but all uniting in a soft, impurpled radiance. He now knelt by his wife's side, watching her earnestly, but without alarm; for he was confident in his science, and felt that he could draw a magic circle round her within which no evil might intrude.

"Where am I? Ah, I remember," said Georgiana, faintly; and she placed her hand over her cheek to hide the terrible mark from her husband's eyes.

"Fear not, dearest!" exclaimed he. "Do not shrink from me! Believe me, Georgiana, I even rejoice in this single imperfection, since it will be such a rapture to remove it."

"Oh, spare me!" sadly replied his wife. "Pray do not look at it again. I never can forget that convulsive shudder."

In order to soothe Georgiana, and, as it were, to release her mind from the burden of actual things, Aylmer now put in practice some of the light and playful secrets which science had taught him among its profounder lore. Airy figures, absolutely bodiless ideas, and forms of unsubstantial beauty came and danced before her, imprinting their momentary footsteps on beams of light. Though she had some indistinct idea of the method of these optical phenomena, still the illusion was almost perfect enough to warrant the belief that her husband possessed sway over the spiritual world. Then again, when she felt a wish to look forth from her seclusion, immediately, as if her thoughts were answered, the procession of external existence flitted across a screen. The scenery and the figures of actual life were perfectly represented, but with that bewitching, yet indescribable difference which always makes a picture, an image, or a shadow so much more attractive than the original. When wearied of this, Aylmer bade her cast her eyes upon a vessel containing a quantity of earth. She did so, with little interest at first; but was soon startled to perceive the germ of a plant shooting upward from the soil. Then came the slender stalk; the leaves gradually unfolded themselves; and amid them was a perfect and lovely flower.

"It is magical!" cried Georgiana. "I dare not touch it."

"Nay, pluck it," answered Aylmer,—"pluck it, and inhale its brief perfume while you may. The flower will wither in a few moments and leave nothing save its brown seed vessels; but thence may be perpetuated a race as ephemeral as itself."

But Georgiana had no sooner touched the flower than the whole plant suffered a blight, its leaves turning coal-black as if by the agency of fire.

"There was too powerful a stimulus," said Aylmer, thoughtfully.

To make up for this abortive experiment, he proposed to take her portrait by a scientific process of his own invention. It was to be effected by rays of light striking upon a polished plate of metal. Georgiana assented; but, on looking at the result, was affrighted to find the features of the portrait blurred and indefinable; while the minute figure of a hand appeared where the cheek should have been. Aylmer snatched the metallic plate and threw it into a jar of corrosive acid.

Soon, however, he forgot these mortifying failures. In the intervals of study and chemical experiment he came to her flushed and exhausted, but seemed invigorated by her presence, and spoke in glowing language of the resources of his art. He gave a history of the long dynasty of the alchemists, who spent so many ages in quest of the universal solvent by which the golden principle might be elicited from all things vile and base. Aylmer appeared to believe that, by the plainest scientific logic, it was altogether within the limits of possibility to discover this

long-sought medium; "but," he added, "a philosopher who should go
deep enough to acquire the power would attain too lofty a wisdom to
stoop to the exercise of it." Not less singular were his opinions in regard
to the elixir vitae. He more than intimated that it was at his option to
concoct a liquid that should prolong life for years, perhaps interminably;
but that it would produce a discord in Nature which all the world, and
chiefly the quaffer of the immortal nostrum, would find cause to curse.

"Aylmer, are you in earnest?" asked Georgiana, looking at him with
amazement and fear. "It is terrible to possess such power, or even to
dream of possessing it."

"Oh, do not tremble, my love," said her husband. "I would not
wrong either you or myself by working such inharmonious effects upon
our lives; but I would have you consider how trifling, in comparison, is
the skill requisite to remove this little hand."

At the mention of the birthmark, Georgiana, as usual, shrank as if a
redhot iron had touched her cheek.

Again Aylmer applied himself to his labors. She could hear his voice in
the distant furnace room giving directions to Aminadab, whose harsh,
uncouth, misshapen tones were audible in response, more like the grunt
or growl of a brute than human speech. After hours of absence, Aylmer
reappeared and proposed that she should now examine his cabinet of
chemical products and natural treasures of the earth. Among the former
he showed her a small vial, in which, he remarked, was contained a gentle yet most powerful fragrance, capable of impregnating all the breezes
that blow across a kingdom. They were of inestimable value, the contents
of that little vial; and, as he said so, he threw some of the perfume into the
air and filled the room with piercing and invigorating delight.

"And what is this?" asked Georgiana, pointing to a small crystal
globe containing a gold-colored liquid. "It is so beautiful to the eye that
I could imagine it the elixir of life."

"In one sense it is," replied Aylmer; "or, rather, the elixir of immortality. It is the most precious poison that ever was concocted in this
world. By its aid I could apportion the lifetime of any mortal at whom
you might point your finger. The strength of the dose would determine
whether he were to linger out years, or drop dead in the midst of a
breath. No king on his guarded throne could keep his life if I, in my private station, should deem that the welfare of millions justified me in
depriving him of it."

"Why do you keep such a terrific drug?" inquired Georgiana in horror.

"Do not mistrust me, dearest," said her husband, smiling; "its virtuous potency is yet greater than its harmful one. But see! here is a powerful cosmetic. With a few drops of this in a vase of water, freckles may be washed away as easily as the hands are cleansed. A stronger infusion would take the blood out of the cheek, and leave the rosiest beauty a pale ghost."

"Is it with this lotion that you intend to bathe my cheek?" asked Georgiana, anxiously.

"Oh, no," hastily replied her husband; "this is merely superficial. Your case demands a remedy that shall go deeper."

In his interviews with Georgiana, Aylmer generally made minute inquiries as to her sensations and whether the confinement of the rooms and the temperature of the atmosphere agreed with her. These questions had such a particular drift that Georgiana began to conjecture that she was already subjected to certain physical influences, either breathed in with the fragrant air or taken with her food. She fancied likewise, but it might be altogether fancy, that there was a stirring up of her system—a strange, indefinite sensation creeping through her veins, and tingling, half painfully, half pleasurably, at her heart. Still, whenever she dared to look into the mirror, there she beheld herself pale as a white rose and with the crimson birthmark stamped upon her cheek. Not even Aylmer now hated it so much as she.

To dispel the tedium of the hours which her husband found it necessary to devote to the processes of combination and analysis, Georgiana turned over the volumes of his scientific library. In many dark old tomes she met with chapters full of romance and poetry. They were the works of philosophers of the middle ages, such as Albertus Magnus, Cornelius Agrippa, Paracelsus, and the famous friar who created the prophetic Brazen Head.[3] All these antique naturalists stood in advance of their centuries, yet were imbued with some of their credulity, and therefore were believed, and perhaps imagined themselves to have acquired from the investigation of Nature a power above Nature, and from physics a sway

---

[3]*Albertus Magnus* (c.1200–1280) and *Cornelius Agrippa* (1486–1535) of Germany, and *Paracelsus* (1490–1541) of Switzerland were all philosophers of the Middle Ages interested in the natural sciences, alchemy, and the supernatural. The *famous friar* is Roger Bacon (c.1214–1294), an English philosopher and scientist who was said to have created a head of brass that could speak with great wisdom.

over the spiritual world. Hardly less curious and imaginative were the early volumes of the Transactions of the Royal Society, in which the members, knowing little of the limits of natural possibility, were continually recording wonders or proposing methods whereby wonders might be wrought.

But to Georgiana the most engrossing volume was a large folio from her husband's own hand, in which he had recorded every experiment of his scientific career, its original aim, the methods adopted for its development, and its final success or failure, with the circumstances to which either event was attributable. The book, in truth, was both the history and emblem of his ardent, ambitious, imaginative, yet practical and laborious life. He handled physical details as if there were nothing beyond them; yet spiritualized them all, and redeemed himself from materialism by his strong and eager aspiration towards the infinite. In his grasp the veriest clod of earth assumed a soul. Georgiana, as she read, reverenced Aylmer and loved him more profoundly than ever, but with a less entire dependence on his judgment than heretofore. Much as he had accomplished, she could not but observe that his most splendid successes were almost invariably failures, if compared with the ideal at which he aimed. His brightest diamonds were the merest pebbles, and felt to be so by himself, in comparison with the inestimable gems which lay hidden beyond his reach. The volume, rich with achievements that had won renown for its author, was yet as melancholy a record as ever mortal hand had penned. It was the sad confession and continual exemplification of the shortcomings of the composite man, the spirit burdened with clay and working in matter, and of the despair that assails the higher nature at finding itself so miserably thwarted by the earthly part. Perhaps every man of genius in whatever sphere might recognize the image of his own experience in Aylmer's journal.

So deeply did these reflections affect Georgiana that she laid her face upon the open volume and burst into tears. In this situation she was found by her husband.

"It is dangerous to read in a sorcerer's books," said he with a smile, though his countenance was uneasy and displeased. "Georgiana, there are pages in that volume which I can scarcely glance over and keep my senses. Take heed lest it prove as detrimental to you."

"It has made me worship you more than ever," said she.

"Ah, wait for this one success," rejoined he, "then worship me if you will. I shall deem myself hardly unworthy of it. But come, I have sought you for the luxury of your voice. Sing to me, dearest."

So she poured out the liquid music of her voice to quench the thirst of his spirit. He then took his leave with a boyish exuberance of gayety, assuring her that her seclusion would endure but a little longer, and that the result was already certain. Scarcely had he departed when Georgiana felt irresistibly impelled to follow him. She had forgotten to inform Aylmer of a symptom which for two or three hours past had begun to excite her attention. It was a sensation in the fatal birthmark, not painful, but which induced a restlessness throughout her system. Hastening after her husband, she intruded for the first time into the laboratory.

The first thing that struck her eye was the furnace, that hot and feverish worker, with the intense glow of its fire, which by the quantities of soot clustered above it seemed to have been burning for ages. There was a distilling apparatus in full operation. Around the room were retorts, tubes, cylinders, crucibles, and other apparatus of chemical research. An electrical machine stood ready for immediate use. The atmosphere felt oppressively close, and was tainted with gaseous odors which had been tormented forth by the processes of science. The severe and homely simplicity of the apartment, with its naked walls and brick pavement, looked strange, accustomed as Georgiana had become to the fantastic elegance of her boudoir. But what chiefly, indeed almost solely, drew her attention, was the aspect of Aylmer himself.

He was pale as death, anxious and absorbed, and hung over the furnace as if it depended upon his utmost watchfulness whether the liquid which it was distilling should be the draught of immortal happiness or misery. How different from the sanguine and joyous mien that he had assumed for Georgiana's encouragement!

"Carefully now, Aminadab; carefully, thou human machine; carefully, thou man of clay!" muttered Aylmer, more to himself than his assistant. "Now, if there be a thought too much or too little, it is all over."

"Ho! ho!" mumbled Aminadab. "Look, master! look!"

Aylmer raised his eyes hastily, and at first reddened, then grew paler than ever, on beholding Georgiana. He rushed towards her and seized her arm with a gripe that left the print of his fingers upon it.

"Why do you come hither? Have you no trust in your husband?" cried he, impetuously. "Would you throw the blight of that fatal birthmark over my labors? It is not well done. Go, prying woman, go!"

"Nay, Aylmer," said Georgiana with the firmness of which she possessed no stinted endowment, "it is not you that have a right to complain. You mistrust your wife; you have concealed the anxiety with which you watch the development of this experiment. Think not so unworthily of me, my husband. Tell me all the risk we run, and fear not that I shall shrink; for my share in it is far less than your own."

"No, no, Georgiana!" said Aylmer, impatiently; "it must not be."

"I submit," replied she calmly. "And, Aylmer, I shall quaff whatever draught you bring me; but it will be on the same principle that would induce me to take a dose of poison if offered by your hand."

"My noble wife," said Aylmer, deeply moved, "I knew not the height and depth of your nature until now. Nothing shall be concealed. Know, then, that this crimson hand, superficial as it seems, has clutched its grasp into your being with a strength of which I had no previous conception. I have already administered agents powerful enough to do aught except to change your entire physical system. Only one thing remains to be tried. If that fail us we are ruined."

"Why did you hesitate to tell me this?" asked she.

"Because, Georgiana," said Aylmer, in a low voice, "there is danger."

"Danger? There is but one danger—that this horrible stigma shall be left upon my cheek!" cried Georgiana. "Remove it, remove it, whatever be the cost, or we shall both go mad!"

"Heaven knows your words are too true," said Aylmer, sadly. "And now, dearest, return to your boudoir. In a little while all will be tested."

He conducted her back and took leave of her with a solemn tenderness which spoke far more than his words how much was now at stake. After his departure Georgiana became rapt in musings. She considered the character of Aylmer, and did it completer justice than at any previous moment. Her heart exulted, while it trembled, at his honorable love—so pure and lofty that it would accept nothing less than perfection nor miserably make itself contented with an earthlier nature than he had dreamed of. She felt how much more precious was such a sentiment than that meaner kind which would have borne with the imperfection for her sake, and have been guilty of treason to holy love by degrading its perfect idea to the level of the actual; and with her whole spirit she prayed that, for a single moment, she might satisfy his highest and deepest conception. Longer than one moment she well knew it could not be; for his spirit was ever on the march, ever ascending, and each instant required something that was beyond the scope of the instant before.

The sound of her husband's footsteps aroused her. He bore a crystal goblet containing a liquor colorless as water, but bright enough to be the draught of immortality. Aylmer was pale; but it seemed rather the consequence of a highly-wrought state of mind and tension of spirit than of fear or doubt.

"The concoction of the draught has been perfect," said he, in answer to Georgiana's look. "Unless all my science have deceived me, it cannot fail."

"Save on your account, my dearest Aylmer," observed his wife, "I might wish to put off this birthmark of mortality by relinquishing mortality itself in preference to any other mode. Life is but a sad possession to those who have attained precisely the degree of moral advancement at which I stand. Were I weaker and blinder it might be happiness. Were I stronger, it might be endured hopefully. But, being what I find myself, methinks I am of all mortals the most fit to die."

"You are fit for heaven without tasting death!" replied her husband. "But why do we speak of dying? The draught cannot fail. Behold its effect upon this plant."

On the window seat there stood a geranium diseased with yellow blotches, which had overspread all its leaves. Aylmer poured a small quantity of the liquid upon the soil in which it grew. In a little time, when the roots of the plant had taken up the moisture, the unsightly blotches began to be extinguished in a living verdure.

"There needed no proof," said Georgiana, quietly. "Give me the goblet. I joyfully stake all upon your word."

"Drink, then, thou lofty creature!" exclaimed Aylmer, with fervid admiration. "There is no taint of imperfection on thy spirit. Thy sensible frame, too, shall soon be all perfect."

She quaffed the liquid and returned the goblet to his hand.

"It is grateful," said she with a placid smile. "Methinks it is like water from a heavenly fountain; for it contains I know not what of unobtrusive fragrance and deliciousness. It allays a feverish thirst that had parched me for many days. Now, dearest, let me sleep. My earthly senses are closing over my spirit like the leaves around the heart of a rose at sunset."

She spoke the last words with a gentle reluctance, as if it required almost more energy than she could command to pronounce the faint and lingering syllables. Scarcely had they loitered through her lips ere she was lost in slumber. Aylmer sat by her side, watching her aspect with the emotions proper to a man the whole value of whose existence was involved in the process now to be tested. Mingled with this mood, however, was the philosophic investigation characteristic of the man of science. Not the minutest symptom escaped him. A heightened flush of the cheek, a slight irregularity of breath, a quiver of the eyelid, a hardly perceptible tremor through the frame,—such were the details which, as the moments passed, he wrote down in his folio volume. Intense thought had set its stamp upon every previous page of that volume, but the thoughts of years were all concentrated upon the last.

While thus employed, he failed not to gaze often at the fatal hand, and not without a shudder. Yet once, by a strange and unaccountable impulse, he pressed it with his lips. His spirit recoiled, however, in the very act; and Georgiana, out of the midst of her deep sleep, moved uneasily and murmured as if in remonstrance. Again Aylmer resumed his watch. Nor was it without avail. The crimson hand, which at first had been strongly visible upon the marble paleness of Georgiana's cheek, now grew more faintly outlined. She remained not less pale than ever; but the birthmark, with every breath that came and went, lost somewhat of its former distinctness. Its presence had been awful; its departure was more awful still. Watch the stain of the rainbow fading out the sky, and you will know how that mysterious symbol passed away.

"By Heaven! it is well-nigh gone!" said Aylmer to himself, in almost irrepressible ecstasy. "I can scarcely trace it now. Success! success! And now it is like the faintest rose color. The lightest flush of blood across her cheek would overcome it. But she is so pale!"

He drew aside the window curtain and suffered the light of natural day to fall into the room and rest upon her cheek. At the same time he heard a gross, hoarse chuckle, which he had long known as his servant Aminadab's expression of delight.

"Ah, clod! ah, earthly mass!" cried Aylmer, laughing in a sort of frenzy, "you have served me well! Matter and spirit—earth and heaven—have both done their part in this! Laugh, thing of the senses! You have earned the right to laugh."

These exclamations broke Georgiana's sleep. She slowly unclosed her eyes and gazed into the mirror which her husband had arranged for that purpose. A faint smile flitted over her lips when she recognized how barely perceptible was now that crimson hand which had once blazed forth with such disastrous brilliancy as to scare away all their happiness. But then her eyes sought Aylmer's face with a trouble and anxiety that he could by no means account for.

"My poor Aylmer!" murmured she.

"Poor? Nay, richest, happiest, most favored!" exclaimed he. "My peerless bride, it is successful! You are perfect!"

"My poor Aylmer," she repeated, with a more than human tenderness, "you have aimed loftily; you have done nobly. Do not repent that with so high and pure a feeling, you have rejected the best the earth could offer. Aylmer, dearest Aylmer, I am dying!"

Alas! it was too true! The fatal hand had grappled with the mystery of life, and was the bond by which an angelic spirit kept itself in union with a mortal frame. As the last crimson tint of the birthmark—that sole token of human imperfection—faded from her cheek, the parting breath of the now perfect woman passed into the atmosphere, and her soul, lingering a moment near her husband, took its heavenward flight. Then a hoarse, chuckling laugh was heard again! Thus ever does the gross fatality of earth exult in its invariable triumph over the immortal essence which, in this dim sphere of half development, demands the completeness of a higher state. Yet, had Aylmer reached a profounder wisdom, he need not thus have flung away the happiness which would have woven his mortal life of the selfsame texture with the celestial. The momentary circumstance was too strong for him; he failed to look beyond the shadowy scope of time, and, living once for all in eternity, to find the perfect future in the present.

—*1846*

*Edgar Allan Poe (1809–1849) has become so much the captive of his own legend that his name summons up visions of a mad genius who has little in common with the meticulous craftsman of criticism, fiction, and poetry whose influence on world literature has been immense. Born in Boston, Poe was the child of actors and orphaned at age two. Nevertheless, he lived a privileged childhood as the ward of John Allan, a wealthy Richmond merchant who gave Poe his middle name. After a profligate year at the University of Virginia, successful military service (under an assumed name), and an abortive stay at West Point, Poe broke with his foster father, married his young cousin, and set about a literary career, succeeding as editor of several prominent magazines. However, his irregular habits and a drinking problem, which grew more pronounced following the death of his wife in 1847, led to his mysterious death in Baltimore at the age of thirty-nine. Poe's poetry and short fiction have influenced writers as diverse as Charles Baudelaire and Stephen King. Similarly, Poe's literary criticism has been extremely influential; his tightly structured "The Cask of Amontillado" is a good example of his theory of the "single effect" produced by a well-crafted short story.*

## Edgar Allan Poe
# The Cask of Amontillado[1]

The thousand injuries of Fortunato I had borne as I best could; but when he ventured upon insult, I vowed revenge. You, who so well know the nature of my soul, will not suppose, however, that I gave utterance to a threat. *At length* I would be avenged; this was a point definitely settled—but the very definitiveness with which it was resolved precluded the idea of risk. I must not only punish, but punish with impunity. A wrong is unredressed when retribution overtakes its redresser. It is equally unredressed when the avenger fails to make himself felt as such to him who has done the wrong.

It must be understood that neither by word nor deed had I given Fortunato cause to doubt my good will. I continued, as was my wont, to smile in his face, and he did not perceive that my smile *now* was at the thought of his immolation.

He had a weak point—this Fortunato—although in other regards he was a man to be respected and even feared. He prided himself on

[1]*Cask:* barrel. *Amontillado:* dry sherry from Montilla, Spain.

his connoisseurship in wine. Few Italians have the true virtuoso spirit. For the most part their enthusiasm is adopted to suit the time and opportunity—to practise imposture upon the British and Austrian *millionaires*. In painting and gemmary Fortunato, like his countrymen, was a quack—but in the matter of old wines he was sincere. In this respect I did not differ from him materially; I was skilful in the Italian vintages myself, and bought largely whenever I could.

It was about dusk, one evening during the supreme madness of the carnival season, that I encountered my friend. He accosted me with excessive warmth, for he had been drinking much. The man wore motley. He had on a tight-fitting parti-striped dress, and his head was surmounted by the conical cap and bells. I was so pleased to see him that I thought I should never have done wringing his hand.

I said to him—'My dear Fortunato, you are luckily met. How remarkably well you are looking to-day! I But I have received a pipe[2] of what passes for Amontillado, and I have my doubts.'

'How?' said he. 'Amontillado? A pipe? Impossible! And in the middle of the carnival!'

'I have my doubts', I replied; 'and I was silly enough to pay the full Amontillado price without consulting you in the matter. You were not to be found, and I was fearful of losing a bargain.'

'Amontillado!'

'I have my doubts.'

'Amontillado!'

'And I must satisfy them.'

'Amontillado!'

'As you are engaged, I am on my way to Luchesi. If any one has a critical turn, it is he. He will tell me—'

'Luchesi cannot tell Amontillado from Sherry.'

'And yet some fools will have it that his taste is a match for your own.'

'Come, let us go.'

'Whither?'

'To your vaults.'

'My friend, no; I will not impose upon your good nature. I perceive you have an engagement. Luchesi—'

'I have no engagement;—come.'

---

[2]*pipe:* large cask holding 477 litres.

'My friend, no. It is not the engagement, but the severe cold with which I perceive you are afflicted. The vaults are insufferably damp. They are encrusted with nitre.'

'Let us go, nevertheless. The cold is merely nothing. Amontillado! You have been imposed upon. And as for Luchesi, he cannot distinguish Sherry from Amontillado.'

Thus speaking, Fortunato possessed himself of my arm. Putting on a mask of black silk, and drawing a *roquelaire*[3] closely about my person, I suffered him to hurry me to my palazzo.

There were no attendants at home; they had absconded to make merry in honor of the time. I had told them that I should not return until the morning, and had given them explicit orders not to stir from the house. These orders were sufficient, I well knew, to insure their immediate disappearance, one and all, as soon as my back was turned.

I took from their sconces two flambeaux, and giving one to Fortunato, bowed him through several suites of rooms to the archway that led into the vaults. I passed down a long and winding staircase, requesting him to be cautious as he followed. We came at length to the foot of the descent, and stood together on the damp ground of the catacombs of the Montresors.

The gait of my friend was unsteady, and the bells upon his cap jingled as he strode.

'The pipe,' said he.

'It is farther on,' said I; 'but observe the white web-work which gleams from these cavern walls.'

He turned towards me, and looked into my eyes with two filmy orbs that distilled the rheum of intoxication.

'Nitre?' he asked, at length.

'Nitre,' I replied. 'How long have you had that cough?'

'Ugh! ugh! ugh!—ugh! ugh! ugh!—ugh! ugh! ugh!—ugh! ugh! ugh!—ugh! ugh! ugh!'

My poor friend found it impossible to reply for many minutes.

'It is nothing', he said, at last.

'Come', I said, with decision, 'we will go back; your health is precious. You are rich, respected, admired, beloved; you are happy, as once I was.

[3]*roquelaire:* knee-length man's cloak.

*Guy de Maupassant (1850–1893)* did not consider a literary career until he was almost thirty years of age. After military service he worked as a French government clerk until 1882. The great influence on his development as a writer was the novelist Gustave Flaubert, who introduced Maupassant to other Parisian literary figures. Maupassant died young, a victim of a self-destructive lifestyle that led to syphilis, attempted suicide, and madness, but during his most productive decade (1880–1890) he produced over three hundred stories, six novels, poetry, travel writing, and a play. Maupassant's focus on the unglamorous realities of both rural and urban life marks him as one of the masters of literary naturalism, and his careful plot construction and attention to detail set high standards for later writers of short fiction.

## Guy de Maupassant
# The Piece of String

Along all the roads around Goderville the peasants and their wives were coming toward the town because it was market day. The men were proceeding with slow steps, the whole body bent forward at each movement of their long twisted legs, deformed by their hard work, by the weight on the plow which, at the same time, raised the left shoulder and swerved the figure, by the reaping of the wheat which made the knees spread to make a firm "purchase," by all the slow and painful labors of the country. Their blouses, blue, "stiff-starched," shining as if varnished, ornamented with a little design in white at the neck and wrists, puffed about their bony bodies, seemed like balloons ready to carry them off. From each of them a head, two arms, and two feet protruded.

Some led a cow or a calf by a cord, and their wives, walking behind the animal, whipped its haunches with a leafy branch to hasten its progress. On their arms they carried large baskets from which, in some cases, chickens and, in others, ducks thrust out their heads. And they walked with a quicker, livelier step than their husbands. Their spare straight figures were wrapped in scanty little shawls, pinned over their flat bosoms, and their heads were enveloped in white cloths glued to the hair and surmounted by caps.

Then a wagon passed at the jerky trot of a nag, shaking strangely, two men seated side by side and a woman in the bottom of the vehicle, the latter holding on to the sides to lessen the hard jolts.

In the public square of Goderville there was a crowd, a throng of human beings and animals mixed together. The horns of the cattle, the tall hats with the long nap of the rich peasant, and the headgear of the peasant women rose above the surface of the assembly. And the clamorous, shrill, screaming voices made a continuous and savage din which sometimes was dominated by the robust lungs of some countryman's laugh, or the long lowing of a cow tied to the wall of a house.

All that smacked of the stable, the dairy and the dirt heap, hay and sweat, giving forth that unpleasant odor, human and animal, peculiar to the people of the field.

Maître Hauchecome, of Breaute, had just arrived at Goderville, and he was directing his steps toward the public square, when he perceived upon the ground a little piece of string. Maître Hauchecome, economical like a true Norman, thought that everything useful ought to be picked up, and he bent painfully, for he suffered from rheumatism. He took the bit of thin cord from the ground and began to roll it carefully when he noticed Maître Malandain, the harness-maker, on the threshold of his door, looking at him. They had heretofore had business together on the subject of a halter, and they were on bad terms, being both good haters. Maître Hauchecome was seized with a sort of shame to be seen thus by his enemy, picking a bit of string out of the dirt. He concealed his "find" quickly under his blouse, then in his trousers' pocket; then he pretended to be still looking on the ground for something which he did not find, and he went toward the market, his head forward, bent double by his pains.

He was soon lost in the noisy and slowly moving crowd, which was busy with interminable bargainings. The peasants milked, went and came, perplexed, always in fear of being cheated, not daring to decide, watching the vendor's eye, ever trying to find the trick in the man and the flaw in the beast.

The women, having placed their great baskets at their feet, had taken out the poultry which lay upon the ground, tied together by the feet, with terrified eyes and scarlet crests.

They heard offers, stated their prices with a dry air and impassive face, or perhaps, suddenly deciding on some proposed reduction, shouted to the customer who was slowly going away: "All right, Maître Authirne, I'll give it to you for that."

Then little by little the square was deserted, and when the Angelus rang at noon, those who had stayed too long, scattered to their shops.

At Jourdain's the great room was full of people eating, as the big court was full of vehicles of all kinds, carts, gigs, wagons, dump carts, yellow with dirt, mended and patched, raising their shafts to the sky like two arms, or perhaps with their shafts in the ground and their backs in the air.

Just opposite the diners seated at the table, the immense fireplace, filled with bright flames, cast a lively heat on the backs of the row on the right. Three spits were turning on which were chickens, pigeons, and legs of mutton; and an appetizing odor of roast beef and gravy dripping over the nicely browned skin rose from the hearth, increased the jovialness, and made everybody's mouth water.

All the aristocracy of the plow ate there, at Maître Jourdain's, tavern keeper and horse dealer, a rascal who had money.

The dishes were passed and emptied, as were the jugs of yellow cider. Everyone told his affairs, his purchases, and sales. They discussed the crops. The weather was favorable for the green things but not for the wheat.

Suddenly the drum beat in the court, before the house. Everybody rose except a few indifferent persons, and ran to the door, or to the windows, their mouths still full and napkins in their hands.

After the public crier had ceased his drum-beating, he called out in a jerky voice, speaking his phrases irregularly:

"It is hereby made known to the inhabitants of Goderville, and in general to all persons present at the market, that there was lost this morning, on the road to Benzeville, between nine and ten o'clock, a black leather pocketbook containing five hundred francs and some business papers. The finder is requested to return same with all haste to the mayor's office or to Maître Fortune Houlbreque of Manneville. There will be twenty francs reward."

Then the man went away. The heavy roll of the drum and the crier's voice were again heard at a distance.

Then they began to talk of this event discussing the chances that Maître Houlbreque had of finding or not finding his pocketbook.

And the meal concluded. They were finishing their coffee when a chief of the gendarmes appeared upon the threshold.

He inquired: "Is Maître Hauchecome, of Breaute, here?"

Maître Hauchecome, seated at the other end of the table, replied: "Here I am."

And the officer resumed: "Maître Hauchecome, will you have the goodness to accompany me to the mayor's office? The mayor would like to talk to you."

The peasant, surprised and disturbed, swallowed at a draught his tiny glass of brandy, rose, and, even more bent than in the morning, for the first steps after each rest were specially difficult, set out, repeating: "Here I am, here I am."

The mayor was awaiting him, seated on an armchair. He was the notary of the vicinity, a stout, serious man, with pompous phrases.

"Maître Hauchecome," said he, "you were seen this morning to pick up, on the road to Benzeville, the pocketbook lost by Maître Houlbreque, of Manneville."

The countryman, astounded, looked at the mayor, already terrified by this suspicion resting on him without his knowing why.

"Me? Me? Me pick up the pocketbook?"

"Yes, you, yourself."

"Word of honor, I never heard of it."

"But you were seen."

"I was seen, me? Who says he saw me?"

"Monsieur Malandain, the harness-maker."

The old man remembered, understood, and flushed with anger.

"Ah, he saw me, the clodhopper, he saw me pick up this string, here, M'sieu' the Mayor." And rummaging in his pocket he drew out the little piece of string.

But the mayor, incredulous, shook his head.

"You will not make me believe, Maître Hauchecome, that Monsieur Malandain, who is a man worthy of credence, mistook this cord for a pocketbook."

The peasant, furious, lifted his hand, spat at one side to attest his honor, repeating: "It is nevertheless the truth of the good God, the sacred truth, M'sieu' the Mayor. I repeat it on my soul and my salvation."

The mayor resumed: "After picking up the object, you stood like a stilt, looking a long while in the mud to see if any piece of money had fallen out."

The good, old man choked with indignation and fear.

"How anyone can tell—how anyone can tell—such lies to take away an honest man's reputation! How can anyone—"

There was no use in his protesting; nobody believed him. He was confronted with Monsieur Malandain, who repeated and maintained his affirmation. They abused each other for an hour. At his own request, Maître Hauchecome was searched; nothing was found on him.

Finally the mayor, very much perplexed, discharged him with the warning that he would consult the public prosecutor and ask for further orders.

The news had spread. As he left the mayor's office, the old man was surrounded and questioned with a serious or bantering curiosity, in which there was no indignation. He began to tell the story of the string. No one believed him. They laughed at him.

He went along, stopping his friends, beginning endlessly his statement and his protestations, showing his pockets turned inside out, to prove that he had nothing.

They said: "Old rascal, get out!"

And he grew angry, becoming exasperated, hot, and distressed at not being believed, not knowing what to do and always repeating himself.

Night came. He must depart. He started on his way with three neighbors to whom he pointed out the place where he had picked up the bit of string; and all along the road he spoke of his adventure.

In the evening he took a turn in the village of Breaute, in order to tell it to everybody. He only met with incredulity.

It made him ill at night.

The next day about one o'clock in the afternoon, Marius Paumelle, a hired man in the employ of Maître Breton, husbandman at Ymanville, returned the pocketbook and its contents to Maître Houlbreque of Manneville.

This man claimed to have found the object in the road; but not knowing how to read, he had carried it to the house and given it to his employer.

The news spread through the neighborhood. Maître Hauchecome was informed of it. He immediately went the circuit and began to recount his story completed by the happy climax. He was in triumph.

"What grieved me so much was not the thing itself, as the lying. There is nothing so shameful as to be placed under a cloud on account of a lie."

He talked of his adventure all day long; he told it on the highway to people who were passing by, in the wine-shop to people who were drinking there, and to persons coming out of church the following Sunday. He stopped strangers to tell them about it. He was calm now, and yet something disturbed him without his knowing exactly what it was. People had the air of joking while they listened. They did not seem convinced. He seemed to feel that remarks were being made behind his back.

On Tuesday of the next week he went to the market at Goderville, urged solely by the necessity he felt of discussing the case.

Malandain, standing at his door, began to laugh on seeing him pass. Why?

He approached a farmer from Crequetot, who did not let him finish, and giving him a thump in the stomach said to his face: "You big rascal."

Then he turned his back on him.

Maître Hauchecome was confused. Why was he called a big rascal?

When he was seated at the table, in Jourdain's tavern he commenced to explain "the affair."

A horse dealer from Monvilliers called to him: "Come, come, old sharper, that's an old trick; I know all about your piece of string!"

Hauchecome stammered: "But since the pocketbook was found."

But the other man replied: "Shut up, papa, there is one that finds, and there is one that reports. At any rate you are mixed up with it."

The peasant stood choking. He understood. They accused him of having had the pocketbook returned by a confederate, by an accomplice.

He tried to protest. All the table began to laugh.

He could not finish his dinner and went away, in the midst of jeers.

He went home ashamed and indignant, choking with anger and confusion, the more dejected that he was capable with his Norman cunning of doing what they had accused him of, and even boasting of it as of a good turn. His innocence to him, in a confused way, was impossible to prove, as his sharpness was known. And he was stricken to the heart by the injustice of the suspicion.

Then he began to recount the adventures again, prolonging his history every day, adding each time new reasons, more energetic protestations, more solemn oaths which he imagined and prepared in his hours of solitude, his whole mind given up to the story of the string. He was believed so much the less as his defense was more complicated and his arguing more subtle.

"Those are lying excuses," they said behind his back.

He felt it, consumed his heart over it, and wore himself out with useless efforts. He wasted away before their very eyes.

She did not stop to ask if it were not a monstrous joy that held her. A clear and exalted perception enabled her to dismiss the suggestion as trivial.

She knew that she would weep again when she saw the kind, tender hands folded in death; the face that had never looked save with love upon her, fixed and gray and dead. But she saw beyond that bitter moment a long procession of years to come that would belong to her absolutely. And she opened and spread her arms out to them in welcome.

There would be no one to live for her during those coming years; she would live for herself. There would be no powerful will bending her in that blind persistence with which men and women believe they have a right to impose a private will upon a fellow creature. A kind intention or a cruel intention made the act seem no less a crime as she looked upon it in that brief moment of illumination.

And yet she had loved him—sometimes. Often she had not. What did it matter! What could love, the unsolved mystery, count for in face of this possession of self-assertion which she suddenly recognized as the strongest impulse of her being.

"Free! Body and soul free!" she kept whispering.

Josephine was kneeling before the closed door with her lips to the keyhole, imploring for admission. "Louise, open the door! I beg; open the door—you will make yourself ill. What are you doing, Louise? For heaven's sake open the door."

"Go away. I am not making myself ill." No; she was drinking in a very elixir of life through that open window.

Her fancy was running riot along those days ahead of her. Spring days and summer days, and all sorts of days that would be her own. She breathed a quick prayer that life might be long. It was only yesterday she had thought with a shudder that life might be long.

She arose at length and opened the door to her sister's importunities. There was a feverish triumph in her eyes, and she carried herself unwittingly like a goddess of Victory. She clasped her sister's waist, and together they descended the stairs. Richards stood waiting for them at the bottom.

Some one was opening the front door with a latchkey. It was Brently Mallard who entered, a little travel-stained, composedly carrying his gripsack and umbrella. He had been far from the scene of the accident, and did not even know there had been one. He stood amazed at Josephine's piercing cry; at Richards' quick motion to screen him from the view of his wife.

But Richards was too late.

When the doctors came they said she had died of heart disease—of joy that kills.

*—1894*

---

**Oscar Wilde (1854–1900)** *was an Irish-born writer best known for his play* The Importance of Being Earnest *(1895); but he also wrote poems and fiction including the novel* The Picture of Dorian Gray *(1891), and beloved fairy tales such as "The Selfish Giant" and "The Happy Prince." In 1895 he was tried for homosexuality and sentenced to imprisonment with hard labour for two years. After his release, crushed financially and physically, Wilde lived out his last years in Paris under an assumed name. In her story "Mr. Wilde's Second Chance," Joanna Russ speculates on the choices open to Wilde in the era in which he lived.*

## Oscar Wilde
# The Sphinx without a Secret: An Etching

One afternoon I was sitting outside the Café de la Paix, watching the splendour and shabbiness of Parisian life, and wondering over my vermouth at the strange panorama of pride and poverty that was passing before me, when I heard some one call my name. I turned round, and saw Lord Murchison. We had not met since we had been at college together, nearly ten years before, so I was delighted to come across him again, and we shook hands warmly. At Oxford we had been great friends. I had liked him immensely, he was so handsome, so high-spirited, and so honourable. We used to say of him that he would be the best of fellows, if he did not always speak the truth, but I think we really admired him all the more for his frankness. I found him a good deal changed. He looked anxious and puzzled, and seemed to be in doubt about something. I felt it could not be modern scepticism, for Murchison was the stoutest of Tories, and believed in the Pentateuch[1] as firmly as he believed in the House of Peers; so I concluded that it was a woman, and asked him if he was married yet.

'I don't understand women well enough,' he answered.

'My dear Gerald,' I said, 'women are meant to be loved, not to be understood.'

'I cannot love where I cannot trust,' he replied.

'I believe you have a mystery in your life, Gerald,' I exclaimed; 'tell me about it.'

'Let us go for a drive,' he answered, 'it is too crowded here. No, not a yellow carriage, any other colour—there, that dark-green one will do;' and in a few moments we were trotting down the boulevard in the direction of the Madeleine.

'Where shall we go to?' I said.

'Oh, anywhere you like!' he answered—'to the restaurant in the Bois; we will dine there, and you shall tell me all about yourself.'

'I want to hear about you first,' I said. 'Tell me your mystery.'

He took from his pocket a little silver-clasped morocco case, and handed it to me. I opened it. Inside there was the photograph of a woman. She was tall and slight, and strangely picturesque with her large vague eyes and loosened hair. She looked like a *clairvoyante*, and was wrapped in rich furs.

'What do you think of that face?' he said; 'is it truthful?'

I examined it carefully. It seemed to me the face of some one who had a secret, but whether that secret was good or evil I could not say. Its beauty was a beauty moulded out of many mysteries—the beauty, in fact, which is psychological, not plastic—and the faint smile that just played across the lips was far too subtle to be really sweet.

'Well,' he cried impatiently, 'what do you say?'

'She is the Gioconda[2] in sables,' I answered. 'Let me know all about her.'

'Not now,' he said; 'after dinner;' and began to talk of other things.

When the waiter brought us our coffee and cigarettes I reminded Gerald of his promise. He rose from his seat, walked two or three times

---

[1]*Pentateuch:* first five books of the Old Testament.
[2]*Gioconda:* Leonardo da Vinci's *Mona Lisa* (1507).

up and down the room, and, sinking into an armchair, told me the following story:—

'One evening,' he said, 'I was walking down Bond Street about five o'clock. There was a terrific crush of carriages, and the traffic was almost stopped. Close to the pavement was standing a little yellow brougham, which, for some reason or other, attracted my attention. As I passed by there looked out from it the face I showed you this afternoon. It fascinated me immediately. All that night I kept thinking of it, and all the next day. I wandered up and down that wretched Row, peering into every carriage, and waiting for the yellow brougham; but I could not find *ma belle inconnue*, and at last I began to think she was merely a dream. About a week afterwards I was dining with Madame de Rastail. Dinner was for eight o'clock; but at half-past eight we were still waiting in the drawing-room. Finally the servant threw open the door, and announced Lady Alroy. It was the woman I had been looking for. She came in very slowly, looking like a moonbeam in grey lace, and, to my intense delight, I was asked to take her in to dinner. After we had sat down I remarked quite innocently, "I think I caught sight of you in Bond Street some time ago, Lady Alroy." She grew very pale, and said to me in a low voice, "Pray do not talk so loud; you may be overheard." I felt miserable at having made such a bad beginning, and plunged recklessly into the subject of the French plays. She spoke very little, always in the same low musical voice, and seemed as if she was afraid of some one listening. I fell passionately, stupidly in love, and the indefinable atmosphere of mystery that surrounded her excited my most ardent curiosity. When she was going away, which she did very soon after dinner, I asked her if I might call and see her. She hesitated for a moment, glanced round to see if any one was near us, and then said, "Yes; to-morrow at a quarter to five." I begged Madame de Rastail to tell me about her; but all that I could learn was that she was a widow with a beautiful house in Park Lane, and as some scientific bore began a dissertation on widows, as exemplifying the survival of the matrimonially fittest, I left and went home.

'The next day I arrived at Park Lane punctual to the moment, but was told by the butler that Lady Alroy had just gone out. I went down to the club quite unhappy and very much puzzled, and after long consideration wrote her a letter, asking if I might be allowed to try my chance some other afternoon. I had no answer for several days, but at last I got a little note saying she would be at home on Sunday at four,

'My dear Gerald,' I answered, 'Lady Alroy was simply a woman with a mania for mystery. She took these rooms for the pleasure of going there with her veil down, and imagining she was a heroine. She had a passion for secrecy, but she herself was merely a Sphinx without a secret.'

'Do you really think so?'

'I am sure of it,' I replied.

He took out the morocco case, opened it, and looked at the photograph. 'I wonder?' he said at last.

*—1891*

---

**Anton Chekhov (1860–1904)** *was the grandchild of Russian serfs but showed great understanding of and sympathy for the upper-class characters, like those in his masterpiece* The Cherry Orchard *(1904), who could see their world ending in the decades before the Russian Revolution. After early education in his native town of Taganrog, Chekhov entered the University of Moscow, where he took a medical degree in 1884. Except for occasional service during epidemics, Chekhov practised only rarely, preferring to earn his living as a regular contributor of stories to humour magazines. His first play,* Ivanov, *was produced in 1887, beginning for Chekhov a career as a dramatist that flourished in the last decade of his life, when he allied himself with the Moscow Art Theatre and its influential director, Konstantin Stanislavsky. Chekhov's early stories were primarily comic, but those of his mature period, like his plays, are remarkable for their emotional depth. Chekhov's objectivity and realism, qualities that he perhaps gained from his medical studies, continue to make him one of the most modern of nineteenth-century authors; there are rarely easy morals in Chekhov's works. The "unheroic heroes and heroines" whom he depicts with sympathy and gentle irony foreshadow many of the key literary themes of the twentieth century.*

## *Anton Chekhov*
# An Upheaval

Mashenka Pavletsky, a young girl who had only just finished her studies at a boarding school, returning from a walk to the house of the Kushkins, with whom she was living as a governess, found the household in a terrible turmoil. Mihailo, the porter who opened the door to her, was excited and red as a crab.

Translated by Constance Garnett.

Loud voices were heard from upstairs.

"Madame Kushkin is in a fit, most likely, or else she has quarrelled with her husband," thought Mashenka.

In the hall and in the corridor she met maidservants. One of them was crying. Then Mashenka saw, running out of her room, the master of the house himself, Nikolay Sergeitch, a little man with a flabby face and a bald head, though he was not old. He was red in the face and twitching all over. He passed the governess without noticing her, and throwing up his arms, exclaimed:

"Oh, how horrible it is! How tactless! How stupid! How barbarous! Abominable!"

Mashenka went into her room, and then, for the first time in her life, it was her lot to experience in all its acuteness the feeling that is so familiar to persons in dependent positions, who eat the bread of the rich and powerful, and cannot speak their minds. There was a search going on in her room. The lady of the house, Fedosya Vassilyevna, a stout, broad-shouldered, uncouth woman with thick black eyebrows, a faintly perceptible moustache, and red hands, who was exactly like a plain, illiterate cook in face and manners, was standing, without her cap on, at the table, putting back into Mashenka's work-bag balls of wool, scraps of materials, and bits of papers. . . . Evidently the governess's arrival took her by surprise, since, on looking round and seeing the girl's pale and astonished face, she was a little taken aback, and muttered:

"*Pardon.* I . . . I upset it accidentally. . . . My sleeve caught in it . . ."

And saying something more, Madame Kushkin rustled her long skirts and went out. Mashenka looked round her room with wondering eyes, and, unable to understand it, not knowing what to think, shrugged her shoulders, and turned cold with dismay. What had Fedosya Vassilyevna been looking for in her work-bag? If she really had, as she said, caught her sleeve in it and upset everything, why had Nikolay Sergeitch dashed out of her room so excited and red in the face? Why was one drawer of the table pulled out a little way? The money-box, in which the governess put away ten kopeck pieces and old stamps, was open. They had opened it, but did not know how to shut it, though they had scratched the lock all over. The whatnot with her books on it, the things on the table, the bed—all bore fresh traces of a search. Her linen-basket, too. The linen had been carefully folded, but it was not in the same order as Mashenka had left it when she went out. So the search had been thorough, most thorough. But what was it for? Why? What had happened? Mashenka remembered the excited porter, the general turmoil which was still going on, the weeping servant-girl; had it not all some connection with the search that had just been made in her room? Was she not mixed up in something dreadful? Mashenka turned pale, and feeling cold all over, sank on to her linen-basket.

A maidservant came into the room.

"Liza, you don't know why they have been rummaging in my room?" the governess asked her.

"Mistress has lost a brooch worth two thousand," said Liza.

"Yes, but why have they been rummaging in my room?"

"They've been searching every one, miss. They've searched all my things, too. They stripped us all naked and searched us. . . . God knows, miss, I never went near her toilet-table, let alone touching the brooch. I shall say the same at the police-station."

"But . . . why have they been rummaging here?" the governess still wondered.

"A brooch has been stolen, I tell you. The mistress has been rummaging in everything with her own hands. She even searched Mihailo, the porter, herself. It's a perfect disgrace! Nikolay Sergeitch simply looks on and cackles like a hen. But you've no need to tremble like that, miss. They found nothing here. You've nothing to be afraid of if you didn't take the brooch."

"But Liza, it's vile . . . it's insulting," said Mashenka, breathless with indignation. "It's so mean, so low! What right had she to suspect me and to rummage in my things?"

"You are living with strangers, miss," sighed Liza. "Though you are a young lady, still you are . . . as it were . . . a servant. . . . It's not like living with your papa and mamma."

Mashenka threw herself on the bed and sobbed bitterly. Never in her life had she been subjected to such an outrage, never had she been so deeply insulted. . . . She, well-educated, refined, the daughter of a teacher, was suspected of theft; she had been searched like a street-walker! She could not imagine a greater insult. And to this feeling of resentment was added an oppressive dread of what would come next. All sorts of absurd ideas came into her mind. If they could suspect her of theft, then they might arrest her, strip her naked, and search her, then lead her through the street with an escort of soldiers, cast her into a cold, dark cell with mice and wood lice, exactly like the dungeon in which Princess Tarakanov was imprisoned. Who would stand up for her? Her parents lived far away in the Provinces; they had not the money to come to her. In the capital she was as solitary as in a desert, without friends or kindred. They could do what they liked with her.

"I will go to all the courts and all the lawyers," Mashenka thought, trembling. "I will explain to them, I will take an oath. . . . They will believe that I could not be a thief!"

Mashenka remembered that under the sheets in her basket she had some sweetmeats, which, following the habits of her schooldays, she had put in her pocket at dinner and carried off to her room. She felt hot all over, and was ashamed at the thought that her little secret was known to the lady of the house; all this terror, shame, resentment, brought on an attack of palpitation of the heart, which set up a throbbing in her temples, in her heart, and deep down in her stomach.

"Dinner is ready," the servant summoned Mashenka.

"Shall I go, or not?"

Mashenka brushed her hair, wiped her face with a wet towel and went into the dining room. There they had already begun dinner. At one end of the table sat Fedosya Vassilyevna with a stupid, solemn, serious face; at the other end Nikolay Sergeitch. At the sides there were the visitors and the children. The dishes were handed by two footmen in swallowtails and white gloves. Everyone knew that there was an upset in the house, that Madame Kushkin was in trouble, and everyone was silent. Nothing was heard but the sound of munching and the rattle of spoons on the plates.

The lady of the house, herself, was the first to speak.

"What is the third course?" she asked the footman in a weary, injured voice.

"*Esturgeon à la russe*,"[1] answered the footman.

"I ordered that, Fenya," Nikolay Sergeitch hastened to observe. "I wanted some fish. If you don't like it, *ma chère*, don't let them serve it. I just ordered it. . . ."

Fedosya Vassilyevna did not like dishes that she had not ordered herself, and now her eyes filled with tears.

"Come, don't let us agitate ourselves," Mamikov, her household doctor, observed in a honeyed voice, just touching her arm, with a smile as

---

[1]*Esturgeon à la russe:* sturgeon, cooked in the Russian manner.

"I know it's not your fault, Nikolay Sergeitch," said Mashenka, looking him full in the face with her big tear-stained eyes. "Why should you worry yourself?"

"Of course, no. . . . But still, don't you . . . go away. I entreat you."

Mashenka shook her head. Nikolay Sergeitch stopped at the window and drummed on a pane with his fingertips.

"Such misunderstandings are simply torture to me," he said. "Why, do you want me to go down on my knees to you, or what? Your pride is wounded, and here you've been crying and packing up to go; but I have pride, too, and you do not spare it! Or do you want me to tell you what I would not tell at Confession? Do you? Listen; you want me to tell you what I won't tell the priest on my deathbed?"

Mashenka made no answer.

"I took my wife's brooch," Nikolay Sergeitch said quickly. "Is that enough now? Are you satisfied? Yes, I . . . took it. . . . But, of course, I count on your discretion. . . . For God's sake, not a word, not half a hint to any one!"

Mashenka, amazed and frightened, went on packing; she snatched her things, crumpled them up, and thrust them anyhow into the box and the basket. Now, after this candid avowal on the part of Nikolay Sergeitch, she could not remain another minute, and could not understand how she could have gone on living in the house before.

"And it's nothing to wonder at," Nikolay Sergeitch went on after a pause. "It's an everyday story! I need money, and she . . . won't give it to me. It was my father's money that bought this house and everything, you know! It's all mine, and the brooch belonged to my mother, and . . . it's all mine! And she took it, took possession of everything. . . . I can't go to law with her, you'll admit. . . . I beg you most earnestly, overlook it . . . stay on. *Tout comprendre, tout pardonner.*[2] Will you stay?"

"No!" said Mashenka resolutely, beginning to tremble. "Let me alone, I entreat you!"

"Well, God bless you!" sighed Nikolay Sergeitch, sitting down on the stool near the box. "I must own I like people who still can feel resentment, contempt, and so on. I could sit here forever and look at your indignant face. . . . So you won't stay, then? I understand. . . . it's bound to be so. . . . Yes, of course. . . . It's all right for you, but for me—wo-o-o-o! . . . I can't

---

[2]*Tout comprendre, tout pardonner:* All is understood, all is forgiven.

stir a step out of this cellar. I'd go off to one of our estates, but in every one of them there are some of my wife's rascals . . . stewards, experts, damn them all! They mortgage and remortgage. . . . You mustn't catch fish, must keep off the grass, mustn't break the trees."

"Nikolay Sergeitch!" his wife's voice called from the drawing-room. "Agnia, call your master!"

"Then you won't stay?" asked Nikolay Sergeitch, getting up quickly and going toward the door. "You might as well stay, really. In the evenings I could come and have a talk with you. Eh? Stay! If you go, there won't be a human face left in the house. It's awful!"

Nikolay Sergeitch's pale, exhausted face besought her, but Mashenka shook her head, and with a wave of his hand he went out.

Half an hour later she was on her way.

—*1917*

---

*Stephen Leacock (1869–1944) was born in Swanmore, England, but immigrated to Ontario with his family in 1876. Though he published in the field of political science, he was best known for his humour writing, most notably* Sunshine Sketches of a Little Town *(1912), a collection of affectionate satires of small-town Canadian life based on Orillia, a town on the shore of Lake Simcoe, where Leacock spent his summer holidays.* Idle Adventures of the Arcadian Rich *(1914), a darker collection based on life in Montreal, where Leacock taught at McGill University, soon followed. The explicitly Canadian content of these accomplished works might have meant that they were not as popular internationally as Leacock's other comic collections, including* Literary Lapses *(1910),* Nonsense Novels *(1911), and* The Dry Pickwick *(1932).*

## Stephen Leacock
# Ho for Happiness: A Plea for Lighter and Brighter Literature

"Why is it," said some one in conversation the other day, "that all the really good short stories seem to contain so much sadness and suffering and to turn so much on crime and wickedness? Why can't they be happy all the time?"

No one present was able to answer the question. But I thought it over afterwards, and I think I see why it is so. A happy story, after all, would make pretty dull reading. It may be all right in real life to have everything come along just right, with happiness and good luck all the time, but in fiction it would never do.

Stop, let me illustrate the idea. Let us make up a story which is happy all the time and contrast it as it goes along with the way things happen in the really good stories.

Harold Herald never forgot the bright October morning when the mysterious letter, which was to alter his whole life, arrived at his downtown office.

His stenographer brought it in to him and laid it on his desk.

"A letter for you," she said. Then she kissed him and went out again.

Harold sat for some time with the letter in front of him. Should he open it? After all, why not?

He opened the letter. Then the idea occurred to him to read it. "I might as well," he thought.

"Dear Mr. Herald" (so ran the letter), "if you will have the kindness to call at this office, we shall be happy to tell you something to your great advantage."

The letter was signed John Scribman. The paper on which it was written bore the heading "Scribman, Scribman & Company, Barristers, Solicitors, etc., No. 13 Yonge St."

A few moments later saw Harold on his way to the lawyers' office. Never had the streets looked brighter and more cheerful than in this perfect October sunshine. In fact, they never had been.

Nor did Harold's heart misgive him and a sudden suspicion enter his mind as Mr. Scribman, the senior partner, rose from his chair to greet him. Not at all. Mr. Scribman was a pleasant, middle-aged man whose countenance behind his gold spectacles beamed with goodwill and good nature.

"Ah, Mr. Harold Herald," he said, "or perhaps, you will let me call you simply Harold. I didn't like to give you too much news in one short letter. The fact is that our firm has been entrusted to deliver to you a legacy, or rather a gift. . . . Stop, stop!" continued the lawyer, as Harold was about to interrupt with questions, " . . . our client's one request was that his name would not be divulged. He thought it would be so much nicer for you just to have the money and not know who gave it to you."

Harold murmured his assent.

Mr. Scribman pushed a bell.

"Mr. Harold Herald's money, if you please," he said.

A beautiful stenographer wearing an American Beauty rose at her waist entered the room carrying a silken bag.

"There is half a million dollars here in five-hundred-dollar bills," said the lawyer. "At least, we didn't count them; but that is what our client said. Did you take any?" he asked the stenographer.

"I took out a few last night to go to the theatre with," admitted the girl with a pretty blush.

"Monkey!" said Mr. Scribman. "But that's all right. Don't bother with a receipt, Harold. Come along with me: my daughter is waiting for us down below in the car to take us to lunch."

Harold thought he had never seen a more beautiful girl than Alicia Scribman. In fact he hadn't. The luxurious motor, the faultless chauffeur, the presence of the girl beside him and the bag of currency under the seat, the sunlit streets filled with happy people with the bright feeling of just going back to work, full of lunch—the sight of all this made Harold feel as if life were indeed a pleasant thing.

"After all," he mused, "how little is needed for our happiness! Half a million dollars, a motor-car, a beautiful girl, youth, health—surely one can be content with that . . ."

It was after lunch at the beautiful country home of the Scribmans that Harold found himself alone for a few minutes with Miss Scribman.

He rose, walked over to her and took her hand, kneeling on one knee and pulling up his pants so as not to make a crease in them.

"Alicia!" he said. "Ever since I first saw you, I have loved you. I want to ask you if you will marry me?"

"Oh, Harold," said Alicia, leaning forward and putting both her arms about his neck with one ear against the upper right-hand end of his cheekbone. "Oh, Harold!"

"I can, as you know," continued Harold, "easily support you."

"Oh, that's all right," said Alicia. "As a matter of fact, I have much more than that of my own, to be paid over to me when I marry."

"Then you will marry me?" said Harold rapturously.

"Yes, indeed," said Alicia, "and it happens so fortunately just now, as papa himself is engaged to marry again and so I shall be glad to have a new home of my own. Papa is marrying a charming girl, but she is so much younger than he is that perhaps she would not want a grown-up stepdaughter."

Harold made his way back to the city in a tumult of happiness. Only for a moment was his delirium of joy brought to a temporary standstill.

As he returned to his own apartment, he suddenly remembered that he was engaged to be married to his cousin Winnie. . . . The thing had been entirely washed out of his mind by the flood-tide of his joy.

He seized the telephone.

"Winnie," he said, "I am so terribly sorry. I want to ask you to release me from our engagement. I want to marry someone else."

"That's all right, Hal!" came back Winnie's voice cheerfully. "As a matter of fact, I want to do the same thing myself. I got engaged last week to the most charming man in the world, a little older, in fact quite a bit older than I am, but ever so nice. He is a wealthy lawyer and his name is Walter Scribman. . . ."

The double wedding took place two weeks later, the church being smothered with chrysanthemums and the clergyman buried under Canadian currency. Harold and Alicia built a beautiful country home at the other side—the farthest-away side—of the city from the Scribmans'. A year or so after their marriage, they had a beautiful boy, and then another, then a couple of girls (twins), and then they lost count.

There. Pretty dull reading it makes. And yet, I don't know. There's something about it, too. In the real stories Mr. Scribman would have been a crook, and Harold would have either murdered Winnie or been accused of it, and the stenographer with the rose would have stolen the money instead of just taking it, and it wouldn't have happened in bright, clear October weather but in dirty old November—oh, no, let us have romance and happiness, after all. It may not be true, but it's better.

*—1932*

## Emily Carr
# Kitwancool

When the Indians told me about the Kitwancool totem poles, I said:

"How can I get to Kitwancool?"

"Dunno," the Indians replied.

White men told me about the Kitwancool poles too, but when I told them I wanted to go there, they advised me—"Keep out." But the thought of those old Kitwancool poles pulled at me. I was at Kitwangak, twenty or so miles from Kitwancool.

Then a halfbreed at Kitwangak said to me, "The young son of the Kitwancool Chief is going in tomorrow with a load of lumber. I asked if he would take you; he will."

"How can I get out again?"

"The boy is coming back to Kitwangak after two days."

The Chief's son Aleck was shy, but he spoke good English. He said I was to be at the Hudson's Bay store at eight the next morning.

I bought enough food and mosquito oil to last me two days; then I sat in front of the Hudson's Bay store from eight to eleven o'clock, waiting. I saw Aleck drive past to load his lumber. The wagon had four wheels and a long pole. He tied the lumber to the pole and a sack of oats to the lumber; I was to sit on the oats. Rigged up in front somehow was a place for the driver—no real seat, just a couple of coal-oil boxes bound to some boards. Three men sat on the two boxes. The road was terrible. When we bumped, the man on the down side of the boxes fell off.

A sturdy old man trudged behind the wagon. Sometimes he rode a bit on the end of the long pole, which tossed him up and down like a see-saw. The old man carried a gun and walked most of the way.

The noon sun burnt fiercely on our heads. The oat-sack gave no support to my back, and my feet dangled. I had to clutch the corner of the oat-sack with one hand to keep from falling off—with the other I held my small griffon dog. Every minute I thought we would be pitched off the pole. You could seldom see the old man because of clouds of yellow dust rolling behind the wagon. The scrub growth at the road-side smelt red hot.

The scraggy ponies dragged their feet heavily; sweat cut rivers through the dust that was caked on their sides.

One of the three men on the front seat of the wagon seemed to be a hero. The other men questioned him all the way, though generally Indians do not talk as they travel. When one of the men fell off the seat he ran round the wagon to the high side and jumped up again and all the while he did not stop asking the hero questions. There were so many holes in the road and the men fell off so often that they were always changing places, like birds on a roost in cold weather.

Suddenly we gave such an enormous bump that we all fell off together, and the horses stopped. When the wheels were not rattling any more we could hear water running. Then the old man came out of the clouds of dust behind us and said there was a stream close by.

We threw ourselves on-to our stomachs, put our lips to the water and drank like horses. The Indians took the bits out of their horses' mouths and gave them food. Then the men crawled under the wagon to eat their lunch in its shade; I sat by the shadiest wheel. It was splendid to put my legs straight out and have the earth support them and the wheel support my back. The old man went to sleep.

After he woke and after the horses had pulled the wagon out of the big hole, we rumbled on again.

When the sun began to go down we were in woods, and the clouds of mosquitoes were as thick as the clouds of dust, but more painful. We let them eat us because, after bumping for seven hours, we were too tired to fight.

At last we came to a great dip where the road wound around the edge of a ravine shaped like an oblong bowl. There were trees growing in this earth bowl. It seemed to be bottomless. We were level with the tree-tops as we looked down. The road was narrow—its edges broken.

I was afraid and said, "I want to walk."

Aleck waved his hand across the ravine. "Kitwancool," he said and I saw some grey roofs on the far side of the hollow. After we had circled the ravine and climbed the road on the other side we would be there, unless we were lying dead in that deep bowl.

I said again, "I want to walk."

"Village dogs will kill you and the little dog," said Aleck. But I did walk around the bend and up the hill, until the village was near. Then I rode into Kitwancool on the oat-sack.

The dogs rushed out in a pack. The village people came out too. They made a fuss over the hero-man, clustering about him and jabbering. They paid no more attention to me than to the oat-sack. All of them went into the nearest house taking Aleck, the hero, the old man and the other man with them, and shut the door.

I wanted to cry, sticking alone up there on top of the oats and lumber, the sagging horses in front and the yapping dogs all round, nobody to ask about anything and very tired. Aleck had told me I could sleep on the verandah of his father's house, because I only had a cot and a tent-fly with me, and bears came into the village often at night. But how did I know which was his father's house? The dogs would tear me if I got down and there was no one to ask, anyway.

Suddenly something at the other end of the village attracted the dogs. The pack tore off and the dust hid me from them.

Aleck came out of the house and said, "We are going to have dinner in this house now." Then he went in again and shut the door.

The wagon was standing in the new part of the village. Below us, on the right, I could see a row of old houses. They were dim, for the light was going, but above them, black and clear against the sky stood the old totem poles of Kitwancool. I jumped down from the wagon and came to them. That part of the village was quite dead. Between the river and the poles was a flat of green grass. Above, stood the houses, grey and broken. They were in a long, wavering row, with wide, windowless fronts. The totem poles stood before them there on the top of a little bank above the green flat. There were a few poles down on the flat too, and some graves that had fences round them and roofs over the tops.

When it was almost dark I went back to the wagon.

The house of Aleck's father was the last one at the other end of the new village. It was one great room like a hall and was built of new logs. It had seven windows and two doors; all the windows were propped open with blue castor-oil bottles.

I was surprised to find that the old man who had trudged behind our wagon was Chief Douse—Aleck's father.

Mrs. Douse was more important than Mr. Douse; she was a chieftain-ess in her own right, and had great dignity. Neither of them spoke to me that night. Aleck showed me where to put my bed on the verandah and I hung the fly over it. I ate a dry scrap of food and turned into my blankets. I had no netting, and the mosquitoes tormented me.

My heart said into the thick dark, "Why did I come?"

And the dark answered, "You know."

In the morning the hero-man came to me and said, "My mother-in-law wishes to speak with you. She does not know English words so she will talk through my tongue."

I stood before the tall, cold woman. She folded her arms across her body and her eyes searched my face. They were as expressive as if she were saying the words herself instead of using the hero's tongue.

"My mother-in-law wishes to know why you have come to our village."

"I want to make some pictures of the totem poles."

"What do you want our totem poles for?"

"Because they are beautiful. They are getting old now, and your people make very few new ones. The young people do not value the poles as the old ones did. By and by there will be no more poles. I want to make pictures of them, so that your young people as well as the white people will see how fine your totem poles used to be."

Mrs. Douse listened when the young man told her this. Her eyes raked my face to see if I was talking "straight". Then she waved her hand towards the village.

"Go along," she said through the interpreter, "and I shall see." She was neither friendly nor angry. Perhaps I was going to be turned out of this place that had been so difficult to get into.

The air was hot and heavy. I turned towards the old village with the pup Ginger Pop at my heels. Suddenly there was a roar of yelpings, and I saw my little dog putting half a dozen big ones to rout down the village street. Their tails were flat, their tongues lolled and they yelped. The Douses all rushed out of their house to see what the noise was about, and we laughed together so hard that the strain, which before had been between us, broke.

The sun enriched the old poles grandly. They were carved elaborately and with great sincerity. Several times the figure of a woman that held a child was represented. The babies had faces like wise little old men. The mothers expressed all womanhood—the big wooden hands holding the child were so full of tenderness they had to be distorted enormously in order to contain it all. Womanhood was strong in Kitwancool. Perhaps, after all, Mrs. Douse might let me stay.

I sat in front of a totem mother and began to draw—so full of her strange, wild beauty that I did not notice the storm that was coming, till the totem poles went black, flashed vividly white and then went black again. Bang upon bang, came the claps of thunder. The hills on one side tossed it to the hills on the other; sheets of rain washed over me. I was beside a grave down on the green flat; some of the pickets of its fence were gone, so I crawled through on to the grave with Ginger Pop in my arms to shelter under its roof. Stinging nettles grew on top of the grave with mosquitoes hiding under their leaves. While I was beating down the nettles with my easel, it struck the head of a big wooden bear squatted on the grave. He startled me. He was painted red. As I sat down upon him my foot hit something that made a hollow rattling noise. It was a shaman's rattle. This then must be a shaman's, a medicine-man's grave, and this the rattle he had used to scare away evil spirits. Shamen worked black magic. His body lay here just a few feet below me in the earth. At the thought I made a dash for the broken community house on the bank above. All the Indian horses had got there first and taken for their shelter the only corner of the house that had any roof over it.

I put my stool near the wall and sat upon it. The water ran down the wall in rivers. The dog shivered under my coat—both of us were wet to the skin. My sketch sack was so full of water that when I emptied it on to the ground it made the pool we sat in bigger.

After two hours the rain stopped suddenly. The horses held their bones stiff and quivered their skins. It made the rain fly out of their coats and splash me. One by one they trooped out through a hole in the wall. When their hooves struck the baseboard there was a sodden thud. Ginger Pop shook himself too, but I could only drip. Water poured from the eyes of the totems and from the tips of their carved noses. New little rivers trickled across the green flat. The big river was whipped to froth. A blur like boiling mist hung over it.

When I got back to the new village I found my bed and things in a corner of the Douses' great room. The hero told me, "My mother-in-law says you may live in her house. Here is a rocking-chair for you."

Mrs. Douse acknowledged my gratitude stolidly. I gave Mr. Douse a dollar and asked if I might have a big fire to dry my things and make tea. There were two stoves—the one at their end of the room was alight. Soon, mine too was roaring and it was cosy. When the Indians accepted me as one of themselves, I was very grateful.

The people who lived in that big room of the Douses were two married daughters, their husbands and children, the son Aleck and an orphan girl called Lizzie. The old couple came and went continually, but they ate and slept in a shanty at the back of the new house. This little place had been made round them. The floor was of earth and the walls were of cedar. The fire on the ground sent its smoke through a smoke-hole in the roof. Dried salmon hung on racks. The old people's mattress was on the floor. The place was full of themselves—they had breathed themselves into it as a bird, with its head under its wing, breathes itself into its own cosiness. The Douses were glad for their children to have the big fine house and be modern but this was the right sort of place for themselves.

Life in the big house was most interesting. A baby swung in its cradle from the rafters; everyone tossed the cradle as he passed and the baby cooed and gurgled. There was a crippled child of six—pinched and white under her brown skin; she sat in a chair all day. And there was Orphan Lizzie who would slip out into the wet bushes and come back with a wild strawberry or a flower in her grubby little hand, and, kneeling by the sick child's chair, would open her fingers suddenly on the surprise.

There was no rush, no scolding, no roughness in this household. When anyone was sleepy he slept; when they were hungry they ate; if they were sorry they cried, and if they were glad they sang. They enjoyed Ginger Pop's fiery temper, the tilt of his nose and particularly the way he kept the house free of Indian dogs. It was Ginger who bridged the gap between their language and mine with laughter. Ginger's snore was the only sound in that great room at night. Indians sleep quietly.

Orphan Lizzie was shy as a rabbit but completely unselfconscious. It was she who set the food on the big table and cleared away the dishes. There did not seem to be any particular meal-times. Lizzie always took a long lick at the top of the jam-tin as she passed it.

The first morning I woke at the Douses', I went very early to wash myself in the creek below the house. I was kneeling on the stones brushing my teeth. It was very cold. Suddenly I looked up—Lizzie was close by me watching. When I looked up, she darted away like a fawn, leaving her water pails behind. Later, Mrs. Douse came to my corner of the house, carrying a tin basin; behind her was Lizzie with a tiny glass cream pitcher full of water, and behind Lizzie was the hero.

"My mother-in-law says the river is too cold for you to wash in. Here is water and a basin for you."

Everyone watched my washing next morning. The washing of my ears interested them most.

One day after work I found the Douse family all sitting round on the floor. In the centre of the group was Lizzie. She was beating something in a pail, beating it with her hands; her arms were blobbed with pink froth to the elbows. Everyone stuck his hand into Lizzie's pail and hooked out some of the froth in the crook of his fingers, then took long delicious licks. They invited me to lick too. It was "soperlallie", or soap berry. It grows in the woods; when you beat the berry it froths up and has a queer bitter taste. The Indians love it.

For two days from dawn till dark I worked down in the old part of the village. On the third day Aleck was to take me back to Kitwangak. But that night it started to rain. It rained for three days and three nights without stopping; the road was impossible. I had only provisioned for two days, had been here five and had given all the best bits from my box to the sick child. All the food I had left for the last three days was hard tack and raisins. I drank hot water, and rocked my hunger to the tune of the rain beating on the window. Ginger Pop munched hard tack unconcerned—amusing everybody.

The Indians would have shared the loaf and jam-tin with me, but I did not tell them that I had no food. The thought of Lizzie's tongue licking the jam-tin stopped me.

When it rained, the Indians drowsed like flies, heavy as the day itself.

On the sixth day of my stay in Kitwancool the sun shone again, but we had to wait a bit for the puddles to drain.

I straightened out my obligations and said goodbye to Mr. and Mrs. Douse. The light wagon that was taking me out seemed luxurious after the thing I had come in on. I climbed up beside Aleck. He gathered his reins and "giddapped".

Mrs. Douse, followed by her husband, came out of the house and waved a halt. She spoke to Aleck.

"My mother wants to see your pictures."

"But I showed her every one before they were packed."

At the time I had thought her stolidly indifferent.

"My mother wishes to see the pictures again."

I clambered over the back of the wagon, unpacked the wet canvases and opened the sketchbooks. She went through them all. The two best poles in the village belonged to Mrs. Douse. She argued and discussed with her husband. I told Aleck to ask if his mother would like to have me give her pictures of her poles. If so, I would send them through the Hudson's Bay store at Kitwangak. Mrs. Douse's neck loosened. Her head nodded violently and I saw her smile for the first time.

Repacking, I climbed over the back of the seat to Aleck.

"Giddap!"

The reins flapped: we were off. The dust was laid; everything was keen and fresh; indeed the appetites of the mosquitoes were very keen.

When I got back to Kitwangak the Mounted Police came to see me.

"You have been in to Kitwancool?"

"Yes."

"How did the Indians treat you?"

"Splendidly."

"Learned their lesson, eh?" said the man. "We have had no end of trouble with those people—chased missionaries out and drove surveyors off with axes—simply won't have whites in their village. I would never have advised anyone going in—particularly a woman. No, I would certainly have said, 'Keep out'."

"Then I am glad I did not ask for your advice," I said. "Perhaps it is because I am a woman that they were so good to me."

"One of the men who went in on the wagon with you was straight from jail, a fierce, troublesome customer."

Now I knew who the hero was.

—*1941*

---

*Lucy Maud Montgomery (1874–1942) was born and raised in Prince Edward Island, the setting for most of her books, including* Anne of Green Gables *(1908), the international best-seller about the red-haired heroine with the vivid imagination.* The Story Girl *(1911) was the last of her books to be written on the Island, and includes the experiences of her own great-grandmother. After her marriage in 1911, Montgomery moved to Ontario, where she lived for the remainder of her life, continuing to write prolifically, producing twenty-two books of fiction and hundreds of short stories and poems, as well as extensive journals.*

## *Lucy Maud Montgomery*
# How Betty Sherman Won a Husband

The rest of us did not share the Story Girl's enthusiasm regarding our call on Mr. Campbell. We secretly dreaded it. If, as was said, he detested children, who knew what sort of a reception we might meet?

Mr. Campbell was a rich, retired farmer, who took life easily. He had visited New York and Boston, Toronto and Montreal; he had even been as far as the Pacific coast. Therefore he was regarded in Carlisle as a much travelled man; and he was known to be "well read" and intelligent. But it was also known that Mr. Campbell was not always in a good humour. If he liked you there was nothing he would not do for you; if he disliked you—well, you were not left in ignorance of it. In short, we had the impression that Mr. Campbell resembled the famous little girl with the curl in the middle of her forehead. "When he was good, he was very, very good, and when he was bad he was horrid." What if this were one of his horrid days?

"He can't *do* anything to us, you know," said the Story Girl. "He may be rude, but that won't hurt any one but himself."

"Hard words break no bones," observed Felix philosophically.

"But they hurt your feelings. *I* am afraid of Mr. Campbell," said Cecily candidly.

"Perhaps we'd better give up and go home," suggested Dan.

"You can go home if you like," said the Story Girl scornfully. "But *I* am going to see Mr. Campbell. I know I can manage him. But if I have to go alone, and he gives me anything, I'll keep it all for my own collection, mind you."

That settled it. We were not going to let the Story Girl get ahead of us in the matter of collecting.

Mr. Campbell's housekeeper ushered us into his parlour and left us. Presently Mr. Campbell himself was standing in the doorway, looking us over. We took heart of grace. It seemed to be one of his good days, for there was a quizzical smile on his broad, clean-shaven, strongly-featured face. Mr. Campbell was a tall man, with a massive head, well thatched with thick, black hair, gray-streaked. He had big, black eyes, with many wrinkles around them, and a thin, firm, long-lipped mouth. We thought him handsome, for an old man.

His gaze wandered over us with uncomplimentary indifference until it fell on the Story Girl, leaning back in an armchair. She looked like a slender red lily in the unstudied grace of her attitude. A spark flashed into Mr. Campbell's black eyes.

"Is this a Sunday School deputation?" he inquired rather ironically.

"No. We have come to ask a favour of you," said the Story Girl.

The magic of her voice worked its will on Mr. Campbell, as on all others. He came in, sat down, hooked his thumb into his vest pocket, and smiled at her.

"What is it?" he asked.

"We are collecting for our school library, and we have called to ask you for a contribution," she replied.

"Why should *I* contribute to your school library?" demanded Mr. Campbell.

This was a poser for us. Why should he, indeed? But the Story Girl was quite equal to it. Leaning forward, and throwing an indescribable witchery into tone and eyes and smile, she said,

"Because a lady asks you."

Mr. Campbell chuckled.

"The best of all reasons," he said. "But see here, my dear young lady, I'm an old miser and curmudgeon, as you may have heard. I *hate* to part with my money, even for a good reason. And I *never* part with any of it, unless I am to receive some benefit from the expenditure. Now, what earthly good could I get from your three by six school library? None whatever. But I shall make you a fair offer. I have heard from my housekeeper's urchin of a son that you are a 'master hand' to tell stories. Tell me one, here and now. I shall pay you in proportion to the entertainment you afford me. Come now, and do your prettiest."

There was a fine mockery in his tone that put the Story Girl on her mettle instantly. She sprang to her feet, an amazing change coming over her. Her eyes flashed and burned; crimson spots glowed in her cheeks.

"I shall tell you the story of the Sherman girls, and how Betty Sherman won a husband," she said.

We gasped. Was the Story Girl crazy? Or had she forgotten that Betty Sherman was Mr. Campbell's own great-grandmother, and that her method of winning a husband was not exactly in accordance with maidenly traditions.

But Mr. Campbell chuckled again.

"An excellent test," he said. "If you can amuse *me* with that story you must be a wonder. I've heard it so often that it has no more interest for me than the alphabet."

"One cold winter day, eighty years ago," began the Story Girl without further parley, "Donald Fraser was sitting by the window of his new house, playing his fiddle for company, and looking out over the white, frozen bay before his door. It was bitter, bitter cold, and a storm was brewing. But, storm, or no storm, Donald meant to go over the bay that evening to see Nancy Sherman. He was thinking of her as he played 'Annie Laurie,' for Nancy was more beautiful than the lady of the song. 'Her face, it is the fairest that e'er the sun shone on,' hummed Donald— and oh, he thought so, too! He did not know whether Nancy cared for him or not. He had many rivals. But he knew that if she would not come to be the mistress of his new house no one else ever should. So he sat there that afternoon and dreamed of her, as he played sweet old songs and rollicking jigs on his fiddle.

"While he was playing a sleigh drove up to the door, and Neil Campbell came in. Donald was not overly glad to see him, for he suspected where he was going. Neil Campbell, who was Highland Scotch and lived down at Berwick, was courting Nancy Sherman, too; and, what was far worse, Nancy's father favoured him, because he was a richer man than Donald Fraser. But Donald was not going to show all he thought—Scotch people never do—and he pretended to be very glad to see Neil, and made him heartily welcome.

"Neil sat down by the roaring fire, looking quite well satisfied with himself. It was ten miles from Berwick to the bay shore, and a call at a half way house was just the thing. Then Donald brought out the whisky. They always did that eighty years ago, you know. If you were a woman, you could give your visitors a dish of tea; but if you were a man and did not offer them a 'taste' of whisky, you were thought either very mean or very ignorant.

" 'You look cold,' said Donald, in his great, hearty voice. 'Sit nearer the fire, man, and put a bit of warmth in your veins. It's bitter cold the day. And now tell me the Berwick news. Has Jean McLean made up with her man yet? And is it true that Sandy McQuarrie is to marry Kate Ferguson? 'Twill be a match now! Sure, with her red hair, Sandy will not be like to lose his bride past finding.'

"Neil had plenty of news to tell. And the more whisky he drank the more he told. He didn't notice that Donald was not taking much. Neil talked on and on, and of course he soon began to tell things it would have been much wiser not to tell. Finally he told Donald that he was going over the bay to ask Nancy Sherman that very night to marry him. And if she would have him, then Donald and all the folks should see a wedding that *was* a wedding.

"Oh, wasn't Donald taken aback! This was more than he had expected. Neil hadn't been courting Nancy very long, and Donald never dreamed he would propose to her *quite* so soon.

"At first Donald didn't know what to do. He felt sure deep down in his heart, that Nancy liked *him*. She was very shy and modest, but you know a girl can let a man see she likes him without going out of her way. But Donald knew that if Neil proposed first he would have the

best chance. Neil was rich and the Shermans were poor, and old Elias
Sherman would have the most to say in the matter. If he told Nancy she
must take Neil Campbell she would never dream of disobeying him.
Old Elias Sherman was a man who had to be obeyed. But if Nancy had
only promised some one else first her father would not make her break
her word.

"Wasn't it a hard plight for poor Donald? But he was a Scotchman,
you know, and it's pretty hard to stick a Scotchman long. Presently
a twinkle came into his eyes, for he remembered that all was fair in love
and war. So he said to Neil, oh, so persuasively,

" 'Have some more, man, have some more. 'Twill keep the heart in
you in the teeth of that wind. Help yourself. There's plenty more where
that came from.'

"Neil didn't want *much* persuasion. He took some more, and said
slyly,

" 'Is it going over the bay the night that yourself will be doing?'

"Donald shook his head.

" 'I had thought of it,' he owned, 'but it looks a wee like a storm,
and my sleigh is at the blacksmith's to be shod. If I went it must be on
Black Dan's back, and he likes a canter over the ice in a snow-storm as
little as I. His own fireside is the best place for a man to-night,
Campbell. Have another taste, man, have another taste.'

"Neil went on 'tasting,' and that sly Donald sat there with a sober
face, but laughing eyes, and coaxed him on. At last Neil's head fell forward on his breast, and he was sound asleep. Donald got up, put on his
overcoat and cap, and went to the door.

" 'May your sleep be long and sweet, man,' he said, laughing softly,
'and as for the waking, 'twill be betwixt you and me.'

"With that he untied Neil's horse, climbed into Neil's sleigh, and
tucked Neil's buffalo robe about him.

" 'Now, Bess, old girl, do your bonniest,' he said. 'There's more than
you know hangs on your speed. If the Campbell wakes too soon Black Dan
could show you a pair of clean heels for all your good start. On, my girl.'

"Brown Bess went over the ice like a deer, and Donald kept thinking
of what he should say to Nancy—and more still of what she would say
to him. *Suppose* he was mistaken. *Suppose* she said 'no!'

" 'Neil will have the laugh on me then. Sure he's sleeping well. And
the snow is coming soon. There'll be a bonny swirl on the bay ere long.

I hope no harm will come to the lad if he starts to cross. When he wakes up he'll be in such a fine Highland temper that he'll never stop to think of danger. Well, Bess, old girl, here we are. Now, Donald Fraser, pluck up heart and play the man. Never flinch because a slip of a lass looks scornful at you out of the bonniest dark-blue eyes on earth.'

"But in spite of his bold words Donald's heart was thumping as he drove into the Sherman yard. Nancy was there, milking a cow by the stable door, but she stood up when she saw Donald coming. Oh, she was very beautiful! Her hair was like a skein of golden silk, and her eyes were as blue as the gulf water when the sun breaks out after a storm. Donald felt more nervous than ever. But he knew he must make the most of his chance. He might not see Nancy alone again before Neil came. He caught her hand and stammered out,

" 'Nan, lass, I love you. You may think 'tis a hasty wooing, but that's a story I can tell you later maybe. I know well I'm not worthy of you, but if true love could make a man worthy there'd be none before me. Will you have me, Nan?'

"Nancy didn't *say* she would have him. She just *looked* it, and Donald kissed her right there in the snow.

"The next morning the storm was over. Donald knew that Neil must be soon on his track. He did not want to make the Sherman house the scene of a quarrel, so he resolved to get away before the Campbell came. He persuaded Nancy to go with him to visit some friends in another settlement. As he brought Neil's sleigh up to the door he saw a black speck far out on the bay and laughed.

" 'Black Dan goes well, but he'll not be quick enough,' he said.

"Half an hour later Neil Campbell rushed into the Sherman kitchen and oh, how angry he was! There was nobody there but Betty Sherman, and Betty was not afraid of him. She was never afraid of anybody. She was very handsome, with hair as brown as October nuts and black eyes and crimson cheeks; and she had always been in love with Neil Campbell herself.

" 'Good morning, Mr. Campbell,' she said, with a toss of her head. 'It's early abroad you are. And on Black Dan, no less! Was I mistaken in thinking that Donald Fraser said once that his favourite horse should never be backed by any man but him? But doubtless a fair exchange is no robbery, and Brown Bess is a good mare in her way.'

" 'Where is Donald Fraser?' said Neil, shaking his fist. 'It's him I'm seeking, and it's him I will be finding. Where is he, Betty Sherman?'

" 'Donald Fraser is far enough away by this time,' mocked Betty. 'He is a prudent fellow, and has some quickness of wit under that sandy thatch of his. He came here last night at sunset, with a horse and sleigh not his own, or lately gotten, and he asked Nan in the stable yard to marry him. Did a man ask *me* to marry him at the cow's side, with a milking pail in my hand, it's a cold answer he'd get for his pains. But Nan thought differently, and they sat late together last night, and 'twas a bonny story Nan wakened me to hear when she came to bed—the story of a braw lover who let his secret out when the whisky was above the wit, and then fell asleep while his rival was away to woo and win his lass. Did you ever hear a like story, Mr. Campbell?'

" 'Oh, yes,' said Neil fiercely. 'It is laughing at me over the country side and telling that story that Donald Fraser will be doing, is it? But when I meet him it is not laughing he will be doing. Oh, no. There will be another story to tell!'

" 'Now, don't meddle with the man,' cried Betty. 'What a state to be in because one good-looking lass likes sandy hair and gray eyes better than Highland black and blue! You have not the spirit of a wren, Neil Campbell. Were I you, I would show Donald Fraser that I could woo and win a lass as speedily as any Lowlander of them all; that I would! There's many a girl would gladly say "yes" for your asking. And here stands one! Why not marry *me*, Neil Campbell? Folks say I'm as bonny as Nan—and I could love you as well as Nan loves her Donald—ay, and ten times better!'

"What do you suppose the Campbell did? Why, just the thing he ought to have done. He took Betty at her word on the spot; and there was a double wedding soon after. And it is said that Neil and Betty were the happiest couple in the world—happier even than Donald and Nancy. So all was well because it ended well!'"

The Story Girl curtsied until her silken skirts swept the floor. Then she flung herself in her chair and looked at Mr. Campbell, flushed, triumphant, daring.

The story was old to us. It had once been published in a Charlottetown paper, and we had read in Aunt Olivia's scrap-book, where the Story Girl had learned it. But we had listened entranced.

I have written down the bare words of the story, as she told it; but I can never reproduce the charm and colour and spirit she infused into it. It *lived* for us. Donald and Neil, Nancy and Betty, were there in that room with us. We saw the flashes of expression on their faces, we heard their voices, angry or tender, mocking or merry, in Lowland and Highland accent. We realized all the mingled coquetry and feeling and defiance and archness in Betty Sherman's daring speech. We had even forgotten all about Mr. Campbell.

That gentleman, in silence, took out his wallet, extracted a note therefrom, and handed it gravely to the Story Girl.

"There are five dollars for you," he said, "and your story was well worth it. You *are* a wonder. Some day you will make the world realize it. I've been about a bit, and heard some good things, but I've never enjoyed anything more than that threadbare old story I heard in my cradle. And now, will you do me a favour?"

"Of course," said the delighted Story Girl.

"Recite the multiplication table for me," said Mr. Campbell.

We stared. Well might Mr. Campbell be called eccentric. What on earth did he want the multiplication table recited for? Even the Story Girl was surprised. But she began promptly, with twice one and went through it to twelve times twelve. She repeated it simply, but her voice changed from one tone to another as each in succession grew tired. We had never dreamed that there was so much in the multiplication table. As she announced it, the fact that three times three was nine was exquisitely ridiculous, five times six almost brought the tears to our eyes, eight times seven was the most tragic and frightful thing ever heard of, and twelve times twelve rang like a trumpet call to victory.

Mr. Campbell nodded his satisfaction.

"I thought you could do it," he said. "The other day I found this statement in a book. 'Her voice would have made the multiplication table charming!' I thought of it when I heard yours. I didn't believe it before, but I do now."

Then he let us go.

"You see," said the Story Girl as we went home, "you need never be afraid of people."

"But we are not all Story Girls," said Cecily.

That night we heard Felicity talking to Cecily in their room.

"Mr. Campbell never noticed one of us except the Story Girl," she said, "but if *I* had put on *my* best dress as she did maybe she wouldn't have taken all the attention."

"Could you ever do what Betty Sherman did, do you suppose?" asked Cecily absently.

"No; but I believe the Story Girl could," answered Felicity rather snappishly.

*—1911*

---

*James Joyce (1882–1941) is best known for his masterpiece,* Ulysses, *the complex modernist novel of a single day in the life of Dublin that shortly after its appearance in 1922 became both a classic and the subject of a landmark censorship case, which its publishers eventually won. Joyce's lifelong quarrel with the provincial concerns of Irish religious, cultural, and literary life (all touched on in his long story "The Dead") led him to permanent Continental self-exile in Zurich and Paris. Most readers would associate Joyce with his pioneering of experimental techniques such as the fragmentary observations found in his early* Epiphanies *(posthumously published in 1956), his use of interior monologue and stream-of-consciousness, and the complicated linguistic games of* Finnegan's Wake *(1939), forgetting that his earlier works lie squarely in the realm of traditional fiction.* Dubliners *(1914), his collection of short stories of life in his native city, remains an imposing achievement, as does his autobiographical novel,* A Portrait of the Artist as a Young Man *(1916).*

## James Joyce
# Araby

North Richmond Street, being blind, was a quiet street except at the hour when the Christian Brothers' School set the boys free. An uninhabited house of two storeys stood at the blind end, detached from its neighbours in a square ground. The other houses of the street, conscious of decent lives within them, gazed at one another with brown imperturbable faces.

The former tenant of our house, a priest, had died in the back drawing-room. Air, musty from having been long enclosed, hung in all the rooms, and the waste room behind the kitchen was littered with old useless papers. Among these I found a few paper-covered books, the pages of which were curled and damp: *The Abbot*, by Walter Scott, *The Devout Communicant* and *The Memoirs of Vidocq*. I liked the last best because its leaves were yellow. The wild garden behind the house contained a central apple-tree and a few straggling bushes under one of which I found the late tenant's rusty bicycle-pump. He had been a very charitable priest; in his will he had left all his money to institutions and the furniture of his house to his sister.

When the short days of winter came dusk fell before we had well eaten our dinners. When we met in the street the houses had grown sombre. The space of sky above us was the colour of ever-changing violet and towards it the lamps of the street lifted their feeble lanterns. The cold air stung us and we played till our bodies glowed. Our shouts echoed in the silent street. The career of our play brought us through the dark muddy lanes behind the houses where we ran the gantlet of the rough tribes from the cottages, to the back doors of the dark dripping gardens where odours arose from the ashpits, to the dark odorous stables where a coachman smoothed and combed the horse or shook music from the buckled harness. When we returned to the street light from the kitchen windows had filled the areas. If my uncle was seen turning the corner we hid in the shadow until we had seen him safely housed. Or if Mangan's sister came out on the doorstep to call her brother in to his tea we watched her from our shadow peer up and down the street. We waited to see whether she would remain or go in and, if she remained, we left our shadow and walked up to Mangan's steps resignedly. She was waiting for us, her figure defined by the light from the half-opened door. Her brother always teased her before he obeyed and I stood by the railings looking at her. Her dress swung as she moved her body and the soft rope of her hair tossed from side to side.

Every morning I lay on the floor in the front parlour watching her door. The blind was pulled down to within an inch of the sash so that I could not be seen. When she came out on the doorstep my heart leaped. I ran to the hall, seized my books and followed her. I kept her brown figure always in my eye and, when we came near the point at which our ways diverged, I quickened my pace and passed her. This happened morning after morning. I had never spoken to her, except for a few casual words, and yet her name was like a summons to all my foolish blood.

Her image accompanied me even in places the most hostile to romance. On Saturday evenings when my aunt went marketing I had to go to carry some of the parcels. We walked through the flaring streets, jostled by drunken men and bargaining women, amid the curses of labourers, the shrill litanies of shop-boys who stood on guard by the barrels of pigs' cheeks, the nasal chanting of street-singers, who sang a *come-all-you* about O'Donovan Rossa, or a ballad about the troubles in our native land. These noises converged in a single sensation of life for me: I imagined that I bore my chalice safely through a throng of foes. Her name sprang to my lips at moments in strange prayers and praises which I myself did not understand. My eyes were often full of tears (I could not tell why) and at times a flood from my heart seemed to pour itself out into my bosom. I thought little of the future. I did not know whether I would ever speak to her or not or, if I spoke to her, how I could tell her of my confused adoration. But my body was like a harp and her words and gestures were like fingers running upon the wires.

One evening I went into the back drawing-room in which the priest had died. It was a dark rainy evening and there was no sound in the house. Through one of the broken panes I heard the rain impinge upon the earth, the fine incessant needles of water playing in the sodden beds. Some distant lamp or lighted window gleamed below me. I was thankful that I could see so little. All my senses seemed to desire to veil themselves and, feeling that I was about to slip from them, I pressed the palms of my hands together until they trembled, murmuring: *O love! O love!* many times.

At last she spoke to me. When she addressed the first words to me I was so confused that I did not know what to answer. She asked me was I going to *Araby*. I forget whether I answered yes or no. It would be a splendid bazaar, she said; she would love to go.

—And why can't you? I asked.

While she spoke she turned a silver bracelet round and round her wrist. She could not go, she said, because there would be a retreat that week in her convent. Her brother and two other boys were fighting for their caps and I was alone at the railings. She held one of the spikes, bowing her head towards me. The light from the lamp opposite our door caught the white curve of her neck, lit up her hair that rested there and, falling, lit up the hand upon the railing. It fell over one side of her dress and caught the white border of a petticoat, just visible as she stood at ease.

—It's well for you, she said.

—If I go, I said, I will bring you something.

What innumerable follies laid waste my waking and sleeping thoughts after that evening! I wished to annihilate the tedious intervening days. I chafed against the work of school. At night in my bedroom and by day in the classroom her image came between me and the page I strove to read. The syllables of the word *Araby* were called to me through the silence in which my soul luxuriated and cast an Eastern enchantment over me. I asked for leave to go to the bazaar Saturday night. My aunt was surprised and hoped it was not some Freemason affair. I answered few questions in class. I watched my master's face pass from amiability to sternness; he hoped I was not beginning to idle. I could not call my wandering thoughts together. I had hardly any patience with the serious work of life which, now that it stood between me and my desire, seemed to me child's play, ugly monotonous child's play.

On Saturday morning I reminded my uncle that I wished to go to the bazaar in the evening. He was fussing at the hallstand, looking for the hat-brush, and answered me curtly:

—Yes, boy, I know.

As he was in the hall I could not go into the front parlour and lie at the window. I left the house in bad humour and walked slowly towards the school. The air was pitilessly raw and already my heart misgave me.

When I came home to dinner my uncle had not yet been home. Still it was early. I sat staring at the clock for some time and, when its ticking began to irritate me, I left the room. I mounted the staircase and gained the upper part of the house. The high cold empty gloomy rooms liberated me and I went from room to room singing. From the front window I saw my companions playing below in the street. Their cries reached me weakened and indistinct and, leaning my forehead against the cool glass, I looked over at the dark house where she lived. I may have stood there for an hour, seeing nothing but the brown-clad figure cast by my imagination, touched discreetly by the lamplight at the curved neck, at the hand upon the railings and at the border below the dress.

When I came downstairs again I found Mrs Mercer sitting at the fire. She was an old garrulous woman, a pawnbroker's widow, who collected used stamps for some pious purpose. I had to endure the gossip of the tea-table. The meal was prolonged beyond an hour and still my uncle did not come. Mrs Mercer stood up to go: she was sorry she couldn't wait any longer, but it was after eight o'clock and she did not like to be out late, as the night air was bad for her. When she had gone I began to walk up and down the room, clenching my fists. My aunt said:

—I'm afraid you may put off your bazaar for this night of Our Lord.

At nine o'clock I heard my uncle's latchkey in the hall-door. I heard him talking to himself and heard the hallstand rocking when it had received the weight of his overcoat. I could interpret these signs. When he was midway through his dinner I asked him to give me the money to go to the bazaar. He had forgotten.

—The people are in bed and after their first sleep now, he said.

I did not smile. My aunt said to him energetically:

—Can't you give him the money and let him go? You've kept him late enough as it is.

My uncle said he was very sorry he had forgotten. He said he believed in the old saying: *All work and no play makes Jack a dull boy*. He asked me where I was going and, when I had told him a second time he asked me did I know *The Arab's Farewell to his Steed*. When I left the kitchen he was about to recite the opening lines of the piece to my aunt.

I held a florin tightly in my hand as I strode down Buckingham Street towards the station. The sight of the streets thronged with buyers and glaring with gas recalled to me the purpose of my journey. I took my seat in a third-class carriage of a deserted train. After an intolerable delay the train moved out of the station slowly. It crept onward among ruinous houses and over the twinkling river. At Westland Row Station a crowd of people pressed to the carriage doors; but the porters moved them back, saying that it was a special train for the bazaar. I remained alone in the bare carriage. In a few minutes the train drew up beside an improvised wooden platform. I passed out on to the road and saw by the lighted dial of a clock that it was ten minutes to ten. In front of me was a large building which displayed the magical name.

I could not find any sixpenny entrance and, fearing that the bazaar would be closed, I passed in quickly through a turnstile, handing a shilling to a weary-looking man. I found myself in a big hall girdled at half its height by a gallery. Nearly all the stalls were closed and the greater part of the hall was in darkness. I recognised a silence like that which pervades a church after a service. I walked into the centre of the bazaar timidly. A few people were gathered about the stalls which were still open. Before a curtain, over which the words *Café Chantant* were written in coloured lamps, two men were counting money on a salver. I listened to the fall of the coins.

Remembering with difficulty why I had come I went over to one of the stalls and examined porcelain vases and flowered tea-sets. At the door of the stall a young lady was talking and laughing with two young gentlemen. I remarked their English accents and listened vaguely to their conversation.

—O, I never said such a thing!

—O, but you did!

—O, but I didn't!

—Didn't she say that?

—Yes. I heard her.

—O, there's a . . . fib!

Observing me the young lady came over and asked me did I wish to buy anything. The tone of her voice was not encouraging; she seemed to have spoken to me out of a sense of duty. I looked humbly at the great jars that stood like eastern guards at either side of the dark entrance to the stall and murmured:

—No, thank you.

The young lady changed the position of one of the vases and went back to the two young men. They began to talk of the same subject. Once or twice the young lady glanced at me over her shoulder.

I lingered before her stall, though I knew my stay was useless, to make my interest in her wares seem the more real. Then I turned away slowly and walked down the middle of the bazaar. I allowed the two pennies to fall against the sixpence in my pocket. I heard a voice call from one end of the gallery that the light was out. The upper part of the hall was now completely dark.

Gazing up into the darkness I saw myself as a creature driven and derided by vanity; and my eyes burned with anguish and anger.

*—1914*

*Virginia Woolf (1882–1941) was born Virginia Stephen into a literary household in London, England. Despite not receiving the education granted to her brothers, she became an important writer, critic, and essayist who, along with her husband, Leonard Woolf, founded a press that published early works of Katherine Mansfield and T. S. Eliot and translations of Sigmund Freud. She was an innovator in the form of prose fiction known as stream-of-consciousness in novels such as* Mrs. Dalloway *(1925),* To the Lighthouse *(1927), and* The Waves *(1931), and in her short fiction gathered in* Monday and Tuesday *(1921) and* A Haunted House *(1944). Her feminist concerns appear in non-fiction books such as* A Room of One's Own *(1929) and* Three Guineas *(1938). Struggling with the fragile mental health that had plagued her for much of her life, she drowned herself in 1941.*

## Virginia Woolf
# A Haunted House

Whatever hour you woke there was a door shutting. From room to room they went, hand in hand, lifting here, opening there, making sure—a ghostly couple.

"Here we left it," she said. And he added, "Oh, but here too!" "It's upstairs," she murmured. "And in the garden," he whispered. "Quietly," they said, "or we shall wake them."

But it wasn't that you woke us. Oh, no. "They're looking for it; they're drawing the curtain," one might say, and so read on a page or two. "Now they've found it," one would be certain, stopping the pencil on the margin. And then, tired of reading, one might rise and see for oneself, the house all empty, the doors standing open, only the wood pigeons bubbling with content and the hum of the threshing machine sounding from the farm. "What did I come in here for? What did I want to find?" My hands were empty. "Perhaps it's upstairs then?" The apples were in the loft. And so down again, the garden still as ever, only the book had slipped into the grass.

But they had found it in the drawing-room. Not that one could ever see them. The window panes reflected apples, reflected roses; all the leaves were green in the glass. If they moved in the drawing-room, the apple only turned its yellow side. Yet, the moment after, if the door was opened, spread about the floor, hung upon the walls, pendant from the ceiling—what? My hands were empty. The shadow of a thrush crossed the carpet; from the deepest wells of silence the wood pigeon drew its bubble of sound. "Safe, safe, safe," the pulse of the house beat softly. "The treasure buried; the room . . ." the pulse stopped short. Oh, was that the buried treasure?

A moment later the light had faded. Out in the garden then? But the trees spun darkness for a wandering beam of sun. So fine, so rare, coolly sunk beneath the surface the beam I sought always burnt behind the glass. Death was the glass; death was between us; coming to the woman first, hundreds of years ago, leaving the house, sealing all the windows; the rooms were darkened. He left it, left her, went North, went East, saw the stars turned in the Southern sky; sought the house, found it dropped beneath the Downs. "Safe, safe, safe," the pulse of the house beat gladly. "The Treasure yours."

The wind roars up the avenue. Trees stoop and bend this way and that. Moonbeams splash and spill wildly in the rain. But the beam of the lamp falls straight from the window. The candle burns stiff and still. Wandering through the house, opening the windows, whispering not to wake us, the ghostly couple seek their joy.

"Here we slept," she says. And he adds, "Kisses without number." "Waking in the morning—" "Silver between the trees—" "Upstairs—" "In the garden—" "When summer came—" "In winter snowtime—" The doors go shutting far in the distance, gently knocking like the pulse of a heart.

Nearer they come; cease at the doorway. The wind falls, the rain slides silver down the glass. Our eyes darken; we hear no steps beside us; we see no lady spread her ghostly cloak. His hands shield the lantern. "Look," he breathes. "Sound asleep. Love upon their lips."

Stooping, holding their silver lamp above us, long they look and deeply. Long they pause. The wind drives straightly; the flame stoops slightly. Wild beams of moonlight cross both floor and wall, and, meeting, stain the faces bent; the faces pondering; the faces that search the sleepers and seek their hidden joy.

"Safe, safe, safe," the heart of the house beats proudly. "Long years—" he sighs. "Again you found me." "Here," she murmurs, "sleeping; in the garden reading; laughing, rolling apples in the loft. Here we left our treasure—" Stooping, their light lifts the lids upon my eyes. "Safe! safe! safe!" the pulse of the house beats wildly. Waking, I cry "Oh, is this *your* buried treasure? The light in the heart."

*—1921*

*D. H. Lawrence (1885–1930) was born in Nottinghamshire, England, the son of a coal miner and a teacher. His first novel,* The White Peacock *(1911), was followed by* Sons and Lovers *(1913),* The Rainbow *(1915), and* Women in Love *(1920). His interest in Freudian psychology and human sexuality made him controversial during his career and perhaps still overshadows his skills as a chronicler of English life in villages forever altered by the Industrial Revolution.* Lady Chatterley's Lover *(1928), with its frank language and depictions of sex, remains a landmark in the battle against literary censorship, and an unexpurgated edition did not appear in England until thirty years after the author's death. Lawrence also published numerous collections of poetry and short stories. "The Horse Dealer's Daughter" reflects both his interest in the dynamics of desire and his symbolic technique.*

## D. H. Lawrence

# The Horse Dealer's Daughter

"Well, Mabel, and what are you going to do with yourself?" asked Joe, with foolish flippancy. He felt quite safe himself. Without listening for an answer, he turned aside, worked a grain of tobacco to the tip of his tongue, and spat it out. He did not care about anything, since he felt safe himself.

The three brothers and the sister sat round the desolate breakfast-table, attempting some sort of desultory consultation. The morning's post had given the final tap to the family fortunes, and all was over. The dreary dining-room itself, with its heavy mahogany furniture, looked as if it were waiting to be done away with.

But the consultation amounted to nothing. There was a strange air of ineffectuality about the three men, as they sprawled at table, smoking and reflecting vaguely on their own condition. The girl was alone, a rather short, sullen-looking young woman of twenty-seven. She did not share the same life as her brothers. She would have been good-looking, save for the impressive fixity of her face, 'bull-dog', as her brothers called it.

There was a confused tramping of horses' feet outside. The three men all sprawled round in their chairs to watch. Beyond the dark holly bushes that separated the strip of lawn from the high-road, they could see a cavalcade of shire horses swinging out of their own yard, being taken for exercise. This was the last time. These were the last horses that would go through their hands. The young men watched with critical, callous look. They were all frightened at the collapse of their lives, and the sense of disaster in which they were involved left them no inner freedom.

Yet they were three fine, well-set fellows enough. Joe, the eldest, was a man of thirty-three, broad and handsome in a hot, flushed way. His face was red, he twisted his black moustache over a thick finger, his eyes were shallow and restless. He had a sensual way of uncovering his teeth when he laughed, and his bearing was stupid. Now he watched the horses with a glazed look of helplessness in his eyes, a certain stupor of downfall.

The great draught-horses swung past. They were tied head to tail, four of them, and they heaved along to where a lane branched off from the high-road, planting their great hoofs floutingly in the fine black mud, swinging their great rounded haunches sumptuously, and trotting a few sudden steps as they were led into the lane, round the corner. Every movement showed a massive, slumbrous strength, and a stupidity which held them in subjection. The groom at the head looked back, jerking the leading rope. And the cavalcade moved out of sight up the lane, the tail of the last horse, bobbed up tight and stiff, held out taut from the swinging great haunches as they rocked behind the hedges in a motion-like sleep.

Joe watched with glazed hopeless eyes. The horses were almost like his own body to him. He felt he was done for now. Luckily he was engaged to a woman as old as himself, and therefore her father, who was steward of a neighbouring estate, would provide him with a job. He would marry and go into harness. His life was over, he would be a subject animal now.

He turned uneasily aside, the retreating steps of the horses echoing in his ears. Then, with foolish restlessness, he reached for the scraps of bacon-rind from the plates, and making a faint whistling sound, flung them to the terrier that lay against the fender. He watched the dog swallow them, and waited till the creature looked into his eyes. Then a faint grin came on his face, and in a high, foolish voice he said:

"You won't get much more bacon, shall you, you little b——?"

The dog faintly and dismally wagged its tail, then lowered its haunches, circled round, and lay down again.

There was another helpless silence at the table. Joe sprawled uneasily in his seat, not willing to go till the family conclave was dissolved. Fred Henry, the second brother, was erect, clean-limbed, alert. He had watched the passing of the horses with more *sang-froid*.[1] If he was an animal, like Joe, he was an animal which controls, not one which is controlled. He was master of any horse, and he carried himself with a well-tempered air of mastery. But he was not master of the situations of life. He pushed his coarse brown moustache upwards, off his lip, and glanced irritably at his sister, who sat impassive and inscrutable.

"You'll go and stop with Lucy for a bit, shan't you?" he asked. The girl did not answer.

"I don't see what else you can do," persisted Fred Henry.

"Go as a skivvy," Joe interpolated laconically.

The girl did not move a muscle.

"If I was her, I should go in for training for a nurse," said Malcolm, the youngest of them all. He was the baby of the family, a young man of twenty-two, with a fresh, jaunty *museau*.[2]

But Mabel did not take any notice of him. They had talked at her and round her for so many years, that she hardly heard them at all.

The marble clock on the mantelpiece softly chimed the half-hour, the dog rose uneasily from the hearth-rug and looked at the party at the breakfast-table. But still they sat on in ineffectual conclave.

"Oh, all right," said Joe suddenly, apropos of nothing. "I'll get a move on."

He pushed back his chair, straddled his knees with a downward jerk, to get them free, in horsey fashion, and went to the fire. Still he did not go out of the room; he was curious to know what the others would do or say. He began to charge his pipe, looking down at the dog and saying in a high, affected voice:

"Going wi' me? Going wi' me are ter? Tha'rt goin' further than tha counts on just now, dost hear?"

The dog faintly wagged its tail, the man stuck out his jaw and covered his pipe with his hands, and puffed intently, losing himself in the tobacco, looking down all the while at the dog with an absent brown eye. The dog looked up at him in mournful distrust. Joe stood with his knees stuck out, in real horsey fashion.

[1]*sang-froid*: literally "cold blood," with cool indifference.
[2]*museau*: face.

"Have you had a letter from Lucy?" Fred Henry asked of his sister.

"Last week," came the neutral reply.

"And what does she say?"

There was no answer.

"Does she *ask* you to go and stop there?" persisted Fred Henry.

"She says I can if I like."

"Well, then, you'd better. Tell her you'll come on Monday."

This was received in silence.

"That's what you'll do then, is it?" said Fred Henry, in some exasperation.

But she made no answer. There was a silence of futility and irritation in the room. Malcolm grinned fatuously.

"You'll have to make up your mind between now and next Wednesday," said Joe loudly, "or else find yourself lodgings on the kerbstone."

The face of the young woman darkened, but she sat on immutable.

"Here's Jack Ferguson!" exclaimed Malcolm, who was looking aimlessly out of the window.

"Where?" exclaimed Joe loudly.

"Just gone past."

"Coming in?"

Malcolm craned his neck to see the gate.

"Yes," he said.

There was a silence. Mabel sat on like one condemned, at the head of the table. Then a whistle was heard from the kitchen. The dog got up and barked sharply. Joe opened the door and shouted:

"Come on."

After a moment a young man entered. He was muffled up in overcoat and a purple woollen scarf, and his tweed cap, which he did not remove, was pulled down on his head. He was of medium height, his face was rather long and pale, his eyes looked tired.

"Hello, Jack! Well, Jack!" exclaimed Malcolm and Joe. Fred Henry merely said: "Jack."

"What's doing?" asked the newcomer, evidently addressing Fred Henry.

"Same. We've got to be out by Wednesday. Got a cold?"

"I have—got it bad, too."

"Why don't you stop in?"

"*Me* stop in? When I can't stand on my legs, perhaps I shall have a chance." The young man spoke huskily. He had a slight Scotch accent.

"It's a knock-out, isn't it," said Joe, boisterously, "if a doctor goes round croaking with a cold. Looks bad for the patients, doesn't it?"

The young doctor looked at him slowly.

"Anything the matter with *you*, then?" he asked sarcastically.

"Not as I know of. Damn your eyes, I hope not. Why?"

"I thought you were very concerned about the patients, wondered if you might be one yourself."

"Damn it, no, I've never been patient to no flaming doctor, and hope I never shall be," returned Joe.

At this point Mabel rose from the table, and they all seemed to become aware of her existence. She began putting the dishes together. The young doctor looked at her, but did not address her. He had not greeted her. She went out of the room with the tray, her face impassive and unchanged.

"When are you off then, all of you?" asked the doctor.

"I'm catching the eleven-forty," replied Malcolm. "Are you goin' down wi' th' trap, Joe?"

"Yes, I've told you I'm going down wi' th' trap, haven't I?"

"We'd better be getting her in then. So long, Jack, if I don't see you before I go," said Malcolm, shaking hands.

He went out, followed by Joe, who seemed to have his tail between his legs.

"Well, this is the devil's own," exclaimed the doctor, when he was left alone with Fred Henry. "Going before Wednesday, are you?"

"That's the orders," replied the other.

"Where, to Northampton?"

"That's it."

"The devil!" exclaimed Fergusson, with quiet chagrin.

And there was silence between the two.

"All settled up, are you?" asked Fergusson.

"About."

There was another pause.

"Well, I shall miss yer, Freddy, boy," said the young doctor.

"And I shall miss thee, Jack," returned the other.

"Miss you like hell," mused the doctor.

Fred Henry turned aside. There was nothing to say. Mabel came in again, to finish clearing the table.

"What are *you* going to do, then, Miss Pervin?" asked Fergusson. "Going to your sister's, are you?"

Mabel looked at him with her steady, dangerous eyes, that always made him uncomfortable, unsettling his superficial ease.

"No," she said.

"Well, what in the name of fortune *are* you going to do? Say what you mean to do," cried Fred Henry, with futile intensity.

But she only averted her head, and continued her work. She folded the white table-cloth, and put on the chenille cloth.

"The sulkiest bitch that ever trod!" muttered her brother.

But she finished her task with perfectly impassive face, the young doctor watching her interestedly all the while. Then she went out.

Fred Henry stared after her, clenching his lips, his blue eyes fixing in sharp antagonism, as he made a grimace of sour exasperation.

"You could bray her into bits, and that's all you'd get out of her," he said, in a small, narrowed tone.

The doctor smiled faintly.

"What's she *going* to do, then?" he asked.

"Strike me if *I* know!" returned the other.

There was a pause. Then the doctor stirred.

"I'll be seeing you to-night, shall I?" he said to his friend.

"Ay—where's it to be? Are we going over to Jessdale?"

"I don't know. I've got such a cold on me. I'll come round to the 'Moon and Stars', anyway."

"Let Lizzie and May miss their night for once, eh?"

"That's it—if I feel as I do now."

"All's one——"

The two young men went through the passage and down to the back door together. The house was large, but it was servantless now, and desolate. At the back was a small bricked house-yard and beyond that a big square, gravelled fine and red, and having stables on two sides. Sloping, dank, winter-dark fields stretched away on the open sides.

But the stables were empty. Joseph Pervin, the father of the family, had been a man of no education, who had become a fairly large horse dealer. The stables had been full of horses, there was a great turmoil and come-and-go of horses and of dealers and grooms. Then the kitchen was full of servants. But of late things had declined. The old man had married a second time, to retrieve his fortunes. Now he was dead and everything was gone to the dogs, there was nothing but debt and threatening.

For months, Mabel had been servantless in the big house, keeping the home together in penury for her ineffectual brothers. She had kept house for ten years. But previously it was with unstinted means. Then, however brutal and coarse everything was, the sense of money had kept her proud, confident. The men might be foul-mouthed, the women in the kitchen might have bad reputations, her brothers might have illegitimate children. But so long as there was money, the girl felt herself established, and brutally proud, reserved.

No company came to the house, save dealers and coarse men. Mabel had no associates of her own sex, after her sister went away. But she did not mind. She went regularly to church, she attended to her father. And she lived in the memory of her mother, who had died when she was fourteen, and whom she had loved. She had loved her father, too, in a different way, depending upon him, and feeling secure in him, until at the age of fifty-four he married again. And then she had set hard against him. Now he had died and left them all hopelessly in debt.

She had suffered badly during the period of poverty. Nothing, however, could shake the curious, sullen, animal pride that dominated each member of the family. Now, for Mabel, the end had come. Still she would not cast about her. She would follow her own way just the same. She would always hold the keys of her own situation. Mindless and persistent, she endured from day to day. Why should she think? Why should she answer anybody? It was enough that this was the end, and there was no way out. She need not pass any more darkly along the main street of the small town, avoiding every eye. She need not demean herself any more, going into the shops and buying the cheapest food. This was at an end. She thought of nobody, not even of herself. Mindless and persistent, she seemed in a sort of ecstasy to be coming nearer to her fulfilment, her own glorification, approaching her dead mother, who was glorified.

In the afternoon she took a little bag, with shears and sponge and a small scrubbing-brush, and went out. It was a grey, wintry day, with saddened, dark green fields and an atmosphere blackened by the smoke of foundries not far off. She went quickly, darkly along the causeway, heeding nobody, through the town to the churchyard.

There she always felt secure, as if no one could see her, although as a matter of fact she was exposed to the stare of everyone who passed along under the churchyard wall. Nevertheless, once under the shadow of the great looming church, among the graves, she felt immune from the world, reserved within the thick churchyard wall as in another country.

Carefully she clipped the grass from the grave, and arranged the pinky white, small chrysanthemums in the tin cross. When this was done, she took an empty jar from a neighbouring grave, brought water, and carefully, most scrupulously sponged the marble headstone and the coping-stone.

It gave her sincere satisfaction to do this. She felt in immediate contact with the world of her mother. She took minute pains, went through the park in a state bordering on pure happiness, as if in performing this task she came into a subtle, intimate connection with her mother. For the life she followed here in the world was far less real than the world of death she inherited from her mother.

The doctor's house was just by the church. Fergusson, being a mere hired assistant, was slave to the country-side. As he hurried now to attend to the out-patients in the surgery, glancing across the graveyard with his quick eye, he saw the girl at her task at the grave. She seemed so intent and remote, it was like looking into another world. Some mystical element was touched in him. He slowed down as he walked, watching her as if spellbound.

She lifted her eyes, feeling him looking. Their eyes met. And each looked again at once, each feeling, in some way, found out by the other. He lifted his cap and passed on down the road. There remained distinct in his consciousness, like a vision, the memory of her face, lifted from the tombstone in the churchyard; and looking at him with slow, large, portentous eyes. It *was* portentous, her face. It seemed to mesmerise him. There was a heavy power in her eyes which laid hold of his whole being, as if he had drunk some powerful drug. He had been feeling weak and done before. Now the life came back into him, he felt delivered from his own fretted, daily self.

He finished his duties at the surgery as quickly as might be, hastily filling up the bottles of the waiting people with cheap drugs. Then, in perpetual haste, he set off again to visit several cases in another part of his round, before tea-time. At all times he preferred to walk if he could, but particularly when he was not well. He fancied the motion restored him.

The afternoon was falling. It was grey, deadened, and wintry, with a slow, moist, heavy coldness sinking in and deadening all the faculties. But why should he think or notice? He hastily climbed the hill and turned across the dark green fields, following the black cinder-track. In the distance, across a shallow dip in the country, the small town was clustered like smouldering ash, a tower, a spire, a heap of low, raw, extinct houses. And on the nearest fringe of the town, sloping into the dip, was Oldmeadow, the Pervins' house. He could see the stables and the outbuildings distinctly, as they lay towards him on the slope. Well, he would not go there many more times! Another resource would be lost to him, another place gone: the only company he cared for in the alien, ugly little town he was losing. Nothing but work, drudgery, constant hastening from dwelling to dwelling among the colliers and the iron-workers. It wore him out, but at the same time he had a craving for it. It was a stimulant to him to be in the homes of the working people, moving, as it were, through the innermost body of their life. His nerves were excited and gratified. He could come so near, into the very lives of the rough, inarticulate, powerfully emotional men and women. He grumbled, he said he hated the hellish hole. But as a matter of fact it excited him, the contact with the rough, strongly-feeling people was a stimulant applied direct to his nerves.

Below Oldmeadow, in the green, shallow, soddened hollow of fields, lay a square, deep pond. Roving across the landscape, the doctor's quick eye detected a figure in black passing through the gate of the field, down towards the pond. He looked again. It would be Mabel Pervin. His mind suddenly became alive and attentive.

Why was she going down there? He pulled up on the path on the slope above, and stood staring. He could just make sure of the small black figure moving in the hollow of the failing day. He seemed to see her in the midst of such obscurity, that he was like a clairvoyant, seeing rather with the mind's eye than with ordinary sight. Yet he could see her positively enough, whilst he kept his eye attentive. He felt, if he looked away from her, in the thick, ugly falling dusk, he would lose her altogether.

He followed her minutely as she moved, direct and intent, like something transmitted rather than stirring in voluntary activity, straight down the field towards the pond. There she stood on the bank for a moment. She never raised her head. Then she waded slowly into the water.

He stood motionless as the small black figure walked slowly and deliberately towards the centre of the pond, very slowly, gradually moving deeper into the motionless water, and still moving forward as the water got up to her breast. Then he could see her no more in the dusk of the dead afternoon.

"There!" he exclaimed. "Would you believe it?"

And he hastened straight down, running over the wet, soddened fields, pushing through the hedges, down into the depression of callous wintry obscurity. It took him several minutes to come to the pond. He stood on the bank, breathing heavily. He could see nothing. His eyes seemed to penetrate the dead water. Yes, perhaps that was the dark shadow of her black clothing beneath the surface of the water.

He slowly ventured into the pond. The bottom was deep, soft clay, he sank in, and the water clasped dead cold round his legs. As he stirred he could smell the cold, rotten clay that fouled up into the water. It was objectionable in his lungs. Still, repelled and yet not heeding, he moved deeper into the pond. The cold water rose over his thighs, over his loins, upon his abdomen. The lower part of his body was all sunk in the hideous cold element. And the bottom was so deeply soft and uncertain, he was afraid of pitching with his mouth underneath. He could not swim, and was afraid.

He crouched a little, spreading his hands under the water and moving them round, trying to feel for her. The dead cold pond swayed upon his chest. He moved again, a little deeper, and again, with his hands underneath, he felt all around under the water. And he touched her clothing. But it evaded his fingers. He made a desperate effort to grasp it.

And so doing he lost his balance and went under, horribly, suffocating in the foul earthy water, struggling madly for a few moments. At last, after what seemed an eternity, he got his footing, rose again into the air and looked around. He gasped, and knew he was in the world. Then he looked at the water. She had risen near him. He grasped her clothing, and drawing her nearer, turned to take his way to land again.

He went very slowly, carefully, absorbed in the slow progress. He rose higher, climbing out of the pond. The water was now only about his legs; he was thankful, full of relief to be out of the clutches of the pond. He lifted her and staggered on to the bank, out of the horror of wet, grey clay.

He laid her down on the bank. She was quite unconscious and running with water. He made the water come from her mouth, he worked to restore her. He did not have to work very long before he could feel the breathing begin again in her; she was breathing naturally. He worked a little longer. He could feel her live beneath his hands; she was coming back. He wiped her face, wrapped her in his overcoat, looked round into the dim, dark grey world, then lifted her and staggered down the bank and across the fields.

It seemed an unthinkably long way, and his burden so heavy he felt he would never get to the house. But at last he was in the stable-yard, and then in the house-yard. He opened the door and went into the house. In the kitchen he laid her down on the hearth-rug and called. The house was empty. But the fire was burning in the grate.

Then again he kneeled to attend to her. She was breathing regularly, her eyes were wide open and as if conscious, but there seemed something missing in her look. She was conscious in herself, but unconscious of her surroundings.

He ran upstairs, took blankets from a bed, and put them before the fire to warm. Then he removed her saturated, earthy-smelling clothing, rubbed her dry with a towel, and wrapped her naked in the blankets. Then he went into the dining-room, to look for spirits. There was a little whisky. He drank a gulp himself, and put some into her mouth.

The effect was instantaneous. She looked full into his face, as if she had been seeing him for some time, and yet had only just become conscious of him.

"Dr. Fergusson?" she said.

"What?" he answered.

He was divesting himself of his coat, intending to find some dry clothing upstairs. He could not bear the smell of the dead, clayey water, and he was mortally afraid for his own health.

"What did I do?" she asked.

"Walked into the pond," he replied. He had begun to shudder like one sick, and could hardly attend to her. Her eyes remained full on him, he seemed to be going dark in his mind, looking back at her helplessly.

The shuddering became quieter in him, his life came back to him, dark and unknowing, but strong again.

"Was I out of my mind?" she asked, while her eyes were fixed on him all the time.

"Maybe, for the moment," he replied. He felt quiet, because his strength had come back. The strange fretful strain had left him.

"Am I out of my mind now?" she asked.

"Are you?" he reflected a moment. "No," he answered truthfully, "I don't see that you are." He turned his face aside. He was afraid now, because he felt dazed, and felt dimly that her power was stronger than his, in this issue. And she continued to look at him fixedly all the time. "Can you tell me where I shall find some dry things to put on?" he asked.

"Did you dive into the pond for me?" she asked.

"No," he answered. "I walked in. But I went in overhead as well."

There was silence for a moment. He hesitated. He very much wanted to go upstairs to get into dry clothing. But there was another desire in him. And she seemed to hold him. His will seemed to have gone to sleep, and left him, standing there slack before her. But he felt warm inside himself. He did not shudder at all, though his clothes were sodden on him.

"Why did you?" she asked.

"Because I didn't want you to do such a foolish thing," he said.

"It wasn't foolish," she said, still gazing at him as she lay on the floor, with a sofa cushion under her head. "It was the right thing to do. *I* knew best, then."

"I'll go and shift these wet things," he said. But still he had not the power to move out of her presence, until she sent him. It was as if she had the life of his body in her hands, and he could not extricate himself. Or perhaps he did not want to.

Suddenly she sat up. Then she became aware of her own immediate condition. She felt the blankets about her, she knew her own limbs. For a moment it seemed as if her reason were going. She looked round, with wild eye, as if seeking something. He stood still with fear. She saw her clothing lying scattered.

"Who undressed me?" she asked, her eyes resting full and inevitable on his face.

"I did," he replied, "to bring you round."

For some moments she sat and gazed at him awfully, her lips parted. "Do you love me, then?" she asked.

He only stood and stared at her, fascinated. His soul seemed to melt.

She shuffled forward on her knees, and put her arms round him, round his legs, as he stood there, pressing her breasts against his knees and thighs, clutching him with strange, convulsive certainty, pressing his thighs against her, drawing him to her face, her throat, as she looked up at him with flaring, humble eyes of transfiguration, triumphant in first possession.

"You love me," she murmured, in strange transport, yearning and triumphant and confident. "You love me. I know you love me, I know."

And she was passionately kissing his knees, through the wet clothing, passionately and indiscriminately kissing his knees, his legs, as if unaware of everything.

He looked down at the tangled wet hair, the wild, bare, animal shoulders. He was amazed, bewildered, and afraid. He had never thought of loving her. He had never wanted to love her. When he rescued her and restored her, he was a doctor, and she was a patient. He had had no single personal thought of her. Nay, this introduction of the personal element was very distasteful to him, a violation of his professional honour. It was horrible to have her there embracing his knees. It was horrible. He revolted from it, violently. And yet—and yet—he had not the power to break away.

She looked at him again, with the same supplication of powerful love, and that same transcendent, frightening light of triumph. In view of the delicate flame which seemed to come from her face like a light, he was powerless. And yet he had never intended to love her. He had never intended. And something stubborn in him could not give way.

"You love me," she repeated, in a murmur of deep, rhapsodic assurance. "You love me."

Her hands were drawing him, drawing him down to her. He was afraid, even a little horrified. For he had, really, no intention of loving her. Yet her hands were drawing him towards her. He put out his hand quickly to steady himself, and grasped her bare shoulder. A flame seemed to burn the hand that grasped her soft shoulder. He had no intention of loving her: his whole will was against his yielding. It was horrible. And yet wonderful was the touch of her shoulders, beautiful the shining of her face. Was she perhaps mad? He had a horror of yielding to her. Yet something in him ached also.

He had been staring away at the door, away from her. But his hand remained on her shoulder. She had gone suddenly very still. He looked down at her. Her eyes were now wide with fear, with doubt, the light was dying from her face, a shadow of terrible greyness was returning. He could not bear the touch of her eyes' question upon him, and the look of death behind the question.

With an inward groan he gave way, and let his heart yield towards her. A sudden gentle smile came on his face. And her eyes, which never left his face, slowly, slowly filled with tears. He watched the strange water rise in her eyes, like some slow fountain coming up. And his heart seemed to burn and melt away in his breast.

He could not bear to look at her any more. He dropped on his knees and caught her head with his arms and pressed her face against his throat. She was very still. His heart, which seemed to have broken, was burning with a kind of agony in his breast. And he felt her slow, hot tears wetting his throat. But he could not move.

He felt the hot tears wet his neck and the hollows of his neck, and he remained motionless, suspended through one of man's eternities. Only now it had become indispensable to him to have her face pressed close to him; he could never let her go again. He could never let her head go away from the close clutch of his arm. He wanted to remain like that for ever, with his heart hurting him in a pain that was also life to him. Without knowing, he was looking down on her damp, soft brown hair.

Then, as it were suddenly, he smelt the horrid stagnant smell of that water. And at the same moment she drew away from him and looked at him. Her eyes were wistful and unfathomable. He was afraid of them, and he fell to kissing her, not knowing what he was doing. He wanted her eyes not to have that terrible, wistful, unfathomable look.

When she turned her face to him again, a faint delicate flush was glowing, and there was again dawning that terrible shining of joy in her eyes, which really terrified him, and yet which he now wanted to see, because he feared the look of doubt still more.

"You love me?" she said, rather faltering.

"Yes." The word cost him a painful effort. Not because it wasn't true. But because it was too newly true, the *saying* seemed to tear open again his newly-torn heart. And he hardly wanted it to be true, even now.

She lifted her face to him, and he bent forward and kissed her on the mouth, gently, with the one kiss that is an eternal pledge. And as he kissed her his heart strained again in his breast. He never intended to love her. But now it was over. He had crossed over the gulf to her, and all that he had left behind had shrivelled and become void.

After the kiss, her eyes again slowly filled with tears. She sat still, away from him, with her face drooped aside, and her hands folded in her lap. The tears fell very slowly. There was complete silence. He too sat there motionless and silent on the hearth-rug. The strange pain of his heart that was broken seemed to consume him. That he should love her? That this was love! That he should be ripped open in this way! Him, a doctor! How they would all jeer if they knew! It was agony to him to think they might know.

In the curious naked pain of the thought he looked again to her. She was sitting there drooped into a muse. He saw a tear fall, and his heart flared hot. He saw for the first time that one of her shoulders was quite uncovered, one arm bare, he could see one of her small breasts; dimly, because it had become almost dark in the room.

"Why are you crying?" he asked, in an altered voice.

She looked up at him, and behind her tears the consciousness of her situation for the first time brought a dark look of shame to her eyes.

"I'm not crying, really," she said, watching him, half frightened.

He reached his hand, and softly closed it on her bare arm.

"I love you! I love you!" he said in a soft, low vibrating voice, unlike himself.

She shrank, and dropped her head. The soft, penetrating grip of his hand on her arm distressed her. She looked up at him.

"I want to go," she said. "I want to go and get you some dry things."

"Why?" he said. "I'm all right."

"But I want to go," she said. "And I want you to change your things."

He released her arm, and she wrapped herself in the blanket, looking at him rather frightened. And still she did not rise.

"Kiss me," she said wistfully.

He kissed her, but briefly, half in anger.

Then, after a second, she rose nervously, all mixed up in the blanket. He watched her in her confusion as she tried to extricate herself and wrap herself up so that she could walk. He watched her relentlessly, as she knew. And as she went, the blanket trailing, and as he saw a glimpse of her feet and her white leg, he tried to remember her as she was when he had wrapped her in the blanket. But then he didn't want to remember, because she had been nothing to him then, and his nature revolted from remembering her as she was when she was nothing to him.

A tumbling, muffled noise from within the dark house startled him. Then he heard her voice: "There are clothes." He rose and went to the foot of the stairs, and gathered up the garments she had thrown down. Then he came back to the fire, to rub himself down and dress. He grinned at his own appearance when he had finished.

The fire was sinking, so he put on coal. The house was now quite dark, save for the light of a street-lamp that shone in faintly from beyond the holly trees. He lit the gas with matches he found on the mantelpiece. Then he emptied the pockets of his own clothes, and threw all his wet things in a heap into the scullery. After which he gathered up her sodden clothes, gently, and put them in a separate heap on the copper-top in the scullery.

It was six o'clock on the clock. His own watch had stopped. He ought to go back to the surgery. He waited, and still she did not come down. So he went to the foot of the stairs and called:

"I shall have to go."

Almost immediately he heard her coming down. She had on her best dress of black voile, and her hair was tidy, but still damp. She looked at him—and in spite of herself, smiled.

"I don't like you in those clothes," she said.

"Do I look a sight?" he answered.

They were shy of one another.

"I'll make you some tea," she said.

"No, I must go."

"Must you?" And she looked at him again with the wide, strained, doubtful eyes. And again, from the pain of his breast, he knew how he loved her. He went and bent to kiss her, gently, passionately, with his heart's painful kiss.

"And my hair smells so horrible," she murmured in distraction. "And I'm so awful, I'm so awful! Oh no, I'm too awful." And she broke into bitter, heart-broken sobbing. "You can't want to love me, I'm horrible."

"Don't be silly, don't be silly," he said, trying to comfort her, kissing her, holding her in his arms. "I want you, I want to marry you, we're going to be married, quickly, quickly—to-morrow if I can."

But she only sobbed terribly, and cried:

"I feel awful. I feel awful. I feel I'm horrible to you."

"No, I want you, I want you," was all he answered, blindly, with that terrible intonation which frightened her almost more than her horror lest he should *not* want her.

*—1922*

---

*Katherine Mansfield (1888–1923) was born in Wellington, New Zealand, and chose the short story as her primary vehicle for exploring the psychological lives of her characters, particularly women and children. Her collections include* Bliss *(1920) and* The Garden Party *(1922), in which this story appears. Influenced by Chekhov, she was interested in the significance of small details, and the aptness of expression. Of "Miss Brill" she wrote, "I chose not only the length of every sentence, but even the sound of every sentence—I chose the rise and fall of every paragraph to fit her—and to fit her on that day at that very moment." Mansfield lived an unconventional life as a New Woman travelling throughout England, France, and Italy, making friends with D. H. Lawrence and Virginia Woolf. She died of tuberculosis at age thirty-five.*

# Katherine Mansfield
## Miss Brill

Although it was so brilliantly fine—the blue sky powdered with gold and great spots of light like white wine splashed over the Jardins Publiques—Miss Brill was glad that she had decided on her fur. The air was motionless, but when you opened your mouth there was just a faint chill, like a chill from a glass of iced water before you sip, and now and again a leaf came drifting—from nowhere, from the sky. Miss Brill put up her hand and touched her fur. Dear little thing! It was nice to feel it again. She had taken it out of its box that afternoon, shaken out the moth-powder, given it a good brush, and rubbed the life back into the dim little eyes. "What has been happening to me?" said the sad little eyes. Oh, how sweet it was to see them snap at her again from the red eiderdown! . . . But the nose, which was of some black composition, wasn't at all firm. It must have had a knock, somehow. Never mind—a little dab of black sealing-wax when the time came—when it was absolutely necessary. . . . Little rogue! Yes, she really felt like that about it. Little rogue biting its tail just by her left ear. She could have taken it off and laid it on her lap and stroked it. She felt a tingling in her hands and arms, but that came from walking, she supposed. And when she breathed, something light and sad—no, not sad, exactly—something gentle seemed to move in her bosom.

There were a number of people out this afternoon, far more than last Sunday. And the band sounded louder and gayer. That was because the Season had begun. For although the band played all the year round on Sundays, out of season it was never the same. It was like some one playing with only the family to listen; it didn't care how it played if there weren't any strangers present. Wasn't the conductor wearing a new coat, too? She was sure it was new. He scraped with his foot and flapped his arms like a rooster about to crow, and the bandsmen sitting in the green rotunda blew out their cheeks and glared at the music. Now there came a little "flutey" bit—very pretty!—a little chain of bright drops. She was sure it would be repeated. It was; she lifted her head and smiled.

Only two people shared her "special" seat: a fine old man in a velvet coat, his hands clasped over a huge carved walking-stick, and a big old woman, sitting upright, with a roll of knitting on her embroidered apron. They did not speak. This was disappointing, for Miss Brill always looked forward to the conversation. She had become really quite expert, she thought, at listening as though she didn't listen, at sitting in other people's lives just for a minute while they talked round her.

She glanced, sideways, at the old couple. Perhaps they would go soon. Last Sunday, too, hadn't been as interesting as usual. An Englishman and his wife, he wearing a dreadful Panama hat and she button boots. And she'd gone on the whole time about how she ought to wear spectacles; she knew she needed them; but that it was no good getting any; they'd be sure to break and they'd never keep on. And he'd been so patient. He'd suggested everything—gold rims, the kind that curved round your ears, little pads inside the bridge. No, nothing would please her. "They'll always be sliding down my nose!" Miss Brill had wanted to shake her.

The old people sat on the bench, still as statues. Never mind, there was always the crowd to watch. To and fro, in front of the flower-beds and the band rotunda, the couples and groups paraded, stopped to talk, to greet, to buy a handful of flowers from the old beggar who had his tray fixed to the railings. Little children ran among them, swooping and laughing; little boys with big white silk bows under their chins, little girls, little French dolls, dressed up in velvet and lace. And sometimes a tiny staggerer came suddenly rocking into the open from under the trees, stopped, stared, as suddenly sat down "flop," until its small high-stepping mother, like a young hen, rushed scolding to its rescue. Other people sat on the benches and green chairs, but they were nearly always the same, Sunday after Sunday, and—Miss Brill had often noticed—there was something funny about nearly all of them. They were odd, silent, nearly all old, and from the way they stared they looked as though they'd just come from dark little rooms or even—even cupboards!

Behind the rotunda the slender trees with yellow leaves down drooping, and through them just a line of sea, and beyond the blue sky with gold-veined clouds.

Tum-tum-tum tiddle-um! tiddle-um! tum tiddley-um tum ta! blew the band.

Two young girls in red came by and two young soldiers in blue met them, and they laughed and paired and went off arm-in-arm. Two peasant women with funny straw hats passed, gravely, leading beautiful smoke-coloured donkeys. A cold, pale nun hurried by. A beautiful woman came along and dropped her bunch of violets, and a little boy ran after to hand them to her, and she took them and threw them away as if they'd been poisoned. Dear me! Miss Brill didn't know whether to admire that or not! And now an ermine toque and a gentleman in grey met just in front of her. He was tall, stiff, dignified, and she was wearing the ermine toque she'd bought when her hair was yellow. Now everything, her hair, her face, even her eyes, was the same colour as the shabby ermine, and her hand, in its cleaned glove, lifted to dab her lips, was a tiny yellowish paw. Oh, she was so pleased to see him—delighted! She rather thought they were going to meet that afternoon. She described where she'd been—everywhere, here, there, along by the sea. The day was so charming—didn't he agree? And wouldn't he, perhaps? . . . But he shook his head, lighted a cigarette, slowly breathed a great deep puff into her face, and, even while she was still talking and laughing, flicked the match away and walked on. The ermine toque was alone; she smiled more brightly than ever. But even the band seemed to know what she was feeling and played more softly, played tenderly, and the drum beat, "The Brute! The Brute!" over and over. What would she do? What was going to happen now? But as Miss Brill wondered, the ermine toque turned, raised her hand as though she'd seen some one else, much nicer, just over there, and pattered away. And the band changed again and played more quickly, more gaily than ever, and the old couple on Miss Brill's seat got up and marched away, and such a funny old man with long whiskers hobbled along in time to the music and was nearly knocked over by four girls walking abreast.

Oh, how fascinating it was! How she enjoyed it! How she loved sitting here, watching it all! It was like a play. It was exactly like a play. Who could believe the sky at the back wasn't painted? But it wasn't till a little brown dog trotted on solemn and then slowly trotted off, like a little "theatre" dog, a little dog that had been drugged, that Miss Brill discovered what it was that made it so exciting. They were all on the stage. They weren't only the audience, not only looking on; they were acting. Even she had a part and came every Sunday. No doubt somebody would have noticed if she hadn't been there; she was part of the performance after all. How strange she'd never thought of it like that before! And yet it explained why she made such a point of starting from home at just the same time each week—so as not to be late for the performance—and it also explained why she had quite a queer, shy feeling at telling her English pupils how she spent her Sunday afternoons. No wonder! Miss Brill nearly laughed out loud. She was on the stage. She thought of the old invalid gentleman to whom she read the newspaper four afternoons a week while he slept in the garden. She had got quite used to the frail head on the cotton pillow, the hollowed eyes, the open mouth and the high pinched nose. If he'd been dead she mightn't have noticed for weeks; she wouldn't have minded. But suddenly he knew he was having the paper read to him by an actress! "An actress!" The old head lifted; two points of light quivered in the old eyes. "An actress—are ye?" And Miss Brill smoothed the newspaper as though it were the manuscript of her part and said gently: "Yes, I have been an actress for a long time."

The band had been having a rest. Now they started again. And what they played was warm, sunny, yet there was just a faint chill—a something, what was it?—not sadness—no, not sadness—a something that made you want to sing. The tune lifted, lifted, the light shone; and it seemed to Miss Brill that in another moment all of them, all the whole company, would begin singing. The young ones, the laughing ones who were moving together, they would begin, and the men's voices, very resolute and brave, would join them. And then she too, she too, and the others on the benches—they would come in with a kind of accompaniment—something low, that scarcely rose or fell, something so beautiful—moving. . . . And Miss Brill's eyes filled with tears and she looked smiling at all the other members of the company. Yes, we understand, we understand, she thought—though what they understood she didn't know.

Just at that moment a boy and a girl came and sat down where the old couple had been. They were beautifully dressed; they were in love. The hero and heroine, of course, just arrived from his father's yacht. And still soundlessly singing, still with that trembling smile, Miss Brill prepared to listen.

"No, not now," said the girl. "Not here, I can't."

"But why? Because of that stupid old thing at the end there?" asked the boy. "Why does she come here at all—who wants her? Why doesn't she keep her silly old mug at home?"

"It's her fu-fur which is so funny," giggled the girl. "It's exactly like a fried whiting."

"Ah, be off with you!" said the boy in an angry whisper. Then: "Tell me, ma petite chérie—"

"No, not here," said the girl. "Not *yet.*"

On her way home she usually bought a slice of honey-cake at the baker's. It was her Sunday treat. Sometimes there was an almond in her slice, sometimes not. It made a great difference. If there was an almond it was like carrying home a tiny present—a surprise—something that might very well not have been there. She hurried on the almond Sundays and struck the match for the kettle in quite a dashing way.

But to-day she passed the baker's by, climbed the stairs, went into the little dark room—her room like a cupboard—and sat down on the red eiderdown. She sat there for a long time. The box that the fur came out of was on the bed. She unclasped the necklet quickly; quickly, without looking, laid it inside. But when she put the lid on she thought she heard something crying.

*—1922*

*Ernest Hemingway (1899–1961) completely embodied the public image of the successful writer for so long that nearly half a century after his suicide it is difficult to separate the celebrity from the serious artist, the sportsman from the stylist whose influence on the short story and novel continues to be felt. The terse, stripped-down quality of his prose renders modern alienation with stark, concrete details. Born the son of a doctor in a middle-class suburb of Chicago, wounded as a volunteer ambulance driver in Italy during World War I, he worked as a reporter in Kansas and Toronto, moving to Paris in the early 1920s, where he was at the centre of a group of American expatriate writers referred to as the "Lost Generation." Sojourns in Europe, Africa, America, and Cuba inspired his long fiction—from his first successful novel,* The Sun Also Rises *(1926), to his Pulitzer Prize–winning* The Old Man and the Sea *(1952)—as well as several collections of short fiction and nonfiction. He won the Nobel Prize in 1954.*

## *Ernest Hemingway*
# Hills like White Elephants

The hills across the valley of the Ebro were long and white. On this side there was no shade and no trees and the station was between two lines of rails in the sun. Close against the side of the station there was the warm shadow of the building and a curtain, made of strings of bamboo beads, hung across the open door into the bar, to keep out flies. The American and the girl with him sat at a table in the shade, outside the building. It was very hot and the express from Barcelona would come in forty minutes. It stopped at this junction for two minutes and went on to Madrid.

"What should we drink?" the girl asked. She had taken off her hat and put it on the table.

"It's pretty hot," the man said.

"Let's drink beer."

"*Dos cervezas,*" the man said into the curtain.

"Big ones?" a woman asked from the doorway.

"Yes. Two big ones."

The woman brought two glasses of beer and two felt pads. She put the felt pads and the beer glasses on the table and looked at the man and the girl. The girl was looking off at the line of hills. They were white in the sun and the country was brown and dry.

"They look like white elephants," she said.

"I've never seen one," the man drank his beer.

"No, you wouldn't have."

"I might have," the man said. "Just because you say I wouldn't have doesn't prove anything."

The girl looked at the bead curtain. "They've painted something on it," she said. "What does it say?"

"Anis del Toro. It's a drink."

"Could we try it?"

The man called "Listen" through the curtain. The woman came out from the bar.

"Four reales."

"We want two Anis del Toro."

"With water?"

"Do you want it with water?"

"I don't know," the girl said. "Is it good with water?"

"It's all right."

"You want them with water?" asked the woman.

"Yes, with water."

"It tastes like licorice," the girl said and put the glass down.

"That's the way with everything."

"Yes," said the girl. "Everything tastes of licorice. Especially all the things you've waited so long for, like absinthe."

"Oh, cut it out."

"You started it," the girl said. "I was being amused. I was having a fine time."

"Well, let's try and have a fine time."

"All right. I was trying. I said the mountains looked like white elephants. Wasn't that bright?"

"That was bright."

"I wanted to try this new drink: That's all we do, isn't it—look at things and try new drinks?"

"I guess so."

The girl looked across at the hills.

"They're lovely hills," she said. "They don't really look like white elephants. I just meant the coloring of their skin through the trees."

"Should we have another drink?"

"All right."

The warm wind blew the bead curtain against the table.

"The beer's nice and cool," the man said.

"It's lovely," the girl said.

"It's really an awfully simple operation, Jig," the man said. "It's not really an operation at all."

The girl looked at the ground the table legs rested on.

"I know you wouldn't mind it, Jig. It's really not anything. It's just to let the air in."

The girl did not say anything.

"I'll go with you and I'll stay with you all the time. They just let the air in and then it's all perfectly natural."

"Then what will we do afterward?"

"We'll be fine afterward. Just like we were before."

"What makes you think so?"

"That's the only thing that bothers us. It's the only thing that's made us unhappy."

The girl looked at the bead curtain, put her hand out and took hold of two of the strings of beads.

"And you think then we'll be all right and be happy."

"I know we will. You don't have to be afraid. I've known lots of people that have done it."

"So have I," said the girl. "And afterward they were all so happy."

"Well," the man said, "if you don't want to you don't have to. I wouldn't have you do it if you didn't want to. But I know it's perfectly simple."

"And you really want to?"

"I think it's the best thing to do. But I don't want you to do it if you don't really want to."

"And if I do it you'll be happy and things will be like they were and you'll love me?"

"I love you now. You know I love you."

"I know. But if I do it, then it will be nice again if I say things are like white elephants, and you'll like it?"

"I'll love it. I love it now but I just can't think about it. You know how I get when I worry."

"If I do it you won't ever worry?"

"I won't worry about that because it's perfectly simple."

"Then I'll do it. Because I don't care about me."

"What do you mean?"

"I don't care about me."

"Well, I care about you."

"Oh, yes. But I don't care about me. And I'll do it and then every-thing will be fine."

"I don't want you to do it if you feel that way."

The girl stood up and walked to the end of the station. Across, on the other side, were fields of grain and trees along the banks of the Ebro. Far away, beyond the river, were mountains. The shadow of a cloud moved across the field of grain and she saw the river through the trees.

"And we could have all this," she said. "And we could have every-thing and every day we make it more impossible."

"What did you say?"

"I said we could have everything."

"We can have everything."

"No, we can't."

"We can have the whole world."

"No, we can't."

"We can go everywhere."

"No, we can't. It isn't ours any more."

"It's ours."

"No, it isn't. And once they take it away, you never get it back."

"But they haven't taken it away."

"We'll wait and see."

"Come on back in the shade," he said. "You mustn't feel that way."

"I don't feel any way," the girl said. "I just know things."

"I don't want you to do anything that you don't want to do———"

"Nor that isn't good for me," she said. "I know. Could we have another beer?"

"All right. But you've got to realize———"

"I realize," the girl said. "Can't we maybe stop talking?"

They sat down at the table and the girl looked across at the hills on the dry side of the valley and the man looked at her and at the table.

"You've got to realize," he said, "that I don't want you to do it if you don't want to. I'm perfectly willing to go through with it if it means anything to you."

"Doesn't it mean anything to you? We could get along."

"Of course it does. But I don't want anybody but you. I don't want any one else. And I know it's perfectly simple."

"Yes, you know it's perfectly simple."

"It's all right for you to say that, but I do know it."

"Would you do something for me now?"

"I'd do anything for you."

"Would you please please please please please please please stop talking?"

He did not say anything but looked at the bags against the wall of the station. There were labels on them from all the hotels where they had spent nights.

"But I don't want you to," he said, "I don't care anything about it."

"I'll scream," the girl said.

The woman came out through the curtains with two glasses of beer and put them down on the damp felt pads. "The train comes in five minutes," she said.

"What did she say?" asked the girl.

"That the train is coming in five minutes."

The girl smiled brightly at the woman, to thank her.

"I'd better take the bags over to the other side of the station," the man said. She smiled at him.

"All right. Then come back and we'll finish the beer."

He picked up the two heavy bags and carried them around the station to the other tracks. He looked up the tracks but could not see the train. Coming back, he walked through the barroom, where people waiting for the train were drinking. He drank an Anis at the bar and looked at the people. They were all waiting reasonably for the train. He went out through the bead curtain. She was sitting at the table and smiled at him.

"Do you feel better?" he asked.

"I feel fine," she said. "There's nothing wrong with me. I feel fine."

*—1927*

*Jorge Luis Borges (1899–1986) is perhaps the most original writer in Spanish of the twentieth century, and many of his experiments anticipate the "metafiction" and "cyberpunk" techniques of today's avant-garde. Born in Buenos Aires, Borges was caught with his parents in Switzerland during World War I, a circumstance that happily led to a multilingual education. Borges was equally fluent in English (he was an expert in Anglo-Saxon literature) and his native Spanish, and he also learned French, German, and Latin. In his early career he was associated with a group of avant-garde experimental poets who attempted, in the pages of literary magazines like* Sur, *to connect the provincial Argentine reading public with the main currents of modernism. Borges himself translated the works of complex American poets like e. e. cummings and Wallace Stevens into Spanish. Borges turned to fiction in his forties, and his paradoxical allegories of time and being, although widely discussed, were never aimed at large popular audiences. A vocal opponent of the Nazis (who had many supporters in Argentina) and of the Perón dictatorship, Borges was dismissed from several positions because of his politics. After the fall of Perón in 1955, Borges served a distinguished term as director of Argentina's national library, despite progressive deterioration of his sight, which left him almost totally blind. In his later years he travelled and lectured in the United States and oversaw the translation of his works into English.*

## Jorge Luis Borges
# The Book of Sand

. . . thy rope of sands . . . [1]

—George Herbert (1593–1623)

The line consists of an infinite number of points; the plane, of an infinite number of lines; the volume, of an infinite number of planes; the hypervolume, of an infinite number of volumes . . . No—this, *more geometrico*, is decidedly not the best way to begin my tale. To say that the story is true is by now a convention of every fantastic tale; mine, nevertheless, *is* true.

I live alone, in a fifth-floor apartment on Calle Belgrano. One evening a few months ago, I heard a knock at my door. I opened it, and a stranger stepped in. He was a tall man, with blurred, vague features, or perhaps my nearsightedness made me see him that way. Everything about him spoke of honest poverty: he was dressed in gray, and carried a gray valise. I immediately sensed that he was a foreigner. At first

[1]*thy rope of sands:* line from Herbert's poem "The Collar" (1633).

I thought he was old; then I noticed that I had been misled by his sparse hair, which was blond, almost white, like the Scandinavians'. In the course of our conversation, which I doubt lasted more than an hour, I learned that he hailed from the Orkneys.

I pointed the man to a chair. He took some time to begin talking. He gave off an air of melancholy, as I myself do now.

"I sell Bibles," he said at last.

"In this house," I replied, not without a somewhat stiff, pedantic note, "there are several English Bibles, including the first one, Wyclif's. I also have Cipriano de Valera's, Luther's (which is, in literary terms, the worst of the lot), and a Latin copy of the Vulgate. As you see, it isn't exactly Bibles I might be needing."

After a brief silence he replied.

"It's not only Bibles I sell. I can show you a sacred book that might interest a man such as yourself. I came by it in northern India, in Bikaner."

He opened his valise and brought out the book. He laid it on the table. It was a clothbound octavo volume that had clearly passed through many hands. I examined it; the unusual heft of it surprised me. On the spine was printed *Holy Writ*, and then *Bombay*.

"Nineteenth century, I'd say," I observed.

"I don't know," was the reply. "Never did know."

I opened it at random. The characters were unfamiliar to me. The pages, which seemed worn and badly set, were printed in double columns, like a Bible. The text was cramped, and composed into versicles. At the upper corner of each page were Arabic numerals. I was struck by an odd fact: the even-numbered page would carry the number 40,514, let us say, while the odd-numbered page that followed it would be 999. I turned the page; the next page bore an eight-digit number. It also bore a small illustration, like those one sees in dictionaries: an anchor drawn in pen and ink, as though by the unskilled hand of a child.

It was at that point that the stranger spoke again.

"Look at it well. You will never see it again."

There was a threat in the words, but not in the voice.

I took note of the page, and then closed the book. Immediately I opened it again. In vain I searched for the figure of the anchor, page after page. To hide my discomfiture, I tried another tack.

"This is a version of Scripture in some Hindu language, isn't that right?"

"No," he replied.

Then he lowered his voice, as though entrusting me with a secret.

"I came across this book in a village on the plain, and I traded a few rupees and a Bible for it. The man who owned it didn't know how to read. I suspect he saw the Book of Books as an amulet. He was of the lowest caste; people could not so much as step on his shadow without being defiled. He told me his book was called the Book of Sand because neither sand nor this book has a beginning or an end."

He suggested I try to find the first page.

I took the cover in my left hand and opened the book, my thumb and forefinger almost touching. It was impossible: several pages always lay between the cover and my hand. It was as though they grew from the very book.

"Now try to find the end."

I failed there as well.

"This can't be," I stammered, my voice hardly recognizable as my own.

"It can't be, yet it *is*," the Bible peddler said, his voice little more than a whisper. "The number of pages in this book is literally infinite. No page is the first page; no page is the last. I don't know why they're numbered in this arbitrary way, but perhaps it's to give one to understand that the terms of an infinite series can be numbered any way whatever."

Then, as though thinking out loud, he went on.

"If space is infinite, we are anywhere, at any point in space. If time is infinite, we are at any point in time."

His musings irritated me. "You," I said, "are a religious man, are you not?"

"Yes, I'm Presbyterian. My conscience is clear. I am certain I didn't cheat that native when I gave him the Lord's Word in exchange for his diabolic book."

I assured him he had nothing to reproach himself for, and asked whether he was just passing through the country. He replied that he planned to return to his own country within a few days. It was then that I learned he was a Scot, and that his home was in the Orkneys. I told him I had great personal fondness for Scotland because of my love for Stevenson and Hume.

"And Robbie Burns," he corrected.

As we talked I continued to explore the infinite book.

"Had you intended to offer this curious specimen to the British Museum, then?" I asked with feigned indifference.

"No," he replied, "I am offering it to you," and he mentioned a great sum of money.

I told him, with perfect honesty, that such an amount of money was not within my ability to pay. But my mind was working; in a few moments I had devised my plan.

"I propose a trade," I said. "You purchased the volume with a few rupees and the Holy Scripture; I will offer you the full sum of my pension, which I have just received, and Wyclif's black-letter Bible. It was left to me by my parents."

"A black-letter Wyclif!" he murmured.

I went to my bedroom and brought back the money and the book. With a bibliophile's zeal he turned the pages and studied the binding.

"Done," he said.

I was astonished that he did not haggle. Only later was I to realize he had entered my house already determined to sell the book. He did not count the money, but merely put the bills into his pocket.

We chatted about India, the Orkneys, and the Norwegian jarls that had once ruled those islands. Night was falling when the man left. I have never seen him since, nor do I know his name.

I thought of putting the Book of Sand in the space left by the Wyclif, but I chose at last to hide it behind some imperfect volumes of the *Thousand and One Nights*.

I went to bed but could not sleep. At three or four in the morning I turned on the light. I took out the impossible book and turned its pages. On one, I saw an engraving of a mask. There was a number in the corner of the page—I don't remember now what it was—raised to the ninth power.

I showed no one my treasure. To the joy of possession was added the fear that it would be stolen from me, and to that, the suspicion that it might not be truly infinite. Those two points of anxiety aggravated my already habitual misanthropy. I had but few friends left, and those, I stopped seeing. A prisoner of the Book, I hardly left my house. I examined the worn binding and the covers with a magnifying glass, and rejected the possibility of some artifice. I found that the small illustrations were spaced at two-thousand-page intervals. I began noting them down in an alphabetized notebook, which was very soon filled. They never repeated themselves. At night, during the rare intervals spared me by insomnia, I dreamed of the book.

Summer was drawing to a close, and I realized that the book was monstrous. It was cold consolation to think that I, who looked upon it with my eyes and fondled it with my ten flesh-and-bone fingers, was no less monstrous than the book. I felt it was a nightmare thing, an obscene thing, and that it defiled and corrupted reality.

I considered fire, but I feared that the burning of an infinite book might be similarly infinite, and suffocate the planet in smoke.

I remembered reading once that the best place to hide a leaf is in the forest. Before my retirement I had worked in the National Library, which contained nine hundred thousand books; I knew that to the right of the lobby a curving staircase descended into the shadows of the basement, where the maps and periodicals are kept. I took advantage of the librarians' distraction to hide the Book of Sand on one of the library's damp shelves; I tried not to notice how high up, or how far from the door.

I now feel a little better, but I refuse even to walk down the street the library's on.[2]

*—1971*

---

[2]In Spanish, the story ends with "Calle Mexico," the street location of Argentina's National Library, where Borges was director, but the allusion has been explained for foreign readers.

*John Cheever (1912–1982) was associated with* The New Yorker *for most of his creative life. It was the magazine that first published most of his short stories. Cheever's examinations of the tensions of life in white-collar suburbia take many forms—from naturalism to outright fantasy—but virtually all of his fiction is suffused with a melancholy that is often fuelled by marital tensions, failed social aspirations, and what one story aptly calls "the sorrows of gin." Born in Quincy, Massachusetts, Cheever was expelled from Thayer Academy at seventeen, an event that formed the subject of his first published story, and he worked almost exclusively as a writer of fiction for the rest of his life, with occasional periods spent teaching at universities and writing for television. His most original writing is arguably in his short stories, but novels like the National Book Award-winning* The Wapshot Chronicle *(1957),* The Wapshot Scandal *(1964),* Bullet Park *(1969), and* Falconer *(1977) brought him to the attention of large audiences.* The Stories of John Cheever *won the Pulitzer Prize in 1979. In recent years his daughter, Susan Cheever, has published a memoir,* Home Before Dark, *and an edition of her father's journals, both of which chronicle Cheever's long struggles with alcoholism and questions of sexual identity.*

## John Cheever
# Reunion

The last time I saw my father was in Grand Central Station. I was going from my grandmother's in the Adirondacks to a cottage on the Cape that my mother had rented, and I wrote my father that I would be in New York between trains for an hour and a half, and asked if we could have lunch together. His secretary wrote to say that he would meet me at the information booth at noon, and at twelve o'clock sharp I saw him coming through the crowd. He was a stranger to me—my mother divorced him three years ago and I hadn't been with him since—but as soon as I saw him I felt that he was my father, my flesh and blood, my future and my doom. I knew that when I was grown I would be something like him; I would have to plan my campaigns within his limitations. He was a big, good-looking man, and I was terribly happy to see him again. He struck me on the back and shook my hand. "Hi, Charlie," he said. "Hi, boy. I'd like to take you up to my club, but it's in the Sixties, and if you have to catch an early train I guess we'd better get something to eat around here." He put his arm around me, and I smelled my father the way my mother sniffs a rose. It was a rich compound of whiskey, after-shave lotion, shoe polish, woolens, and the rankness of a mature male. I hoped that someone would see us together. I wished that we could be photographed. I wanted some record of our having been together.

We went out of the station and up a side street to a restaurant. It was still early, and the place was empty. The bartender was quarreling with a delivery boy, and there was one very old waiter in a red coat down by the kitchen door. We sat down, and my father hailed the waiter in a loud voice. "*Kellner!*" he shouted. "*Garçon! Cameriere! You!*" His boisterousness in the empty restaurant seemed out of place. "Could we have a little service here!" he shouted. "Chop-chop." Then he clapped his hands. This caught the waiter's attention, and he shuffled over to our table.

"Were you clapping your hands at me?" he asked.

"Calm down, calm down, *sommelier*," my father said. "If it isn't too much to ask of you—if it wouldn't be too much above and beyond the call of duty, we would like a couple of Beefeater Gibsons."

"I don't like to be clapped at," the waiter said.

"I should have brought my whistle," my father said. "I have a whistle that is audible only to the ears of old waiters. Now, take out your little pad and your little pencil and see if you can get this straight: two Beefeater Gibsons. Repeat after me: two Beefeater Gibsons."

"I think you'd better go somewhere else," the waiter said quietly.

"That," said my father, "is one of the most brilliant suggestions I have ever heard. Come on, Charlie, let's get the hell out of here!"

I followed my father out of that restaurant into another. He was not so boisterous this time. Our drinks came, and he cross-questioned me about the baseball season. He then struck the edge of his empty glass with his knife and began shouting again. "*Garçon! Kellner! Cameriere! You!* Could we trouble you to bring us two more of the same."

"How old is the boy?" the waiter asked.

"That," my father said, "is none of your God-damned business."

"I'm sorry, sir," the waiter said, "but I won't serve the boy another drink."

"Well, I have some news for you," my father said. "I have some very interesting news for you. This doesn't happen to be the only restaurant in New York. They've opened another on the corner. Come on, Charlie."

He paid the bill, and I followed him out of that restaurant into another. Here the waiters wore pink jackets like hunting coats, and there was a lot of horse tack on the walls. We sat down, and my father began to shout again. "Master of the hounds! Tallyhoo and all that sort of thing. We'd like a little something in the way of a stirrup cup. Namely, two Bibson Geefeaters."

"Two Bibson Geefeaters?" the waiter asked, smiling.

"You know damned well what I want," my father said angrily. "I want two Beefeater Gibsons, and make it snappy. Things have changed in jolly old England. So my friend the duke tells me. Let's see what England can produce in the way of a cocktail."

"This isn't England," the waiter said.

"Don't argue with me," my father said. "Just do as you're told."

"I just thought you might like to know where you are," the waiter said.

"If there is one thing I cannot tolerate," my father said, "it is an impudent domestic. Come on, Charlie."

The fourth place we went to was Italian. *"Buon giorno,"* my father said. *"Per favore, possiamo avere due cocktail americani, forti, forti. Molto gin, poco vermut."*[1]

"I don't understand Italian," the waiter said.

"Oh, come off it," my father said. "You understand Italian, and you know damned well you do. *Vogliamo due cocktail americani. Subito."*

The waiter left us and spoke with the captain, who came over to our table and said, "I'm sorry, sir, but this table is reserved."

"All right," my father said. "Get us another table."

"All the tables are reserved," the captain said.

"I get it," my father said. "You don't desire our patronage. Is that it? Well, the hell with you. *Vada all' inferno.* Let's go, Charlie."

"I have to get my train," I said.

"I'm sorry, sonny," my father said. "I'm terribly sorry." He put his arm around me and pressed me against him. "I'll walk you back to the station. If there had only been time to go up to my club."

"That's all right, Daddy," I said.

"I'll get you a paper," he said. "I'll get you a paper to read on the train."

Then he went up to a newsstand and said, "Kind sir, will you be good enough to favor me with one of your God-damned, no-good,

---

[1]The father is ordering drinks in Italian.

ten-cent afternoon papers?" The clerk turned away from him and stared at a magazine cover. "Is it asking too much, kind sir," my father said, "is it asking too much for you to sell me one of your disgusting specimens of yellow journalism?"

"I have to go, Daddy," I said. "It's late."

"Now, just wait a second, sonny," he said. "I want to get a rise out of this chap."

"Goodbye, Daddy," I said, and I went down the stairs and got my train, and that was the last time I saw my father.

*—1962*

---

*Maya Angelou (b. 1928) was born Marguerite Ann Johnson in St. Louis, Missouri, but went in 1931 to live with her grandmother in Stamps, Arkansas, a childhood she describes in the best-seller* I Know Why the Caged Bird Sings *(1970). Five more volumes of autobiography followed, culminating with* A Song Flung Up to Heaven *(2002). While working as a nightclub singer, Angelou adopted her professional name, which combined a childhood nickname with the name of her first husband. She has published more than thirty books, including several collections of poetry and plays, books for children, and personal essays. She is also an actor, director, educator, and civil rights activist.*

## Maya Angelou
# *from* I Know Why the Caged Bird Sings

The Angel of the candy counter had found me out at last, and was exacting excruciating penance for all the stolen Milky Ways, Mounds, Mr. Goodbars and Hersheys with Almonds. I had two cavities that were rotten to the gums. The pain was beyond the bailiwick of crushed aspirins or oil of cloves. Only one thing could help me, so I prayed earnestly that I'd be allowed to sit under the house and have the building collapse on my left jaw. Since there was no Negro dentist in Stamps, nor doctor either, for that matter, Momma had dealt with previous toothaches by pulling them out (a string tied to the tooth with the other end looped over her fist), pain killers and prayer. In this particular instance the medicine had proved ineffective; there wasn't enough enamel left to hook a string on, and the prayers were being ignored because the Balancing Angel was blocking their passage.

I lived a few days and nights in blinding pain, not so much toying with as seriously considering the idea of jumping in the well, and Momma decided I had to be taken to a dentist. The nearest Negro dentist was in Texarkana, twenty-five miles away, and I was certain that I'd be dead long before we reached half the distance. Momma said we'd go to Dr. Lincoln, right in Stamps, and he'd take care of me. She said he owed her a favor.

I knew that there were a number of whitefolks in town that owed her favors. Bailey and I had seen the books which showed how she had lent money to Blacks and whites alike during the Depression, and most still owed her. But I couldn't aptly remember seeing Dr. Lincoln's name, nor had I ever heard of a Negro's going to him as a patient. However, Momma said we were going, and put water on the stove for our baths. I had never been to a doctor, so she told me that after the bath (which would make my mouth feel better) I had to put on freshly starched and ironed underclothes from inside out. The ache failed to respond to the bath, and I knew then that the pain was more serious than that which anyone had ever suffered.

Before we left the Store, she ordered me to brush my teeth and then wash my mouth with Listerine. The idea of even opening my clamped jaws increased the pain, but upon her explanation that when you go to a doctor you have to clean yourself all over, but most especially the part that's to be examined, I screwed up my courage and unlocked my teeth. The cool air in my mouth and the jarring of my molars dislodged what little remained of my reason. I had frozen to the pain, my family nearly had to tie me down to take the toothbrush away. It was no small effort to get me started on the road to the dentist. Momma spoke to all the passers-by, but didn't stop to chat. She explained over her shoulder that we were going to the doctor and she'd "pass the time of day" on our way home.

Until we reached the pond the pain was my world, an aura that haloed me for three feet around. Crossing the bridge into whitefolks' country, pieces of sanity pushed themselves forward. I had to stop moaning and start walking straight. The white towel, which was drawn under my chin and tied over my head, had to be arranged. If one was dying, it had to be done in style if the dying took place in whitefolks' part of town.

On the other side of the bridge the ache seemed to lessen as if a whitebreeze blew off the whitefolks and cushioned everything in their neighborhood—including my jaw. The gravel road was smoother, the stones smaller and the tree branches hung down around the path and nearly covered us. If the pain didn't diminish then, the familiar yet strange sights hypnotized me into believing that it had.

But my head continued to throb with the measured insistence of a bass drum, and how could a toothache pass the calaboose,[1] hear the songs of the prisoners, their blues and laughter, and not be changed? How could one or two or even a mouthful of angry tooth roots meet a wagonload of powhite-trash children, endure their idiotic snobbery and not feel less important?

Behind the building which housed the dentist's office ran a small path used by servants and those tradespeople who catered to the butcher and Stamps' one restaurant. Momma and I followed that lane to the backstairs of Dentist Lincoln's office. The sun was bright and gave the day a hard reality as we climbed up the steps to the second floor.

Momma knocked on the back door and a young white girl opened it to show surprise at seeing us there. Momma said she wanted to see Dentist Lincoln and to tell him Annie was there. The girl closed the door firmly. Now the humiliation of hearing Momma describe herself as if she had no last name to the young white girl was equal to the physical pain. It seemed terribly unfair to have a toothache and a headache and have to bear at the same time the heavy burden of Blackness.

It was always possible that the teeth would quiet down and maybe drop out of their own accord. Momma said we would wait. We leaned in the harsh sunlight on the shaky railings of the dentist's back porch for over an hour.

He opened the door and looked at Momma. "Well, Annie, what can I do for you?"

He didn't see the towel around my jaw or notice my swollen face.

Momma said, "Dentist Lincoln. It's my grandbaby here. She got two rotten teeth that's giving her a fit."

She waited for him to acknowledge the truth of her statement. He made no comment, orally or facially.

---

[1] *calaboose:* prison.

"She had this toothache purt' near four days now, and today I said, 'Young lady, you going to the Dentist.' "

"Annie?"

"Yes, sir, Dentist Lincoln."

He was choosing words the way people hunt for shells. "Annie, you know I don't treat nigra, colored people."

"I know, Dentist Lincoln. But this here is just my little grandbaby, and she ain't gone be no trouble to you . . ."

"Annie, everybody has a policy. In this world you have to have a policy. Now, my policy is I don't treat colored people."

The sun had baked the oil out of Momma's skin and melted the Vaseline in her hair. She shone greasily as she leaned out of the dentist's shadow.

"Seem like to me, Dentist Lincoln, you might look after her, she ain't nothing but a little mite. And seems like maybe you owe me a favor or two."

He reddened slightly. "Favor or no favor. The money has all been repaid to you and that's the end of it. Sorry, Annie." He had his hand on the doorknob. "Sorry." His voice was a bit kinder on the second "Sorry," as if he really was.

Momma said, "I wouldn't press on you like this for myself but I can't take No. Not for my grandbaby. When you come to borrow my money you didn't have to beg. You asked me, and I lent it. Now, it wasn't my policy. I ain't no moneylender, but you stood to lose this building and I tried to help you out."

"It's been paid, and raising your voice won't make me change my mind. My policy . . ." He let go of the door and stepped nearer Momma. The three of us were crowded on the small landing. "Annie, my policy is I'd rather stick my hand in a dog's mouth than in a nigger's."

He had never once looked at me. He turned his back and went through the door into the cool beyond. Momma backed up inside herself for a few minutes. I forgot everything except her face which was almost a new one to me. She leaned over and took the doorknob, and in her everyday soft voice she said, "Sister, go on downstairs. Wait for me. I'll be there directly."

Under the most common of circumstances I knew it did no good to argue with Momma. So I walked down the steep stairs, afraid to look back and afraid not to do so. I turned as the door slammed, and she was gone.

Momma walked in that room as if she owned it. She shoved that silly nurse aside with one hand and strode into the dentist's office. He was sitting in his chair, sharpening his mean instruments and putting extra sting into his medicines. Her eyes were blazing like live coals and her arms had doubled themselves in length. He looked up at her just before she caught him by the collar of his white jacket.

"Stand up when you see a lady, you contemptuous scoundrel." Her tongue had thinned and the words rolled off well enunciated. Enunciated and sharp like little claps of thunder.

The dentist had no choice but to stand at R.O.T.C.[2] attention. His head dropped after a minute and his voice was humble. "Yes, ma'am, Mrs. Henderson."

"You knave, do you think you acted like a gentleman, speaking to me like that in front of my granddaughter?" She didn't shake him, although she had the power. She simply held him upright.

"No, ma'am, Mrs. Henderson."

"No, ma'am, Mrs. Henderson, what?" Then she did give him the tiniest of shakes, but because of her strength the action set his head and arms to shaking loose on the ends of his body. He stuttered much worse than Uncle Willie. "No, ma'am. Mrs. Henderson, I'm sorry."

With just an edge of her disgust showing, Momma slung him back in his dentist's chair. "Sorry is as sorry does, and you're about the sorriest dentist I ever laid my eyes on." (She could afford to slip into the vernacular because she had such eloquent command of English.)

"I didn't ask you to apologize in front of Marguerite, because I don't want her to know my power, but I order you, now and herewith. Leave Stamps by sundown."

"Mrs. Henderson, I can't get my equipment . . ." He was shaking terribly now.

"Now, that brings me to my second order. You will never again practice dentistry. Never! When you get settled in your next place, you will be a vegetarian caring for dogs with the mange, cats with the cholera and cows with the epizootic.[3] Is that clear?"

The saliva ran down his chin and his eyes filled with tears. "Yes, ma'am. Thank you for not killing me. Thank you, Mrs. Henderson."

[2]*R.O.T.C.:* Reserve Officers' Training Corps.
[3]*epizootic:* cattle plague.

*Momma pulled herself back from being ten feet tall with eight-foot arms and said, "You're welcome for nothing, you varlet, I wouldn't waste a killing on the likes of you."*

*On her way out she waved her handkerchief at the nurse and turned her into a crocus sack of chicken feed.*

Momma looked tired when she came down the stairs, but who wouldn't be tired if they had gone through what she had. She came close to me and adjusted the towel under my jaw (I had forgotten the toothache; I only knew that she made her hands gentle in order not to awaken the pain). She took my hand. Her voice never changed. "Come on, Sister."

I reckoned we were going home where she would concoct a brew to eliminate the pain and maybe give me new teeth too. New teeth that would grow overnight out of my gums. She led me toward the drug-store, which was in the opposite direction from the Store. "I'm taking you to Dentist Baker in Texarkana."

I was glad after all that that I had bathed and put on Mum and Cashmere Bouquet talcum powder. It was a wonderful surprise. My toothache had quieted to solemn pain, Momma had obliterated the evil white man, and we were going on a trip to Texarkana, just the two of us.

On the Greyhound she took an inside seat in the back, and I sat beside her. I was so proud of being her granddaughter and sure that some of her magic must have come down to me. She asked if I was scared. I only shook my head and leaned over on her cool brown upper arm. There was no chance that a dentist, especially a Negro dentist, would dare hurt me then. Not with Momma there. The trip was uneventful, except that she put her arm around me, which was very unusual for Momma to do.

The dentist showed me the medicine and the needle before he dead-ened my gums, but if he hadn't I wouldn't have worried. Momma stood right behind him. Her arms were folded and she checked on everything he did. The teeth were extracted and she bought me an ice cream cone from the side window of a drug counter. The trip back to Stamps was quiet, except that I had to spit into a very small empty snuff can which she had gotten for me and it was difficult with the bus humping and jerking on our country roads.

At home, I was given a warm salt solution, and when I washed out my mouth I showed Bailey the empty holes, where the clotted blood sat like filling in a pie crust. He said I was quite brave, and that was my cue to reveal our confrontation with the peckerwood[4] dentist and Momma's incredible powers.

I had to admit that I didn't hear the conversation, but what else could she have said than what I said she said? What else done? He agreed with my analysis in a lukewarm way, and I happily (after all, I'd been sick) flounced into the Store. Momma was preparing our evening meal and Uncle Willie leaned on the door sill. She gave her version.

"Dentist Lincoln got right uppity. Said he'd rather put his hand in a dog's mouth. And when I reminded him of the favor, he brushed it off like a piece of lint. Well, I sent Sister downstairs and went inside. I hadn't never been in his office before, but I found the door to where he takes out teeth, and him and the nurse was in there thick as thieves. I just stood there till he caught sight of me." Crash bang the pots on the stove. "He jumped just like he was sitting on a pin. He said, 'Annie, I done tole you, I ain't gonna mess around in no niggah's mouth.' I said, 'Somebody's got to do it then,' and he said, 'Take her to Texarkana to the colored dentist' and that's when I said, 'If you paid me my money I could afford to take her.' He said, 'It's all been paid.' I tole him everything but the interest had been paid. He said, "Twasn't no interest.' I said, "Tis now. I'll take ten dollars as payment in full.' You know, Willie, it wasn't no right thing to do, 'cause I lent that money without thinking about it.

"He tole that little snippity nurse of his'n to give me ten dollars and make me sign a 'paid in full' receipt. She gave it to me and I signed the papers. Even though by rights he was paid up before, I figger, he gonna be that kind of nasty, he gonna have to pay for it."

Momma and her son laughed and laughed over the white man's evilness and her retributive sin.

I preferred, much preferred, my version.

*—1969*

---

[4]*peckerwood:* slang for white person.

*Gabriel García Márquez (b. 1928) is the author of a brilliant serio-comic historical novel,* One Hundred Years of Solitude *(1967). It is one of the landmarks of contemporary fiction, and rapidly became an international best-seller. "Magic realism" is the term that is often used to describe the author's unique blend of folklore, historical fact, naturalism, and fantasy, much of it occurring in the fictional village of Macondo. A native of Colombia, García Márquez, the eldest of twelve children, was born in Aracéataca, a small town that is the model for the isolated, decaying settlements found in his fiction. Trained as a journalist, García Márquez has lived in France, Spain, and Mexico, where he has written collections of short fiction and non-fiction as well as novels. He was awarded the Nobel Prize in 1982, and his novels* Love in the Time of Cholera *(1988) and* Memories of My Melancholy Whores *(2005) have reached a wide audience.*

# Gabriel García Márquez
# A Very Old Man with Enormous Wings

On the third day of rain they had killed so many crabs inside the house that Pelayo had to cross his drenched courtyard and throw them into the sea, because the newborn child had a temperature all night and they thought it was due to the stench. The world had been sad since Tuesday. Sea and sky were a single ash-gray thing and the sands of the beach, which on March nights glimmered like powdered light, had become a stew of mud and rotten shellfish. The light was so weak at noon that when Pelayo was coming back to the house after throwing away the crabs, it was hard for him to see what it was that was moving and groaning in the rear of the courtyard. He had to go very close to see that it was an old man, a very old man, lying face down in the mud, who, in spite of his tremendous efforts, couldn't get up, impeded by his enormous wings.

Frightened by that nightmare, Pelayo ran to get Elisenda, his wife, who was putting compresses on the sick child, and he took her to the rear of the courtyard. They both looked at the fallen body with mute stupor. He was dressed like a ragpicker. There were only a few faded hairs left on his bald skull and very few teeth in his mouth, and his pitiful condition of a drenched great-grandfather had taken away any sense

Translated by Gregory Rabassa.

of grandeur he might have had. His huge buzzard wings, dirty and half-plucked, were forever entangled in the mud. They looked at him so long and so closely that Pelayo and Elisenda very soon overcame their surprise and in the end found him familiar. Then they dared speak to him, and he answered in an incomprehensible dialect with a strong sailor's voice. That was how they skipped over the inconvenience of the wings and quite intelligently concluded that he was a lonely castaway from some foreign ship wrecked by the storm. And yet, they called in a neighbor woman who knew everything about life and death to see him, and all she needed was one look to show them their mistake.

"He's an angel," she told them. "He must have been coming for the child, but the poor fellow is so old that the rain knocked him down."

On the following day everyone knew that a flesh-and-blood angel was held captive in Pelayo's house. Against the judgment of the wise neighbor woman, for whom angels in those times were the fugitive survivors of a celestial conspiracy, they did not have the heart to club him to death. Pelayo watched over him all afternoon from the kitchen, armed with his bailiff's club, and before going to bed he dragged him out of the mud and locked him up with the hens in the wire chicken coop. In the middle of the night, when the rain stopped, Pelayo and Elisenda were still killing crabs. A short time afterward the child woke up without a fever and with a desire to eat. Then they felt magnanimous and decided to put the angel on a raft with fresh water and provisions for three days and leave him to his fate on the high seas. But when they went out into the courtyard with the first light of dawn, they found the whole neighborhood in front of the chicken coop having fun with the angel, without the slightest reverence, tossing him things to eat through the openings in the wire as if he weren't a supernatural creature but a circus animal.

Father Gonzaga arrived before seven o'clock, alarmed at the strange news. By that time onlookers less frivolous than those at dawn had already arrived and they were making all kinds of conjectures concerning the captive's future. The simplest among them thought that he should be named mayor of the world. Others of sterner mind felt that he should be promoted to the rank of five-star general in order to win all wars. Some visionaries hoped that he could be put to stud in order to implant on earth a race of winged wise men who could take charge of the universe. But Father Gonzaga, before becoming a priest, had been a robust woodcutter. Standing by the wire, he reviewed his catechism in an instant and asked them to open the door so that he could take a close look at that pitiful man who looked more like a huge decrepit hen among the fascinated chickens. He was lying in a corner drying his open wings in the sunlight among the fruit peels and breakfast leftovers that the early risers had thrown him. Alien to the impertinences of the world, he only lifted his antiquarian eyes and murmured something in his dialect when Father Gonzaga went into the chicken coop and said good morning to him in Latin. The parish priest had his first suspicion of an impostor when he saw that he did not understand the language of God or know how to greet His ministers. Then he noticed that seen close up he was much too human: he had an unbearable smell of the outdoors, the back side of his wings was strewn with parasites and his main feathers had been mistreated by terrestrial winds, and nothing about him measured up to the proud dignity of angels. Then he came out of the chicken coop and in a brief sermon warned the curious against the risks of being ingenuous. He reminded them that the devil had the bad habit of making use of carnival tricks in order to confuse the unwary. He argued that if wings were not the essential element in determining the difference between a hawk and an airplane, they were even less so in the recognition of angels. Nevertheless, he promised to write a letter to his bishop so that the latter would write to his primate so that the latter would write to the Supreme Pontiff in order to get the final verdict from the highest courts.

His prudence fell on sterile hearts. The news of the captive angel spread with such rapidity that after a few hours the courtyard had the bustle of a marketplace and they had to call in troops with fixed bayonets to disperse the mob that was about to knock the house down. Elisenda, her spine all twisted from sweeping up so much marketplace trash, then got the idea of fencing in the yard and charging five cents admission to see the angel.

The curious came from far away. A traveling carnival arrived with a flying acrobat who buzzed over the crowd several times, but no one paid any attention to him because his wings were not those of an angel but, rather, those of a sidereal[1] bat. The most unfortunate invalids on earth came in search of health: a poor woman who since childhood had been counting her heartbeats and had run out of numbers, a Portuguese man

---

[1]*sidereal:* coming from the stars.

who couldn't sleep because the noise of the stars disturbed him, a sleep-walker who got up at night to undo the things he had done while awake; and many others with less serious ailments. In the midst of that shipwreck disorder that made the earth tremble, Pelayo and Elisenda were happy with fatigue, for in less than a week they had crammed their rooms with money and the line of pilgrims waiting their turn to enter still reached beyond the horizon.

The angel was the only one who took no part in his own act. He spent his time trying to get comfortable in his borrowed nest, befuddled by the hellish heat of the oil lamps and sacramental candles that had been placed along the wire. At first they tried to make him eat some mothballs, which according to the wisdom of the wise neighbor woman, were the food prescribed for angels. But he turned them down, just as he turned down the papal lunches that the penitents brought him, and they never found out whether it was because he was an angel or because he was an old man that in the end he ate nothing but eggplant mush. His only supernatural virtue seemed to be patience. Especially during the first days, when the hens pecked at him, searching for the stellar parasites that proliferated in his wings, and the cripples pulled out feathers to touch their defective parts with, and even the most merciful threw stones at him, trying to get him to rise so they could see him standing. The only time they succeeded in arousing him was when they burned his side with an iron for branding steers, for he had been motionless for so many hours that they thought he was dead. He awoke with a start, ranting in his hermetic language and with tears in his eyes, and he flapped his wings a couple of times, which brought on a whirl-wind of chicken dung and lunar dust and a gale of panic that did not seem to be of this world. Although many thought that his reaction had been one not of rage but of pain, from then on they were careful not to annoy him, because the majority understood that his passivity was not that of a hero taking his ease but that of a cataclysm in repose.

Father Gonzaga held back the crowd's frivolity with formulas of maidservant inspiration while awaiting the arrival of a final judgment on the nature of the captive. But the mail from Rome showed no sense of urgency. They spent their time finding out if the prisoner had a navel, if his dialect had any connection with Aramaic, how many times he could fit on the head of a pin, or whether he wasn't just a Norwegian with wings. Those meager letters might have come and gone until the end of time if a providential event had not put an end to the priest's tribulations.

It so happened that during those days, among so many other carnival attractions, there arrived in town the traveling show of the woman who had been changed into a spider for having disobeyed her parents. The admission to see her was not only less than the admission to see the angel, but people were permitted to ask her all manner of questions about her absurd state and to examine her up and down so that no one would ever doubt the truth of her honor. She was a frightful tarantula the size of a ram and with the head of a sad maiden. What was most heart-rending, however, was not her outlandish shape but the sincere affliction with which she recounted the details of her misfortune. While still practically a child she had sneaked out of her parents' house to go to a dance, and while she was coming back through the woods after having danced all night without permission, a fearful thunderclap rent the sky in two and through the crack came the lightning bolt of brimstone that changed her into a spider. Her only nourishment came from the meatballs that charitable souls chose to toss into her mouth. A spectacle like that, full of so much human truth and with such a fearful lesson, was found to defeat without even trying that of a haughty angel who scarcely deigned to look at mortals. Besides, the few miracles attributed to the angel showed a certain mental disorder, like the blind man who didn't recover his sight but grew three new teeth, or the paralytic who didn't get to walk, but almost won the lottery, and the leper whose sores sprouted sunflowers. Those consolation miracles, which were more like mocking fun, had already ruined the angel's reputation when the woman who had been changed into a spider finally crushed him completely. That was how Father Gonzaga was cured forever of his insomnia and Pelayo's courtyard went back to being as empty as during the time it had rained for three days and crabs walked through the bedrooms.

The owners of the house had no reason to lament. With the money they saved they built a two-story mansion with balconies and gardens and high netting so that crabs wouldn't get in during the winter, and with iron bars on the windows so that angels wouldn't get in. Pelayo also set up a rabbit warren close to town and gave up his job as bailiff for good, and Elisenda bought some satin pumps with high heels and many dresses of iridescent silk, the kind worn on Sunday by the most desirable women in those times. The chicken coop was the only thing that didn't receive any attention. If they washed it down with creolin and burned tears of myrrh inside it every so often, it was not in homage to the angel but to drive away the dungheap stench that still hung everywhere like a ghost and was turning the new house into an old one. At first, when the child learned to walk, they were careful that he not get too close to the chicken coop. But then they began to lose their fears and got used to the smell, and before the child got his second teeth he'd gone inside the chicken coop to play, where the wires were falling apart. The angel was no less standoffish with him than with other mortals, but he tolerated the most ingenious infamies with the patience of a dog who had no illusions. They both came down with chicken pox at the same time. The doctor who took care of the child couldn't resist the temptation to listen to the angel's heart, and he found so much whistling in the heart and so many sounds in his kidneys that it seemed impossible for him to be alive. What surprised him most, however, was the logic of his wings. They seemed so natural on that completely human organism that he couldn't understand why other men didn't have them too.

When the child began school it had been some time since the sun and rain had caused the collapse of the chicken coop. The angel went dragging himself about here and there like a stray dying man. They would drive him out of the bedroom with a broom and a moment later find him in the kitchen. He seemed to be in so many places at the same time that they grew to think that he'd been duplicated, that he was reproducing himself all through the house, and the exasperated and unhinged Elisenda shouted that it was awful living in that hell full of angels. He could scarcely eat and his antiquarian eyes had also become so foggy that he went about bumping into posts. All he had left were the bare cannulae[2] of his last feathers. Pelayo threw a blanket over him and extended him the charity of letting him sleep in the shed, and only then did they notice that he had a temperature at night, and was delirious with the tongue twisters of an old Norwegian. That was one of the few times they became alarmed, for they thought he was going to die and not even the wise neighbor woman had been able to tell them what to do with dead angels.

---

[2]*cannulae:* the tubular pieces by which feathers are attached to a body.

And yet he not only survived his worst winter, but seemed improved with the first sunny days. He remained motionless for several days in the farthest corner of the courtyard, where no one would see him, and at the beginning of December some large, stiff feathers began to grow on his wings, the feathers of a scarecrow, which looked more like another misfortune of decrepitude. But he must have known the reason for those changes, for he was quite careful that no one should notice them, that no one should hear the sea chanteys that he sometimes sang under the stars. One morning Elisenda was cutting some bunches of onions for lunch when a wind that seemed to come from the high seas blew into the kitchen. Then she went to the window and caught the angel in his first attempts at flight. They were so clumsy that his fingernails opened a furrow in the vegetable patch and he was on the point of knocking the shed down with the ungainly flapping that slipped on the light and couldn't get a grip on the air. But he did manage to gain altitude. Elisenda let out a sigh of relief, for herself and for him, when she saw him pass over the last houses, holding himself up in some way with the risky flapping of a senile vulture. She kept watching him even when she was through cutting the onions and she kept on watching until it was no longer possible for her to see him, because then he was no longer an annoyance in her life but an imaginary dot on the horizon of the sea.

*—1968*

*Ursula K. Le Guin (b. 1929), the daughter of an anthropologist and a folklorist, is often called a science fiction writer because of classics like* The Left Hand of Darkness *(1969) and the* Earthsea *books; but her work might best be termed speculative fiction, in which she ponders important questions about the meaning of culture, gender, language, and survival. She uses a variety of techniques such as fantasy, realism, and magic realism in her novels and collections of short fiction, which include* The Compass Rose *(1982) and* Changing Planes *(2003). Le Guin has also published many works for children and collections of poetry, including* Incredible Good Fortune: New Poems *(2006).*

# *Ursula K. Le Guin*

# Sur[1]

## A Summary Report of the *Yelcho* Expedition
## to the Antarctic, 1909–1910

Although I have no intention of publishing this report, I think it would be nice if a grandchild of mine, or somebody's grandchild, happened to find it some day; so I shall keep it in the leather trunk in the attic, along with Rosita's christening dress and Juanito's silver rattle and my wedding shoes and finneskos.[2]

The first requisite for mounting an expedition—money—is normally the hardest to come by. I grieve that even in a report destined for a trunk in the attic of a house in a very quiet suburb of Lima I dare not write the name of the generous benefactor, the great soul without whose unstinting liberality the *Yelcho*[3] Expedition would never have been more than the idlest excursion into daydream. That our equipment was the best and most modern—that our provisions were plentiful and fine—that a ship of the Chilean Government, with her brave officers and gallant crew, was twice sent halfway round the world for our convenience: all this is due to that benefactor whose name, alas! I must not say, but whose happiest debtor I shall be till death.

When I was little more than a child my imagination was caught by a newspaper account of the voyage of the *Belgica*, which, sailing south from Tierra del Fuego, became beset by ice in the Bellingshausen Sea

---

[1]*Sur:* Spanish for "south."
[2]*finneskos:* reindeer-skin boots.
[3]*Yelcho:* Chilean steamer that later rescued the stranded crew of Ernest Shackleton in 1916.

and drifted a whole year with the floe, the men aboard her suffering a great deal from want of food and from the terror of the unending winter darkness. I read and reread that account, and later followed with excitement the reports of the rescue of Dr. Nordenskjold from the South Shetland Isles by the dashing Captain Irizar of the *Uruguay*, and the adventures of the *Scotia* in the Weddell Sea. But all these exploits were

### The Map in the Attic[4]

[4]The female explorers rename places after women such as pioneer British nurse **Florence Nightingale** (1820–1910), or South American figures such as **Concolorcorvo**, pseudonym of Alonso Carrio de la Vandera (1715–1778), who wrote *El Lazarillo: A Guide for Inexperienced Travellers*; **Garcilaso** (1539–1616), writer and son of a Spanish conquistador and Inca princess; Spanish poet **Ercilla** (1533–1595); and South American revolutionaries **Francisco de Miranda** (1750–1816) and **Simon Bolivar** (1783–1830). The treeless plains of South America are called **pampas**.

to me but forerunners of the British National Antarctic Expedition of 1902–1904, in the *Discovery*, and the wonderful account of that expedition by Captain Scott.[5] This book, which I ordered from London and reread a thousand times, filled me with longing to see with my own eyes that strange continent, last Thule of the South, which lies on our maps and globes like a white cloud, a void, fringed here and there with scraps of coastline, dubious capes, supposititious islands, headlands that may or may not be there: Antarctica. And the desire was as pure as the polar snows: to go, to see—no more, no less. I deeply respect the scientific accomplishments of Captain Scott's expedition, and have read with passionate interest the findings of physicists, meteorologists, biologists, etc.; but having had no training in any science, nor any opportunity for such training, my ignorance obliged me to forego any thought of adding to the body of scientific knowledge concerning Antarctica; and the same is true for all the members of my expedition. It seems a pity; but there was nothing we could do about it. Our goal was limited to observation and exploration. We hoped to go a little farther, perhaps, and see a little more; if not, simply to go and to see. A simple ambition, I think, and essentially a modest one.

Yet it would have remained less than an ambition, no more than a longing, but for the support and encouragement of my dear cousin and friend Juana —— ——. (I use no surnames, lest this report fall into strangers' hands at last, and embarrassment or unpleasant notoriety thus be brought upon unsuspecting husbands, sons, etc.) I had lent Juana my copy of *The Voyage of the Discovery*; and it was she who, as we strolled beneath our parasols across the Plaza de Armas after Mass one Sunday in 1908, said, "Well, if Captain Scott can do it, why can't we?"

It was Juana who proposed that we write Carlota —— in Valparaiso. Through Carlota we met our benefactor, and so obtained our money, our ship, and even the plausible pretext of going on retreat in a Bolivian convent, which some of us were forced to employ (while the rest of us said we were going to Paris for the winter season). And it was my Juana who in the darkest moments remained resolute, unshaken in her determination to achieve our goal.

---

[5]*Captain Scott:* British explorer Robert Falcon Scott (1866–1912) made two expeditions to Antarctica, the second ending in death.

And there were dark moments, especially in the early months of 1909—times when I did not see how the Expedition would ever become more than a quarter ton of pemmican gone to waste and a lifelong regret. It was so very hard to gather our expeditionary force together! So few of those we asked even knew what we were talking about—so many thought we were mad, or wicked, or both! And of those few who shared our folly, still fewer were able, when it came to the point, to leave their daily duties and commit themselves to a voyage of at least six months, attended with not inconsiderable uncertainty and danger. An ailing parent; an anxious husband beset by business cares; a child at home with only ignorant or incompetent servants to look after it: these are not responsibilities lightly to be set aside. And those who wished to evade such claims were not the companions we wanted in hard work, risk, and privation.

But since success crowned our efforts, why dwell on the setbacks and delays, or the wretched contrivances and downright lies that we all had to employ? I look back with regret only to those friends who wished to come with us but could not, by any contrivance, get free—those we had to leave behind to a life without danger, without uncertainty, without hope.

On the seventeenth of August, 1909, in Punta Arenas, Chile, all the members of the Expedition met for the first time: Juana and I, the two Peruvians; from Argentina, Zoe, Berta, and Teresa; and our Chileans, Carlota and her friends Eva, Pepita, and Dolores. At the last moment I had received word that Maria's husband, in Quito, was ill, and she must stay to nurse him, so we were nine, not ten. Indeed, we had resigned ourselves to being but eight, when, just as night fell, the indomitable Zoe arrived in a tiny pirogue manned by Indians, her yacht having sprung a leak just as it entered the Strait of Magellan.

That night before we sailed we began to get to know one another; and we agreed, as we enjoyed our abominable supper in the abominable seaport inn of Punta Arenas, that if a situation arose of such urgent danger that one voice must be obeyed without present question, the unenviable honor of speaking with that voice should fall first upon myself: if I were incapacitated, upon Carlota: if she, then upon Berta. We three were then toasted as "Supreme Inca," "La Araucana," and "The Third Mate," among a lot of laughter and cheering. As it came out, to my very great pleasure and relief, my qualities as a "leader" were

never tested; the nine of us worked things out amongst us from beginning to end without any orders being given by anybody, and only two or
three times with recourse to a vote by voice or show of hands. To be
sure, we argued a good deal. But then, we had time to argue. And one
way or another the arguments always ended up in a decision, upon
which action could be taken. Usually at least one person grumbled
about the decision, sometimes bitterly. But what is life without grumbling, and the occasional opportunity to say, "I told you so"? How could
one bear housework, or looking after babies, let alone the rigors of
sledge-hauling in Antarctica, without grumbling? Officers—as we came
to understand aboard the *Yelcho*—are forbidden to grumble; but we
nine were, and are, by birth and upbringing, unequivocally and irrevoc-
ably, all crew.

Though our shortest course to the southern continent, and that originally urged upon us by the captain of our good ship, was to the South
Shetlands and the Bellingshausen Sea, or else by the South Orkneys into
the Weddell Sea, we planned to sail west to the Ross Sea, which Captain
Scott had explored and described, and from which the brave Ernest
Shackleton had returned only the previous autumn. More was known
about this region than any other portion of the coast of Antarctica, and
though that more was not much, yet it served as some insurance of the
safety of the ship, which we felt we had no right to imperil. Captain
Pardo had fully agreed with us after studying the charts and our
planned itinerary; and so it was westward that we took our course out of
the Strait next morning.

Our journey half round the globe was attended by fortune. The little
*Yelcho* steamed cheerily along through gale and gleam, climbing up and
down those seas of the Southern Ocean that run unbroken round the
world. Juana, who had fought bulls and the far more dangerous cows on
her family's *estancia*,[6] called the ship "*la vaca valiente*," because she
always returned to the charge. Once we got over being seasick we all
enjoyed the sea voyage, though oppressed at times by the kindly but
officious protectiveness of the captain and his officers, who felt that we
were only "safe" when huddled up in the three tiny cabins which they
had chivalrously vacated for our use.

---

[6]*estancia:* Spanish for ranch.
[7]"*la vaca valiente*": courageous cow.

We saw our first iceberg much farther south than we had looked for it, and saluted it with Veuve Clicquot at dinner. The next day we entered the ice pack, the belt of floes and bergs, broken loose from the land ice and winter-frozen seas of Antarctica, which drifts northward in the spring. Fortune still smiled on us: our little steamer, incapable, with her unreinforced metal hull, of forcing a way into the ice, picked her way from lane to lane without hesitation, and on the third day we were through the pack, in which ships have sometimes struggled for weeks and been obliged to turn back at last. Ahead of us now lay the dark grey waters of the Ross Sea, and beyond that, on the horizon, the remote glimmer, the cloud-reflected whiteness of the Great Ice Barrier.

Entering the Ross Sea a little east of Longitude West 160°, we came in sight of the Barrier at the place where Captain Scott's party, finding a bight in the vast wall of ice, had gone ashore and sent up their hydrogen-gas balloon for reconnaissance and photography. The towering face of the Barrier, its sheer cliffs and azure and violet water-worn caves, all were as described, but the location had changed: instead of a narrow bight there was a considerable bay, full of the beautiful and terrific orca whales playing and spouting in the sunshine of that brilliant southern spring.

Evidently masses of ice many acres in extent had broken away from the Barrier (which—at least for most of its vast extent—does not rest on land but floats on water) since the *Discovery*'s passage in 1902. This put our plan to set up camp on the Barrier itself in a new light; and while we were discussing alternatives, we asked Captain Pardo to take the ship west along the Barrier face towards Ross Island and McMurdo Sound. As the sea was clear of ice and quite calm, he was happy to do so, and, when we sighted the smoke plume of Mount Erebus, to share in our celebration—another half case of Veuve Clicquot.

The *Yelcho* anchored in Arrival Bay, and we went ashore in the ship's boat. I cannot describe my emotions when I set foot on the earth, on that earth, the barren, cold gravel at the foot of the long volcanic slope. I felt elation, impatience, gratitude, awe, familiarity. I felt that I was home at last. Eight Adélie penguins immediately came to greet us with many exclamations of interest not unmixed with disapproval. "Where on earth have you been? What took you so long? The Hut is around this way. Please come this way. Mind the rocks!" They insisted on our going to visit Hut Point, where the large structure built by Captain Scott's party stood, looking just as in the photographs and drawings that illustrate his book. The area about it, however, was disgusting—a kind of graveyard of seal skins, seal bones, penguin bones, and rubbish, presided over by the mad, screaming skua gulls. Our escorts waddled past the slaughterhouse in all tranquillity, and one showed me personally to the door, though it would not go in.

The interior of the hut was less offensive, but very dreary. Boxes of supplies had been stacked up into a kind of room within the room; it did not look as I had imagined it when the *Discovery* party put on their melodramas and minstrel shows in the long winter night. (Much later, we learned that Sir Ernest had rearranged it a good deal when he was there just a year before us.) It was dirty, and had about it a mean disorder. A pound tin of tea was standing open. Empty meat tins lay about; biscuits were spilled on the floor; a lot of dog turds were underfoot—frozen, of course, but not a great deal improved by that. No doubt the last occupants had had to leave in a hurry, perhaps even in a blizzard. All the same, they could have closed the tea tin. But housekeeping, the art of the infinite, is no game for amateurs.

Teresa proposed that we use the hut as our camp. Zoe counterproposed that we set fire to it. We finally shut the door and left it as we had found it. The penguins appeared to approve, and cheered us all the way to the boat.

McMurdo Sound was free of ice, and Captain Pardo now proposed to take us off Ross Island and across to Victoria Land, where we might camp at the foot of the Western Mountains, on dry and solid earth. But those mountains, with their storm-darkened peaks and hanging cirques and glaciers, looked as awful as Captain Scott had found them on his western journey, and none of us felt much inclined to seek shelter among them.

Aboard the ship that night we decided to go back and set up our base as we had originally planned, on the Barrier itself. For all available reports indicated that the clear way south was across the level Barrier surface until one could ascend one of the confluent glaciers to the high plateau which appears to form the whole interior of the continent. Captain Pardo argued strongly against this plan, asking what would become of us if the Barrier "calved"—if our particular acre of ice broke away and started to drift northward. "Well," said Zoe, "then you won't have to come so far to meet us." But he was so persuasive on this theme that he persuaded himself into leaving one of the *Yelcho*'s boats with us when we camped, as a means of escape. We found it useful for fishing, later on.

My first steps on Antarctic soil, my only visit to Ross Island, had not been pleasure unalloyed. I thought of the words of the English poet:

> *Though every prospect pleases,*
> *And only Man is vile.*[8]

But then, the backside of heroism is often rather sad; women and servants know that. They know also that the heroism may be no less real for that. But achievement is smaller than men think. What is large is the sky, the earth, the sea, the soul. I looked back as the ship sailed east again that evening. We were well into September now, with ten hours or more of daylight. The spring sunset lingered on the twelve-thousand-foot peak of Erebus and shone rosy gold on her long plume of steam. The steam from our own small funnel faded blue on the twilit water as we crept along under the towering pale wall of ice.

On our return to "Orca Bay"—Sir Ernest, we learned years later, had named it the Bay of Whales—we found a sheltered nook where the Barrier edge was low enough to provide fairly easy access from the ship. The *Yelcho* put out her ice anchor, and the next long, hard days were spent in unloading our supplies and setting up our camp on the ice, a half kilometer in from the edge: a task in which the *Yelcho*'s crew lent us invaluable aid and interminable advice. We took all the aid gratefully, and most of the advice with salt.

The weather so far had been extraordinarily mild for spring in this latitude; the temperature had not yet gone below $-20°$ Fahrenheit, and there was only one blizzard while we were setting up camp. But Captain Scott had spoken feelingly of the bitter south winds on the Barrier, and we had planned accordingly. Exposed as our camp was to every wind, we built no rigid structures above ground. We set up tents to shelter in while we dug out a series of cubicles in the ice itself, lined them with hay insulation and pine boarding, and roofed them with canvas over bamboo poles, covered with snow for weight and insulation. The big central room was instantly named Buenos Aires by our Argentineans, to whom the center, wherever one is, is always Buenos Aires. The heating

---

[8]*And only Man is vile:* lines from the hymn "From Greenland's Icy Mountains" (1819) by Reginald Heber.

and cooking stove was in Buenos Aires. The storage tunnels and the privy (called Punta Arenas) got some back heat from the stove. The sleeping cubicles opened off Buenos Aires, and were very small, mere tubes into which one crawled feet first; they were lined deeply with hay and soon warmed by one's body warmth. The sailors called them "coffins" and "wormholes," and looked with horror on our burrows in the ice. But our little warren or prairie-dog village served us well, permitting us as much warmth and privacy as one could reasonably expect under the circumstances. If the *Yelcho* was unable to get through the ice in February, and we had to spend the winter in Antarctica, we certainly could do so, though on very limited rations. For this coming summer, our base—Sudamérica del Sur, South South America, but we generally called it the Base—was intended merely as a place to sleep, to store our provisions, and to give shelter from blizzards.

To Berta and Eva, however, it was more than that. They were its chief architect-designers, its most ingenious builder-excavators, and its most diligent and contented occupants, forever inventing an improvement in ventilation, or learning how to make skylights, or revealing to us a new addition to our suite of rooms dug in the living ice. It was thanks to them that our stores were stowed so handily, that our stove drew and heated so efficiently, and that Buenos Aires, where nine people cooked, ate, worked, conversed, argued, grumbled, painted, played the guitar and banjo, and kept the Expedition's library of books and maps, was a marvel of comfort and convenience. We lived there in real amity; and if you simply had to be alone for a while, you crawled into your sleeping hole head first.

Berta went a little farther. When she had done all she could to make South South America livable, she dug out one more cell just under the ice surface, leaving a nearly transparent sheet of ice like a greenhouse roof; and there, alone, she worked at sculptures. They were beautiful forms, some like a blending of the reclining human figure with the subtle curves and volumes of the Weddell seal, others like the fantastic shapes of ice cornices and ice caves. Perhaps they are there still, under the snow, in the bubble in the Great Barrier. There where she made them they might last as long as stone. But she could not bring them north. That is the penalty for carving in water.

Captain Pardo was reluctant to leave us, but his orders did not permit him to hang about the Ross Sea indefinitely, and so at last, with many earnest injunctions to us to stay put—make no journeys—take no risks—beware of frostbite—don't use edge tools—look out for cracks in the ice—and a heartfelt promise to return to Orca Bay on the twentieth of February, or as near that date as wind and ice would permit, the good man bade us farewell, and his crew shouted us a great goodbye cheer as they weighed anchor. That evening, in the long orange twilight of October, we saw the topmast of the *Yelcho* go down the north horizon, over the edge of the world, leaving us to ice, and silence, and the Pole.

That night we began to plan the Southern Journey.

The ensuing month passed in short practice trips and depot-laying. The life we had led at home, though in its own way strenuous, had not fitted any of us for the kind of strain met with in sledge-hauling at ten or twenty degrees below freezing. We all needed as much working-out as possible before we dared undertake a long haul.

My longest exploratory trip, made with Dolores and Carlota, was southwest towards Mount Markham, and it was a nightmare—blizzards and pressure ice all the way out, crevasses and no view of the mountains when we got there, and white weather and sastrugi[9] all the way back. The trip was useful, however, in that we could begin to estimate our capacities; and also in that we had started out with a very heavy load of provisions, which we depoted at 100 and 130 miles SSW of Base. Thereafter other parties pushed on farther, till we had a line of snow cairns and depots right down to Latitude 83° 43', where Juana and Zoe, on an exploring trip, had found a kind of stone gateway opening on a great glacier leading south. We established these depots to avoid, if possible, the hunger that had bedevilled Captain Scott's Southern Party, and the consequent misery and weakness. And we also established to our own satisfaction—intense satisfaction—that we were sledgehaulers at least as good as Captain Scott's husky dogs. Of course we could not have expected to pull as much or as fast as his men. That we did so was because we were favored by much better weather than Captain Scott's party ever met on the Barrier; and also the quantity and quality of our food made a very considerable difference. I am sure that the fifteen percent of dried fruits in our pemmican helped prevent scurvy; and the potatoes, frozen and dried according to an ancient Andean Indian method, were very nourishing yet very light and compact—perfect

[9]*sastrugi:* wind-formed ridges of snow.

sledging rations. In any case, it was with considerable confidence in our capacities that we made ready at last for the Southern Journey.

The Southern Party consisted of two sledge teams: Juana, Dolores, and myself; Carlota, Pepita, and Zoe. The support team of Berta, Eva, and Teresa set out before us with a heavy load of supplies, going right up onto the glacier to prospect routes and leave depots of supplies for our return journey. We followed five days behind them, and met them returning between Depot Ercilla and Depot Miranda (see map). That "night"—of course there was no real darkness—we were all nine together in the heart of the level plain of ice. It was the fifteenth of November, Dolores's birthday. We celebrated by putting eight ounces of pisco in the hot chocolate, and became very merry. We sang. It is strange now to remember how thin our voices sounded in that great silence. It was overcast, white weather, without shadows and without visible horizon or any feature to break the level; there was nothing to see at all. We had come to that white place on the map, that void, and there we flew and sang like sparrows.

After sleep and a good breakfast the Base Party continued north, and the Southern Party sledged on. The sky cleared presently. High up, thin clouds passed over very rapidly from southwest to northeast, but down on the Barrier it was calm and just cold enough, five or ten degrees below freezing, to give a firm surface for hauling.

On the level ice we never pulled less than eleven miles, seventeen kilometers, a day, and generally fifteen or sixteen miles, twenty-five kilometers. (Our instruments, being British made, were calibrated in feet, miles, degrees Fahrenheit, etc., but we often converted miles to kilometers because the larger numbers sounded more encouraging.) At the time we left South America, we knew only that Mr. Shackleton had mounted another expedition to the Antarctic in 1908, had tried to attain the Pole but failed, and had returned to England in June of the current year, 1909. No coherent report of his explorations had yet reached South America when we left; we did not know what route he had gone, or how far he had got. But we were not altogether taken by surprise when, far across the featureless white plain, tiny beneath the mountain peaks and the strange silent flight of the rainbow-fringed cloud wisps, we saw a fluttering dot of black. We turned west from our course to visit it: a snow heap nearly buried by the winter's storms—a flag on a bamboo pole, a mere shred of threadbare cloth—an empty oilcan—and a few footprints standing some inches above the ice. In some conditions of weather the snow compressed under one's weight remains when the surrounding soft snow melts or is scoured away by the wind; and so these reversed footprints had been left standing all these months, like rows of cobbler's lasts—a queer sight.

We met no other such traces on our way. In general I believe our course was somewhat east of Mr. Shackleton's. Juana, our surveyor, had trained herself well and was faithful and methodical in her sightings and readings, but our equipment was minimal—a theodolite on tripod legs, a sextant with artificial horizon, two compasses, and chronometers. We had only the wheel meter on the sledge to give distance actually travelled.

In any case, it was the day after passing Mr. Shackleton's waymark that I first saw clearly the great glacier among the mountains to the southwest, which was to give us a pathway from the sea level of the Barrier up to the altiplano, ten thousand feet above. The approach was magnificent: a gateway formed by immense vertical domes and pillars of rock. Zoe and Juana had called the vast ice river that flowed through that gateway the Florence Nightingale Glacier, wishing to honor the British, who had been the inspiration and guide of our expedition; that very brave and very peculiar lady seemed to represent so much that is best, and strangest, in the island race. On maps, of course, this glacier bears the name Mr. Shackleton gave it, the Beardmore.

The ascent of the Nightingale was not easy. The way was open at first, and well marked by our support party, but after some days we came among terrible crevasses, a maze of hidden cracks, from a foot to thirty feet wide and from thirty to a thousand feet deep. Step by step we went, and step by step, and the way always upward now. We were fifteen days on the glacier. At first the weather was hot, up to 20° F., and the hot nights without darkness were wretchedly uncomfortable in our small tents. And all of us suffered more or less from snowblindness just at the time when we wanted clear eyesight to pick our way among the ridges and crevasses of the tortured ice, and to see the wonders about and before us. For at every day's advance more great, nameless peaks came into view in the west and southwest, summit beyond summit, range beyond range, stark rock and snow in the unending noon.

We gave names to these peaks, not very seriously, since we did not expect our discoveries to come to the attention of geographers. Zoe had a gift for naming, and it is thanks to her that certain sketch maps in various suburban South American attics bear such curious features as "Bolívar's Big Nose," "I Am General Rosas," "The Cloudmaker," "Whose Toe?" and "Throne of Our Lady of the Southern Cross." And when at last we got up onto the altiplano, the great interior plateau, it was Zoe who called it the pampa, and maintained that we walked there among vast herds of invisible cattle, transparent cattle pastured on the spindrift snow, their gauchos, the restless, merciless winds. We were by then all a little crazy with exhaustion and the great altitude—twelve thousand feet—and the cold and the wind blowing and the luminous circles and crosses surrounding the suns, for often there were three or four suns in the sky, up there.

That is not a place where people have any business to be. We should have turned back; but since we had worked so hard to get there, it seemed that we should go on, at least for a while.

A blizzard came with very low temperatures, so we had to stay in the tents, in our sleeping bags, for thirty hours, a rest we all needed; though it was warmth we needed most, and there was no warmth on that terrible plain anywhere at all but in our veins. We huddled close together all that time. The ice we lay on is two miles thick.

It cleared suddenly and became, for the plateau, good weather: twelve below zero and the wind not very strong. We three crawled out of our tent and met the others crawling out of theirs. Carlota told us then that her group wished to turn back. Pepita had been feeling very ill; even after the rest during the blizzard, her temperature would not rise above 94°. Carlota was having trouble breathing. Zoe was perfectly fit, but much preferred staying with her friends and lending them a hand in difficulties to pushing on towards the Pole. So we put the four ounces of pisco which we had been keeping for Christmas into the breakfast cocoa, and dug out our tents, and loaded our sledges, and parted there in the white daylight on the bitter plain.

Our sledge was fairly light by now. We pulled on to the south. Juana calculated our position daily. On the twenty-second of December, 1909, we reached the South Pole. The weather was, as always, very cruel. Nothing of any kind marked the dreary whiteness. We discussed leaving some kind of mark or monument, a snow cairn, a tent pole and flag; but there seemed no particular reason to do so. Anything we could do, anything we were, was insignificant, in that awful place. We put up the tent for shelter for an hour and made a cup of tea, and then struck

"90° Camp."[10] Dolores, standing patient as ever in her sledging harness, looked at the snow; it was so hard frozen that it showed no trace of our footprints coming, and she said, "Which way?"

"North," said Juana.

It was a joke, because at that particular place there is no other direction. But we did not laugh. Our lips were cracked with frostbite and hurt too much to let us laugh. So we started back, and the wind at our backs pushed us along, and dulled the knife edges of the waves of frozen snow.

All that week the blizzard wind pursued us like a pack of mad dogs. I cannot describe it. I wished we had not gone to the Pole. I think I wish it even now. But I was glad even then that we had left no sign there, for some man longing to be first might come some day, and find it, and know then what a fool he had been, and break his heart.

We talked, when we could talk, of catching up to Carlota's party, since they might be going slower than we. In fact they had used their tent as a sail to catch the following wind and had got far ahead of us. But in many places they had built snow cairns or left some sign for us; once Zoe had written on the lee side of a ten-foot sastrugi, just as children write on the sand of the beach at Miraflores, "This Way Out!" The wind blowing over the frozen ridge had left the words perfectly distinct.

In the very hour that we began to descend the glacier, the weather turned warmer, and the mad dogs were left to howl forever tethered to the Pole. The distance that had taken us fifteen days going up we covered in only eight days going down. But the good weather that had aided us descending the Nightingale became a curse down on the Barrier ice, where we had looked forward to a kind of royal progress from depot to depot, eating our fill and taking our time for the last three hundred-odd miles. In a tight place on the glacier I lost my goggles—I was swinging from my harness at the time in a crevasse— and then Juana had broken hers when we had to do some rock climbing coming down to the Gateway. After two days in bright sunlight with only one pair of snow goggles to pass amongst us, we were all suffering badly from snowblindness. It became acutely painful to keep lookout for landmarks or depot flags, to take sightings, even to study the compass, which had to be laid down on the snow to steady the needle. At Concolorcorvo Depot, where there was a particularly good

[10]*"90° camp"*: location of the South Pole at 90 degrees latitude, 0 degrees longitude.

supply of food and fuel, we gave up, crawled into our sleeping bags with bandaged eyes, and slowly boiled alive like lobsters in the tent exposed to the relentless sun. The voices of Berta and Zoe were the sweetest sound I ever heard. A little concerned about us, they had skied south to meet us. They led us home to Base.

We recovered quite swiftly, but the altiplano left its mark. When she was very little, Rosita asked if a dog "had bitted Mama's toes." I told her Yes, a great, white, mad dog named Blizzard! My Rosita and my Juanito heard many stories when they were little, about that fearful dog and how it howled, and the transparent cattle of the invisible gauchos, and a river of ice eight thousand feet high called Nightingale, and how Cousin Juana drank a cup of tea standing on the bottom of the world under seven suns, and other fairy tales.

We were in for one severe shock when we reached Base at last. Teresa was pregnant. I must admit that my first response to the poor girl's big belly and sheepish look was anger—rage—fury. That one of us should have concealed anything, and such a thing, from the others! But Teresa had done nothing of the sort. Only those who had concealed from her what she most needed to know were to blame. Brought up by servants, with four years' schooling in a convent, and married at sixteen, the poor girl was still so ignorant at twenty years of age that she had thought it was "the cold weather" that made her miss her periods. Even this was not entirely stupid, for all of us on the Southern Journey had seen our periods change or stop altogether as we experienced increasing cold, hunger, and fatigue. Teresa's appetite had begun to draw general attention; and then she had begun, as she said pathetically, "to get fat." The others were worried at the thought of all the sledge-hauling she had done, but she flourished, and the only problem was her positively insatiable appetite. As well as could be determined from her shy references to her last night on the hacienda with her husband, the baby was due at just about the same time as the *Yelcho*, the twentieth of February. But we had not been back from the Southern Journey two weeks when, on February 14, she went into labor.

Several of us had borne children and had helped with deliveries, and anyhow most of what needs to be done is fairly self-evident; but a first labor can be long and trying, and we were all anxious, while Teresa was frightened out of her wits. She kept calling for her José till she was as hoarse as a skua. Zoe lost all patience at last and said, "By God, Teresa, if you say 'José!' once more I hope you have a penguin!" But what she had, after twenty long hours, was a pretty little red-faced girl.

Many were the suggestions for that child's name from her eight proud midwife-aunts: Polita, Penguina, McMurdo, Victoria. . . . But Teresa announced, after she had had a good sleep and a large serving of pemmican, "I shall name her Rosa—Rosa del Sur," Rose of the South. That night we drank the last two bottles of Veuve Clicquot (having finished the pisco at 88° 30' South) in toasts to our little Rose.

On the nineteenth of February, a day early, my Juana came down into Buenos Aires in a hurry. "The ship," she said, "the ship has come," and she burst into tears—she who had never wept in all our weeks of pain and weariness on the long haul.

Of the return voyage there is nothing to tell. We came back safe.

In 1912 all the world learned that the brave Norwegian Amundsen[11] had reached the South Pole; and then, much later, came the accounts of how Captain Scott and his men had come there after him, but did not come home again.

Just this year, Juana and I wrote to the captain of the *Yelcho*, for the newspapers have been full of the story of his gallant dash to rescue Sir Ernest Shackleton's men from Elephant Island, and we wished to congratulate him, and once more to thank him. Never one word has he breathed of our secret. He is a man of honor, Luis Pardo.

I add this last note in 1929. Over the years we have lost touch with one another. It is very difficult for women to meet, when they live so far apart as we do. Since Juana died, I have seen none of my old sledge-mates, though sometimes we write. Our little Rosa del Sur died of the scarlet fever when she was five years old. Teresa had many other children. Carlota took the veil in Santiago ten years ago. We are old women now, with old husbands, and grown children, and grandchildren who might some day like to read about the Expedition. Even if they are rather ashamed of having such a crazy grandmother, they may enjoy sharing in the secret. But they must not let Mr. Amundsen know! He would be terribly embarrassed and disappointed. There is no need for him or anyone else outside the family to know. We left no footprints, even.

*—1982*

[11]*Amundsen:* Roald Amundsen (1872–1928) of Norway was the first man to reach the South Pole, on December 14, 1911.

*Timothy Finðley (1930–2002) was born in Toronto, and moved from an acting to a writing career that included ten novels, three short-story collections, and several plays. Violence and the human struggle to survive it have been among his most enduring subjects, from his third novel,* The Wars *(1977), which earned him his first Governor General's Award, to this story from the collection* Stones *(1988). Whether in work that is self-reflexive and surreal or work that is more closely tied to history, Finðley maintains that fiction is all about "achieving the clarity obscured by facts."*

## Timothy Finðley
# Stones

We lived on the outskirts of Rosedale, over on the wrong side of Yonge Street. This was the impression we had, at any rate. Crossing the street-car tracks put you in another world.

One September, my sister, Rita, asked a girl from Rosedale over to our house after school. Her name was Allison Pritchard and she lived on Cluny Drive. When my mother telephoned to see if Allison Pritchard could stay for supper, Mrs Pritchard said she didn't think it would be appropriate. That was the way they talked in Rosedale: very polite; oblique and cruel.

Over on our side—the west side—of Yonge Street, there were merchants—and this, apparently, made the difference to those whose houses were in Rosedale. People of class were not meant to live in the midst of commerce.

Our house was on Gibson Avenue, a cul-de-sac with a park across the road. My bedroom window faced a hockey rink in winter and a football field in summer. Cy, my brother, was a star in either venue. I was not. My forte, then, was the tricycle.

Up at the corner, there was an antique store on one side and a variety shop on the other. In the variety shop, you could spend your allowance on penny candy, Eskimo pies and an orange drink I favoured then called *Stubby. Stubby* came in short, fat bottles and aside from everything else—the thick orange flavour and the ginger in the bubbles —there was something wonderfully satisfying in the fact that it took both hands to hold it up to your lips and tip it down your throat.

Turning up Yonge Street, beyond the antique store, you came to The Women's Bakery, Adam's Grocery, Oskar Schickel, the butcher and

Max's Flowers. We were Max's Flowers. My mother and my father wore green aprons when they stood behind the counter or went back into the cold room where they made up wreaths for funerals, bouquets for weddings and corsages for dances at the King Edward Hotel. Colonel Matheson, retired, would come in every morning on his way downtown and pick out a boutonnière from the jar of carnations my mother kept on the counter near the register. Once, when I was four, I caused my parents untold embarrassment by pointing out that Colonel Matheson had a large red growth on the end of his nose. The "growth" was nothing of the sort, of course, but merely the result of Colonel Matheson's predilection for gin.

Of the pre-war years, my overall memory is one of perfect winters, heavy with snow and the smell of coal- and wood-smoke mingling with the smell of bread and cookies rising from The Women's Bakery. The coal-smoke came from our furnaces and the wood-smoke—mostly birch and maple—came to us from the chimneys of Rosedale, where it seemed that every house must have a fireplace in every room.

Summers all smelled of grass being cut in the park and burning tar from the road crews endlessly patching the potholes in Yonge Street. The heat of these summers was heroic and the cause of many legends. Mister Schickel, the butcher, I recall once cooked an egg on the sidewalk outside his store. My father, who was fond of Mister Schickel, made him a bet of roses it could not be done. I think Mister Schickel's part of the bet was pork chops trimmed of excess fat. When the egg began to sizzle, my father slapped his thigh and whistled and he sent my sister, Rita, in to get the flowers. Mister Schickel, however, was a graceful man and when he placed his winnings in the window of his butcher shop, he also placed a card that read: *Thanks to Max's Flowers one dozen roses.*

The Great Depression held us all in thrall, but its effects on those of us who were used to relative poverty—living on the west side of Yonge Street—were not so debilitating as they were on the far side in Rosedale. The people living there regarded money as something you had—as opposed to something you went out and got—and they were slower to adjust to what, for them, was the unique experience of deprivation.

I remember, too, that there always seemed to be a tramp at the door: itinerants asking if—for the price of a meal, or the meal itself—they could carry out the ashes, sweep the walks or pile the baskets and pails in which my father brought his flowers from the market and the greenhouse.

Our lives continued in this way until about the time I was five—in August of 1939. Everyone's life, I suppose, has its demarcation lines—its latitudes and longitudes passing through time. Some of these lines define events that everyone shares—others are confined to personal—even to secret lives. But the end of summer 1939 is a line drawn through the memory of everyone who was then alive. We were all about to be pitched together into a melting pot of violence from which a few of us would emerge intact and the rest of us would perish.

My father joined the army even before the war had started. He went downtown one day and didn't come back till after suppertime. I noticed that he hadn't taken the truck but had ridden off on the streetcar. I asked my mother why he had worn his suit on a weekday and she replied *because today is special.* But that was all she said.

At the table, eating soufflé and salad, my brother, Cy—who was nine years old that summer—talked about the World's Fair in New York City and pictures he'd seen of the future in magazines. The Great World's Fair was a subject that had caught all our imaginations with its demonstrations of new appliances, aeroplanes and motor cars. Everything was "streamlined" in 1939; everything designed with swept-back lines as if we were all preparing to shoot off into space. Earlier that summer, the King and Queen of England had come to Canada, riding on a stream-lined train whose blue-painted engine was sleek and slim as something in a silver glove. In fact, the King and Queen had arrived in Toronto just up Yonge Street from where we lived. We got permission from the Darrow family, who lived over Max's Flowers, to stand on the roof and watch the parade with its Mounties in scarlet and its Black Watch Band and the King and Queen, all blue and white and smiling, sitting in an open Buick called a *McLaughlin—built,* according to Cy, *right here in Canada!* For one brief moment while all these symbols of who we were went marching past, the two communities—one on either side of Yonge Street—were united in a surge of cheering and applause. But after the King and Queen were gone, the ribbon of Yonge Street divided us again. It rained.

Now, Cy and Rita were arguing over the remnants in the soufflé dish. Cy held the classic belief that what was in the dish was his by virtue of his being the eldest child. He also held the classic belief that girls were meant to be second in everything. Rita, who was always hungry but never seemed to gain an ounce, held none of these beliefs and was capable of fighting Cy for hours on end when our parents weren't present. With Mother at the table, however, the argument was silenced by her announcement that the soufflé dish and all the delicious bits of cheese and egg that clung to its sides would be set aside for our father.

Then—or shortly thereafter—our father did indeed arrive, but he said he wasn't hungry and he wanted to be left alone with Mother.

In half an hour the children were called from the kitchen where we had been doing the dishes and scooping up the remains of the meal. I— the child my mother called *The Rabbit*—had been emptying the salad bowl, stuffing my mouth with lettuce, tomatoes and onion shards and nearly choking in the process. We all went into the sitting-room with food on our lips and tea towels in our hands: Father's three little Maxes —Cy and Rita and Ben. He looked at us then, as he always did, with a measure of pride he could never hide and a false composure that kept his lips from smiling, but not his eyes. I look back now on that moment with some alarm when I realize my father was only twenty-seven years old—an age I have long survived and doubled.

"Children, I have joined the army," he said—in his formal way, as if we were his customers. "I am going to be a soldier."

Our mother had been weeping before we entered the room, but she had dried her eyes because she never allowed us to witness her tears. Now, she was smiling and silent. After a moment, she left the room and went out through the kitchen into the garden where, in the twilight, she found her favourite place and sat in a deck-chair amidst the flowers.

Cy, for his part, crowed with delight and yelled with excitement. He wanted to know if the war would last until he was a man and could join our father at the front.

Father, I remember, told him the war had not yet begun and the reason for his enlistment was precisely so that Cy and I could not be soldiers. "There will be no need for that," he said.

Cy was immensely disappointed. He begged our father to make the war go on till 1948, when he would be eighteen.

Our father only laughed at that.

"The war," he said, "will be over in 1940."

I went out then and found our mother in the garden.

"What will happen to us while he's away?" I asked.

"Nothing," she said. And then she said: "come here."

I went and leaned against her thigh and she put her arm around my shoulder and I could smell the roses somewhere behind us. It was getting dark.

"Look up there," she said. "The stars are coming out. Why don't you count them?"

This was her way of distracting me whenever my questions got out of hand. Either she told me to count the stars or go outside and dig for China. *There's a shovel in the shed,* she would tell me. *You get started and I will join you.* Just as if we would be in China and back by suppertime.

But that night in August, 1939, I wasn't prepared to bite. I didn't want to dig for China and I didn't want to count the stars. I'd dug for China so many times and had so many holes in the yard that I knew I would never arrive; it was much too far and, somehow, she was making a fool of me. As for the stars: "I counted them last night," I told her. "And the night before."

"Oh?" she said—and I felt her body tense, though she went on trying to inject a sense of ease when she spoke. "So tell me," she said. "How many are there?"

"Twelve," I said.

"Ah," she said. And sighed. "Just twelve. I thought there might be more than twelve."

"I mean twelve zillion," I said with great authority.

"Oh," she said. "I see. And you counted them all?"

"Unh-hunh."

For a moment she was quiet. And then she said: "what about that one there?"

One week later, the war began. But my father had already gone.

On the 14th of February, 1943, my father was returned. He came back home from the war. He did this on a Sunday and I recall the hush that fell upon our house, as indeed it seemed to have fallen over all the city. Only the sparrows out in the trees made sound.

We had gone downtown to the Exhibition Grounds to meet him. The journey on the streetcar took us over an hour, but Mother had splurged and hired a car and driver to take us all home. The car, I remember, embarrassed me. I was afraid some friend would see me being driven— sitting up behind a chauffeur.

A notice had come that told us the families of all returning soldiers would be permitted to witness their arrival. I suspect the building they used for this was the one now used to house the Royal Winter Fair and other equestrian events. I don't remember what it was called and I'm not inclined to inquire. It was enough that I was there that once—and once remains enough.

We sat in the bleachers, Cy and Rita and Mother and me, and there was a railing holding us back. There must have been over a thousand people waiting to catch a glimpse of someone they loved—all of them parents, children or wives of the men returning. I was eight years old that February—almost nine and feeling I would never get there. Time was like a field of clay and all the other children I knew appeared to have cleared it in a single bound while I was stuck in the mud and barely able to lift my feet. I hated being eight and dreaded being nine. I wanted to be ten—the only dignified age a child could be, it seemed to me. Cy, at ten, had found a kind of silence I admired to the point of worship. Rita, who in fact was ten that year and soon to be eleven, had also found a world of silence in which she kept her self secreted—often behind closed doors. Silence was a sign of valour.

The occasion was barely one for public rejoicing. The men who were coming home were mostly casualties whose wounds, we had been warned, could be distressing and whose spirit, we had equally been warned, had been damaged in long months of painful recuperation. Plainly, it was our job to lift their spirits and to deny the severity of their wounds. Above all else, they must not be allowed to feel they could not rejoin society at large. A man with no face must not be stared at.

Our father's wounds were greater by far than we had been told. There was not a mark on his body, but—far inside—he had been destroyed. His mind had been severely damaged and his spirit had been broken. No one had told me what this might have made of him. No one had said *he may never be kind again.* No one had said *he will never sleep again without the aid of alcohol.* No one had said *he will try to kill your mother.* No one had said *you will not be sure it's him when you see him.* Yet all these things were true.

I had never seen a military parade without a band. The effect was eerie and upsetting. Two or three officers came forward into the centre of the oval. Somebody started shouting commands and a sergeant-major, who could not yet be seen, was heard outside the building counting off the steps.

I wanted drums. I wanted bugles. Surely this ghostly, implacable sound of marching feet in the deadening sand was just a prelude to everyone standing up and cheering and the music blaring forth. But, no. We all stood up, it is true, the minute the first of the columns rounded the wooden corner of the bleachers and came into sight. But no one uttered a sound. One or two people threw their hands up over their mouths—as if to stifle cries—but most of us simply stood there—staring in disbelief.

Nurses came with some of the men, supporting them. Everyone was pale in the awful light—and the colours of their wounds and bruises were garish and quite unreal. There was a predominance of yellow flesh and dark maroon scars and of purple welts and blackened scabs. Some men wore bandages—some wore casts and slings. Others used canes and crutches to support themselves. A few had been the victims of fire, and these wore tight, blue skull-caps and collarless shirts and their faces and other areas of uncovered skin were bright with shining oint-ments and dressings.

It took a very great while for all these men and women—perhaps as many as two hundred of them—to arrive inside the building and make their way into the oval. They were being lined up in order of columns—several long lines, and each line punctuated here and there with atten-dant nurses. The voices of the sergeant-major and of the adjutant who was taking the parade were swallowed up in the dead acoustics, and—far above us—pigeons and sparrows moved among the girders and beams that supported the roof. I still had not seen Father.

At last, because my panic was spreading out of control, I tugged my mother's elbow and whispered that I couldn't see him. Had there been a mistake and he wasn't coming at all?

"No," she told me—looking down at me sideways and turning my head with her ungloved fingers. "There he is, there," she said. "But don't say anything yet. He may not know we're here."

My father's figure could only be told because of his remarkable height. He was six feet four and had always been, to me, a giant. But now his height seemed barely greater than the height of half a dozen other men who were gathered out in the sand. His head was bowed, though once or twice he lifted his chin when he heard the commands.

His shoulders, no longer squared, were rounded forward and dipping towards his centre. His neck was so thin I thought that someone or something must have cut over half of it away. I studied him solemnly and then looked up at my mother.

She had closed her eyes against him because she could not bear to look.

Later on that night, when everyone had gone to bed but none of us had gone to sleep, I said to Cy: "what is it?"

"What?"

"That's happened to Dad. . . ."

Cy didn't answer for a moment and then he said: "Dieppe."

I didn't understand. I thought it was a new disease.

We were told the next day not to mention at school that our father had come back home. Nothing was said about why it must be kept a secret. That was a bitter disappointment. Other children whose fathers had returned from overseas were always the centre of attention. Teachers, beaming smiles and patting heads, would congratulate them just as if they had won a prize. Classmates pestered them with questions: *what does he look like? Have you seen his wounds? How many Germans did he kill?* But we had none of this. All we got was: *what did you do on the weekend?*

*Nothing.*

All day Monday, Father remained upstairs. Our parents' bedroom was on the second floor directly over the sitting-room. Also, directly underneath the bedroom occupied by Cy and me. We had heard our mother's voice long into the night, apparently soothing him, telling him over and over again that everything was going to be all right.

We could not make out her words, but the tone of her voice was familiar. Over time, she had sat with each of us, deploying her comforts in all the same cadences and phrases, assuring us that pains and aches and sicknesses would pass.

Because we could not afford to lose the sale of even one flower, neither the single rose bought once a week by Edna Holmes to cheer her ailing sister, nor the daily boutonnière of Colonel Matheson—our mother had persuaded Mrs Adams, the grocer's wife, to tend the store while she "nipped home" once every hour to see to Father's needs.

It was only later that we children realized what those needs entailed. He was drinking more or less constantly in every waking hour, and our mother's purpose was first to tempt him with food—which he refused—and then to make certain that his matches and cigarettes did not set fire to the house.

On the Wednesday, Father emerged from his shell around two o'clock in the afternoon. We were all at school, of course, and I have only the account of what follows from my mother. When she returned at two, Mother found that Father had come down into the hallway, fully dressed in civilian clothes. He had already donned his greatcoat when she arrived. She told me that, at first, he had seemed to be remarkably sober. He told her he wanted to go outside and walk in the street. He wanted to go and see the store, he said.

"But you can't wear your greatcoat, David," she told him.

"Why?"

"Because you're in civilian dress. You know that's not allowed. A man was arrested just last week."

"I wasn't here last week," said my father.

"Nevertheless," my mother told him, "this man was arrested because it is not allowed."

"But I'm a soldier!" my father yelled.

My mother had to play this scene with all the care and cunning she could muster. The man who had been arrested had been a deserter. All that winter, desertions had been increasing and there had been demonstrations of overt disloyalty. People had shouted *down with the King!* and had booed the Union Jack. There were street gangs of youths who called themselves *Zombies* and they hung around the Masonic Temple on Yonge Street and the Palais Royale at Sunnyside. Some of these young men were in uniform, members of the Home Guard: reserves who had been promised, on joining up, they would not be sent overseas. They may have disapproved of the war, but they did not disapprove of fighting. They waited outside the dancehalls, excessively defensive of their manhood, challenging the servicemen who were dancing inside to *come out fighting and show us your guts!* Men had been killed in such encounters and the encounters had been increasing. The government was absolutely determined to stamp these incidents out before they spread across the country. These were the darkest hours of the war and morale, both in and out of the Forces, was at its lowest ebb. If my father had appeared on the street with his military greatcoat worn over his civilian clothes, it would have been assumed he was a *Zombie* or a deserter and he would have been arrested instantly. Our neighbours would have turned him in, no matter who he was. Our patriotism had come to that.

"I don't have a civilian overcoat," my father said. "And don't suggest that I put on my uniform, because I won't. My uniform stinks of sweat and I hate it."

"Well, you aren't going out like that," my mother said. "That's all there is to it. Why not come to the kitchen and I'll fix you a sandwich. . . ."

"I don't want a goddamned sandwich," my father yelled at her. "I want to see the store!"

At this point, he tore off his greatcoat and flung it onto the stairs. And then, before my mother could prevent him, he was out the door and running down the steps.

My mother—dressed in her green shop apron and nothing but a scarf to warm her—raced out after him.

What would the neighbours think? What would the neighbours say? How could she possibly explain?

By the time she had reached the sidewalk, my father had almost reached the corner. But, when she got to Yonge Street, her fears were somewhat allayed. My father had not gone into Max's Flowers but was standing one door shy of it, staring into the butcher's window.

"What's going on here?" he said, as my mother came abreast of him.

Mother did not know what he meant.

"Where is Mister Schickel, Lily?" he asked her.

She had forgotten that, as well.

"Mister Schickel has left," she told him—trying to be calm—trying to steer my father wide of the butcher's window and in towards their own front stoop.

"Left?" my father shouted. "He's only just managed to pay off his mortgage! And who the hell is this imposter, Reilly?"

"Reilly?"

"Arthur Reilly the bloody butcher!" My father pointed at and read the sign that had replaced *Oskar Schickel, Butcher* in the window.

"Mister Reilly has been there most of the winter, David. Didn't I write and tell you that?" She knew very well she hadn't.

My father blinked at the meagre cuts of rationed meat displayed beyond the glass and said: "what happened to Oskar, Lily? Tell me."

And so, she had to tell him, like it or not.

Mister Schickel's name was disagreeable—stuck up there on Yonge Street across from Rosedale—and someone from Park Road had thrown a stone through the window.

There. It was said.

"But Oskar wasn't a German," my father whispered. "He was a Canadian."

"But his name was German, David."

My father put his fingers against the glass and did not appear to respond to what my mother had said.

At last my mother pulled at his arm. "Why not come back home," she said. "You can come and see the shop tomorrow."

My father, while my mother watched him, concentrated very hard and moved his finger over the dusty glass of Oskar Schickel's store.

"What are you doing, David?"

"Nothing," said my father. "Setting things right, that's all."

Then he stepped back and said to her: "now—we'll go home."

What he had written was:

*Oskar Schickel: Proprietor in absentia.*

Mother said that Mrs Reilly rushed outside as soon as they had reached the corner and she washed the window clean.

This was the only remaining decent thing my father did until the day he died.

The rest was all a nightmare.

I had never seen Dieppe. I had seen its face in photographs. I had read all the books and heard all the stories. The battle, of which my father had been a victim, had taken place in August of 1942—roughly six months before he was returned to us. Long since then, in my adult years, I have seen that battle, or seen its parts, through the medium of documentary film. It was only after Cy and Rita had vetted these films that I was able to watch. Till then, I had been afraid I would catch my father's image unawares—fearful that somehow our eyes would meet in that worst of moments. I couldn't bear the thought of seeing him destroyed. So, I had seen all this—the photographs, the books, the films—but I had never seen the town of Dieppe itself until that day in May of 1987 when I took my father's ashes there to scatter them.

Before I can begin this ending, I have to make it clear that the last thing I want to provoke is the sentimental image of a wind-blown stretch of rocky beach with a rainbow of ashes arching over the stones and blowing out to sea. If you want that image, let me tell you that had been the way it was when Cy, my brother, and Rita, my sister, and I went walking, wading into the ocean south of Lunenburg, Nova Scotia—where our mother had been born—to cast her ashes into the air above the Atlantic. Then there was almost music and we rejoiced because our mother had finally gained her freedom from a life that had become intolerable. But in Dieppe, when I shook my father's ashes out of their envelope, there was no rejoicing. None.

I felt, in fact, as if I had brought the body of an infidel into a holy place and laid it down amongst the true believers. Still, this was what my father had wanted—and how could I refuse him? Neither Cy nor Rita would do it for him. *Gone*, they had said. *Good riddance.*

And so it fell to me.

I was always the least informed. I was always the most inquisitive. During my childhood, nobody told me—aside from the single word *Dieppe*—what it was that had happened to my father. And yet, perhaps because I knew the least and because I was the youngest and seemed the most naïve and willing, it was more than often me he focused on.

His tirades would begin in silence—the silence we had been warned of when he first returned. He would sit at the head of the table, eating a piece of fish and drinking from a glass of beer. The beer was always dark in colour. Gold.

Our dining-room had a window facing west. Consequently, winter sunsets in particular got in his eyes.

*Curtain*, he would say at his plate—and jab his fork at me.

If I didn't understand because his mouth was full, my mother would reach my sleeve and pull it with her fingers. *The curtain, Ben*, she would say. *Your father's eyes.*

*Yes, ma'am.* Down I'd get and pull the curtain.

Then, no sooner would I be reseated than my father—still addressing his plate—would mumble *lights*. And I would rise and turn on the lights. Then, when I was back at last in my chair, he would look at me and say, without apparent rancour, *why don't you tell me to shove the goddamn curtain up my ass?*

You will understand my silence in response to this if you understand that—before he went away—the worst my father had ever said in our presence had been *damn* and *hell*. The ultimate worst had been *Christ!* when he'd nearly sliced his finger off with a knife. Then, however, he hadn't known that anyone was listening. And so, when he started to talk this way—and perhaps especially at table—it paralyzed me.

Cy or Mother would sometimes attempt to intervene, but he always cut them off with something worse than he'd said to me. Then he would turn his attention back in my direction and continue. He urged me to refuse his order, then to upbraid him, finally to openly defy him—call him the worst of the words he could put in my mouth and hit him. Of course, I never did any of these things, but the urging, the cajoling and ultimately the begging never ceased.

One night, he came into the bedroom where I slept in the bunk-bed over Cy and he shouted at me *why don't you fight back?* Then he dragged my covers off and threw me onto the floor against the bureau. All this was done in the dark, and after my mother had driven me down in the truck to the Emergency Ward of Wellesley Hospital, the doctors told her that my collar-bone was broken. I heard my mother saying *yes, he fell out of bed.*

Everyone—even I—conspired to protect him. The trouble was, my father had no wish to protect himself. At least, it seemed that way until a fellow veteran of Dieppe turned up one day in the shop and my father turned on him with a pair of garden shears and tried to drive him back onto Yonge Street. Far from being afraid of my father, the other man took off his jacket and threw it in my father's face and all the while he stood there, the man was yelling at my father: *Coward! Coward! Yellow Bastard!*

Then, he turned around and walked away. The victor.

Thinking for sure the police would come, my mother drew the blind and closed the shop for the rest of the day.

But that was not the end of it. She gathered us together out on the porch and Cy was told to open a can of pork and beans and to make what our mother called a *passel of toast.* He and Rita and I were to eat this meal in the kitchen, after which Cy, who'd been handed a dollar bill my mother had lifted from the till, was to take us down to the Uptown

Theatre where an Abbott and Costello film was playing. All these ordinary things we did. Nonetheless, we knew that our father had gone mad.

It was summer then and when the movie was over, I remember Cy and Rita and I stood on the street and the sidewalks gave off heat and the air around us smelled of peanuts and popcorn and Cy said: "I don't think it's safe to go home just yet." For almost an hour, we wandered on Yonge Street, debating what we should do and, at last, we decided we would test the waters by going and looking at the house and listening to see if there was any yelling.

Gibson Avenue only has about twenty houses, most of them semi-detached—and all of them facing south and the park. The porches and the stoops that night were filled with our neighbours drinking beer from coffee cups and fanning themselves with paper plates and folded bits of the *Daily Star.* They were drinking out of cups—you could smell the beer—because the law back then forbade the public consumption, under any circumstance, of alcohol. Whatever you can hide does not exist.

Passing, we watched our neighbours watching us—the Matlocks and the Wheelers and the Conrads and the Bolts—and we knew they were thinking *there go the Max kids and David Max, their father, tried to kill a man today in his store with gardening shears. . . .*

"Hello, Cy."

"Hello."

"Ben. Rita."

"Hi."

"Good-night . . ."

We went and stood together on the sidewalk out in front of our house.

Inside, everything seemed to be calm and normal. The lights were turned on in their usual distribution—most of them downstairs. The radio was playing. Someone was singing *Praise the Lord and Pass the Ammunition.*

Cy went up the steps and turned the handle. He was brave—but I'd always known that. Rita and I were told to wait on the porch.

Two minutes passed—or five—or ten—and finally Cy returned. He was very white and his voice was dry, but he wasn't shaking and all he said was: "you'd best come in. I'm calling the police."

Our father had tried to kill our mother with a hammer. She was lying on the sofa and her hands were broken because she had used them trying to fend off the blows.

Father had disappeared. The next day, he turned himself in because, as he told the doctors, he had come to his senses. He was kept for a year and a half—almost until the war was over—at the Asylum for the Insane on Queen Street. None of us children was allowed to visit him there—but our mother went to see him six months after he had been committed. She told me they sat in a long, grey room with bars on all the windows. My father wore a dressing gown and hadn't shaved. Mother said he couldn't look her in the eyes. She told him that she forgave him for what he had done. But my father never forgave himself. My mother said she never saw his eyes again.

Two weeks after our father had tried to kill our mother, a brick was thrown through the window of Max's Flowers. On the brick, a single word was printed in yellow chalk.

*Murderer.*

Mother said: "there's no way around this, now. I'm going to have to explain."

That was how we discovered what had gone wrong with our father at Dieppe.

Our mother had known this all along, and I still have strong suspicions Cy had found it out and maybe Rita before our mother went through the formal procedure of sitting us down and telling us all together. Maybe they had thought I was just too young to understand. Maybe Cy and maybe Rita hadn't known. Maybe they had only guessed. At any rate, I had a very strong sense that I was the only one who received our mother's news in a state of shock.

Father had risen, since his enlistment in 1939, all the way up from an NCO to the rank of captain. Everyone had adored him in the army. He was what they called a natural leader. His men were particularly fond of him and they would, as the saying goes, have followed him anywhere. Then came Dieppe. All but a handful of those who went into battle there were Canadians. This was our Waterloo. Our Gettysburg.

There isn't a single history book you can read—there isn't a single man who was there who won't tell you—there isn't a single scrap of evidence in any archive to suggest that the battle of Dieppe was anything but a total and appalling disaster. Most have called it a slaughter.

Dieppe is a port and market town on the coast of Normandy in northern France. In 1942, the British High Command had chosen it to be the object of a practice raid in preparation for the invasion of Europe. The Allies on every front were faltering, then. A gesture was needed, and even the smallest of victories would do.

And so, on the 19th of August, 1942, the raid on Dieppe had taken place—and the consequent carnage had cost the lives of over a thousand Canadians. Over two thousand were wounded or taken prisoner. Five thousand set out; just over one thousand came back.

My father never left his landing craft.

He was to have led his men ashore in the second wave of troops to follow the tanks—but, seeing the tanks immobilized, unable to move because the beaches were made of stone and the stones had jammed the tank tracks—and seeing the evident massacre of the first wave of troops whose attempt at storming the shore had been repulsed by machine-gun fire from the cliffs above the town—my father froze in his place and could not move. His men—it is all too apparent—did not know what to do. They had received no order to advance and yet, if they stayed, they were sitting ducks.

In the end, though a handful escaped by rushing forward into the water, the rest were blown to pieces when their landing craft was shelled. In the meantime, my father had recovered enough of his wits to crawl back over the end of the landing craft, strip off his uniform and swim out to sea where he was taken on board a British destroyer sitting offshore.

The destroyer, H.M.S. *Berkley*, was ultimately hit and everyone on board, including my father—no one knowing who he was—was transferred to another ship before the *Berkley* was scuttled where she sat. My father made it all the way back to England, where his burns and wounds were dressed and where he debated taking advantage of the chaos to disappear, hoping that, in the long run, he would be counted among the dead.

His problem was, his conscience had survived. He stayed and, as a consequence, he was confronted by survivors who knew his story. He was dishonourably discharged and sent home to us. Children don't understand such things. The only cowards they recognize are figures cut from comic books or seen on movie screens.

Fathers cannot be cowards.

It is impossible.

His torment and his grief were to lead my father all the way to the grave. He left our mother, in the long run, though she would not have wished him to do so and he lived out his days in little bars and back-street beer parlours, seeking whatever solace he could find with whores and derelicts whose stories might have matched his own. The phone would ring and we would dread it. Either it was him or news of him—either his drunken harangue or the name of his most recent jail.

He died in the Wellesley Hospital, the place where I was born—and when he was dying he asked to see his children. Cy and Rita "could not be reached," but I was found—where he'd always found me—sitting within yelling distance. Perhaps this sounds familiar to other children—of whatever age—whose parents, whether one of them or both of them, have made the mistake of losing faith too soon in their children's need to love.

I would have loved a stone.

If only he had known.

He sensed it, maybe, in the end. He told me he was sorry for everything—and meant it. He told me the names of all his men and he said he had walked with them all through hell, long since their deaths, to do them honour. He hoped they would understand him, now.

I said they might.

He asked if his ashes could be put with theirs.

*Why not*, I thought. *A stone among stones.*

The beaches at Dieppe can throw you off balance. The angle at which they slope into the water is both steep and dangerous. At high tide you can slide into the waves and lose your footing before you've remembered how to swim. The stones are treacherous. But they are also beautiful.

My father's ashes were contraband. You can't just walk about with someone's remains, in whatever form, in your suitcase. Stepping off the *Sealink* ferry, I carried my father in an envelope addressed to myself in Canada. This was only in case I was challenged. There was hardly more than a handful of him there. I had thrown the rest of him into the English Channel as the coast of Normandy was coming into view. It had been somewhat more than disconcerting to see the interest his ashes caused amongst the gulls and other sea birds. I had hoped to dispose of him in a private way, unnoticed. But a woman with two small children came and stood beside me at the railing and I heard her explain that *this nice gentleman is taking care of our feathered friends.* I hoped that, if my father was watching, he could laugh. I had to look away.

The ferry arrived in the early afternoon and—once I had booked myself into La Présidence Hotel—I went for a walk along the promenade above the sea-wall. It being May, the offshore breeze was warm and filled with the faintest scent of apple trees in bloom.

I didn't want to relive the battle. I hadn't come to conjure ghosts. But the ghosts and the battle are palpable around you there, no matter what your wishes are. The sound of the tide rolling back across the stones is all the cue you need to be reminded of that summer day in 1942. I stood that evening, resting my arms along the wall and thinking *at last, my father has come ashore.*

In the morning, before the town awoke, I got up in the dark and was on the beach when the sun rose inland beyond the cliffs. I wore a thick woollen sweater, walking shorts and a pair of running shoes. The envelope was in my pocket.

The concierge must have thought I was just another crazy North American off on my morning run. He grunted as I passed and I pretended not to know that he was there. Out on the beach, I clambered over retaining walls and petrified driftwood until I felt I was safely beyond the range of prying eyes.

The stones at Dieppe are mostly flint—and their colours range from white through yellow to red. The red stones look as if they have been washed in blood and the sight of them takes your breath away. I hunkered down above them, holding all that remained of my father in my fist. He felt like a powdered stone—pummelled and broken.

I let him down between my fingers, feeling him turn to paste— watching him divide and disappear.

He is dead and he is gone.

Weekends, our parents used to take us walking under the trees on Crescent Road. This was on the Rosedale side of Yonge Street. My brother Cy and I were always dressed in dark blue suits whose rough wool shorts would chafe against our thighs. Our knee socks—also blue—were turned down over thick elastic garters. Everything itched and smelled of Sunday. Cy had cleats on his shoes because he walked in such a way as to wear his heels *to the bone,* as my mother said— and causing much expense. The cleats made a wondrous clicking noise and you could always hear him coming. I wanted cleats, but I was refused because, no matter how I tried, I couldn't walk like that.

The houses sat up neat as pins beyond their lawns—blank-eyed windows, steaming chimneys—havens of wealth and all the mysteries of wealth.

Father often walked behind us. I don't know why. Mother walked in front with Rita. Rita always wore a dress that was either red or blue beneath her princess coat and in the wintertime she wore a sort of woollen cloche that was tied with a knitted string beneath her chin. Her Mary Jane shoes were just like Shirley Temple's shoes—which, for a while, was pleasing to Rita; then it was not. Rita always had an overpowering sense of image.

After the advent of our father's return, she said from the corner of her mouth one Sunday as we walked on Crescent Road that she and Cy and I had been named as if we were manufactured products: *Cy Max Office Equipment; Rita Max Household Appliances* and *Ben Max Watches.* This, she concluded, was why our father had always walked behind us. Proudly, he was measuring our performance. Now, he had ceased to walk behind us and our mother led us forward dressed in black.

*Tick. Tick. Tick.* That's me. The Ben Max Watch.

I have told our story. But I think it best—and I like it best—to end with all of us moving there beneath the trees in the years before the war. Mister and Mrs David Max out walking with their children any Sunday afternoon in any kind of weather but the rain.

Colonel Matheson, striding down his walk, is caught and forced to grunt acknowledgment that we are there. He cannot ignore us, after all. We have seen him every weekday morning, choosing his boutonnière and buying it from us.

*—1988*

*Chinua Achebe (b. 1930) was born in Ogidi, Nigeria, and, after graduation from University College in Ibadan and study at London University, was employed by the Nigerian Broadcasting Service, where he served for years as a producer. After the appearance of his first novel,* Things Fall Apart, *in 1958 (the title is taken from William Butler Yeats's apocalyptic poem "The Second Coming") he became one of the most widely acclaimed writers to emerge from the former British colonies of Africa. The author of several novels as well as a collection of short stories, Achebe draws heavily on the oral traditions of his native country, but he has been successful in adapting European fictional techniques to deal with subjects like the degradations imposed by colonialism and the relative failure of most post-colonial governments to materially improve on the past for the betterment of the lives of their citizens.*

## *Chinua Achebe*
# Dead Men's Path

Michael Obi's hopes were fulfilled much earlier than he had expected. He was appointed headmaster of Ndume Central School in January 1949. It had always been an unprogressive school, so the Mission authorities decided to send a young and energetic man to run it. Obi accepted this responsibility with enthusiasm. He had many wonderful ideas and this was an opportunity to put them into practice. He had had sound secondary school education which designated him a "pivotal teacher" in the official records and set him apart from the other head-masters in the mission field. He was outspoken in his condemnation of the narrow views of these older and often less-educated ones.

"We shall make a good job of it, shan't we?" he asked his young wife when they first heard the joyful news of his promotion.

"We shall do our best," she replied. "We shall have such beautiful gardens and everything will be just *modern* and delightful. . . ." In their two years of married life she had become completely infected by his passion for "modern methods" and his denigration of "these old and super-annuated people in the teaching field who would be better employed as traders in the Onitsha market." She began to see herself already as the admired wife of the young headmaster, the queen of the school.

The wives of the other teachers would envy her position. She would set the fashion in everything. . . . Then, suddenly, it occurred to her that there might not be other wives. Wavering between hope and fear, she asked her husband, looking anxiously at him.

"All our colleagues are young and unmarried," he said with enthusiasm which for once she did not share. "Which is a good thing," he continued.

"Why?"

"Why? They will give all their time and energy to the school."

Nancy was downcast. For a few minutes she became skeptical about the new school; but it was only for a few minutes. Her little personal misfortune could not blind her to her husband's happy prospects. She looked at him as he sat folded up in a chair. He was stoop-shouldered and looked frail. But he sometimes surprised people with sudden bursts of physical energy. In his present posture, however, all his bodily strength seemed to have retired behind his deep-set eyes, giving them an extraordinary power of penetration. He was only twenty-six, but looked thirty or more. On the whole, he was not unhandsome.

"A penny for your thoughts, Mike," said Nancy after a while, imitating the woman's magazine she read.

"I was thinking what a grand opportunity we've got at last to show these people how a school should be run."

Ndume School was backward in every sense of the word. Mr. Obi put his whole life into the work, and his wife hers too. He had two aims. A high standard of teaching was insisted upon, and the school compound was to be turned into a place of beauty. Nancy's dream-gardens came to life with the coming of the rains, and blossomed. Beautiful hibiscus and allamanda hedges in brilliant red and yellow marked out the carefully tended school compound from the rank neighborhood bushes.

One evening as Obi was admiring his work he was scandalized to see an old woman from the village hobble right across the compound, through a marigold flower-bed and the hedges. On going up there he found faint signs of an almost disused path from the village across the school compound to the bush on the other side.

"It amazes me," said Obi to one of his teachers who had been three years in the school, "that you people allowed the villagers to make use of this footpath. It is simply incredible." He shook his head.

"The path," said the teacher apologetically, "appears to be very important to them. Although it is hardly used, it connects the village shrine with their place of burial."

"And what has that got to do with the school?" asked the headmaster.

"Well, I don't know," replied the other with a shrug of the shoulders. "But I remember there was a big row some time ago when we attempted to close it."

"That was some time ago. But it will not be used now," said Obi as he walked away. "What will the Government Education Officer think of this when he comes to inspect the school next week? The villagers might, for all I know, decide to use the schoolroom for a pagan ritual during the inspection."

Heavy sticks were planted closely across the path at the two places where it entered and left the school premises. These were further strengthened with barbed wire.

Three days later the village priest of *Ani* called on the headmaster. He was an old man and walked with a slight stoop. He carried a stout walking-stick which he usually tapped on the floor, by way of emphasis, each time he made a new point in his argument.

"I have heard," he said after the usual exchange of cordialities, "that our ancestral footpath has recently been closed. . . ."

"Yes," replied Mr. Obi. "We cannot allow people to make a highway of our school compound."

"Look here, my son," said the priest bringing down his walking-stick, "this path was here before you were born and before your father was born. The whole life of this village depends on it. Our dead relatives depart by it and our ancestors visit us by it. But most important, it is the path of children coming in to be born. . . ."

Mr. Obi listened with a satisfied smile on his face.

"The whole purpose of our school," he said finally, "is to eradicate just such beliefs as that. Dead men do not require footpaths. The whole idea is just fantastic. Our duty is to teach your children to laugh at such ideas."

"What you say may be true," replied the priest, "but we follow the practices of our fathers. If you reopen the path we shall have nothing to quarrel about. What I always say is: let the hawk perch and let the eagle perch." He rose to go.

"I am sorry," said the young headmaster. "But the school compound cannot be a thoroughfare. It is against our regulations. I would suggest your constructing another path, skirting our premises. We can even get our boys to help in building it. I don't suppose the ancestors will find the little detour too burdensome."

"I have no more words to say," said the old priest, already outside.

Two days later a young woman in the village died in childbed. A diviner was immediately consulted and he prescribed heavy sacrifices to propitiate ancestors insulted by the fence.

Obi woke up next morning among the ruins of his work. The beautiful hedges were torn up not just near the path but right round the school, the flowers trampled to death and one of the school buildings pulled down. . . . That day, the white Supervisor came to inspect the school and wrote a nasty report on the state of the premises but more seriously about the "tribal-war situation developing between the school and the village, arising in part from the misguided zeal of the new headmaster."

*—1953*

*Alice Munro (b. 1931) was born on a farm in Wingham, Ontario, and educated at the University of Western Ontario, where she received her degree in 1952. Her first book,* Dance of the Happy Shades, *appeared in 1968, and she has continued regularly to publish collections of short stories. Asked about her devotion to short fiction, Munro told* Contemporary Authors: *"I never intended to be a short story writer — I started writing them because I didn't have time to write anything else — I had three children. And then I got used to writing short stories, so I see my materials that way, and now I don't think I'll ever write a novel." Parent–child and marital relations and the discovery of personal freedom are constant themes in Munro's work. Munro has won both the Governor General's Award and the Canadian Booksellers' Award, befitting her status as one of Canada's most distinguished writers.* Selected Stories *appeared in 1996, and* The Love of a Good Woman *was published in 1998. Her collection* Runaway *won the 2004 Giller Prize and she was named one of the world's most influential people in 2005 by* Time *magazine.*

## *Alice Munro*
# Boys and Girls

My father was a fox farmer. That is, he raised silver foxes, in pens; and in the fall and early winter, when their fur was prime, he killed them and skinned them and sold their pelts to the Hudson's Bay Company or the Montreal Fur Traders. These companies supplied us with heroic calendars to hang, one on each side of the kitchen door. Against a background of cold blue sky and black pine forests and treacherous northern rivers, plumed adventurers planted the flags of England or of France; magnificent savages bent their backs to the portage.

For several weeks before Christmas, my father worked after supper in the cellar of our house. The cellar was whitewashed, and lit by a hundred-watt bulb over the worktable. My brother Laird and I sat on the top step and watched. My father removed the pelt inside-out from the body of the fox, which looked surprisingly small, mean and rat-like, deprived of its arrogant weight of fur. The naked, slippery bodies were collected in a sack and buried at the dump. One time the hired man, Henry Bailey, had taken a swipe at me with this sack, saying, "Christmas present!" My mother thought that was not funny. In fact she disliked the whole pelting operation—that was what the killing, skinning, and preparation of the furs was called—and wished it did not have to take place in the house. There was the smell. After the pelt had been stretched inside-out on a long board my father scraped away delicately, removing the little clotted webs of blood vessels, the bubbles of fat; the smell of blood and animal fat, with the strong primitive odour of the fox itself, penetrated all parts of the house. I found it reassuringly seasonal, like the smell of oranges and pine needles.

Henry Bailey suffered from bronchial troubles. He would cough and cough until his narrow face turned scarlet, and his light blue, derisive eyes filled up with tears; then he took the lid off the stove, and, standing well back, shot out a great clot of phlegm—hsss—straight into the heart of the flames. We admired him for this performance and for his ability to make his stomach growl at will, and for his laughter, which was full of high whistlings and gurglings and involved the whole faulty machinery of his chest. It was sometimes hard to tell what he was laughing at, and always possible that it might be us.

After we had been sent to bed we could still smell fox and still hear Henry's laugh, but these things, reminders of the warm, safe, brightly lit downstairs world, seemed lost and diminished, floating on the stale cold air upstairs. We were afraid at night in the winter. We were not afraid of *outside* though this was the time of year when snowdrifts curled around our house like sleeping whales and the wind harassed us all night, coming up from the buried fields, the frozen swamp, with its old bugbear chorus of threats and misery. We were afraid of *inside*, the room where we slept. At this time the upstairs of our house was not finished. A brick chimney went up one wall. In the middle of the floor was a square hole, with a wooden railing around it; that was where the stairs came up. On the other side of the stairwell were the things that nobody had any use for any more—a soldiery roll of linoleum, standing on end, a wicker baby carriage, a fern basket, china jugs and basins with cracks in them, a picture of the Battle of Balaclava, very sad to look at. I had told Laird, as soon as he was old enough to understand such things, that bats and skeletons lived over there; whenever a man escaped from the county jail, twenty miles away, I imagined that he had somehow let himself in the window and was hiding behind the linoleum. But we had rules to keep us safe. When the light was on, we were safe as long as we did not step off the square of worn carpet which defined our bedroom-space; when the light was off no place was safe but the beds themselves. I had to turn out the light kneeling on the end of my bed, and stretching as far as I could to reach the cord.

In the dark we lay on our beds, our narrow life rafts, and fixed our eyes on the faint light coming up the stairwell, and sang songs. Laird sang "Jingle Bells," which he would sing any time, whether it was Christmas or not, and I sang "Danny Boy." I loved the sound of my own voice, frail and supplicating, rising in the dark. We could make out the tall frosted shapes of the windows now, gloomy and white. When I came to the part, *When I am dead, as dead I well may be*—a fit of shivering caused not by the cold sheets but by pleasurable emotion almost silenced me. *You'll kneel and say, an Ave there above me*—What was an Ave? Every day I forgot to find out.

Laird went straight from singing to sleep. I could hear his long, satisfied, bubbly breaths. Now for the time that remained to me, the most perfectly private and perhaps the best time of the whole day, I arranged myself tightly under the covers and went on with one of the stories I was telling myself from night to night. These stories were about myself, when I had grown a little older; they took place in a world that was recognizably mine, yet one that presented opportunities for courage, boldness and self-sacrifice, as mine never did. I rescued people from a bombed building (it discouraged me that the real war had gone on so far away from Jubilee). I shot two rabid wolves who were menacing the schoolyard (the teachers cowered terrified at my back). I rode a fine horse spiritedly down the main street of Jubilee, acknowledging the townspeople's gratitude for some yet-to-be-worked-out piece of heroism (nobody ever rode a horse there, except King Billy in the Orangemen's Day parade). There was always riding and shooting in these stories, though I had only been on a horse twice—bareback because we did not own a saddle—and the second time I had slid right around and dropped under the horse's feet; it had stepped placidly over me. I really was learning to shoot, but I could not hit anything yet, not even tin cans on fence posts.

Alive, the foxes inhabited a world my father made for them. It was surrounded by a high guard fence, like a medieval town, with a gate that was padlocked at night. Along the streets of this town were ranged large, sturdy pens. Each of them had a real door that a man could go through, a wooden ramp along the wire, for the foxes to run up and down on, and a kennel—something like a clothes chest with airholes—where they slept and stayed in winter and had their young. There were feeding and watering dishes attached to the wire in such a way that they could be emptied and cleaned from the outside. The dishes were made of old tin cans, and the ramps and kennels of odds and ends of old lumber. Everything was tidy and ingenious; my father was tirelessly inventive and his favourite book in the world was *Robinson Crusoe*. He had fitted a tin drum on a wheelbarrow, for bringing water down to the pens. This was my job in summer, when the foxes had to have water twice a day. Between nine and ten o'clock in the morning, and again after supper, I filled the drum at the pump and trundled it down through the barnyard to the pens, where I parked it, and filled my watering can and went along the streets. Laird came too, with his little cream and green gardening can, filled too full and knocking against his legs and slopping water on his canvas shoes. I had the real watering can, my father's, though I could only carry it three-quarters full.

The foxes all had names, which were printed on a tin plate and hung beside their doors. They were not named when they were born, but when they survived the first year's pelting and were added to the breeding stock. Those my father had named were called names like Prince, Bob, Wally and Betty. Those I had named were called Star or Turk, or Maureen or Diana. Laird named one Maud after a hired girl we had when he was little, one Harold after a boy at school, and one Mexico, he did not say why.

Naming them did not make pets out of them, or anything like it. Nobody but my father ever went into the pens, and he had twice had blood-poisoning from bites. When I was bringing them their water they prowled up and down on the paths they had made inside their pens, barking seldom—they saved that for nighttime, when they might get up a chorus of community frenzy—but always watching me, their eyes burning, clear gold, in their pointed, malevolent faces. They were beautiful for their delicate legs and heavy, aristocratic tails and the bright fur sprinkled on dark down their backs—which gave them their name—but especially for their faces, drawn exquisitely sharp in pure hostility, and their golden eyes.

Besides carrying water I helped my father when he cut the long grass, and the lamb's quarter and flowering money-musk, that grew between the pens. He cut with the scythe and I raked into piles. Then he took a pitchfork and threw fresh-cut grass all over the top of the pens, to keep the foxes cooler and shade their coats, which were browned by too much sun. My father did not talk to me unless it was about the job we were doing. In this he was quite different from my mother, who, if she was feeling cheerful, would tell me all sorts of things—the name of a dog she had had when she was a little girl, the names of boys she had gone out with later on when she was grown up, and what certain dresses of hers had looked like—she could not imagine now what had become of them. Whatever thoughts and stories my father had were private, and I was shy of him and would never ask him questions. Nevertheless I worked willingly under his eyes, and with a feeling of pride. One time a feed salesman came down into the pens to talk to him and my father said, "Like to have you meet my new hired man." I turned away and raked furiously, red in the face with pleasure.

"Could of fooled me," said the salesman. "I thought it was only a girl."

After the grass was cut, it seemed suddenly much later in the year. I walked on stubble in the earlier evening, aware of the reddening skies, the entering silences, of fall. When I wheeled the tank out of the gate and put the padlock on, it was almost dark. One night at this time I saw my mother and father standing talking on the little rise of ground we called the gangway, in front of the barn. My father had just come from the meathouse; he had his stiff bloody apron on, and a pail of cut-up meat in his hand.

It was an odd thing to see my mother down at the barn. She did not often come out of the house unless it was to do something—hang out the wash or dig potatoes in the garden. She looked out of place, with her bare lumpy legs, not touched by the sun, her apron still on and damp across the stomach from the supper dishes. Her hair was tied up in a kerchief, wisps of it falling out. She would tie her hair up like this in the morning, saying she did not have time to do it properly, and it would stay tied up all day. It was true, too; she really did not have time. These days our back porch was piled with baskets of peaches and grapes and pears, bought in town, and onions and tomatoes and cucumbers grown at home, all waiting to be made into jelly and jam and preserves, pickles and chili sauce. In the kitchen there was a fire in the stove all day, jars clinked in boiling water, sometimes a cheesecloth bag was strung on a pole between two chairs, straining blue-black grape pulp for jelly. I was

given jobs to do and I would sit at the table peeling peaches that had
been soaked in the hot water, or cutting up onions, my eyes smarting
and streaming. As soon as I was done I ran out of the house, trying to
get out of earshot before my mother thought of what she wanted me to
do next. I hated the hot dark kitchen in summer, the green blinds and
the flypapers, the same old oilcloth table and wavy mirror and bumpy
linoleum. My mother was too tired and preoccupied to talk to me, she
had no heart to tell about the Normal School Graduation Dance; sweat
trickled over her face and she was always counting under her breath,
pointing at jars, dumping cups of sugar. It seemed to me that work in
the house was endless, dreary and peculiarly depressing; work done out
of doors, and in my father's service, was ritualistically important.

I wheeled the tank up to the barn, where it was kept, and I heard my
mother saying, "Wait till Laird gets a little bigger, then you'll have a
real help."

What my father said I did not hear. I was pleased by the way he
stood listening, politely as he would to a salesman or a stranger, but
with an air of wanting to get on with his real work. I felt my mother had
no business down here and I wanted him to feel the same way. What did
she mean about Laird? He was no help to anybody. Where was he now?
Swinging himself sick on the swing, going around in circles, or trying to
catch caterpillars. He never once stayed with me till I was finished.

"And then I can use her more in the house," I heard my mother say.
She had a dead-quiet, regretful way of talking about me that always
made me uneasy. "I just get my back turned and she runs off. It's not
like I had a girl in the family at all."

I went and sat on a feed bag in the corner of the barn, not wanting
to appear when this conversation was going on. My mother, I felt, was
not to be trusted. She was kinder than my father and more easily fooled,
but you could not depend on her, and the real reasons for the things she
said and did were not to be known. She loved me, and she sat up late at
night making a dress of the difficult style I wanted, for me to wear when
school started, but she was also my enemy. She was always plotting. She
was plotting now to get me to stay in the house more, although she
knew I hated it (*because* she knew I hated it) and keep me from working for my father. It seemed to me she would do this simply out of per-
versity, and to try her power. It did not occur to me that she could be
lonely, or jealous. No grown-up could be; they were too fortunate. I sat

and kicked my heels monotonously against a feedbag, raising dust, and did not come out till she was gone.

At any rate, I did not expect my father to pay any attention to what she said. Who could imagine Laird doing my work—Laird remembering the padlock and cleaning out the watering-dishes with a leaf on the end of a stick, or even wheeling the tank without it tumbling over? It showed how little my mother knew about the way things really were.

I have forgotten to say what the foxes were fed. My father's bloody apron reminded me. They were fed horsemeat. At this time most farmers still kept horses, and when a horse got too old to work, or broke a leg or got down and would not get up, as they sometimes did, the owner would call my father, and he and Henry went out to the farm in the truck. Usually they shot and butchered the horse there, paying the farmer from five to twelve dollars. If they had already too much meat on hand, they would bring the horse back alive, and keep it for a few days or weeks in our stable, until the meat was needed. After the war the farmers were buying tractors and gradually getting rid of horses altogether, so it sometimes happened that we got a good healthy horse, that there was just no use for any more. If this happened in the winter we might keep the horse in our stable till spring, for we had plenty of hay and if there was a lot of snow—and the plow did not always get our road cleared—it was convenient to be able to go to town with a horse and cutter.

The winter I was eleven years old we had two horses in the stable. We did not know what names they had had before, so we called them Mack and Flora. Mack was an old black workhorse, sooty and indifferent. Flora was a sorrel mare, a driver. We took them both out in the cutter. Mack was slow and easy to handle. Flora was given to fits of violent alarm, veering at cars and even at other horses, but we loved her speed and high-stepping, her general air of gallantry and abandon. On Saturdays we went down to the stable and as soon as we opened the door on its cosy, animal-smelling darkness Flora threw up her head, rolled her eyes, whinnied despairingly and pulled herself through a crisis of nerves on the spot. It was not safe to go into her stall; she would kick.

This winter also I began to hear a great deal more on the theme my mother had sounded when she had been talking in front of the barn. I no longer felt safe. It seemed that in the minds of the people around me there was a steady undercurrent of thought, not to be deflected, on this one subject. The word *girl* had formerly seemed to me innocent and unburdened, like the word *child;* now it appeared that it was no such thing. A girl was not, as I had supposed, simply what I was; it was what I had to become. It was a definition, always touched with emphasis, with reproach and disappointment. Also it was a joke on me. Once Laird and I were fighting, and for the first time ever I had to use all my strength against him; even so, he caught and pinned my arm for a moment, really hurting me. Henry saw this, and laughed, saying, "Oh, that there Laird's gonna show you, one of these days!" Laird was getting a lot bigger. But I was getting bigger too.

My grandmother came to stay with us for a few weeks and I heard other things. "Girls don't slam doors like that." "Girls keep their knees together when they sit down." And worse still, when I asked some questions, "That's none of girls' business." I continued to slam the doors and sit as awkwardly as possible, thinking that by such measures I kept myself free.

When spring came, the horses were let out in the barnyard. Mack stood against the barn wall trying to scratch his neck and haunches, but Flora trotted up and down and reared at the fences, clattering her hooves against the rails. Snow drifts dwindled quickly, revealing the hard grey and brown earth, the familiar rise and fall of the ground, plain and bare after the fantastic landscape of winter. There was a great feeling of opening-out, of release. We just wore rubbers now, over our shoes; our feet felt ridiculously light. One Saturday we went out to the stable and found all the doors open, letting in the unaccustomed sunlight and fresh air. Henry was there, just idling around looking at his collection of calendars which were tacked up behind the stalls in a part of the stable my mother had probably never seen.

"Come to say goodbye to your old friend Mack?" Henry said. "Here, you give him a taste of oats." He poured some oats into Laird's cupped hands and Laird went to feed Mack. Mack's teeth were in bad shape. He ate very slowly, patiently shifting the oats around in his mouth, trying to find a stump of a molar to grind it on. "Poor old Mack," said Henry mournfully. "When a horse's teeth's gone, he's gone. That's about the way."

"Are you going to shoot him today?" I said. Mack and Flora had been in the stable so long I had almost forgotten they were going to be shot.

Henry didn't answer me. Instead he started to sing in a high, trembly, mocking-sorrowful voice, *Oh, there's no more work, for poor Uncle Ned, he's gone where the good darkies go.* Mack's thick, blackish tongue worked diligently at Laird's hand. I went out before the song was ended and sat down on the gangway.

I had never seen them shoot a horse, but I knew where it was done. Last summer Laird and I had come upon a horse's entrails before they were buried. We had thought it was a big black snake, coiled up in the sun. That was around in the field that ran up beside the barn. I thought that if we went inside the barn, and found a wide crack or a knothole to look through, we would be able to see them do it. It was not something I wanted to see; just the same, if a thing really happened, it was better to see it, and know.

My father came down from the house, carrying the gun.

"What are you doing here?" he said.

"Nothing."

"Go on up and play around the house."

He sent Laird out of the stable. I said to Laird, "Do you want to see them shoot Mack?" and without waiting for an answer led him around to the front door of the barn, opened it carefully, and went in. "Be quiet or they'll hear us," I said. We could hear Henry and my father talking in the stable, then the heavy, shuffling steps of Mack being backed out of his stall.

In the loft it was cold and dark. Thin, crisscrossed beams of sunlight fell through the cracks. The hay was low. It was a rolling country, hills and hollows, slipping under our feet. About four feet up was a beam going around the walls. We piled hay up in one corner and I boosted Laird up and hoisted myself. The beam was not very wide; we crept along it with our hands flat on the barn walls. There were plenty of knotholes, and I found one that gave me the view I wanted—a corner of the barnyard, the gate, part of the field. Laird did not have a knothole and began to complain.

I showed him a widened crack between two boards. "Be quiet and wait. If they hear you you'll get us in trouble."

My father came in sight carrying the gun. Henry was leading Mack by the halter. He dropped it and took out his cigarette papers and tobacco; he rolled cigarettes for my father and himself. While this was going on Mack nosed around in the old, dead grass along the fence.

Then my father opened the gate and they took Mack through. Henry led Mack away from the path to a patch of ground and they talked together, not loud enough for us to hear. Mack again began searching for a mouthful of fresh grass, which was not to be found. My father walked away in a straight line, and stopped short at a distance which seemed to suit him. Henry was walking away from Mack too, but sideways, still negligently holding on to the halter. My father raised the gun and Mack looked up as if he had noticed something and my father shot him.

Mack did not collapse at once but swayed, lurched sideways and fell, first on his side; then he rolled over on his back and, amazingly, kicked his legs for a few seconds in the air. At this Henry laughed, as if Mack had done a trick for him. Laird, who had drawn a long, groaning breath of surprise when the shot was fired, said out loud, "He's not dead." And it seemed to me it might be true. But his legs stopped, he rolled on his side again, his muscles quivered and sank. The two men walked over and looked at him in a businesslike way; they bent down and examined his forehead where the bullet had gone in, and now I saw his blood on the brown grass.

"Now they just skin him and cut him up," I said. "Let's go." My legs were a little shaky and I jumped gratefully down into the hay. "Now you've seen how they shoot a horse," I said in a congratulatory way, as if I had seen it many times before. "Let's see if any barn cat's had kittens in the hay." Laird jumped. He seemed young and obedient again. Suddenly I remembered how, when he was little, I had brought him into the barn and told him to climb the ladder to the top beam. That was in the spring, too, when the hay was low. I had done it out of a need for excitement, a desire for something to happen so that I could tell about it. He was wearing a little bulky brown and white checked coat, made down from one of mine. He went all the way up, just as I told him, and sat down on the top beam with the hay far below him on one side, and the barn floor and some old machinery on the other. Then I ran screaming to my father, "Laird's up on the top beam!" My father came, my mother came, my father went up the ladder talking very quietly and brought Laird down under his arm, at which my mother leaned against the ladder and began to cry. They said to me, "Why weren't you watching him?" but nobody ever knew the truth. Laird did not know enough to tell. But whenever I saw the brown and white checked coat hanging in the closet, or at the bottom of the rag bag, which was where it ended up, I felt a weight in my stomach, the sadness of unexorcized guilt.

I looked at Laird who did not even remember this, and I did not like the look on this thin, winter-pale face. His expression was not frightened or upset, but remote, concentrating. "Listen," I said, in an unusually bright and friendly voice, "you aren't going to tell, are you?"

"No," he said absently.

"Promise."

"Promise," he said. I grabbed the hand behind his back to make sure he was not crossing his fingers. Even so, he might have a nightmare; it might come out that way. I decided I had better work hard to get all thoughts of what he had seen out of his mind—which, it seemed to me, could not hold very many things at a time. I got some money I had saved and that afternoon we went into Jubilee and saw a show, with Judy Canova, at which we both laughed a great deal. After that I thought it would be all right.

Two weeks later I knew they were going to shoot Flora. I knew from the night before, when I heard my mother ask if the hay was holding out all right, and my father said, "Well, after tomorrow there'll just be the cow, and we should be able to put her out to grass in another week." So I knew it was Flora's turn in the morning.

This time I didn't think of watching it. That was something to see just one time. I had not thought about it very often since, but sometimes when I was busy, working at school, or standing in front of the mirror combing my hair and wondering if I would be pretty when I grew up, the whole scene would flash into my mind: I would see the easy, practised way my father raised the gun, and hear Henry laughing when Mack kicked his legs in the air. I did not have any great feeling of horror and opposition, such as a city child might have had; I was too used to seeing the death of animals as a necessity by which we lived. Yet I felt a little ashamed, and there was a new wariness, a sense of holding-off, in my attitude to my father and his work.

It was a fine day, and we were going around the yard picking up tree branches that had been torn off in winter storms. This was something we had been told to do, and also we wanted to use them to make a teepee. We heard Flora whinny, and then my father's voice and Henry's shouting, and we ran down to the barnyard to see what was going on.

The stable door was open. Henry had just brought Flora out, and she had broken away from him. She was running free in the barnyard, from one end to the other. We climbed up on the fence. It was exciting to see her running, whinnying, going up on her hind legs, prancing and threatening like a horse in a Western movie, an unbroken ranch horse, though she was just an old driver, an old sorrel mare. My father and Henry ran after her and tried to grab the dangling halter. They tried to work her into a corner, and they had almost succeeded when she made a run between them, wild-eyed, and disappeared around the corner of the barn. We heard the rails clatter down as she got over the fence, and Henry yelled, "She's into the field now!"

That meant she was in the long L-shaped field that ran up by the house. If she got around the center, heading towards the lane, the gate was open; the truck had been driven into the field this morning. My father shouted to me, because I was on the other side of the fence, nearest the lane, "Go shut the gate!"

I could run very fast. I ran across the garden, past the tree where our swing was hung, and jumped across a ditch into the lane. There was the open gate. She had not got out, I could not see her up on the road; she must have run to the other end of the field. The gate was heavy. I lifted it out of the gravel and carried it across the roadway. I had it half-way across when she came in sight, galloping straight towards me. There was just time to get the chain on. Laird came scrambling through the ditch to help me.

Instead of shutting the gate, I opened it as wide as I could. I did not make any decision to do this, it was just what I did. Flora never slowed down; she galloped straight past me, and Laird jumped up and down, yelling, "Shut it, shut it!" even after it was too late. My father and Henry appeared in the field a moment too late to see what I had done. They only saw Flora heading for the township road. They would think I had not got there in time.

They did not waste any time asking about it. They went back to the barn and got the gun and the knives they used, and put these in the truck; then they turned the truck around and came bouncing up the field toward us. Laird called to them, "Let me go too, let me go too!" and Henry stopped the truck and they took him in. I shut the gate after they were all gone.

I supposed Laird would tell. I wondered what would happen to me. I had never disobeyed my father before, and I could not understand why I had done it. Flora would not really get away. They would catch up with her in the truck. Or if they did not catch her this morning somebody would see her and telephone us this afternoon or tomorrow. There was no wild country here for her to run to, only farms. What was more, my father had paid for her, we needed the meat to feed the foxes, we needed the foxes to make our living. All I had done was make more work for my father who worked hard enough already. And when my father found out about it he was not going to trust me any more; he would know that I was not entirely on his side. I was on Flora's side, and that made me no use to anybody, not even to her. Just the same, I did not regret it; when she came running at me and I held the gate open, that was the only thing I could do.

I went back to the house, and my mother said, "What's all the commotion?" I told her that Flora had kicked down the fence and got away. "Your poor father," she said, "now he'll have to go chasing over the countryside. Well, there isn't any use planning dinner before one." She put up the ironing board. I wanted to tell her, but thought better of it and went upstairs and sat on my bed.

Lately I had been trying to make my part of the room fancy, spreading the bed with old lace curtains, and fixing myself a dressing-table with some leftovers of cretonne for a skirt. I planned to put up some kind of barricade between my bed and Laird's, to keep my section separate from his. In the sunlight, the lace curtains were just dusty rags. We did not sing at night any more. One night when I was singing Laird said, "You sound silly," and I went right on but the next night I did not start. There was not so much need to anyway, we were no longer afraid. We knew it was just old furniture over there, old jumble and confusion. We did not keep to the rules. I still stayed awake after Laird was asleep and told myself stories, but even in these stories something different was happening, mysterious alterations took place. A story might start off in the old way, with a spectacular danger, a fire or wild animals, and for a while I might rescue people; then things would change around, and instead, somebody would be rescuing me. It might be a boy from our class at school, or even Mr. Campbell, our teacher, who tickled girls under the arms. And at this point the story concerned itself at great length with what I looked like—how long my hair was, and what kind of dress I had on; by the time I had these details worked out the real excitement of the story was lost.

It was later than one o'clock when the truck came back. The tarpaulin was over the back, which meant there was meat in it. My mother had to heat dinner up all over again. Henry and my father had changed from their bloody overalls into ordinary working overalls in the barn, and they washed their arms and necks and faces at the sink, and splashed water on their hair and combed it. Laird lifted his arm to show off a streak of blood. "We shot old Flora," he said, "and cut her up in fifty pieces."

"Well I don't want to hear about it," my mother said. "And don't come to my table like that."

My father made him go and wash the blood off.

We sat down and my father said grace and Henry pasted his chewing gum on the end of his fork, the way he always did; when he took it off he would have us admire the pattern. We began to pass the bowls of steaming, overcooked vegetables. Laird looked across the table at me and said proudly, distinctly, "Anyway it was her fault Flora got away."

"What?" my father said.

"She could of shut the gate and she didn't. She just open' it up and Flora run out."

"Is that right?" my father said.

Everybody at the table was looking at me. I nodded, swallowing food with great difficulty. To my shame, tears flooded my eyes.

My father made a curt sound of disgust. "What did you do that for?"

I did not answer. I put down my fork and waited to be sent from the table, still not looking up.

But this did not happen. For some time nobody said anything, then Laird said matter-of-factly, "She's crying."

"Never mind," my father said. He spoke with resignation, even good humour, the words which absolved and dismissed me for good. "She's only a girl," he said.

I didn't protest that, even in my heart. Maybe it was true.

*—1968*

**Donald Barthelme (1931–1989)** *was born in Philadelphia but lived in New York City and Texas. An innovator on the frontier between modernism and postmodernism, he produced four novels, including* Snow White *(1967) and* Paradise *(1986), and over one hundred short stories gathered in collections such as* City Life *(1970),* Sixty Stories *(1981), and* Overnight to Many Distant Cities *(1983). His fiction makes use of collage techniques incorporating high and low culture, realism and fable, and the bizarre and familiar fragments that make up the disjointed debris of contemporary life, often without regard to the conventions of plot, character, and setting.*

## *Donald Barthelme*
# The Glass Mountain

1. I was trying to climb the glass mountain.

2. The glass mountain stands at the corner of Thirteenth Street and Eighth Avenue.

3. I had attained the lower slope.

4. People were looking up at me.

5. I was new in the neighborhood.

6. Nevertheless I had acquaintances.

7. I had strapped climbing irons to my feet and each hand grasped a sturdy plumber's friend.

8. I was 200 feet up.

9. The wind was bitter.

10. My acquaintances had gathered at the bottom of the mountain to offer encouragement.

11. "Shithead."

12. "Asshole."

13. Everyone in the city knows about the glass mountain.

14. People who live here tell stories about it.

15. It is pointed out to visitors.

16. Touching the side of the mountain, one feels coolness.

17. Peering into the mountain, one sees sparkling blue-white depths.

18. The mountain towers over that part of Eighth Avenue like some splendid, immense office building.

19. The top of the mountain vanishes into the clouds, or on cloudless days, into the sun.

20. I unstuck the righthand plumber's friend leaving the lefthand one in place.

21. Then I stretched out and reattached the righthand one a little higher up, after which I inched my legs into new positions.

22. The gain was minimal, not an arm's length.

23. My acquaintances continued to comment.

24. "Dumb motherfucker."

25. I was new in the neighborhood.

26. In the streets were many people with disturbed eyes.

27. Look for yourself.

28. In the streets were hundreds of young people shooting up in doorways, behind parked cars.

29. Older people walked dogs.

30. The sidewalks were full of dogshit in brilliant colors: ocher, umber, Mars yellow, sienna, viridian, ivory black, rose madder.

31. And someone had been apprehended cutting down trees, a row of elms broken-backed among the VWs and Valiants.

32. Done with a power saw, beyond a doubt.

33. I was new in the neighborhood yet I had accumulated acquaintances.

34. My acquaintances passed a brown bottle from hand to hand.

35. "Better than a kick in the crotch."

36. "Better than a poke in the eye with a sharp stick."

37. "Better than a slap in the belly with a wet fish."

38. "Better than a thump on the back with a stone."

39. "Won't he make a splash when he falls, now?"

40. "I hope to be here to see it. Dip my handkerchief in the blood."

41. "Fart-faced fool."

42. I unstuck the lefthand plumber's friend leaving the righthand one in place.

43. And reached out.

44. To climb the glass mountain, one first requires a good reason.

45. No one has ever climbed the mountain on behalf of science, or in search of celebrity, or because the mountain was a challenge.

46. Those are not good reasons.

47. But good reasons exist.

48. At the top of the mountain there is a castle of pure gold, and in a room in the castle tower sits . . .

49. My acquaintances were shouting at me.

50. "Ten bucks you bust your ass in the next four minutes!"

51. . . . a beautiful enchanted symbol.

52. I unstuck the righthand plumber's friend leaving the lefthand one in place.

53. And reached out.

54. It was cold there at 206 feet and when I looked down I was not encouraged.

55. A heap of corpses both of horses and riders ringed the bottom of the mountain, many dying men groaning there.

56. "A weakening of the libidinous interest in reality has recently come to a close." (Anton Ehrenzweig)[1]

---

[1]*Anton Ehrenzweig:* the author of the *Hidden Order of Art: A Study in the Psychology of Artistic Imagination.*

57. A few questions thronged into my mind.

58. Does one climb a glass mountain, at considerable personal discomfort, simply to disenchant a symbol?

59. Do today's stronger egos still *need* symbols?

60. I decided that the answer to these questions was "yes."

61. Otherwise what was I doing there, 206 feet above the power-sawed elms, whose white meat I could see from my height?

62. The best way to fail to climb the mountain is to be a knight in full armor—one whose horse's hoofs strike fiery sparks from the sides of the mountain.

63. The following-named knights had failed to climb the mountain and were groaning in the heap: Sir Giles Guilford, Sir Henry Lovell, Sir Albert Denny, Sir Nicholas Vaux, Sir Patrick Grifford, Sir Gisbourne Gower, Sir Thomas Grey, Sir Peter Coleville, Sir John Blunt, Sir Richard Vernon, Sir Walter Willoughby, Sir Stephen Spear, Sir Roger Faulconbridge, Sir Clarence Vaughan, Sir Hubert Ratcliffe, Sir James Tyrrel, Sir Walter Herbert, Sir Robert Brakenbury, Sir Lionel Beaufort, and many others.[2]

64. My acquaintances moved among the fallen knights.

65. My acquaintances moved among the fallen knights, collecting rings, wallets, pocket watches, ladies' favors.

66. "Calm reigns in the country, thanks to the confident wisdom of everyone." (M. Pompidou)[3]

67. The golden castle is guarded by a lean-headed eagle with blazing rubies for eyes.

68. I unstuck the lefthand plumber's friend, wondering if—

69. My acquaintances were prising out the gold teeth of not-yet-dead knights.

---

[2]Names of knights taken from the history plays of William Shakespeare including *The Tragedy of King Richard the Third* and *The Famous History of the Life of King Henry the Eighth.*
[3]*Monsieur Georges Pompidou* (1911–1974): president of France from 1969 to 1974. During the French student–worker revolt of May 1968, he was instrumental in negotiating an end to the strikes and restoring law and order.

70. In the streets were people concealing their calm behind a façade of vague dread.

71. "The conventional symbol (such as the nightingale, often associated with melancholy), even though it is recognized only through agreement, is not a sign (like the traffic light) because, again, it presumably arouses deep feelings and is regarded as possessing properties beyond what the eye alone sees." *(A Dictionary of Literary Terms)*

72. A number of nightingales with traffic lights tied to their legs flew past me.

73. A knight in pale pink armor appeared above me.

74. He sank, his armor making tiny shrieking sounds against the glass.

75. He gave me a sideways glance as he passed me.

76. He uttered the word *"Muerte"*[4] as he passed me.

77. I unstuck the righthand plumber's friend.

78. My acquaintances were debating the question, which of them would get my apartment?

79. I reviewed the conventional means of attaining the castle.

80. The conventional means of attaining the castle are as follows: "The eagle dug its sharp claws into the tender flesh of the youth, but he bore the pain without a sound, and seized the bird's two feet with his hands. The creature in terror lifted him high up into the air and began to circle the castle. The youth held on bravely. He saw the glittering palace, which by the pale rays of the moon looked like a dim lamp; and he saw the windows and balconies of the castle tower. Drawing a small knife from his belt, he cut off both the eagle's feet. The bird rose up in the air with a yelp, and the youth dropped lightly onto a broad balcony. At the same moment a door opened, and he saw a courtyard filled with flowers and trees, and there, the beautiful enchanted princess." *(The Yellow Fairy Book)*[5]

[4]*Muerte:* Spanish for "Death."
[5]*Yellow Fairy Book:* Scottish scholar Andrew Lang (1844–1912) edited numerous volumes of fairy stories named after colours.

81. I was afraid.

82. I had forgotten the Bandaids.

83. When the eagle dug its sharp claws into my tender flesh—

84. Should I go back for the Bandaids?

85. But if I went back for the Bandaids I would have to endure the contempt of my acquaintances.

86. I resolved to proceed without the Bandaids.

87. "In some centuries, his [man's] imagination has made life an intense practice of all the lovelier energies." (John Masefield)[6]

88. The eagle dug its sharp claws into my tender flesh.

89. But I bore the pain without a sound, and seized the bird's two feet with my hands.

90. The plumber's friends remained in place, standing at right angles to the side of the mountain.

91. The creature in terror lifted me high in the air and began to circle the castle.

92. I held on bravely.

93. I saw the glittering palace, which by the pale rays of the moon looked like a dim lamp; and I saw the windows and balconies of the castle tower.

94. Drawing a small knife from my belt, I cut off both the eagle's feet.

95. The bird rose up in the air with a yelp, and I dropped lightly onto a broad balcony.

96. At the same moment a door opened, and I saw a courtyard filled with flowers and trees, and there, the beautiful enchanted symbol.

97. I approached the symbol, with its layers of meaning, but when I touched it, it changed into only a beautiful princess.

---

[6]*John Masefield* (1878–1967): an English poet who wandered the world doing odd jobs including a stint as a bartender's assistant in New York. He was Poet Laureate of England from 1930 until his death.

98. I threw the beautiful princess headfirst down the mountain to my acquaintances.

99. Who could be relied upon to deal with her.

100. Nor are eagles plausible, not at all, not for a moment.

*—1970*

---

*Carol Shields (1935–2003) was born in Oak Park, Illinois, but moved to Canada in her twenties, living primarily in Manitoba and British Columbia. She is best known for her novels, including* The Stone Diaries *(1993), which won both the Governor General's Award and the Pulitzer Prize, and* Unless *(2000). However, she also published a number of short-story collections, including* Various Miracles *(1985) and* Dressing Up for the Carnival *(2001), which explore the extraordinary beneath the ordinary, especially in the unrecorded lives of women.*

## *Carol Shields*
# Words

When the world first started heating up, an international conference was held in Rome to discuss ways of dealing with the situation.

Ian's small northern country—small in terms of population, that is, not in size—sent him to the meetings as a junior observer, and it was there he met Isobel, who was representing her country as a full-fledged delegate. She wore a terrible green dress the first time he saw her, and rather clumsy shoes, but he could see that her neck was slender, her waist narrow and her legs long and brown. For so young a woman, she was astonishingly articulate; in fact, it was her voice more than anything else that he fell in love with—its hills and valleys and its pliant, easy-sided wit. It was a voice that could be distinguished in any gathering, being both sweet and husky and having an edging of contralto merriment that seemed to Ian as rare and fine as a border of gold leaf.

They played truant, missing half the study sessions, the two of them lingering instead over tall, cool drinks in the cafe they found on the Via Traflori. There, under a cheerful striped canopy, Isobel leaned across a little table and placed long, ribbony Spanish phrases into Ian's mouth, encouraging and praising him when he got them right. And he, in his somewhat stiff northern voice, gave back the English equivalents: table, chair, glass, cold, hot, money, street, people, mouth. In the evenings, walking in the gardens in front of the institute where the conference was being held, they turned to each other and promised with their eyes, and in two languages as well, to love each other for ever.

The second International Conference was held ten years later. The situation had become grave. One could use the word *crisis* and not be embarrassed. Ian—by then married to Isobel, who was at home with the children—attended every session, and he listened attentively to the position papers of various physicists, engineers, geographers and linguists from all parts of the world. It was a solemn but distinguished assembly; many eminent men and women took their places at the lectern, including the spidery old Scottish demographer who years earlier had made the first correlation between substrata temperatures and highly verbalized societies. In every case, these speakers presented their concerns with admirable brevity, each word weighted and frugally chosen, and not one of them exceeded the two minute time limitation. For by now no one really doubted that it was the extravagance and proliferation of language that had caused the temperature of the earth's crust to rise, and in places—California, Japan, London—to crack open and form long ragged lakes of fire. The evidence was everywhere and it was incontrovertible; thermal maps and measurements, sonar readings, caloric separations, a network of subterranean monitoring systems—all these had reinforced the integrity of the original Scottish theories.

But the delegates, sitting in the plenary session of the second International Conference, still were reluctant to take regulatory action. It was partly a case of heads-in-the-sand; it was—human nature being what it is—partly a matter of political advantage or commercial gain. There lingered, too, a somewhat surprising nostalgia for traditional liberties and for the old verbal order of the world. Discussion at the conference had gone around and around all week, pointless and wasteful, and it looked very much as though the final meeting would end in yet another welter of indecision and deferral. It was at that point that Ian, seated in the front row, rose and requested permission to speak.

He was granted a one-minute slot on the agenda. In fact, he spoke for several minutes, but his eloquence, his sincerity (and no doubt his strong, boyish appearance, his shaggy hair and his blue eyes) seemed to merit an exception. Certainly not one person sitting in that gathering had any wish to stop him.

It was unfortunate, tragic some thought, that a freak failure in the electronic system—only a plug accidentally pulled from its socket—prevented his exact words from being recorded, but those who were present remembered afterward how passionately he pleaded his love for the planet. (In truth—though who could know this?—he was thinking chiefly of his love for Isobel and his two children.)

We are living in a fool's dream, he told his fellow delegates, and the time has come for us to wake up. Voluntary restraints were no longer adequate to preserve the little earth, which was the only home we know. Halfway measures like the old three-hour *temps tranquilles* were next to useless since they were never, or almost never, enforced. The evening curfew-lingua was ridiculously lenient. Abuses of every sort abounded, particularly the use of highly percussive words or words that were redolent with emotional potency, even though it had been established that these two classes of words were particularly damaging to bedrock and shales. Multilingualism continued to flourish. Wasteful antiphonic structures were actually on the increase in the more heavily populated regions, as was the use of elaborate ceremonial metaphor. It was as though, by refusing to make linguistic sacrifices, the human race had willed its own destruction.

When he finished speaking, the applause was prolonged and powerful. It perhaps held an element of shame, too; this young man had found the courage to say at last what should have been said long before. One after another the delegates rose to their feet, and soon their clapping fell into a steady rhythmic beat which had the effect of holding Ian hostage on the platform. The chairman whispered into his ear, begging him for a few additional words.

He assented. He could not say no. And, in a fever that was remarkably similar to the fever he had suffered as a child during a severe case of measles, or like the fever of love he had succumbed to ten years earlier in Rome, he announced to the audience, holding up a hand for attention, that he would be the first to take a vow of complete silence for the sake of the planet that had fathered him.

Almost at once he regretted his words, but hubris kept him from recanting for the first twenty-four hours and, after that, a kind of stubbornness took over. Isobel met him at the airport with the words, "You went too far." Later, after a miserable, silent attempt at lovemaking, she said, "I'll never forgive you." His children, clamoring to hear about his moment of heroism, poked at him, at his face and chest and arms, as though he were inert. He tried to tell them with his eyes that he was still their father, that he still loved them.

"Leave him alone," Isobel said sharply. "He might as well be a stranger now. He's no different than anyone else."

She became loud and shrewish. When his silent followers arrived at their door—and in time there were thousands of them, each with the same blank face and gold armband—she admitted them with bad grace. She grew garrulous. She rambled on and on, bitter and blaming, sometimes incoherent, sometimes obscene, sometimes reverting to a coarse, primitive schoolyard Spanish, sometimes shouting to herself or cursing into the mirror or chanting oaths—anything to furnish the emptiness of the house with words. She became disoriented. The solid plaster of the walls fell away from her, melting into a drift of vapor. There seemed to be no shadows, no sense of dimension, no delicate separation between one object and another. Privately she pleaded with her husband for an act of apostasy. Later she taunted him. "Show me you're still human," she would say. "Give me just one word." The word *betrayal* came frequently out of her wide mobile mouth, and so did the scornful epithet *martyr*.

But time passes and people forget. She forgot, finally, what it was that had betrayed her. Next she forgot her husband's name. Sometimes she forgot that she had a husband at all, for how could anything be said to exist, she asked herself loudly, hoarsely—even a husband, even one's self—if it didn't also exist in the shape of a word.

He worried that she might be arrested, but for some reason, his position probably, she was always let off with a warning. In their own house she ignored him, passing him on the stairs without a look, or crossing in front of him as though he were a stuffed chair. Often she disappeared for hours, venturing out alone into the heat of the night, and he began to suspect she had taken a lover.

The thought preyed on him, though in fact he had long since forgotten the word for *wife* and also the word for *fidelity*. One night, when she left the house, he attempted to follow her, but clearly she was suspicious because she walked very quickly, looking back over her shoulder, making a series of unnecessary turns and choosing narrow old streets whose curbs were blackened by fire. Within minutes he lost sight of her; soon after that he was driven back by the heat.

The next night he tried again, and this time he saw her disappear into an ancient, dilapidated building, the sort of enclosure, he remembered, where children had once gone to learn to read and write. Unexpectedly he felt a flash of pity; what a sad place for a tryst. He waited briefly, then entered the building and went up a flight of smoldering stairs which seemed on the point of collapse. There he found a dim corridor, thick with smoke, and a single room at one end.

Through the door he heard a waterfall of voices. There must have been a dozen people inside, all of them talking. The talk seemed to be about poetry. Someone—a woman—was giving a lecture. There were interruptions, a discussion, some laughter. He heard his wife's voice, her old gilt-edged contralto, asking a question, and the sound of it made him draw in his breath so sharply that something hard, like a cinder or a particle of gravel, formed in his throat.

It stayed stubbornly lodged there all night. He found it painful to breathe, and even Isobel noticed how he thrashed about in bed, gasping wildly for air. In the morning she called a doctor, who could find nothing wrong, but she remained uneasy, and that evening she stayed home and made him cups of iced honey-and-lemon tea to ease his throat. He took her hand at one point and held it to his lips as though it might be possible to find the air he needed inside the crevices of her skin. By now the scraping in his throat had become terrible, a raw agonizing rasp like a dull knife sawing through limestone. She looked at his face from which the healthy, blood-filled elasticity had gone out and felt herself brushed by a current of air or what might have been the memory of a name.

He began to choke violently, and she heard something grotesque come out of his mouth, a sound that was only half-human, but which rode on a curious rhythmic wave that for some reason stirred her deeply. She imagined it to be the word *Isobel*. "Isobel?" she asked, trying to remember its meaning. He said it a second time, and this time the syllables were more clearly formed.

The light of terror came into his eyes, or perhaps the beginning of a new fever; she managed to calm him by stroking his arm. Then she called the children inside the house, locked the doors and windows against the unbearable heat, and they began, hands linked, at the beginning where they had begun before—with table, chair, bed, cool, else, other, sleep, face, mouth, breath, tongue.

Slowly, patiently.

*—1985*

---

*Alistair MacLeod (b. 1936) was born in Saskatchewan but in 1946 moved back to the family farm in Cape Breton, a place that became the setting for much of his fiction, including two short-story collections,* The Lost Salt Gift of Blood *(1976) and* As Birds Bring Forth the Sun *(1986), as well as the novel* No Great Mischief *(1999), which won the prestigious IMPAC Dublin award. Noted for his exceptional craftsmanship and a generous and humane approach to his characters, he has expressed an interest in literature that rises from and goes back to the people.*

## Alistair MacLeod
# The Boat

There are times even now, when I awake at four o'clock in the morning with the terrible fear that I have overslept; when I imagine that my father is waiting for me in the room below the darkened stairs or that the shorebound men are tossing pebbles against my window while blowing their hands and stomping their feet impatiently on the frozen steadfast earth. There are times when I am half out of bed and fumbling for socks and mumbling for words before I realize that I am foolishly alone, that no one waits at the base of the stairs and no boat rides restlessly in the waters by the pier.

At such times only the grey corpses on the overflowing ashtray beside my bed bear witness to the extinction of the latest spark and silently await the crushing out of the most recent of their fellows. And then because I am afraid to be alone with death, I dress rapidly, make a great to-do about clearing my throat, turn on both faucets in the sink and proceed to make loud splashing ineffectual noises. Later I go out and walk the mile to the all-night restaurant.

In the winter it is a very cold walk and there are often tears in my eyes when I arrive. The waitress usually gives a sympathetic little shiver and says, "Boy, it must be really cold out there; you got tears in your eyes."

"Yes," I say, "it sure is; it really is."

And then the three or four of us who are always in such places at such times make uninteresting little protective chit-chat until the dawn reluctantly arrives. Then I swallow the coffee which is always bitter and leave with a great busy rush because by that time I have to worry about being late and whether I have a clean shirt and whether my car will start and about all the other countless things one must worry about when he teaches at a great Midwestern university. And I know then that that day will go by as have all the days of the past ten years, for the call and the voices and the shapes and the boat were not really there in the early morning's darkness and I have all kinds of comforting reality to prove it. They are only shadows and echoes, the animals a child's hands make on the wall by lamplight, and the voices from the rain barrel; the cuttings from an old movie made in the black and white of long ago.

I first became conscious of the boat in the same way and at almost the same time that I became aware of the people it supported. My earliest recollection of my father is a view from the floor of gigantic rubber boots and then of being suddenly elevated and having my face pressed against the stubble of his cheek, and of how it tasted of salt and of how he smelled of salt from his red-soled rubber boots to the shaggy whiteness of his hair.

When I was very small, he took me for my first ride in the boat. I rode the half-mile from our house to the wharf on his shoulders and I remember the sound of his rubber boots galumphing along the gravel beach, the tune of the indecent little song he used to sing, and the odour of the salt.

The floor of the boat was permeated with the same odour and in its constancy I was not aware of change. In the harbour we made our little circle and returned. He tied the boat by its painter, fastened the stern to its permanent anchor and lifted me high over his head to the solidity of the wharf. Then he climbed up the little iron ladder that led to the wharf's cap, placed me once more upon his shoulders and galumphed off again.

When we returned to the house everyone made a great fuss over my precocious excursion and asked, "How did you like the boat?" "Were you afraid in the boat?" "Did you cry in the boat?" They repeated "the boat" at the end of all their questions and I knew it must be very important to everyone.

My earliest recollection of my mother is of being alone with her in the mornings while my father was away in the boat. She seemed to be always repairing clothes that were "torn in the boat," preparing food "to be eaten in the boat" or looking for "the boat" through our kitchen window which faced upon the sea. When my father returned about noon, she would ask, "Well, how did things go in the boat today?" It was the first question I remember asking: "Well, how did things go in the boat today?" "Well, how did things go in the boat today?"

The boat in our lives was registered at Port Hawkesbury. She was what Nova Scotians called a Cape Island boat and was designed for the small inshore fishermen who sought the lobsters of the spring and the mackerel of summer and later the cod and haddock and hake. She was thirty-two feet long and nine wide, and was powered by an engine from a Chevrolet truck. She had a marine clutch and a high speed reverse gear and was painted light green with the name *Jenny Lynn* stencilled in black letters on her bow and painted on an oblong plate across her stern. Jenny Lynn had been my mother's maiden name and the boat was called after her as another link in the chain of tradition. Most of the boats that berthed at the wharf bore the names of some female member of their owner's household.

I say this now as if I knew it all then. All at once, all about boat dimensions and engines, and as if on the day of my first childish voyage I noticed the difference between a stencilled name and a painted name. But of course it was not that way at all, for I learned it all very slowly and there was not time enough.

I learned first about our house which was one of about fifty which marched around the horseshoe of our harbour and the wharf which was its heart. Some of them were so close to the water that during a storm the sea spray splashed against their windows while others were built farther along the beach as was the case with ours. The houses and their people, like those of the neighbouring towns and villages, were the result of Ireland's discontent and Scotland's Highland Clearances[1] and America's War of Independence. Impulsive emotional Catholic Celts who could not

---

[1]*Highland Clearances:* The sometimes violent removal of tenants so Scottish landowners could introduce sheep in the early 1800s is referred to as the "Highland Clearances."

bear to live with England and shrewd determined Protestant Puritans who, in the years after 1776, could not bear to live without.

The most important room in our house was one of those oblong old-fashioned kitchens heated by a wood- and coal-burning stove. Behind the stove was a box of kindlings and beside it a coal scuttle. A heavy wooden table with leaves that expanded or reduced its dimensions stood in the middle of the floor. There were five wooden homemade chairs which had been chipped and hacked by a variety of knives. Against the east wall, opposite the stove, there was a couch which sagged in the middle and had a cushion for a pillow, and above it a shelf which contained matches, tobacco, pencils, odd fish-hooks, bits of twine, and a tin can filled with bills and receipts. The south wall was dominated by a window which faced the sea and on the north there was a five-foot board which bore a variety of clothes hooks and the burdens of each. Beneath the board there was a jumble of odd footwear, mostly of rubber. There was also, on this wall, a barometer, a map of the marine area and a shelf which held a tiny radio. The kitchen was shared by all of us and was a buffer zone between the immaculate order of ten other rooms and the disruptive chaos of the single room that was my father's.

My mother ran her house as her brothers ran their boats. Everything was clean and spotless and in order. She was tall and dark and powerfully energetic. In later years she reminded me of the women of Thomas Hardy, particularly Eustacia Vye, in a physical way. She fed and clothed a family of seven children, making all of the meals and most of the clothes. She grew miraculous gardens and magnificent flowers and raised broods of hens and ducks. She would walk miles on berry-picking expeditions and hoist her skirts to dig for clams when the tide was low. She was fourteen years younger than my father, whom she had married when she was twenty-six and had been a local beauty for a period of ten years. My mother was of the sea as were all of her people, and her horizons were the very literal ones she scanned with her dark and fearless eyes.

Between the kitchen clothes rack and barometer, a door opened into my father's bedroom. It was a room of disorder and disarray. It was as if the wind which so often clamoured about the house succeeded in entering this single room and after whipping it into turmoil stole quietly away to renew its knowing laughter from without.

My father's bed was against the south wall. It always looked rumpled and unmade because he lay on top of it more than he slept within any folds it might have had. Beside it, there was a little brown table. An archaic goose-necked reading light, a battered table radio, a mound of wooden matches, one or two packages of tobacco, a deck of cigarette papers and an overflowing ashtray cluttered its surface. The brown larvae of tobacco shreds and the grey flecks of ash covered both the table and the floor beneath it. The once-varnished surface of the table was disfigured by numerous black scars and gashes inflicted by the neglected burning cigarettes of many years. They had tumbled from the ashtray unnoticed and branded their statements permanently and quietly into the wood until the odour of their burning caused the snuffing out of their lives. At the bed's foot there was a single window which looked upon the sea.

Against the adjacent wall there was a battered bureau and beside it there was a closet which held his single ill-fitting serge suit, the two or three white shirts that strangled him and the square black shoes that pinched. When he took off his more friendly clothes, the heavy woollen sweaters, mitts and socks which my mother knitted for him and the woollen and doeskin shirts, he dumped them unceremoniously on a single chair. If a visitor entered the room while he was lying on the bed, he would be told to throw the clothes on the floor and take their place upon the chair.

Magazines and books covered the bureau and competed with the clothes for domination of the chair. They further overburdened the heroic little table and lay on top of the radio. They filled a baffling and unknowable cave beneath the bed, and in the corner by the bureau they spilled from the walls and grew up from the floor.

The magazines were the most conventional: *Time, Newsweek, Life, Maclean's Family Herald, Reader's Digest.* They were the result of various cut-rate subscriptions or of the gift subscriptions associated with Christmas, "the two whole years for only $3.50."

The books were more varied. There were a few hard-cover magnificents and bygone Book-of-the-Month wonders and some were Christmas or birthday gifts. The majority of them, however, were used paperbacks which came from those second-hand bookstores which advertise in the backs of magazines: "Miscellaneous Used Paperbacks 10¢ Each." At first he sent for them himself, although my mother resented the expense, but in later years they came more and more often from my sisters who had moved to the cities. Especially at first they were very weird and varied. Mickey Spillane and Ernest Haycox vied with Dostoyevsky and Faulkner, and the Penguin Poets edition of Gerard Manley Hopkins arrived in the same box as a little book on sex technique called *Getting the Most Out of Love*. The former had been assiduously annotated by a very fine hand using a very blue-inked fountain pen while the latter had been studied by someone with very large thumbs, the prints of which were still visible in the margins. At the slightest provocation it would open almost automatically to particularly graphic and well-smudged pages.

When he was not in the boat, my father spent most of his time lying on the bed in his socks, the top two buttons of his trousers undone, his discarded shirt on the ever-ready chair and the sleeves of the woollen Stanfield underwear, which he wore both summer and winter, drawn half way up to his elbows. The pillows propped up the whiteness of his head and the goose-necked lamp illuminated the pages in his hands. The cigarettes smoked and smouldered on the ashtray and on the table and the radio played constantly, sometimes low and sometimes loud. At midnight and at one, two, three and four, one could sometimes hear the radio, his occasional cough, the rustling thud of a completed book being tossed to the corner heap, or the movement necessitated by his sitting on the edge of the bed to roll the thousandth cigarette. He seemed never to sleep, only to doze, and the light shone constantly from his window to the sea.

My mother despised the room and all it stood for and she had stopped sleeping in it after I was born. She despised disorder in rooms and in houses and in hours and in lives, and she had not read a book since high school. There she had read *Ivanhoe* and considered it a colossal waste of time. Still the room remained, like a solid rock of opposition in the sparkling waters of a clear deep harbour, opening off the kitchen where we really lived our lives, with its door always open and its contents visible to all.

The daughters of the room and of the house were very beautiful. They were tall and willowy like my mother and had her fine facial features set off by the reddish copper-coloured hair that had apparently once been my father's before it turned to white. All of them were very clever in school and helped my mother a great deal about the house. When they were young they sang and were very happy and very nice to me because I was the youngest and the family's only boy.

My father never approved of their playing about the wharf like the other children, and they went there only when my mother sent them on an errand. At such times they almost always overstayed, playing screaming games of tag or hide-and-seek in and about the fishing shanties, the piled traps and tubs of trawl, shouting down to the perch that swam languidly about the wharf's algae-covered piles, or jumping in and out of the boats that tugged gently at their lines. My mother was never uneasy about them at such times, and when her husband criticized her she would say, "Nothing will happen to them there," or "They could be doing worse things in worse places."

By about the ninth or tenth grade my sisters one by one discovered my father's bedroom and then the change would begin. Each would go into the room one morning when he was out. She would go with the ideal hope of imposing order or with the more practical objective of emptying the ashtray, and later she would be found spellbound by the volume in her hand. My mother's reaction was always abrupt, bordering on the angry. "Take your nose out of that trash and come and do your work," she would say, and once I saw her slap my youngest sister so hard that the print of her hand was scarletly emblazoned upon her daughter's cheek while the broken-spined paperback fluttered uselessly to the floor.

Thereafter my mother would launch a campaign against what she had discovered but could not understand. At times although she was not overly religious she would bring in God to bolster her arguments, saying, "In the next world God will see to those who waste their lives reading useless books when they should be about their work." Or without theological aid, "I would like to know how books help anyone to live a life." If my father were in, she would repeat the remarks louder than necessary, and her voice would carry into his room where he lay upon his bed. His usual reaction was to turn up the volume of the radio, although that action in itself betrayed the success of the initial thrust.

Shortly after my sisters began to read the books, they grew restless and lost interest in darning socks and baking bread, and all of them eventually went to work as summer waitresses in the Sea Food Restaurant. The restaurant was run by a big American concern from Boston and catered to the tourists that flooded the area during July and August. My mother despised the whole operation. She said the restaurant was not run by "our people," and "our people" did not eat there, and that it was run by outsiders for outsiders.

"Who are these people anyway?" she would ask, tossing back her dark hair, "and what do they, though they go about with their cameras for a hundred years, know about the way it is here, and what do they care about me and mine, and why should I care about them?"

She was angry that my sisters should even conceive of working in such a place and more angry when my father made no move to prevent it, and she was worried about herself and about her family and about her life. Sometimes she would say softly to her sisters, "I don't know what's the matter with my girls. It seems none of them are interested in any of the right things." And sometimes there would be bitter savage arguments. One afternoon I was coming in with three mackerel I'd been given at the wharf when I heard her say, "Well I hope you'll be satisfied when they come home knocked up and you'll have had your way."

It was the most savage thing I'd ever heard my mother say. Not just the words but the way she said them, and I stood there in the porch afraid to breathe for what seemed like the years from ten to fifteen, feeling the damp moist mackerel with their silver glassy eyes growing clammy against my leg.

Through the angle in the screen door I saw my father who had been walking into his room wheel around on one of his rubber-booted heels and look at her with his blue eyes flashing like clearest ice beneath the snow that was his hair. His usually ruddy face was drawn and grey, reflecting the exhaustion of a man of sixty-five who had been working in those rubber boots for eleven hours on an August day, and for a fleeting moment I wondered what I would do if he killed my mother while I stood there in the porch with those three foolish mackerel in my hand. Then he turned and went into his room and the radio blared forth the next day's weather forecast and I retreated under the noise and returned again, stamping my feet and slamming the door too loudly to signal my approach. My mother was busy at the stove when I came in, and did not raise her head when I threw the mackerel in a pan. As I looked into my father's room, I said, "Well how did things go in the boat today?" and he replied, "Oh not too badly, all things considered." He was lying on his back and lighting the first cigarette and the radio was talking about the Virginia coast.

All of my sisters made good money on tips. They bought my father an electric razor which he tried to use for a while and they took out even more magazine subscriptions. They bought my mother a great many clothes of the type she was very fond of, the wide-brimmed hats and the brocaded dresses, but she locked them all in trunks and refused to wear any of them.

On one August day my sisters prevailed upon my father to take some of their restaurant customers for an afternoon ride in the boat. The tourists with their expensive clothes and cameras and sun glasses awkwardly backed down the iron ladder at the wharf's side to where my father waited below, holding the rocking *Jenny Lynn* in snug against the wharf with one hand on the iron ladder and steadying his descending passengers with the other. They tried to look both prim and wind-blown like the girls in the Pepsi-Cola ads and did the best they could, sitting on the thwarts where the newspapers were spread to cover the splattered blood and fish entrails, crowding to one side so that they were in danger of capsizing the boat, taking the inevitable pictures or merely trailing their fingers through the water of their dreams.

All of them liked my father very much and, after he'd brought them back from their circles in the harbour, they invited him to their rented cabins which were located high on a hill overlooking the village to which they were so alien. He proceeded to get very drunk up there with the beautiful view and the strange company and the abundant liquor, and late in the afternoon he began to sing.

I was just approaching the wharf to deliver my mother's summons when he began, and the familiar yet unfamiliar voice that rolled down from the cabins made me feel as I had never felt before in my young life or perhaps as I had always felt without really knowing it, and I was ashamed yet proud, young yet old and saved yet forever lost, and there was nothing I could do to control my legs which trembled nor my eyes which wept for what they could not tell.

The tourists were equipped with tape recorders and my father sang for more than three hours. His voice boomed down the hill and bounced off the surface of the harbour, which was an unearthly blue on that hot August day, and was then reflected to the wharf and the fishing shanties where it was absorbed amidst the men who were baiting their lines for the next day's haul.

He sang all the old sea chanties which had come across from the old world and by which men like him had pulled ropes for generations, and he sang the East Coast sea songs which celebrated the sealing vessels of Northumberland Strait and the long liners of the Grand Banks, and of Anticosti, Sable Island, Grand Manan, Boston Harbor, Nantucket and Block Island. Gradually he shifted to the seemingly unending Gaelic drinking songs with their twenty or more verses and inevitable refrains, and the men in the shanties smiled at the coarseness of some of the verses and at the thought that the singer's immediate audience did not know what they were applauding nor recording to take back to staid old Boston. Later as the sun was setting he switched to the laments and the wild and haunting Gaelic war songs of those spattered Highland ancestors he had never seen, and when his voice ceased, the savage melancholy of three hundred years seemed to hang over the peaceful harbour and the quiet boats and the men leaning in the doorways of their shanties with their cigarettes glowing in the dusk and the women looking to the sea from their open windows with their children in their arms.

When he came home he threw the money he had earned on the kitchen table as he did with all his earnings but my mother refused to touch it and the next day he went with the rest of the men to bait his trawl in the shanties. The tourists came to the door that evening and my mother met them there and told them that her husband was not in although he was lying on the bed only a few feet away with the radio playing and the cigarette upon his lips. She stood in the doorway until they reluctantly went away.

In the winter they sent him a picture which had been taken on the day of the singing. On the back it said, "To Our Ernest Hemingway" and the "Our" was underlined. There was also an accompanying letter telling how much they had enjoyed themselves, how popular the tape was proving and explaining who Ernest Hemingway was. In a way it almost did look like one of those unshaven, taken-in-Cuba pictures of Hemingway. He looked both massive and incongruous in the setting. His bulky fisherman's clothes were too big for the green and white lawn chair in which he sat, and his rubber boots seemed to take up all of the well-clipped grass square. The beach umbrella jarred with his sunburned face and because he had already been singing for some time, his lips which chapped in the winds of spring and burned in the water glare of summer had already cracked in several places, producing tiny flecks of blood at their corners and on the whiteness of his teeth. The bracelets of brass chain which he wore to protect his wrists from chafing seemed abnormally large and his broad leather belt had been slackened and his heavy shirt and underwear were open at the throat revealing an uncultivated wilderness of white chest hair bordering on the semi-controlled stubble of his neck and chin. His blue eyes had looked directly into the camera and his hair was whiter than the two tiny clouds which hung over his left shoulder. The sea was behind him and its immense blue flatness stretched out to touch the arching blueness of the sky. It seemed very far away from him or else he was so much in the foreground that he seemed too big for it.

Each year another of my sisters would read the books and work in the restaurant. Sometimes they would stay out quite late on the hot summer nights and when they came up the stairs my mother would ask them many long and involved questions which they resented and tried to avoid. Before ascending the stairs they would go into my father's room and those of us who waited above could hear them throwing his clothes off the chair before sitting on it or the squeak of the bed as they sat on its edge. Sometimes they would talk to him a long time, the murmur of their voices blending with the music of the radio into a mysterious vapour-like sound which floated softly up the stairs.

I say this again as if it all happened at once and as if all of my sisters were of identical ages and like so many lemmings going into another sea and, again, it was of course not that way at all. Yet go they did, to Boston, to Montreal, to New York with the young men they met during the summers and later married in those far-away cities. The young men were very articulate and handsome and wore fine clothes and drove expensive cars and my sisters, as I said, were very tall and beautiful with their copper-coloured hair and were tired of darning socks and baking bread.

One by one they went. My mother had each of her daughters for fifteen years, then lost them for two and finally forever. None married a fisherman. My mother never accepted any of the young men, for in her eyes they seemed always a combination of the lazy, the effeminate, the dishonest and the unknown. They never seemed to do any physical work and she could not comprehend their luxurious vacations and she did not know whence they came nor who they were. And in the end she did not really care, for they were not of her people and they were not of her sea.

I say this now with a sense of wonder at my own stupidity in thinking I was somehow free and would go on doing well in school and playing and helping in the boat and passing into my early teens while streaks of grey began to appear in my mother's dark hair and my father's rubber boots dragged sometimes on the pebbles of the beach as he trudged home from the wharf. And there were but three of us in the house that had at one time been so loud.

Then during the winter that I was fifteen he seemed to grow old and ill at once. Most of January he lay upon the bed, smoking and reading and listening to the radio while the wind howled about the house and the needle-like snow blistered off the ice-covered harbour and the doors flew out of people's hands if they did not cling to them like death.

In February when the men began overhauling their lobster traps he still did not move, and my mother and I began to knit lobster trap headings in the evenings. The twine was as always very sharp and harsh, and blisters formed upon our thumbs and little paths of blood snaked quietly down between our fingers while the seals that had drifted down from distant Labrador wept and moaned like human children on the ice-floes of the Gulf.

In the daytime my mother's brother who had been my father's partner as long as I could remember also came to work upon the gear. He was a year older than my mother and was tall and dark and the father of twelve children.

By March we were very far behind and although I began to work very hard in the evenings I knew it was not hard enough and that there were but eight weeks left before the opening of the season on May first. And I knew that my mother worried and my uncle was uneasy and that all of our very lives depended on the boat being ready with her gear and two men, by the date of May the first. And I knew then that *David Copperfield* and *The Tempest* and all of those friends I had dearly come to love must really go forever. So I bade them all good-bye.

The night after my first full day at home and after my mother had gone upstairs he called me into his room where I sat upon the chair beside his bed. "You will go back tomorrow," he said simply.

I refused then, saying I had made my decision and was satisfied.

"That is no way to make a decision," he said, "and if you are satisfied I am not. It is best that you go back." I was almost angry then and told him as all children do that I wished he would leave me alone and stop telling me what to do.

He looked at me a long time then, lying there on the same bed on which he had fathered me those sixteen years before, fathered me his only son, out of who knew what emotions when he was already fifty-six and his hair had turned to snow. Then he swung his legs over the edge of the squeaking bed and sat facing me and looked into my own dark eyes with his of crystal blue and placed his hand upon my knee. "I am not telling you to do anything," he said softly, "only asking you."

The next morning I returned to school. As I left, my mother followed me to the porch and said, "I never thought a son of mine would choose useless books over the parents that gave him life."

In the weeks that followed he got up rather miraculously and the gear was ready and the *Jenny Lynn* was freshly painted by the last two weeks of April when the ice began to break up and the lonely screaming gulls returned to haunt the silver herring as they flashed within the sea.

On the first day of May the boats raced out as they had always done, laden down almost to the gunwales with their heavy cargoes of traps. They were almost like living things as they plunged through the waters of the spring and manoeuvred between the still floating icebergs of crystal-white and emerald green on their way to the traditional grounds that they sought out every May. And those of us who sat that day in the high school on the hill, discussing the water imagery of Tennyson, watched them as they passed back and forth beneath us until by afternoon the piles of traps which had been stacked upon the wharf were no longer visible but were spread about the bottoms of the sea. And the *Jenny Lynn* went too, all day, with my uncle tall and dark, like a latter-day Tashtego[2] standing at the tiller with his legs wide apart and guiding her deftly between the floating pans of ice and my father in the stern standing in the same way with his hands upon the ropes that lashed the cargo to the deck. And at night my mother asked, "Well, how did things go in the boat today?"

And the spring wore on and the summer came and school ended in the third week of June and the lobster season on July first and I wished that the two things I loved so dearly did not exclude each other in a manner that was so blunt and too clear.

At the conclusion of the lobster season my uncle said he had been offered a berth on a deep sea dragger and had decided to accept.

[2]*Tashtego:* a Native American harpooner in Herman Melville's novel *Moby-Dick* (1851) about the pursuit of a great white whale.

We all knew that he was leaving the *Jenny Lynn* forever and that before the next lobster season he would buy a boat of his own. He was expecting another child and would be supporting fifteen people by the next spring and could not chance my father against the family that he loved.

I joined my father then for the trawling season, and he made no protest and my mother was quite happy. Through the summer we baited the tubs of trawl in the afternoon and set them at sunset and revisited them in the darkness of the early morning. The men would come tramping by our house at four A.M. and we would join them and walk with them to the wharf and be on our way before the sun rose out of the ocean where it seemed to spend the night. If I was not up they would toss pebbles to my window and I would be very embarrassed and tumble downstairs to where my father lay fully clothed atop his bed, reading his book and listening to his radio and smoking his cigarette. When I appeared he would swing off his bed and put on his boots and be instantly ready and then we would take the lunches my mother had prepared the night before and walk off toward the sea. He would make no attempt to wake me himself.

It was in many ways a good summer. There were few storms and we were out almost every day and we lost a minimum of gear and seemed to land a maximum of fish and I tanned dark and brown after the manner of my uncles.

My father did not tan—he never tanned—because of his reddish complexion, and the salt water irritated his skin as it had for sixty years. He burned and reburned over and over again and his lips still cracked so that they bled when he smiled, and his arms, especially the left, still broke out into the oozing salt-water boils as they had ever since as a child I had first watched him soaking and bathing them in a variety of ineffectual solutions. The chafe-preventing bracelets of brass linked chain that all the men wore about their wrists in early spring were his the full season and he shaved but painfully and only once a week.

And I saw then, that summer, many things that I had seen all my life as if for the first time and I thought that perhaps my father had never been intended for a fisherman either physically or mentally. At least not in the manner of my uncles; he had never really loved it. And I remembered that, one evening in his room when we were talking about *David Copperfield*, he had said that he had always wanted to go to the university and I had dismissed it then in the way one dismisses his father's saying he would like to be a tight-rope walker, and we had gone on to talk about the Peggottys and how they loved the sea.

And I thought then to myself that there were many things wrong with all of us and all our lives and I wondered why my father, who was himself an only son, had not married before he was forty and then I wondered why he had. I even thought that perhaps he had had to marry my mother and checked the dates on the flyleaf of the Bible where I learned that my oldest sister had been born a prosaic eleven months after the marriage, and I felt myself then very dirty and debased for my lack of faith and for what I had thought and done.

And then there came into my heart a very great love for my father and I thought it was very much braver to spend a life doing what you really do not want rather than selfishly following forever your own dreams and inclinations. And I knew then that I could never leave him alone to suffer the iron-tipped harpoons which my mother would forever hurl into his soul because he was a failure as a husband and a father who had retained none of his own. And I felt that I had been very small in a little secret place within me and that even the completion of high school was for me a silly shallow selfish dream.

So I told him one night very resolutely and very powerfully that I would remain with him as long as he lived and we would fish the sea together. And he made no protest but only smiled through the cigarette smoke that wreathed his bed and replied, "I hope you will remember what you've said."

The room was now so filled with books as to be almost Dickensian, but he would not allow my mother to move or change them and he continued to read them, sometimes two or three a night. They came with great regularity now, and there were more hard covers, sent by my sisters who had gone so long ago and now seemed so distant and so prosperous, and sent also pictures of small red-haired grandchildren with baseball bats and dolls which he placed upon his bureau and which my mother gazed at wistfully when she thought no one would see. Red-haired grandchildren with baseball bats and dolls who would never know the sea in hatred or in love.

And so we fished through the heat of August and into the cooler days of September when the water was so clear we could almost see the bottom and the white mists rose like delicate ghosts in the early morning dawn. And one day my mother said to me, "You have given added years to his life."

And we fished on into October when it began to roughen and we could no longer risk night sets but took our gear out each morning and returned at the first sign of the squalls; and on into November when we lost three tubs of trawl and the clear blue water turned to a sullen grey and the trochoidal[3] waves rolled rough and high and washed across our bows and decks as we ran within their troughs. We wore heavy sweaters now and the awkward rubber slickers and the heavy woollen mitts which soaked and froze into masses of ice that hung from our wrists like the limbs of gigantic monsters until we thawed them against the exhaust pipe's heat. And almost every day we would leave for home before noon, driven by the blasts of the northwest wind, coating our eyebrows with ice and freezing our eyelids closed as we leaned into a visibility that was hardly there, charting our course from the compass and the sea, running with the waves and between them but never confronting their towering might.

And I stood at the tiller now, on these homeward lunges, stood in the place and in the manner of my uncle, turning to look at my father and to shout over the roar of the engine and the slop of the sea to where he stood in the stern, drenched and dripping with the snow and the salt and the spray and his bushy eyebrows caked in ice. But on November twenty-first, when it seemed we might be making the final run of the season, I turned and he was not there and I knew even in that instant that he would never be again.

On November twenty-first the waves of the grey Atlantic are very very high and the waters are very cold and there are no signposts on the surface of the sea. You cannot tell where you have been five minutes before and in the squalls of snow you cannot see. And it takes longer than you would believe to check a boat that has been running before a gale and turn her ever so carefully in a wide and stupid circle, with timbers creaking and straining, back into the face of storm. And you know that it is useless and that your voice does not carry the length of the boat and that even if you knew the original spot, the relentless waves would carry such a burden perhaps a mile or so by the time you could return. And you know also, the final irony, that

---

[3]In geometry, a trochoid is a curve connected to a rolling circle.

your father like your uncles and all the men that form your past, cannot swim a stroke.

The lobster beds off the Cape Breton coast are still very rich and now, from May to July, their offerings are packed in crates of ice, and thundered by the gigantic transport trucks, day and night, through New Glasgow, Amherst, Saint John and Bangor and Portland and into Boston where they are tossed still living into boiling pots of water, their final home.

And though the prices are higher and the competition tighter, the grounds to which the *Jenny Lynn* once went remain untouched and unfished as they have for the last ten years. For if there are no signposts on the sea in storm there are certain ones in calm and the lobster bottoms were distributed in calm before any of us can remember and the grounds my father fished were those his father fished before him and there were others before and before and before. Twice the big boats have come from forty and fifty miles, lured by the promise of the grounds, and strewn the bottom with their traps and twice they have returned to find their buoys cut adrift and their gear lost and destroyed. Twice the Fisheries Officer and the Mounted Police have come and asked many long and involved questions and twice they have received no answers from the men leaning in the doors of their shanties and the women standing at their windows with their children in their arms. Twice they have gone away saying: "There are no legal boundaries in the Marine area"; "No one can own the sea"; "Those grounds don't wait for anyone."

But the men and the women, with my mother dark among them, do not care for what they say, for to them the grounds are sacred and they think they wait for me.

It is not an easy thing to know that your mother lives alone on an inadequate insurance policy and that she is too proud to accept any other aid. And that she looks through her lonely window onto the ice of winter and the hot flat calm of summer and the rolling waves of fall. And that she lies awake in the early morning's darkness when the rubber boots of the men scrunch upon the gravel as they pass beside her house on their way down to the wharf. And she knows that the footsteps never stop, because no man goes from her house, and she alone of all the Lynns has neither son nor son-in-law that walks toward the boat that will take him to the sea. And it is not an easy thing to know that your mother looks upon the sea with love and on you with bitterness because the one has been so constant and the other so untrue.

But neither is it easy to know that your father was found on November twenty-eighth, ten miles to the north and wedged between two boulders at the base of the rock-strewn cliffs where he had been hurled and slammed so many many times. His hands were shredded ribbons as were his feet which had lost their boots to the suction of the sea, and his shoulders came apart in our hands when we tried to move him from the rocks. And the fish had eaten his testicles and the gulls had pecked out his eyes and the white-green stubble of his whiskers had continued to grow in death, like the grass on graves, upon the purple, bloated mass that was his face. There was not much left of my father, physically, as he lay there with the brass chains on his wrists and the seaweed in his hair.

—*1976*

---

*Roch Carrier (b. 1937) is best known for his short story "The Hockey Sweater," an excerpt of which appears on the Canadian five-dollar bill. Born in the village of Sainte-Justine, Quebec, he continued his education in New Brunswick, Montreal, and Paris. In 1968, he published the novel* La Guerre, Yes Sir! *and later went on to publish more than a dozen other novels and collections of short short stories, or contes—as they are called in the French-Canadian tradition. He has also worked as a teacher, a dramatist, and the National Librarian of Canada.*

## Roch Carrier
# Perhaps the Trees Do Travel

There were those who had travelled like migratory birds and those who lived rooted to the earth, like trees. Some had gone very far. I remember hearing the story of a man who had gone to the place where the sky meets the earth: he'd had to bend down so he wouldn't bump his head against the sky. The man had suddenly felt lonely and he'd written to his wife. The stamp cost a thousand dollars. Some people had gone to New York; another visited a brother in Montana; my grandfather had sailed on the Atlantic Ocean; a family had migrated to Saskatchewan; and men went to cut timber in the forests of Maine or Abitibi. When these people came home in their new clothes, even the trees on the main street were a little envious of the travellers.

And there were those who had never gone away. Like old Herménégilde. He was so old he'd seen the first house being built in our village. He was old, but his mustache was still completely black. It was a huge mustache that hid his nose, his mouth and his chin. I can still see old Herménégilde's mustache like a big black cloud over our village. Our parents used to say of him that he was healthy as a horse; all the storms of life had been unable to bend his upright, solid pride. At the end of his life he possessed nothing but a small frame house. All his children were gone. Old Herménégilde had spent his whole life without ever going outside the village limits. And he was very proud of having lived that way, rooted to the soil of our village. To indicate the full extent of his pride he would say:

'I've lived my whole life and never needed strangers!'

Old Herménégilde had never gone running off to the distant forests, he had never gone to the neighbouring villages to buy or sell animals. He'd found his wife in the village. Old Herménégilde used to say:

'The good Lord gave us everything we need to get by right here in our village! How come people have to go running off somewheres else where it ain't no better?'

He recalled a proverb written by a very old French poet and repeated it in his own way:

'The fellow next door's grass always looks a heck of a lot greener than your own.'

Old Herménégilde had never been inside an automobile.

'I'm in no rush to die,' he said. 'I want to do it on foot, like a man.'

One morning a black car longer than the one driven by Monsieur Cassidy, the undertaker, stopped with a jolt in front of old Herménégilde's house. A son he hadn't seen for a good many years got out of the car, all dressed in black, as Monsieur Cassidy usually was.

'You coming to my burial, my boy?' asked old Herménégilde.

'No,' said the son. 'I came to take you on a trip.'

Moving from one trade, one job to another, the son had become the private chauffeur to a businessman from Montreal; before he could ask himself what was happening, old Herménégilde, who had never been in a car before, was pushed onto the leather seat of a Cadillac that pawed the ground like a horse.

'Father,' said the son, 'you can't die before you see the world a little.'

'I've seen everything a man needs to see,' said old Herménégilde.

The son's long black car carried him off at a speed he'd never experienced. To avoid seeing that he was going beyond the village limits, old Herménégilde closed his eyes. And with his eyes closed the old man didn't see that he was driving through the neighbouring village, where a number of old men had gone to get their wives; he didn't see Mont Orignal, the highest mountain in the region; he didn't see the ten villages the black car drove through at a speed no runaway horse had ever reached. Tobie, his son, was talking, but he didn't want to listen.

'I'm your son and I know you've spent your whole life as if you were in jail. But you gotta see the world before you die and I'm the one that'll take you out of that jail. Nowadays there's no such thing as distance. My boss, he gets up in Montreal, he opens his eyes in Toronto, he eats his breakfast in New York and then comes back to Montreal to go to sleep. That's what I call living! You gotta keep up with the times. We know the world turns. And you gotta turn with it. I never stop travelling. I know the world. I know life. But you, you've never lived in modern times. It's something you gotta see.'

'A man can go as far as he wants,' said old Herménégilde, 'but he always stays in the same pair of boots.'

'I'm not what you'd call a good son,' said Tobie, 'but I'm the one that's gonna show you the world. That'll be one good thing I've done in my life.'

So then old Herménégilde understood that he was no longer allowed to keep his eyes closed. They had entered Quebec City. In a single glance the old man took in houses taller than the church, more people in the street than for a religious procession and cars swarming everywhere, like ants. His son drove him in front of an immense château, a real château whose name he'd heard when people talked about the rich—the Château Frontenac; then he showed him something much older than he was, older even than his late father—the houses built by the first Frenchmen.

The black car stopped in front of a large garden. Tobie helped his father get out.

'Now people won't be able to say you died without ever setting foot on the Plains of Abraham. This is where we lost our country . . . '

And then it was time to go home. In the car, the son noticed the old Herménégilde was keeping his eyes closed.

'Father, don't shut your eyes, look at the people.'

'I seen too much,' said the old man, 'you showed me too many things today.'

As soon as the son had left old Herménégilde at his house, he hurried off again in the long black car, summoned by other journeys in the vast modern world.

For long months, behind his big black mustache and his closed eyes, old Herménégilde waited for the long black car to return.

—*1979*

---

*Joanna Russ (b. 1937) was born in New York. She has combined feminism and speculative fiction in novels such as* The Female Man *(1975) and* The Two of Them *(1978). Her short-story collections include* Extra (Ordinary) People *(1984) and* The Hidden Side of the Moon *(1987). She has also published nonfiction works, including* How to Suppress Women's Writing *(1983) and* The Country You Have Never Seen *(2005). In 1895, the Irish writer Oscar Wilde was imprisoned for homosexuality, and Russ speculates on what choice he might have made had he been given a second chance.*

## *Joanna Russ*

# Mr. Wilde's Second Chance

*This is a tale told to me by a friend after the Cointreau and the music as we sat in the dusk waiting for the night to come.*

When Oscar Wilde (he said) died, his soul was found too sad for heaven and too happy for hell. A tattered spirit with the look of a debased street imp led him through miles of limbo into a large, foggy room, very like (for what he could see of it) a certain club in London. His small, grimy scud of a guide went up to a stand something like that used by ladies for embroidery or old men for chess, and there it stopped, spinning like a top.

"Yours!" it squeaked.

"Mine?"

But it was gone. On the stand was a board like the kind used for children's games, and nearby a dark lady in wine-colored silk moved pieces over a board of her own. The celebrated writer bent to watch her—she chanced to look up—it was Ada R—, the victim of the most celebrated scandal of the last decade. She had died of pneumonia or a broken heart in Paris; no one knew which. She gave him, out of her black eyes, a look so tragic, so shrinking, so haunted, that the poet (the most courteous of men, even when dead) bowed and turned away. The board before him was a maze of colored squares and meandering lines, and on top was written "O. O'F. Wilde" in coronet script, for this was his life's pattern and each man or woman in the room labored over a board on which was figured the events of his life. Each was trying to rearrange his life into a beautiful and ordered picture, and when he had done that he would be free to live again. As you can imagine, it was both exciting and horribly anxious, this reliving, this being down on the board and at the same time a dead—if not damned—soul in a room the size of all Aetna,[1] but queerly like a London club when it has just got dark and they have lit the lamps. The lady next to Wilde was pale as glass. She was almost finished. She raised one arm—her dark sleeve swept across the board—and in an instant her design was in ruins. Mr. Wilde picked up several of the pieces that had fallen and handed them to the lady.

"If you please," she said. "You are still holding my birthday and my visits to my children."

The poet returned them.

"You are generous," said she. "But then everyone here is generous. They provide everything. They provide all of one's life."

The poet bowed.

"Of course, it is not easy," said the lady. "I try very hard. But I cannot seem to finish anything. I am not sure if it is the necessary organizing ability that I lack or perhaps the aesthetic sense; something ugly always seems to intrude. . . ." She raised her colored counters in both hands, with the grace that had once made her a favorite of society.

"I have tried several times before," she said.

It was at this point that the poet turned and attempted to walk away from his second chance, but wherever he went the board preceded him.

---

[1]*Aetna:* the Latin spelling of Etna (from the Greek for "I burn"), the highest active volcano in Europe, situated on the east coast of Sicily.

It interposed itself between him and old gentlemen in velvet vests; it hovered in front of ladies; it even blossomed briefly at the elbow of a child. Then the poet seemed to regain his composure; he began to work at the game; he sorted and matched and disposed, although with what public in view it was not possible to tell. The board—which had been heavily overlaid in black and purple (like a drawing by one of Mr. Wilde's contemporaries)—began to take on the most delicate stipple of color. It breathed wind and shadow like the closes of a park in June. It spread itself like a fan.

O. O'F. Wilde, the successful man of letters, was strolling with his wife in Hyde Park in the year nineteen-twenty-five. He was sixty-nine years old. He had written twenty books where Oscar Wilde had written one, fifteen plays where the degenerate and debauché had written five, innumerable essays, seven historical romances, three volumes of collected verse, had given many public addresses (though not in the last few years), and had received a citation (this was long in the past) from Queen Victoria herself. The tulips of Hyde Park shone upon the Wildes with a mild and equable light. O. O'F. Wilde, who had written twenty books, and—needless to say—left his two sons an unimpeachable reputation, started, clutched at his heart, and died.

"That is beautiful, sir, beautiful," said a voice in the poet's ear. A gentleman—who was not a *gentleman*—stood at his elbow. "Seldom," said the voice, "have we had one of our visitors, as you might say, complete a work in such a short time, and such a beautiful work, too. And such industry, sir!" The gentleman was beside himself. "Such enthusiasm! Such agreeable docility! You know, of course, that few of our guests display such an excellent attitude. Most of our guests—"

"Do you think so?" said Mr. Wilde curiously.

"Lovely, sir! Such agreeable color. Such delicacy."

"I see," said Mr. Wilde.

"I'm so glad you do, sir. Most of our guests don't. Most of our guests, if you'll permit me the liberty of saying so, are not genteel. Not genteel at all. But you, sir—"

Oscar Wilde, poet, dead at forty-four, took his second chance from the table before him and broke the board across his knee. He was a tall, strong man for all his weight, nearly six feet tall.

*"And then?" I said.*

*"And then," said my friend, "I do not know what happened."*

"*Perhaps,*" *said I,* "*they gave him his second chance, after all. Perhaps they had to.*"

"*Perhaps,*" *said my friend,* "*they did nothing of the kind. . . .*"

"*I wish I knew,*" *he added.* "*I only wish I knew!*"

And there we left it.

—*1981*

***Raymond Carver (1938–1988)*** *built a reputation as a master of the contemporary short story that was still growing at the end of his life, which came prematurely after a long struggle with cancer. A native of Clatskanie, Oregon, Carver worked at a number of unskilled jobs in his early years. Married and the father of two before he was twenty, he knew the working class more intimately than have most American writers. Carver's publishing career is bracketed by collections of poetry, and the compression of language he learned as a poet may in part account for the lean quality of his prose, which has been called, perhaps unfairly and inaccurately, "minimalist." Loving the "brevity and intensity" of the short story, he published five collections, including* What We Talk About When We Talk About Love *(1981) and* Elephant *(1988). He felt the title story of the collection* Cathedral *(1983) marked a turning point in his writing in a different, more detailed and hopeful direction, perhaps reflecting his personal victory over alcoholism, his successful relationship with the poet Tess Gallagher, and increasing critical acclaim.*

## *Raymond Carver*
# Cathedral

This blind man, an old friend of my wife's, he was on his way to spend the night. His wife had died. So he was visiting the dead wife's relatives in Connecticut. He called my wife from his in-laws'. Arrangements were made. He would come by train, a five-hour trip, and my wife would meet him at the station. She hadn't seen him since she worked for him one summer in Seattle ten years ago. But she and the blind man had kept in touch. They made tapes and mailed them back and forth. I wasn't enthusiastic about his visit. He was no one I knew. And his being blind bothered me. My idea of blindness came from the movies. In the movies, the blind moved slowly and never laughed. Sometimes they were led by seeing-eye dogs. A blind man in my house was not something I looked forward to.

That summer in Seattle she had needed a job. She didn't have any money. The man she was going to marry at the end of the summer was in officers' training school. He didn't have any money, either. But she was in love with the guy, and he was in love with her, etc. She'd seen something in the paper: HELP WANTED—*Reading to Blind Man*, and a telephone number. She phoned and went over, was hired on the spot. She'd worked with this blind man all summer. She read stuff to him, case studies, reports, that sort of thing. She helped him organize his little office in the county social-service department. They'd become good friends, my wife and the blind man. How do I know these things? She told me. And she told me something else. On her last day in the office, the blind man asked if he could touch her face. She agreed to this. She told me he touched his fingers to every part of her face, her nose—even her neck! She never forgot it. She even tried to write a poem about it. She was always trying to write a poem. She wrote a poem or two every year, usually after something really important had happened to her.

When we first started going out together, she showed me the poem. In the poem, she recalled his fingers and the way they had moved around over her face. In the poem, she talked about what she had felt at the time, about what went through her mind when the blind man touched her nose and lips. I can remember I didn't think much of the poem. Of course, I didn't tell her that. Maybe I just don't understand poetry. I admit it's not the first thing I reach for when I pick up something to read.

Anyway, this man who'd first enjoyed her favors, the officer-to-be, he'd been her childhood sweetheart. So okay. I'm saying that at the end of the summer she let the blind man run his hands over her face, said goodbye to him, married her childhood etc., who was now a commissioned officer, and she moved away from Seattle. But they'd kept in touch, she and the blind man. She made the first contact after a year or so. She called him up one night from an Air Force base in Alabama. She wanted to talk. They talked. He asked her to send him a tape and tell him about her life. She did this. She sent the tape. On the tape, she told the blind man about her husband and about their life together in the military. She told the blind man she loved her husband but she didn't like it where they lived and she didn't like it that he was a part of the military-industrial thing. She told the blind man she'd written a poem and he was in it. She told him that she was writing a poem about what it was like to be an Air Force officer's wife. The poem wasn't finished yet. She was still writing it. The blind man made a tape. He sent her the tape. She made a tape. This went on for years. My wife's officer was posted to one base and then another. She sent tapes from Moody AFB, McGuire, McConnell, and finally Travis, near Sacramento, where one night she got to feeling lonely and cut off from people she kept losing in that moving-around life. She got to feeling she couldn't go it another step. She went in and swallowed all the pills and capsules in the medicine chest and washed them down with a bottle of gin. Then she got into a hot bath and passed out.

But instead of dying, she got sick. She threw up. Her officer—why should he have a name? he was the childhood sweetheart, and what more does he want?—came home from somewhere, found her, and called the ambulance. In time, she put it all on a tape and sent the tape to the blind man. Over the years, she put all kinds of stuff on tapes and sent the tapes off lickety-split. Next to writing a poem every year, I think it was her chief means of recreation. On one tape, she told the blind man she'd decided to live away from her officer for a time. On another tape, she told him about her divorce. She and I began going out, and of course she told her blind man about it. She told him everything, or so it seemed to me. Once she asked me if I'd like to hear the latest tape from the blind man. This was a year ago. I was on the tape, she said. So I said okay, I'd listen to it. I got us drinks and we settled down in the living room. We made ready to listen. First she inserted the tape into the player and adjusted a couple of dials. Then she pushed a lever. The tape squeaked and someone began to talk in this loud voice. She lowered the volume. After a few minutes of harmless chitchat, I heard my own name in the mouth of this stranger, this blind man I didn't even know! And then this: "From all you've said about him, I can only conclude—" But we were interrupted, a knock at the door, something, and we didn't ever get back to the tape. Maybe it was just as well. I'd heard all I wanted to.

Now this same blind man was coming to sleep in my house.

"Maybe I could take him bowling," I said to my wife. She was at the draining board doing scalloped potatoes. She put down the knife she was using and turned around.

"If you love me," she said, "you can do this for me. If you don't love me, okay. But if you had a friend, any friend, and the friend came to visit, I'd make him feel comfortable." She wiped her hands with the dish towel.

"I don't have any blind friends," I said.

"You don't have *any* friends," she said. "Period. Besides," she said, "goddamn it, his wife's just died! Don't you understand that? The man's lost his wife!"

I didn't answer. She'd told me a little about the blind man's wife. Her name was Beulah. Beulah! That's a name for a colored woman.

"Was his wife a Negro?" I asked.

"Are you crazy?" my wife said. "Have you just flipped or something?" She picked up a potato. I saw it hit the floor, then roll under the stove. "What's wrong with you?" she said. "Are you drunk?"

"I'm just asking," I said.

Right then my wife filled me in with more detail than I cared to know. I made a drink and sat at the kitchen table to listen. Pieces of the story began to fall into place.

Beulah had gone to work for the blind man the summer after my wife had stopped working for him. Pretty soon Beulah and the blind man had themselves a church wedding. It was a little wedding—who'd want to go to such a wedding in the first place?—just the two of them, plus the minister and the minister s wife. But it was a church wedding just the same. It was what Beulah had wanted, he'd said. But even then Beulah must have been carrying the cancer in her glands. After they had been inseparable for eight years—my wife's word, *inseparable*—Beulah's health went into a rapid decline. She died in a Seattle hospital room, the blind man sitting beside the bed and holding on to her hand. They'd married, lived and worked together, slept together—had sex, sure—and then the blind man had to bury her. All this without his having ever seen what the goddamned woman looked like. It was beyond my understanding. Hearing this, I felt sorry for the blind man for a little bit. And then I found myself thinking what a pitiful life this woman must have led. Imagine a woman who could never see herself as she was seen in the eyes of her loved one. A woman who could go on day after day and never receive the smallest compliment from her beloved. A woman whose husband could never read the expression on her face, be it misery or something better. Someone who could wear makeup or not—what difference to him? She could, if she wanted, wear green eye-shadow around one eye, a straight pin in her nostril, yellow slacks and purple shoes, no matter. And then to slip off into death, the blind man's hand on her hand, his blind eyes streaming tears—I'm imagining now—her last thought maybe this: that he never even knew what she looked like, and she on an express to the grave. Robert was left with a small insurance policy and half of a twenty-peso Mexican coin. The other half of the coin went into the box with her. Pathetic.

So when the time rolled around, my wife went to the depot to pick him up. With nothing to do but wait—sure, I blamed him for that— I was having a drink and watching the TV when I heard the car pull into the drive. I got up from the sofa with my drink and went to the window to have a look.

I saw my wife laughing as she parked the car. I saw her get out of the car and shut the door. She was still wearing a smile. Just amazing. She went around to the other side of the car to where the blind man was already starting to get out. This blind man, feature this, he was wearing a full beard! A beard on a blind man! Too much, I say. The blind man reached into the back seat and dragged out a suitcase. My wife took his arm, shut the car door, and, talking all the way, moved him down the drive and then up the steps to the front porch. I turned off the TV. I finished my drink, rinsed the glass, dried my hands. Then I went to the door.

My wife said, "I want you to meet Robert. Robert, this is my husband. I've told you all about him." She was beaming. She had this blind man by his coat sleeve.

The blind man let go of his suitcase and up came his hand.

I took it. He squeezed hard, held my hand, and then he let it go.

"I feel like we've already met," he boomed.

"Likewise," I said. I didn't know what else to say. Then I said, "Welcome. I've heard a lot about you." We began to move then, a little group, from the porch into the living room, my wife guiding him by the arm. The blind man was carrying his suitcase in his other hand. My wife said things like, "To your left here, Robert. That's right. Now watch it, there's a chair. That's it. Sit down right here. This is the sofa. We just bought this sofa two weeks ago."

I started to say something about the old sofa. I'd liked that old sofa. But I didn't say anything. Then I wanted to say something else, small-talk, about the scenic ride along the Hudson. How going *to* New York, you should sit on the right-hand side of the train, and coming *from* New York, the left-hand side.

"Did you have a good train ride?" I said. "Which side of the train did you sit on, by the way?"

"What a question, which side!" my wife said. "What's it matter which side?" she said.

"I just asked," I said.

"Right side," the blind man said. "I hadn't been on a train in nearly forty years. Not since I was a kid. With my folks. That's been a long time. I'd nearly forgotten the sensation. I have winter in my beard now," he said. "So I've been told, anyway. Do I look distinguished, my dear?" the blind man said to my wife.

"You look distinguished, Robert," she said. "Robert," she said. "Robert, it's just so good to see you."

My wife finally took her eyes off the blind man and looked at me. I had the feeling she didn't like what she saw. I shrugged.

I've never met, or personally known, anyone who was blind. This blind man was late forties, a heavy-set, balding man with stooped shoulders, as if he carried a great weight there. He wore brown slacks, brown shoes, a light-brown shirt, a tie, a sports coat. Spiffy. He also had this full beard. But he didn't use a cane and he didn't wear dark glasses. I'd always thought dark glasses were a must for the blind. Fact was, I wished he had a pair. At first glance, his eyes looked like anyone else's eyes. But if you looked close, there was something different about them. Too much white in the iris, for one thing, and the pupils seemed to move around in the sockets without his knowing it or being able to stop it. Creepy. As I stared at his face, I saw the left pupil turn in toward his nose while the other made an effort to keep in one place. But it was only an effort, for that eye was on the roam without his knowing it or wanting it to be.

I said, "Let me get you a drink. What's your pleasure? We have a little of everything. It's one of our pastimes."

"Bub, I'm a Scotch man myself," he said fast enough in this big voice.

"Right," I said. Bub! "Sure you are. I knew it."

He let his fingers touch his suitcase, which was sitting alongside the sofa. He was taking his bearings. I didn't blame him for that.

"I'll move that up to your room," my wife said.

"No, that's fine," the blind man said loudly. "It can go up when I go up."

"A little water with the Scotch?" I said.

"Very little," he said.

"I knew it," I said.

He said, "Just a tad. The Irish actor, Barry Fitzgerald? I'm like that fellow. When I drink water, Fitzgerald said, I drink water. When I drink whiskey, I drink whiskey." My wife laughed. The blind man brought his hand up under his beard. He lifted his beard slowly and let it drop.

I did the drinks, three big glasses of Scotch with a splash of water in each. Then we made ourselves comfortable and talked about Robert's travels. First the long flight from the West Coast to Connecticut, we covered that. Then from Connecticut up here by train. We had another drink concerning that leg of the trip.

I remembered having read somewhere that the blind didn't smoke because, as speculation had it, they couldn't see the smoke they exhaled. I thought I knew that much and that much only about blind people. But this blind man smoked his cigarette down to the nubbin and then lit another one. This blind man filled his ashtray and my wife emptied it.

When we sat down at the table for dinner, we had another drink. My wife heaped Robert's plate with cube steak, scalloped potatoes, green beans. I buttered him up two slices of bread. I said, "Here's bread and butter for you." I swallowed some of my drink. "Now let us pray," I said, and the blind man lowered his head. My wife looked at me, her mouth agape. "Pray the phone won't ring and the food doesn't get cold," I said.

We dug in. We ate everything there was to eat on the table. We ate like there was no tomorrow. We didn't talk. We ate. We scarfed. We grazed that table. We were into serious eating. The blind man had right away located his foods, he knew just where everything was on his plate. I watched with admiration as he used his knife and fork on the meat. He'd cut two pieces of meat, fork the meat into his mouth, and then go all out for the scalloped potatoes, the beans next, and then he'd tear off a hunk of buttered bread and eat that. He'd follow this up with a big drink of milk. It didn't seem to bother him to use his fingers once in a while, either.

We finished everything, including half a strawberry pie. For a few moments, we sat as if stunned. Sweat beaded on our faces. Finally, we got up from the table and left the dirty plates. We didn't look back. We took ourselves into the living room and sank into our places again.

Robert and my wife sat on the sofa. I took the big chair. We had us two or three more drinks while they talked about the major things that had come to pass for them in the past ten years. For the most part, I just listened. Now and then I joined in. I didn't want him to think I'd left the room, and I didn't want her to think I was feeling left out. They talked of things that had happened to them—to them!—these past ten years. I waited in vain to hear my name on my wife's sweet lips: "And then my dear husband came into my life"—something like that. But I heard nothing of the sort. More talk of Robert. Robert had done a little of everything, it seemed, a regular blind jack-of-all-trades. But most recently he and his wife had had an Amway distributorship, from which, I gathered, they'd earned their living, such as it was. The blind man was also a ham radio operator. He talked in his loud voice about conversations he'd had with fellow operators in Guam, in the Philippines, in Alaska, and even in Tahiti. He said he'd have a lot of friends there if he ever wanted to go visit those places. From time to time, he'd turn his blind face toward me, put his hand under his beard, ask me something. How long had I been in my present position? (Three years.) Did I like my work? (I didn't.) Was I going to stay with it? (What were the options?) Finally, when I thought he was beginning to run down, I got up and turned on the TV.

My wife looked at me with irritation. She was heading toward a boil. Then she looked at the blind man and said, "Robert, do you have a TV?"

The blind man said, "My dear, I have two TVs. I have a color set and a black-and-white thing, an old relic. It's funny, but if I turn the TV on, and I'm always turning it on, I turn on the color set. It's funny, don't you think?"

I didn't know what to say to that. I had absolutely nothing to say to that. No opinion. So I watched the news program and tried to listen to what the announcer was saying.

"This is a color TV," the blind man said. "Don't ask me how, but I can tell."

"We traded up a while ago," I said.

The blind man had another taste of his drink. He lifted his beard, sniffed it, and let it fall. He leaned forward on the sofa. He positioned his ashtray on the coffee table, then put the lighter to his cigarette. He leaned back on the sofa and crossed his legs at the ankles.

My wife covered her mouth, and then she yawned. She stretched. She said, "I think I'll go upstairs and put on my robe. I think I'll change into something else. Robert, you make yourself comfortable," she said.

"I'm comfortable," the blind man said.

"I want you to feel comfortable in this house," she said.

"I am comfortable," the blind man said.

After she'd left the room, he and I listened to the weather report and then to the sports roundup. By that time, she'd been gone so long I didn't know if she was going to come back. I thought she might have gone to bed. I wished she'd come back downstairs. I didn't want to be left alone with a blind man. I asked him if he wanted another drink, and he said sure. Then I asked if he wanted to smoke some dope with me. I said I'd just rolled a number. I hadn't, but I planned to do so in about two shakes.

"I'll try some with you," he said.

"Damn right," I said. "That's the stuff."

I got our drinks and sat down on the sofa with him. Then I rolled us two fat numbers. I lit one and passed it. I brought it to his fingers. He took it and inhaled.

"Hold it as long as you can," I said. I could tell he didn't know the first thing.

My wife came back downstairs wearing her pink robe and her pink slippers.

"What do I smell?" she said.

"We thought we'd have us some cannabis," I said.

My wife gave me a savage look. Then she looked at the blind man and said, "Robert, I didn't know you smoked."

He said, "I do now, my dear. There's a first time for everything. But I don't feel anything yet."

"This stuff is pretty mellow," I said. "This stuff is mild. It's dope you can reason with," I said. "It doesn't mess you up."

"Not much it doesn't, bub," he said, and laughed.

My wife sat on the sofa between the blind man and me. I passed her the number. She took it and toked and then passed it back to me. "Which way is this going?" she said. Then she said, "I shouldn't be smoking this. I can hardly keep my eyes open as it is. That dinner did me in. I shouldn't have eaten so much."

"It was the strawberry pie," the blind man said. "That's what did it," he said, and he laughed his big laugh. Then he shook his head.

"There's more strawberry pie," I said.

"Do you want some more, Robert?" my wife said.

"Maybe in a little while," he said.

We gave our attention to the TV. My wife yawned again. She said, "Your bed is made up when you feel like going to bed, Robert. I know you must have had a long day. When you're ready to go to bed, say so." She pulled his arm. "Robert?"

He came to and said, "I've had a real nice time. This beats tapes, doesn't it?"

I said, "Coming at you," and I put the number between his fingers. He inhaled, held the smoke, and then let it go. It was like he'd been doing it since he was nine years old.

"Thanks, bub," he said. "But I think this is all for me. I think I'm beginning to feel it," he said. He held the burning roach out for my wife.

"Same here," she said. "Ditto. Me, too." She took the roach and passed it to me. "I may just sit here for a while between you two guys with my eyes closed. But don't let me bother you, okay? Either one of you. If it bothers you, say so. Otherwise, I may just sit here with my eyes closed until you're ready to go to bed," she said. "Your bed's made up, Robert, when you're ready. It's right next to our room at the top of the stairs. We'll show you up when you're ready. You wake me up now, you guys, if I fall asleep." She said that and then she closed her eyes and went to sleep.

The news program ended. I got up and changed the channel. I sat back down on the sofa. I wished my wife hadn't pooped out. Her head lay across the back of the sofa, her mouth open. She'd turned so that her robe had slipped away from her legs, exposing a juicy thigh. I reached to draw her robe back over her, and it was then that I glanced at the blind man. What the hell! I flipped the robe open again.

"You say when you want some strawberry pie," I said.

"I will," he said.

I said, "Are you tired? Do you want me to take you up to your bed? Are you ready to hit the hay?"

"Not yet," he said. "No, I'll stay up with you, bub. If that's all right. I'll stay up until you're ready to turn in. We haven't had a chance to talk. Know what I mean? I feel like me and her monopolized the evening." He lifted his beard and he let it fall. He picked up his cigarettes and his lighter.

"That's all right," I said. Then I said, "I'm glad for the company."

And I guess I was. Every night I smoked dope and stayed up as long as I could before I fell asleep. My wife and I hardly ever went to bed at the same time. When I did go to sleep, I had these dreams. Sometimes I'd wake up from one of them, my heart going crazy.

Something about the church and the Middle Ages was on the TV. Not your run-of-the-mill TV fare. I wanted to watch something else. I turned to the other channels. But there was nothing on them, either. So I turned back to the first channel and apologized.

"Bub, it's all right," the blind man said. "It's fine with me. Whatever you want to watch is okay. I'm always learning something. Learning never ends. It won't hurt me to learn something tonight. I got ears," he said.

We didn't say anything for a time. He was leaning forward with his head turned at me, his right ear aimed in the direction of the set. Very disconcerting. Now and then his eyelids drooped and then they snapped open again. Now and then he put his fingers into his beard and tugged, like he was thinking about something he was hearing on the television.

On the screen, a group of men wearing cowls was being set upon and tormented by men dressed in skeleton costumes and men dressed as devils. The men dressed as devils wore devil masks, horns, and long tails. This pageant was part of a procession. The Englishman who was narrating the thing said it took place in Spain once a year. I tried to explain to the blind man what was happening.

"Skeletons," he said. "I know about skeletons," he said, and he nodded.

The TV showed this one cathedral. Then there was a long, slow look at another one. Finally, the picture switched to the famous one in Paris, with its flying buttresses and its spires reaching up to the clouds. The camera pulled away to show the whole of the cathedral rising above the skyline.

There were times when the Englishman who was telling the thing would shut up, would simply let the camera move around over the cathedrals. Or else the camera would tour the countryside, men in fields walking behind oxen. I waited as long as I could. Then I felt I had to say something. I said, "They're showing the outside of this cathedral now.

Gargoyles. Little statues carved to look like monsters. Now I guess they're in Italy. Yeah, they're in Italy. There's paintings on the walls of this one church."

"Are those fresco paintings, bub?" he asked, and he sipped from his drink.

I reached for my glass. But it was empty. I tried to remember what I could remember. "You're asking me are those frescoes?" I said, "That's a good question. I don't know."

The camera moved to a cathedral outside Lisbon. The differences in the Portuguese cathedral compared with the French and Italian were not that great. But they were there. Mostly the interior stuff. Then something occurred to me, and I said, "Something has occurred to me. Do you have any idea what a cathedral is? What they look like, that is? Do you follow me? If somebody says cathedral to you, do you have any notion what they're talking about? Do you know the difference between that and a Baptist church, say?"

He let the smoke dribble from his mouth. "I know they took hundreds of workers fifty or a hundred years to build," he said. "I just heard the man say that, of course. I know generations of the same families worked on a cathedral. I heard him say that, too. The men who began their life's work on them, they never lived to see the completion of their work. In that wise, bub, they're no different from the rest of us, right?" He laughed. Then his eyelids drooped again. His head nodded. He seemed to be snoozing. Maybe he was imagining himself in Portugal. The TV was showing another cathedral now. This one was in Germany. The Englishman's voice droned on. "Cathedrals," the blind man said. He sat up and rolled his head back and forth. "If you want the truth, bub, that's about all I know. What I just said. What I heard him say. But maybe you could describe one to me? I wish you'd do it. I'd like that. If you want to know, I really don't have a good idea."

I stared hard at the shot of the cathedral on the TV. How could I even begin to describe it? But say my life depended on it. Say my life was being threatened by an insane guy who said I had to do it or else.

I stared some more at the cathedral before the picture flipped off into the countryside. There was no use. I turned to the blind man and said, "To begin with, they're very tall." I was looking around the room for clues. "They reach way up. Up and up. Toward the sky. They're so big, some of them, they have to have these supports. To help hold them up, so to speak. These supports are called buttresses. They remind me of viaducts, for some reason. But maybe you don't know viaducts, either? Sometimes the cathedrals have devils and such carved into the front. Sometimes lords and ladies. Don't ask me why this is," I said.

He was nodding. The whole upper part of his body seemed to be moving back and forth.

"I'm not doing so good, am I?" I said.

He stopped nodding and leaned forward on the edge of the sofa. As he listened to me, he was running his fingers through his beard. I wasn't getting through to him, I could see that. But he waited for me to go on just the same. He nodded, like he was trying to encourage me. I tried to think what else to say. "They're really big," I said. "They're massive. They're built of stone. Marble, too, sometimes. In those olden days, when they built cathedrals, men wanted to be close to God. In those olden days, God was an important part of everyone's life. You could tell this from their cathedral-building. I'm sorry," I said, "but it looks like that's the best I can do for you. I'm just no good at it."

"That's all right, bub," the blind man said. "Hey, listen. I hope you don't mind my asking you. Can I ask you something? Let me ask you a simple question, yes or no. I'm just curious and there's no offense. You're my host. But let me ask if you are in any way religious? You don't mind my asking?"

I shook my head. He couldn't see that, though. A wink is the same as a nod to a blind man. "I guess I don't believe in it. In anything. Sometimes it's hard. You know what I'm saying?"

"Sure, I do," he said.

"Right," I said.

The Englishman was still holding forth. My wife sighed in her sleep. She drew a long breath and went on with her sleeping.

"You'll have to forgive me," I said. "But I can't tell you what a cathedral looks like. It just isn't in me to do it. I can't do any more than I've done."

The blind man sat very still, his head down, as he listened to me.

I said, "The truth is, cathedrals don't mean anything special to me. Nothing. Cathedrals. They're something to look at on late-night TV. That's all they are."

It was then that the blind man cleared his throat. He brought something up. He took a handkerchief from his back pocket. Then he said,

"I get it, bub. It's okay. It happens. Don't worry about it," he said. "Hey, listen to me. Will you do me a favor? I got an idea. Why don't you find us some heavy paper? And a pen. We'll do something. We'll draw one together. Get us a pen and some heavy paper. Go on, bub, get the stuff," he said.

So I went upstairs. My legs felt like they didn't have any strength in them. They felt like they did after I'd done some running. In my wife's room, I looked around. I found some ballpoints in a little basket on her table. And then I tried to think where to look for the kind of paper he was talking about.

Downstairs, in the kitchen, I found a shopping bag with onion skins in the bottom of the bag. I emptied the bag and shook it. I brought it into the living room and sat down with it near his legs. I moved some things, smoothed the wrinkles from the bag, spread it out on the coffee table.

The blind man got down from the sofa and sat next to me on the carpet.

He ran his fingers over the paper. He went up and down the sides of the paper. The edges, even the edges. He fingered the corners.

"All right," he said. "All right, let's do her."

He found my hand, the hand with the pen. He closed his hand over my hand. "Go ahead, bub, draw," he said. "Draw. You'll see. I'll follow along with you. It'll be okay. Just begin now like I'm telling you. You'll see. Draw," the blind man said.

So I began. First I drew a box that looked like a house. It could have been the house I lived in. Then I put a roof on it. At either end of the roof, I drew spires. Crazy.

"Swell," he said. "Terrific. You're doing fine," he said. "Never thought anything like this could happen in your lifetime, did you, bub? Well, it's a strange life, we all know that. Go on now. Keep it up."

I put in windows with arches. I drew flying buttresses. I hung great doors. I couldn't stop. The TV station went off the air. I put down the pen and closed and opened my fingers. The blind man felt around over the paper. He moved the tips of his fingers over the paper, all over what I had drawn, and he nodded.

"Doing fine," the blind man said.

I took up the pen again, and he found my hand. I kept at it. I'm no artist. But I kept drawing just the same.

My wife opened up her eyes and gazed at us. She sat up on the sofa, her robe hanging open. She said, "What are you doing? Tell me, I want to know."

I didn't answer her.

The blind man said, "We're drawing a cathedral. Me and him are working on it. Press hard," he said to me. "That's right. That's good," he said. "Sure. You got it, bub. I can tell. You didn't think you could. But you can, can't you? You're cooking with gas now. You know what I'm saying? We're going to really have us something here in a minute. How's the old arm?" he said. "Put some people in there now. What's a cathedral without people?"

My wife said, "What's going on? Robert, what are you doing? What's going on?"

"It's all right," he said to her. "Close your eyes now," the blind man said to me.

I did it. I closed them just like he said.

"Are they closed?" he said. "Don't fudge."

"They're closed," I said.

"Keep them that way," he said. He said, "Don't stop now. Draw."

So we kept on with it. His fingers rode my fingers as my hand went over the paper. It was like nothing else in my life up to now.

Then he said, "I think that's it. I think you got it," he said. "Take a look. What do you think?"

But I had my eyes closed. I thought I'd keep them that way for a little longer. I thought it was something I ought to do.

"Well?" he said. "Are you looking?"

My eyes were still closed. I was in my house. I knew that. But I didn't feel like I was inside anything.

"It's really something," I said.

*—1981*

*Margaret Atwood (b. 1939) is a leading figure among Canadian writers, with a huge international following. Equally skilled as a poet and fiction writer, she has used her considerable reputation to support a variety of causes, including PEN International. Born in Ottawa, Ontario, she graduated from the University of Toronto in 1962, and later did graduate work at Radcliffe and Harvard. She has authored over a dozen poetry collections, a dozen novels, including the dystopias* The Handmaid's Tale *(1985) and* Oryx and Crake *(2003), and half a dozen collections of short fiction, including* The Tent *(2006). She has also written literary criticism, including* Survival: A Thematic Guide to Canadian Literature *(1972), and several books for children. Her long list of awards includes the Giller Prize, the Man Booker Prize, and the Governor General's Award. She continues to be an inventive and prolific writer of works that reflect her feminist concerns, her interest in classical and popular mythology, and her increasing concern for the future of humanity.*

# Margaret Atwood
# Happy Endings

John and Mary meet.
What happens next?
If you want a happy ending, try A.

### A

John and Mary fall in love and get married. They both have worthwhile and remunerative jobs which they find stimulating and challenging. They buy a charming house. Real estate values go up. Eventually, when they can afford live-in help, they have two children, to whom they are devoted. The children turn out well. John and Mary have a stimulating and challenging sex life and worthwhile friends. They go on fun vacations together. They retire. They both have hobbies which they find stimulating and challenging. Eventually they die. This is the end of the story.

### B

Mary falls in love with John but John doesn't fall in love with Mary. He merely uses her body for selfish pleasure and ego gratification of a tepid kind. He comes to her apartment twice a week and she cooks him dinner, you'll notice that he doesn't even consider her worth the price of a dinner out, and after he's eaten the dinner he fucks her and after that he falls asleep, while she does the dishes so he won't think she's untidy, having all those dirty dishes lying around, and puts on fresh lipstick so she'll look good when he wakes up, but when he wakes up he doesn't even notice, he puts on his socks and his shorts and his pants and his shirt and his tie and his shoes, the reverse order from the one in which he took them off. He doesn't take off Mary's clothes, she takes them off herself, she acts as if she's dying for it every time, not because she likes sex exactly, she doesn't, but she wants John to think she does because if they do it often enough surely he'll get used to her, he'll come to depend on her and they will get married, but John goes out the door with hardly so much as a good-night and three days later he turns up at six o'clock and they do the whole thing over again.

Mary gets run-down. Crying is bad for your face, everyone knows that and so does Mary but she can't stop. People at work notice. Her friends tell her John is a rat, a pig, a dog, he isn't good enough for her, but she can't believe it. Inside John, she thinks, is another John, who is much nicer. This other John will emerge like a butterfly from a cocoon, a Jack from a box, a pit from a prune, if the first John is only squeezed enough.

One evening John complains about the food. He has never complained about the food before. Mary is hurt.

Her friends tell her they've seen him in a restaurant with another woman, whose name is Madge. It's not even Madge that finally gets to Mary: it's the restaurant. John has never taken Mary to a restaurant. Mary collects all the sleeping pills and aspirins she can find, and takes them and a half a bottle of sherry. You can see what kind of a woman she is by the fact that it's not even whiskey. She leaves a note for John. She hopes he'll discover her and get her to the hospital in time and repent and then they can get married, but this fails to happen and she dies.

John marries Madge and everything continues as in A.

## C

John, who is an older man, falls in love with Mary, and Mary, who is only twenty-two, feels sorry for him because he's worried about his hair falling out. She sleeps with him even though she's not in love with him. She met him at work. She's in love with someone called James, who is twenty-two also and not yet ready to settle down.

John on the contrary settled down long ago: this is what is bothering him. John has a steady, respectable job and is getting ahead in his field, but Mary isn't impressed by him, she's impressed by James, who has a motorcycle and a fabulous record collection. But James is often away on his motorcycle, being free. Freedom isn't the same for girls, so in the meantime Mary spends Thursday evenings with John. Thursdays are the only days John can get away.

John is married to a woman called Madge and they have two children, a charming house which they bought just before the real estate values went up, and hobbies which they find stimulating and challenging, when they have the time. John tells Mary how important she is to him, but of course he can't leave his wife because a commitment is a commitment. He goes on about this more than is necessary and Mary finds it boring, but older men can keep it up longer so on the whole she has a fairly good time.

One day James breezes in on his motorcycle with some top-grade California hybrid and James and Mary get higher than you'd believe possible and they climb into bed. Everything becomes very underwater, but along comes John, who has a key to Mary's apartment. He finds them stoned and entwined. He's hardly in any position to be jealous, considering Madge, but nevertheless he's overcome with despair. Finally he's middle-aged, in two years he'll be bald as an egg and he can't stand it. He purchases a handgun, saying he needs it for target practice—this is the thin part of the plot, but it can be dealt with later—and shoots the two of them and himself.

Madge, after a suitable period of mourning, marries an understanding man called Fred and everything continues as in A, but under different names.

### D

Fred and Madge have no problems. They get along exceptionally well and are good at working out any little difficulties that may arise. But their charming house is by the seashore and one day a giant tidal wave approaches. Real estate values go down. The rest of the story is about what caused the tidal wave and how they escape from it. They do, though thousands drown, but Fred and Madge are virtuous and lucky. Finally on high ground they clasp each other, wet and dripping and grateful, and continue as in A.

E

Yes, but Fred has a bad heart. The rest of the story is about how kind and understanding they both are until Fred dies. Then Madge devotes herself to charity work until the end of A. If you like, it can be "Madge," "cancer," "guilty and confused," and "bird watching."

F

If you think this is all too bourgeois, make John a revolutionary and Mary a counterespionage agent and see how far that gets you. Remember, this is Canada. You'll still end up with A, though in between you may get a lustful brawling saga of passionate involvement, a chronicle of our times, sort of.

You'll have to face it, the endings are the same however you slice it. Don't be deluded by any other endings, they're all fake, either deliberately fake, with malicious intent to deceive, or just motivated by excessive optimism if not by downright sentimentality.

The only authentic ending is the one provided here:

*John and Mary die. John and Mary die. John and Mary die.*

So much for endings. Beginnings are always more fun. True connoisseurs, however, are known to favor the stretch in between, since it's the hardest to do anything with.

That's about all that can be said for plots, which anyway are just one thing after another, a what and a what and a what.

Now try How and Why.

—*1983*

*Ama Ata Aidoo (b. 1942) was born the daughter of a chief in central Ghana and went on to study at the University of Ghana, where she produced her first play. She has since become an important African writer, producing plays, poems, short stories, and novels that explore questions of political and cultural autonomy as well as women's liberation. Though Ghana received independence in 1957, the period that followed was one of disillusionment. In "The Message," a story from* No Sweetness Here *(1970), Aidoo explores the challenging intersection between Western and African cultures with wit and insight.*

## *Ama Ata Aidoo*
# The Message

"Look here my sister, it should not be said but they say they opened her up."

"They opened her up?"

"Yes, opened her up."

"And the baby removed?"

"Yes, the baby removed."

"Yes, the baby removed."

"I say . . ."

"They do not say, my sister."

"Have you heard it?"

"What?"

"This and this and that . . ."

"A-a-ah! that is it . . ."

"*Meewuo!*"

"They don't say *meewuo* . . ."

"And how is she?"

"Am I not here with you? Do I know the highway which leads to Cape Coast?"

"Hmmm . . ."

"And anyway how can she live? What is it like even giving birth with a stomach which is whole . . . eh? . . . I am asking you. And if you are always standing on the brink of death who go to war with a stomach that is whole, then how would she do whose stomach is open to the winds?"

"Oh, *poo*, pity . . ."

"I say . . ."

My little bundle, come. You and I are going to Cape Coast today.

I am taking one of her own cloths with me, just in case. These people on the coast do not know how to do a thing and I am not going to have anybody mishandling my child's body. I hope they give it to me. Horrible things I have heard done to people's bodies. Cutting them up and using them for instructions. Whereas even murderers still have decent burials.

I see Mensima coming. . . . And there is Nkama too . . . and Adwoa Meenu. . . . Now they are coming to . . . *"poo* pity" me. Witches, witches, witches . . . they have picked mine up while theirs prosper around them, children, grandchildren and great-grandchildren—theirs shoot up like mushrooms.

"Esi, we have heard of your misfortune . . ."

"That our little lady's womb has been opened up . . ."

"And her baby removed . . ."

Thank you very much.

"Has she lived through it?"

I do not know.

"Esi, bring her here, back home whatever happens."

*Yoo*, thank you. If the government's people allow it, I shall bring her home.

"And have you got ready your things?"

Yes. . . . No.

I cannot even think well.

It feels so noisy in my head. . . . Oh my little child. . . . I am wasting time. . . . And so I am going . . .

Yes, to Cape Coast.

No, I do not know anyone there now but do you think no one would show me the way to this big hospital . . . if I asked around?

Hmmm . . . it's me has ended up like this. I was thinking that everything was alright now. . . . *Yoo*. And thank you too. Shut the door for me when you are leaving. You may stay too long outside if you wait for me, so go home and be about your business. I will let you know when I bring her in.

"Maami Amfoa, where are you going?"

My daughter, I am going to Cape Coast.

"And what is our old mother going to do with such swift steps? Is it serious?"

My daughter, it is very serious.

"Mother, may God go with you."

*Yoo,* my daughter.

"Eno, and what calls at this hour of the day?"

They want me in Cape Coast.

"Does my friend want to go and see how much the city has changed since we went there to meet the new Wesleyan Chairman, twenty years ago?"

My sister, do you think I have knees to go parading on the streets of Cape Coast?

"Is it heavy?"

Yes, very heavy indeed. They have opened up my grandchild at the hospital, *hi, hi, hi. . . .*

"Eno *due, due, due . . .* I did not know. May God go with you. . . ."

Thank you. *Yaa.*

"O, the world!"

"It's her grandchild. The only daughter of her only son. Do you remember Kojo Amisa who went to sodja and fell in the great war, overseas?"

"Yes, it's his daughter. . . ."

. . . O, *poo,* pity.

"Kobina, run to the street, tell Draba Anan to wait for Nana Amfoa."

". . . Draba Anan, Draba, my mother says I must come and tell you to wait for Nana Amfoa."

"And where is she?"

"There she comes."

"Just look at how she hops like a bird . . . does she think we are going to be here all day? And anyway we are full already . . ."

O, you drivers!

"What have drivers done?"

"And do you think it shows respect when you speak in this way? It is only that things have not gone right; but she could, at least have been your mother. . . ."

"But what have I said? I have not insulted her. I just think that only Youth must be permitted to see Cape Coast, the town of the Dear and Expensive. . . ."

"And do you think she is going on a peaceful journey? The only daughter of her only son has been opened up and her baby removed from her womb."

O . . . God.

O

O

O

*Poo*, pity.

"Me . . . *poo*—pity, I am right about our modern wives I always say they are useless as compared with our mothers."

"You drivers!"

"Now what have your modern wives done?"

"Am I not right what I always say about them?"

"You go and watch them in the big towns. All so thin and dry as sticks—you can literally blow them away with your breath. No decent flesh anywhere. Wooden chairs groan when they meet with their hard exteriors."

"O you drivers. . . ."

"But of course all drivers . . ."

"What have I done? Don't all my male passengers agree with me? These modern girls. . . . Now here is one who cannot even have a baby in a decent way. But must have the baby removed from her stomach. *Tchiaa!*"

"What . . ."

"Here is the old woman."

"Whose grandchild . . . ?"

"Yes."

"Nana, I hear you are coming to Cape Coast with us."

Yes my master.

"We nearly left you behind but we heard it was you and that it is a heavy journey you are making."

Yes my master . . . thank you my master.

"Push up please . . . push up. Won't you push up? Why do you all sit looking at me with such eyes as if I was a block of wood?"

"It is not that there is nowhere to push up to. Five fat women should go on that seat, but look at you!"

"And our own grandmother here is none too plump herself. . . . Nana, if they won't push, come to the front seat with me."

". . . *Hei*, scholar, go to the back. . . ."

". . . And do not scowl on me. I know your sort too well. Something tells me you do not have any job at all. As for that suit you are wearing and looking so grand in, you hired or borrowed it. . . ."

"Oh you drivers!"

Oh you drivers . . .

The scholar who read this telegram thing, said it was made about three days ago. My lady's husband sent it. . . . Three days. . . . God— that is too long ago. Have they buried her . . . where? Or did they cut her up. . . . I should not think about it . . . or something will happen to me. Eleven or twelve . . . Efua Panyin, Okuma, Kwame Gyasi and who else? But they should not have left me here. Sometimes . . . ah, I hate this nausea. But it is this smell of petrol. Now I have remembered I never could travel in a lorry. I always was so sick. But now I hope at least that will not happen. These young people will think it is because I am old and they will laugh. At least if I knew the child of my child was alive, it would have been good. And the little things she sent me. . . . Sometimes some people like Mensima and Nkansa make me feel as if I had been a barren woman instead of only one with whom infant-mortality pledged friendship . . .

I will give her that set of earrings, bracelet and chain which Odwumfo Ata made for me. It is the most beautiful and the most expensive thing I have. . . . It does not hurt me to think that I am going to die very soon and have them and their children gloating over my things. After all what did they swallow my children for? It does not hurt me at all. If I had been someone else, I would have given them all away before I died. But it does not matter. They can share their own curse. Now, that is the end of me and my roots. . . . Eternal death has worked like a warrior rat, with diabolical sense of duty, to gnaw my bottom. Everything is finished now. The vacant lot is swept and the scraps of old sugar-cane pulp, dry sticks and bunches of hair burnt . . . how it reeks, the smoke!

"O, Nana do not weep . . ."

"Is the old woman weeping?"

"If the only child of your only child died, won't you weep?"

"Why do you ask me? Did I know her grandchild is dead?"

"Where have you been, not in this lorry? Where were your ears when we were discussing it?"

"I do not go putting my mouth in other people's affairs . . ."

"So what?"

"So go and die."

"*Hei, hei*, it is prohibited to quarrel in my lorry."

"Draba, here is me, sitting quiet and this lady of muscles and bones being cheeky to me."

"Look, I can beat you."

"Beat me . . . beat me . . . let's see."

"*Hei*, you are not civilised, eh?"

"Keep quiet and let us think, both of you, or I will put you down."

"Nana, do not weep. There is God above."

Thank you my master.

"But we are in Cape Coast already."

*Meewuo!* My God, hold me tight or something will happen to me.

My master, I will come down here.

"O Nana, I thought you said you were going to the hospital. . . . We are not there yet."

I am saying maybe I will get down here and ask my way around.

"Nana, you do not know these people, eh? They are very impudent here. They have no use for old age. So they do not respect it. Sit down, I will take you there."

Are you going there, my master?

"No, but I will take you there."

Ah, my master, your old mother thanks you. Do not shed a tear when you hear of my death . . . my master, your old mother thanks you.

I hear there is somewhere where they keep corpses until their owners claim them . . . if she has been buried, then I must find her husband . . . Esi Amfoa, what did I come to do under this sky? I have buried all my children and now I am going to bury my only grandchild!

"Nana we are there."

Is this the hospital?

"Yes, Nana. What is your child's name?"

Esi Amfoa. Her father named her after me.

"Do you know her European name?"

No, my master.

"What shall we do?"

". . . *Ei* lady, Lady Nurse, we are looking for somebody."

"You are looking for somebody and can you read? If you cannot, you must ask someone what the rules in the hospital are. You can only come and visit people at three o'clock."

Lady, please. She was my only grandchild . . .

"Who? And anyway, it is none of our business."

"Nana, you must be patient . . . and not cry . . ."

"Old woman, why are you crying, it is not allowed here. No one must make any noise . . ."

My lady, I am sorry but she was all I had.

"Who? Oh, are you the old woman who is looking for somebody?"

Yes.

"Who is he?"

She was my granddaughter—the only child of my only son.

"I mean, what was her name?"

Esi Amfoa.

"Esi Amfoa . . . Esi Amfoa. I am sorry, we do not have anyone whom they call like that here."

Is that it?

"Nana, I told you they may know only her European name here."

My master, what shall we do then?

"What is she ill with?"

She came here to have a child . . .

". . . And they say, they opened her stomach and removed the baby."

"Oh . . . oh, I see."

My Lord, hold me tight so that nothing will happen to me now.

"I see. It is the Caesarean case."

"Nurse, you know her?"

And when I take her back, Anona Ebusuafo will say that I did not wait for them to come with me . . .

"Yes. Are you her brother?"

"No. I am only the driver who brought the old woman."

"Did she bring all her clan?"

"No. She came alone."

"Strange thing for a villager to do."

I hope they have not cut her up already.

"Did she bring a whole bag full of cassava and plantain and kenkey?"

"No. She has only her little bundle."

"Follow me. But you must not make any noise. This is not the hour for coming here . . ."

My master, does she know her?

"Yes."

I hear it is very cold where they put them . . .

It was feeding time for new babies. When old Esi Amfoa saw young Esi Amfoa, the latter was all neat and nice. White sheets and all. She did not see the beautiful stitches under the sheets. "This woman is a tough bundle," Dr. Gyamfi had declared after the identical twins had been removed, the last stitches had been threaded off and Mary Koomson, alias Esi Amfoa, had come to.

The old woman somersaulted into the room and lay groaning, not screaming, by the bed. For was not her last pot broken? So they lay them in state even in hospitals and not always cut them up for instruction?

The Nursing Sister was furious. Young Esi Amfoa spoke. And this time old Esi Amfoa wept loud and hard—wept all her tears.

Scrappy nurse-under-training, Jessy Treeson, second-generation-Cape-Coaster-her-grandmother-still-remembered-at-Egyaa No. 7 said, "As for these villagers," and giggled.

Draba Anan looked hard at Jessy Treeson, looked hard at her, all of her: her starched uniform, apron and cap . . . and then dismissed them all. . . . "Such a cassava stick . . . but maybe I will break my toe if I kicked at her buttocks," he thought.

And by the bed the old woman was trying hard to rise and look at the only pot which had refused to get broken.

*—1970*

**Thomas King** *(b. 1943) was born in California of Cherokee and Greek descent. Since 1980 he has spent much of his time in Canada, most recently as professor of Native literature at the University of Guelph. In "A Coyote Columbus Story," originally published for children in 1992, and then in a collection intended for adults,* One Good Story, That One *(1993), he plays with both oral traditions and the Trickster figure of Native mythology. His fiction includes* Medicine River *(1990),* Green Grass, Running Water *(1993),* Truth and Bright Water *(1999), and* A Short History of Indians in Canada: Stories *(2005).*

## *Thomas King*
# A Coyote Columbus Story

You know, Coyote came by my place the other day. She was going to a party. She had her party hat and she had her party whistle and she had her party rattle.

I'm going to a party, she says.

Yes, I says, I can see that.

It is a party for Christopher Columbus, says Coyote. That is the one who found America. That is the one who found Indians.

Boy, that Coyote is one silly Coyote. You got to watch out for her. Some of Coyote's stories have got Coyote tails and some of Coyote's stories are covered with scraggy Coyote fur but all of Coyote's stories are bent.

Christopher Columbus didn't find America, I says. Christopher Columbus didn't find Indians, either. You got a tail on that story.

Oh no, says Coyote. I read it in a book.

Must have been a Coyote book, I says.

No, no, no, no, says Coyote. It was a history book. Big red one. All about how Christopher Columbus sailed the ocean blue looking for America and the Indians.

Sit down, I says. Have some tea. We're going to have to do this story right. We're going to have to do this story now.

It was all Old Coyote's fault, I tell Coyote, and here is how the story goes. Here is what really happened.

So.

Old Coyote loved to play ball, you know. She played ball all day and all night. She would throw the ball and she would hit the ball and she would run and catch the ball. But playing ball by herself was boring, so she sang a song and she danced a dance and she thought about playing ball and pretty soon along came some Indians. Old Coyote and the Indians became very good friends. You are sure a good friend, says those Indians. Yes, that's true, says Old Coyote.

But, you know, whenever Old Coyote and the Indians played ball, Old Coyote always won. She always won because she made up the rules. That sneaky one made up the rules and she always won because she could do that.

That's not fair, says the Indians. Friends don't do that.

That's the rules, says Old Coyote. Let's play some more. Maybe you will win the next time. But they don't.

You keep changing the rules, says those Indians.

No, no, no, no, says Old Coyote. You are mistaken. And then she changes the rules again.

So, after a while, those Indians find better things to do.

Some of them go fishing.

Some of them go shopping.

Some of them go to a movie.

Some of them go on a vacation.

Those Indians got better things to do than play ball with Old Coyote and those changing rules.

So, Old Coyote doesn't have anyone to play with.

So, she has to play by herself.

So, she gets bored.

When Old Coyote gets bored, anything can happen. Stick around. Big trouble is coming, I can tell you that.

Well. That silly one sings a song and she dances a dance and she thinks about playing ball. But she's thinking about changing those rules, too, and she doesn't watch what she is making up out of her head. So pretty soon, she makes three ships.

Hmmmm, says Old Coyote, where did those ships come from?

And pretty soon, she makes some people on those ships.

Hmmmm, says Old Coyote, where did those people come from?

And pretty soon, she makes some people on the beach with flags and funny-looking clothes and stuff.

Hooray, says Old Coyote. You are just in time for the ball game.

Hello, says one of the men in silly clothes and red hair all over his head. I am Christopher Columbus. I am sailing the ocean blue looking for China. Have you seen it?

Forget China, says Old Coyote. Let's play ball.

It must be around here somewhere, says Christopher Columbus. I have a map.

Forget the map, says Old Coyote. I'll bat first and I'll tell you the rules as we go along.

But that Christopher Columbus and his friends don't want to play ball. We got work to do, he says. We got to find China. We got to find things we can sell.

Yes, says those Columbus people, where is the gold?

Yes, they says, where is that silk cloth?

Yes, they says, where are those portable color televisions?

Yes, they says, where are those home computers?

Boy, says Old Coyote, and that one scratches her head. I must have sung that song wrong. Maybe I didn't do the right dance. Maybe I thought too hard. These people I made have no manners. They act as if they have no relations.

And she is right. Christopher Columbus and his friends start jumping up and down in their funny clothes and they shout so loud that Coyote's ears almost fall off.

Boy, what a bunch of noise, says Coyote. What bad manners. You guys got to stop jumping and shouting or my ears will fall off.

We got to find China, says Christopher Columbus. We got to become rich. We got to become famous. Do you think you can help us?

But all Old Coyote can think about is playing ball.

I'll let you bat first, says Old Coyote.

No time for games, says Christopher Columbus.

I'll let you make the rules, cries Old Coyote.

But those Columbus people don't listen. They are too busy running around, peeking under rocks, looking in caves, sailing all over the place. Looking for China. Looking for stuff they can sell.

I got a monkey, says one.

I got a parrot, says another.

I got a fish, says a third.

I got a coconut, says a fourth.

That stuff isn't worth poop, says Christopher Columbus. We can't sell those things in Spain. Look harder.

But all they find are monkeys and parrots and fish and coconuts. And when they tell Christopher Columbus, that one he squeezes his ears and he chews his nose and grinds his teeth. He grinds his teeth so hard, he gets a headache, and, then, he gets cranky.

And then he gets an idea.

Say, says Christopher Columbus. Maybe we could sell Indians.

Yes, says his friends, that's a good idea. We could sell Indians, and they throw away their monkeys and parrots and fish and coconuts.

Wait a minute, says the Indians, that is not a good idea. That is a bad idea. That is a bad idea full of bad manners.

When Old Coyote hears this bad idea, she starts to laugh. Who would buy Indians, she says, and she laughs some more. She laughs so hard, she has to hold her nose on her face with both her hands.

But while that Old Coyote is laughing, Christopher Columbus grabs a big bunch of Indian men and Indian women and Indian children and locks them up in his ships.

When Old Coyote stops laughing and looks around, she sees that some of the Indians are missing. Hey, she says, where are those Indians? Where are my friends?

I'm going to sell them in Spain, says Christopher Columbus. Somebody has to pay for this trip. Sailing over the ocean blue isn't cheap, you know.

But Old Coyote still thinks that Christopher Columbus is playing a trick. She thinks it is a joke. That is a good joke, she says, trying to make me think that you are going to sell my friends. And she starts to laugh again.

Grab some more Indians, says Christopher Columbus.

When Old Coyote sees Christopher Columbus grab some more Indians, she laughs even harder. What a good joke, she says. And she laughs some more. She does this four times and when she is done laughing, all the Indians are gone. And Christopher Columbus is gone and Christopher Columbus's friends are gone, too.

Wait a minute, says old Coyote. What happened to my friends? Where are my Indians? You got to bring them back. Who's going to play ball with me?

But Christopher Columbus didn't bring the Indians back and Old Coyote was real sorry she thought him up. She tried to take him back. But, you know, once you think things like that, you can't take them back. So you have to be careful what you think.

So. That's the end of the story.

Boy, says Coyote. That is one sad story.

Yes, I says. It's sad alright. And things don't get any better, I can tell you that.

What a very sad story, says Coyote. Poor Old Coyote didn't have anyone to play ball with. That one must have been lonely. And Coyote begins to cry.

Stop crying, I says. Old Coyote is fine. Some blue jays come along after that and they play ball with her.

Oh, good, says Coyote. But what happened to the Indians? There was nothing in that red history book about Christopher Columbus and the Indians.

Christopher Columbus sold the Indians, I says, and that one became rich and famous.

Oh, good, says Coyote. I love a happy ending. And that one blows her party whistle and that one shakes her party rattle and that one puts her party hat back on her head. I better get going, she says, I'm going to be late for the party.

Okay, I says. Just remember how that story goes. Don't go messing it up again. Have you got it straight, now?

You bet, says Coyote. But if Christopher Columbus didn't find America and he didn't find Indians, who found these things?

Those things were never lost, I says. Those things were always here. Those things are still here today.

By golly, I think you are right, says Coyote.

Don't be thinking, I says. This world has enough problems already without a bunch of Coyote thoughts with tails and scraggy fur running around bumping into each other.

Boy, that's the truth. I can tell you that.

*—1993*

*Alice Walker (b. 1944) wrote the Pulitzer Prize–winning epistolary novel* The Color Purple *(1982). The book and its 1985 film version have made her the most famous living African-American writer, perhaps the most widely read of any American woman of colour. A native of Eatonton, Georgia, Walker was the eighth child of an impoverished farm couple. She attended Spelman College in Atlanta and Sarah Lawrence College on scholarships, graduating in 1965. Walker began her literary career as a poet, eventually publishing six volumes of verse. Walker's short-story collections and novels, including* The Temple of My Familiar *(1989) and* Possessing the Secret of Joy *(1992), which takes as its subject the controversial practice of female circumcision among African tribes, have continued to reach large audiences and have solidified her reputation as one of the major figures in contemporary literature. Walker has coined the term "womanist" to stand for the Black feminist concerns of much of her fiction. Her latest works include the novel* Now Is the Time to Open Your Heart *(2004), and* Collected Poems *(2005). Like so much of Walker's writing, the story "The Flowers" from* In Love and Trouble *(1973) challenges a myopic world view.*

## Alice Walker
# The Flowers

It seemed to Myop as she skipped lightly from hen house to pigpen to smokehouse that the days had never been as beautiful as these. The air held a keenness that made her nose twitch. The harvesting of the corn and cotton, peanuts and squash, made each day a golden surprise that caused excited little tremors to run up her jaws.

Myop carried a short, knobby stick. She struck out at random at chickens she liked, and worked out the beat of a song on the fence around the pigpen. She felt light and good in the warm sun. She was ten, and nothing existed for her but her song, the stick clutched in her dark brown hand, and the tat-de-ta-ta-ta of accompaniment.

Turning her back on the rusty boards of her family's sharecropper cabin, Myop walked along the fence till it ran into the stream made by the spring. Around the spring, where the family got drinking water, silver ferns and wildflowers grew. Along the shallow banks pigs rooted. Myop watched the tiny white bubbles disrupt the thin black scale of soil and the water that silently rose and slid away down the stream.

She had explored the woods behind the house many times. Often, in late autumn, her mother took her to gather nuts among the fallen leaves.

*Today she made her own path, bouncing this way and that way, vaguely keeping an eye out for snakes. She found, in addition to various common but pretty ferns and leaves, an armful of strange blue flowers with velvety ridges and a sweetsuds bush full of the brown, fragrant buds.*

*By twelve o'clock, her arms laden with sprigs of her findings, she was a mile or more from home. She had often been as far before, but the strangeness of the land made it not as pleasant as her usual haunts. It seemed gloomy in the little cove in which she found herself. The air was damp, the silence close and deep.*

*Myop began to circle back to the house, back to the peacefulness of the morning. It was then she stepped smack into his eyes. Her heel became lodged in the broken ridge between brow and nose, and she reached down quickly, unafraid, to free herself. It was only when she saw his naked grin that she gave a little yelp of surprise.*

*He had been a tall man. From feet to neck covered a long space. His head lay beside him. When she pushed back the leaves and layers of earth and debris Myop saw that he'd had large white teeth, all of them cracked or broken, long fingers, and very big bones. All his clothes had rotted away except some threads of blue denim from his overalls. The buckles of the overalls had turned green.*

*Myop gazed around the spot with interest. Very near where she'd stepped into the head was a wild pink rose. As she picked it to add to her bundle she noticed a raised mound, a ring, around the rose's root. It was the rotted remains of a noose, a bit of shredding plowline, now blending benignly into the soil. Around an overhanging limb of a great spreading oak clung another piece. Frayed, rotted, bleached, and frazzled—barely there—but spinning restlessly in the breeze. Myop laid down her flowers.*

*And the summer was over.*

*—1973*

---

*Lise Bissonnette (b. 1945) was born in Northern Quebec and was for many years the publisher of Montreal's influential newspaper* Le Devoir. *Considered an exceptional journalist and editor, she has also written three novels,* Following the Summer *(1993),* Affairs of Art *(1996), and* An Appropriate Place *(2003), and a collection of stories,* Cruelties *(1998). She is known for her advocacy of feminist and separatist concerns, and now serves as CEO of La Grande Bibliothèque du Québec.*

## *Lise Bissonnette*
# Dresses

It ought to be worn with patent-leather pumps, a string of pearls, and most important, with your hair in a coil, the kind that ripples halfway down the back as it comes undone.

I had high-heeled shoes in a matte, smoky grey-black, harlequin glasses, a rhinestone necklace, and hair as straight as we imagined the nuns' would be under their coifs.

It crossed my mind to throw myself into the water; I tried in vain to feel the urge. On the wire hanger with its scrawny shoulders, the little black dress murmured a call to sin. We'd see.

It had been sewn miles away from the boarding school, during the Christmas holidays. I'd been allowed to choose a Vogue pattern, something my mother consented to only for grand occasions, but on this one we were silent. There comes an age when we pass from taffeta to soft crepe; I wanted it to be dark, she merely warned me not to iron it on the right side, that would make the seams shiny. The hem stopped just below the knee, the sleeves at the elbow, the only fullness was at the bosom, where it was draped over as yet non-existent points. At the last fitting my brother had whistled. The legs, he said, weren't bad.

But now, standing at my bedroom closet, Michèle was gazing at it with the pout of a connoisseur. She'd been dealing with boys for a long time now and if I was able to stand up to her, it was through literature. Jean-Jacques Rousseau was on the Index; I could quote him word for word. Borrowed from the Ottawa library, from which they no longer dared ban us, his *Confessions* under my pillow was considered to be the

Translated by Sheila Fischman.

first licentious book to reach our dormitory. I also claimed to know the loves of Claudel and I invented some for Charles Péguy.[1] I impressed the readers of *Seventeen*, including Michèle, who got along fairly well in Latin too.

My black dress was declared to be too sober. It's true, I didn't dare tell anyone where I'd got the image. That of the wife of Yousuf Karsh,[2] a hieratic beauty I'd brushed up against late that fall. The city was so boring in those days that even Churchill's photographer attended the Jeunesses Musicales concerts. I did mental dictation as I listened to the pianists, an odd little habit that took the soul out of Chopin and left me free to observe this high society among whom she stood alone. So white in her black silk that you could hardly see the pearls around her neck. At intermission, I saw her lean her head towards a man whose chin disappeared into his cravat, a layer of softness for a voice entangled in its accent: "Vould you come mit me to see ze artist after ze concert?" She had the remarkable power of not responding, or of responding so briefly that it seemed she hadn't. I wanted to be long, lithe, and unattainable.

Michèle decided otherwise. Of course I'd wanted this black dress so someone would touch me, while she wanted to correct the faint melancholy of this basic garment, which actually looked rather feminine. In English, and passing ourselves off as a pair of hotheads from Hull, after lengthy explorations we bought first the red shoes and then the matching bag. There was no money left for a perm, but we did that at home quite successfully. Glasses were unthinkable, a myopic gaze being in any case more flattering, and she was going to lend me the earrings and necklace of fake gold I turned out to be allergic to.

On the evening in question, she found a man with dark hair and a friend to take us to the Club Chaudière. I wasn't ugly; a cross between a poodle and a bluish Siamese cat, I felt vague and strong. "You're more sensual than I am," Michèle decreed, promising herself that she'd borrow the dress the following Saturday. We claimed we were going to the movies, a double bill that the chaplain pretended to check on.

---

[1]*Charles Péguy* (1873–1914): French poet and philosopher known for his contribution to French intellectual life, through his writings, his socialist and religious beliefs, and his *Fortnightly Notebooks*, the small but significant journal he founded.
[2]*Yousuf Karsh* (1908–2002): American-Canadian photographer known for his portraits of famous people including Churchill and Hemingway.

The boy was as inane as Péguy would have been at a *bal musette.*[3] He had thick lips and a kiss curl, and he was a compulsive hand-holder (his was damp). Nothing could have been longer than the drive home, complete with the ritual of the backseat Michèle had warned me to go along with.

I came across as a future nun while I dreamed of wantonness in soft crepe. I thought of jumping in the water, I searched in vain for the desire to do so.

Spring came to me on Ste. Catherine Street. A slenderness under woollen clothes, a warm glimmer on a motorbike, an evil thread of violin music through the window of a Tourist Room, dust in an ambulance's wake. I didn't intend to feel provincial for very long.

It was still dark as shopkeepers pushed their displays into the middle of the sidewalk, series of dresses all the same except for the colours in the pattern, hung crowded together on racks, with a piece of cardboard at one end where "$5.00 each/chaque" was written in felt pen. Surrounded by the smells of plastic and of sour winter, squashed into a cupboard where half a mirror jutted out over some packages, I tried on one that moved like daylight itself. Green spangles were woven into the grey weft, the neckline was round, the sleeves short, and the waist was barely caught in the plastic belt, a thin twist in the same green.

Straight and without a fold, it fell like jersey, and it was. Mid-season, I thought, listening to myself in silence. It's fluid, jersey, you grow taller when you pour yourself into it, and its two consonants rub against your skin. You feel like Michelle Tisseyre[4] entertaining in her garden on the first evenings that aren't so cool. "Shall I bring you a sweater?" "No, perhaps another few drops of port." And the man's arm brushes against your shoulder as he pours. There'll always be time to go inside.

I felt as if I were twenty years old; I was dismantling the pleasure of it in advance.

The little man with the moustache was keeping an eye on both the sidewalk and the boutique; he saw none of my beauty, which was

---

[3]*bal musette:* French dance hall with music provided by an accordion band.
[4]*Michelle Tisseyre* (1918– ): Montreal-born star of French radio and television, who worked on the *Encyclopédie de la femme canadienne* (1965) and "La Collection des deux solitudes," intended to bring the work of Canadian English writers to francophone readers.

camouflaged by a winter coat once more when I paid. The jersey would be for other eyes, that very evening.

The bag was light, so light, as far as the corner of the street. For there are limits to frivolity and I had five dollars less for the unexpected—a bookstore that was also displaying its wares in the sun. I spent a long time leafing through the pamphlets published by Éditions du Jour, they were blaring rages unknown in my Ottawa-area boarding school. The door was open and I worked up the courage to go inside as far as the first section of shelves, which disappeared into the half-light of noon. The bookseller was affable and I was terrified by his voice, that of an examiner in search of brilliant students. "You're studying philosophy at your age? Nonsense, I imagine." I hadn't said a word and he was confirming the limits of Thomism,[5] an insight that struck me as original.

It cost me a dollar and twenty cents for the brand-new paperback edition of *The Situation of the Worker*, Simone Weil's journal of her days as a factory worker, a double volume with a red-and-black cover, blood and night. Henri Tranquille had just sold me my first book worthy of the name, and entrance into the world of women who had rebelled, which would lead me later to the world of both George Sand and Rosa Luxemburg.

But I certainly wasn't there yet, though I was in fine form, with my book and my dress in my bookbag. At 101 St. Joseph Boulevard West, I was the last of the regional representatives to take my place at the table where we were to discuss secularism and the Parent report on Quebec's education system. Though at school you couldn't shut me up on the subject, which I used to harass a professor of pedagogy, I would be silent in the presence of the boys, some of whom were about to meet with the minister, Paul Gérin-Lajoie. I would write the press release, however, which only *Le Devoir* would run, abridged: "Through its president, the Presse étudiante nationale (PEN) declares that democratization of the education system must be the primary objective of any reform."

I was thanked as they left the premises for their dinners in Outremont.[6] The only people still there were middle class, the Gestetner operators and stamp-lickers, ready for the night on the town they'd been promised for months. I relinquished Simone Weil and my woollies,

[5]*Thomism:* the doctrines of Thomas Aquinas (c.1225–1274) that synthesize theology and philosophy.
[6]*Outremont:* an attractive and affluent community named for its location beyond (*outre*) Mont Royal, the mountain that gives Montreal its name.

the dress clung tenderly—jersey is uncrushable. Jersey for jazz, jersey for the knee offered under the table. To a skinny boy whose blue eyes were looking elsewhere.

Peel Street, second floor, the trumpet blasting into the piano, the beer as bitter as it was illegal at my age. And I plunged forever into the atrocious solitude of a woman who wanted to be one and wasn't. For what the skinny blue-eyed boy saw all around were Juliettes in black sweaters, black skirts, and black stockings, their hair as straight as the very notion of despair, sooty lashes, souls in hell. My green spangles caught in my throat, and my short sleeves undressed me roughly. The sun was totally out of fashion. I spent hours and a night suffering from the springtime that I'd misread so badly.

On the bus home the next day, Simone Weil taught me about detachment from material goods. In vain. I'd felt as if I were twenty years old, and I had dismantled the pleasure of it in advance.

"You aren't going to wear that for making free love!" Rose-Aimée's cry came not from the heart but from the throat. A fluttering of nerves, hers were fierce and accustomed to scandal. As usual, she was speaking as much to the ceiling as to me, with that way she had of pushing both instruction and morality with her chin, of holding high the tablets of the law. Of all of us, she was the only one who had a boyfriend, a deathly pale member of the Catholic student movement with whom she actively practised purity and preached about it so, she made us loathe it.

Facing the closets we were emptying in preparation for packing our bags in June, she finally encountered evil elsewhere than in sermons. Displayed before her was a long nightgown in which a young woman could die a martyr or live condemned to hell: it was a question of what I might have had in mind when I chose it: deep pink percale, with the bodice cut from a piece of lace crocheted by a grandmother I'd never known. Cream and satin was the ribbon that snaked its way through the lace to cinch the empire waist, and the wide pleats fell like those of Josephine de Beauharnais[7] or St. Cecile, patron of music, depending. Rose-Aimée obviously suspected me of designing this wonder and having it made for purposes other than elegant sleep, especially since I'd never

---

[7]*Josephine de Beauharnais* (1763–1814): After the death of her first husband she became wife to Napoleon Bonaparte and empress of France.

worn it. But she was mistaken. I'd wanted it for no particular reason, for an image, to bring beauty into the tedium of the dormitories.

Still, I was about to wear it for the first time, finally. I'd recently met a young man whose natural shyness went well with my desire to be done with regional activities. His name was Roger, I forgave him for it, and in his slow way of moving one could sense the necessary aptitude for practising existentialism. He was long and pensive, with blue-green eyes and a pianist's hands. During meetings he drew. At the movie he stroked my fingers, on the street his fingers brushed my neck, and he said all kinds of intelligent things about the futility of the world. He'd introduced me to his mother, a mistake. Her enthusiasm had put a little too much colour into the shades of grey where we were silent about our feelings.

He had the use of an apartment that belonged to a friend of his in Montreal, where I was going the next day for a final meeting before the summer holidays. He would be alone, he'd take care of the wine, cheese, and candles, we would eat and sleep there, just the two of us. Not another word had been said. But never was a lace-topped pink night-gown so appropriate as for this occasion. The whole dormitory was in on the secret, and with the exception of Rose-Aimée they all agreed. "Don't forget perfume," Michèle had fussed. She lent it to me with a new reverence. She didn't know any boys who had the use of an apartment; I was the first one to cross that particular threshold.

As for free love, you'd have had to be warped to threaten me with it. There were still so many kisses to discover before I got there, so many acts to perform, so many murmurs to commence. I felt nothing but impatience for a window open onto the noise of Dorchester Boulevard, for a pink gown that moves all down its length, for the bitterness of the wine, for the silence we'd flow into before nightfall, and its hours that would be what they would be. We would open them one by one.

And so there I was at seventeen and a half, draped in pink, drinking Spanish Iago, and chatting about Auguste Comte.[8] I'd become acquainted with him at the same time as with Roger, who considered him to be the spiritual father of Jean-Paul Sartre, and I nearly fell genuinely in love with this long, lean boy buried under his words, who bestowed them on me without vanity. We talked about everything except ourselves, even as

[8]*Auguste Comte* (1798–1857): French thinker known as the founder of sociology and positivism, a philosophical system that confines itself to knowledge gained through the scientific method of observation and experimentation.

we moved closer together in the low armchair that we never dared to abandon for the big bed in the next room. I was excited enough to palpitate a little, I would have untied a ribbon, perhaps I did so just before he finally told me into my hair that his heart was strange and a stranger. He traced the lace with his finger: "I love a boy, this is his place, I can't leave him . . ." His cheek was hollow in the lamplight, his body tense. Was he expecting to see me slip away from him, outside this place, outside of us? But I was filled with contentment. The night passed serenely now, I was fascinated by this man's confession, I was penetrating much deeper than I'd expected into the forbidden, I could put off the decisions of my body, which wasn't serious because it was seventeen years old.

At dawn we went to the mountain to watch the sunrise. The mosquitoes were preparing for a humid day and real summer. We stretched out in the short grass, I imagined us upright and impossible like Tristan and Isolde, who slept with a sword between them.

Roger disturbed the arrangement when he put his hand on my stomach; he was as free now as he was chaste, he could touch a girl.

That was what brought a bellow from the policeman on horseback who was passing by, he drove us from the earthly paradise with words as religious as those of Rose-Aimée. To him I owe the long kiss that my false lover placed defiantly on my neck, love was as free as the air that was gilding both man and beast, we laughed, we were hungry. Life was going to be irresistible.

*—1999*

*Jamaica Kincaid (b. 1949) was born Elaine Potter Richardson in Antigua, a
Caribbean island that did not achieve independence from Britain until 1981. She left
Antigua at seventeen to be an au pair in New York, taking on a new name that was
both a removal and reminder of her ties to the West Indies. "Girl" was first published
in* The New Yorker *and then in the collection* At the Bottom of the River
*(1983). Her style, often closer to poetry than prose, has been compared to that of
Gertrude Stein. Describing writing as a "kind of self-rescuing," she has published
several autobiographical novels, including* Annie John *(1985),* Lucy *(1990),*
Autobiography of My Mother *(1996), and* Mr. Potter *(2002), as well as works
of non-fiction, including* My Brother *(1997) and* Among Flowers: A Walk in
the Himalaya *(2005).*

# Jamaica Kincaid

## Girl

Wash the white clothes on Monday and put them on the stone heap;
wash the color clothes on Tuesday and put them on the clothesline to
dry; don't walk barehead in the hot sun; cook pumpkin fritters in very
hot sweet oil; soak your little cloths right after you take them off; when
buying cotton to make yourself a nice blouse, be sure that it doesn't
have gum on it, because that way it won't hold up well after a wash;
soak salt fish overnight before you cook it; is it true that you sing benna[1]
in Sunday school?; always eat your food in such a way that it won't turn
someone else's stomach; on Sundays try to walk like a lady and not like
the slut you are so bent on becoming; don't sing benna in Sunday
school; you mustn't speak to wharf-rat boys, not even to give directions;
don't eat fruits on the street—flies will follow you; *but I don't sing
benna on Sundays at all and never in Sunday school;* this is how to sew
on a button; this is how to make a buttonhole for the button you have
just sewed on; this is how to hem a dress when you see the hem coming
down and so to prevent yourself from looking like the slut I know you
are so bent on becoming; this is how you iron your father's khaki shirt
so that it doesn't have a crease; this is how you iron your father's khaki
pants so that they don't have a crease; this is how you grow okra—far
from the house, because okra tree harbors red ants; when you are growing dasheen, make sure it gets plenty of water or else it makes your

---

[1]*benna:* popular music, calypso.

throat itch when you are eating it; this is how you sweep a corner; this is how you sweep a whole house; this is how you sweep a yard; this is how you smile to someone you don't like too much; this is how you smile to someone you don't like at all; this is how you smile to someone you like completely; this is how you set a table for tea; this is how you set a table for dinner; this is how you set a table for dinner with an important guest; this is how you set a table for lunch; this is how you set a table for breakfast; this is how to behave in the presence of men who don't know you very well, and this way they won't recognize immediately the slut I have warned you against becoming; be sure to wash every day, even if it is with your own spit; don't squat down to play marbles—you are not a boy, you know; don't pick people's flowers—you might catch something; don't throw stones at blackbirds, because it might not be a blackbird at all; this is how to make a bread pudding; this is how to make doukona;[2] this is how to make pepper pot; this is how to make a good medicine for a cold; this is how to make a good medicine to throw away a child before it even becomes a child; this is how to catch a fish; this is how to throw back a fish you don't like, and that way something bad won't fall on you; this is how to bully a man; this is how a man bullies you; this is how to love a man, and if this doesn't work there are other ways, and if they don't work don't feel too bad about giving up; this is how to spit up in the air if you feel like it, and this is how to move quick so that it doesn't fall on you; this is how to make ends meet; always squeeze bread to make sure it's fresh; *but what if the baker won't let me feel the bread?*; you mean to say that after all you are really going to be the kind of woman who the baker won't let near the bread?

—*1983*

<hr />

[2]*doukona:* a spicy pudding, often made from plantains and wrapped in a plantain or banana leaf.

*Guy Vanderhaeghe (b. 1951) was born in Esterhazy, Saskatchewan, and contin-*
*ues to explore the truth and mythology of Western life in such award-winning novels*
*as* The Englishman's Boy *(1996) and* The Last Crossing *(2001). His debut*
*collection of stories,* Man Descending *(1982), won the Governor General's Award,*
*and he has continued to work in the form, publishing* The Trouble with Heroes
*(1983) and* Things as They Are? *(1992). He counts Alice Munro and John*
*Updike among his influences and combines a love of history, popular culture, and*
*complex characterization in his fiction. Describing himself as a "Big Sky Guy," he*
*credits Saskatoon with making him feel both valued and grounded.*

# Guy Vanderhaeghe
# The Home Place

It was early morning, so early that Gil MacLean loaded the colt into the truck box under a sky still scattered with faint stars. The old man circled the truck once, checking the tailgate, the tires, and the knot in the halter shank, tottering around on legs stiff as stilts, shoulders hunched to keep the chill off him. He was sixty-nine and mostly cold these days.

A hundred yards behind him one window burned yellow in the dark house. That was his son Ronald, asleep under the bare light bulb and the airplanes. Whenever Ronald fled Darlene, the woman Gil MacLean referred to as the "back-pages wife," he slunk back to his father's house in the dead of night to sleep in a room lit up like a Christmas tree. To her father-in-law, Darlene was the back-pages wife because Ronald had found her advertising herself in the classified section of a farm news-paper, right alongside sale notices for second-hand grain augers and doubtful chain-saws.

Dawn found the old man in a temper, a mood. It was the mare he had wanted when he rattled oats in the pail and whistled, but it was the gelding which had been lured. The mare, wiser and warier, had hung back. So this morning he had a green, rough-broke colt to ride. There was nothing for it, though. He needed a horse because his mind was made up to repair Ronald's fences. They were a disgrace.

Generally that was the way to catch what you wanted, shake a little bait. It was what Darlene had done with Ronald, but she hadn't fooled Gil MacLean for a second. He knew how it was.

Four years ago his son and Darlene married after exchanging honeyed letters for six months. Ronald never breathed a word to him about any wedding. When Ronald's mother was alive she used to say Ronald was too much under his father's thumb. But the one time he slipped out from beneath it, look at the result.

One morning Ronald had driven off in the pick-up. Twelve hours later he phoned from Regina to announce that he and his bride were bound for Plentywood, Montana, to honeymoon. Ronald was thirty-eight then, had never been married, had never been engaged, had never even had a date that his father could recollect. It was a shock and a mystery. The way Gil figured it, Ronald must have proposed by mail before he ever met face to face with Darlene. Ronald didn't have it in him to offer himself in the flesh to someone with whom he was actually acquainted. He would be too shy, too embarrassed for that.

The old man folded himself into the cab of the truck, joint by joint. "The best work, the worst sleep," he muttered to Ronald's lighted window as he drove under it. In the east there were mares' tails on the horizon, fine as the vapour trails of jets, reddened by the rising sun.

It was Gil MacLean's speculation that his son married only to get his hands on land. Not land of Darlene's, she was a waif and a pauper and had none, but his land, Gil MacLean's land. He never entertained the idea that Ronald might have married out of loneliness, or lust, or any feeling of the remotest kin to either. Just land. That was why he was sometimes troubled, wondering what share of responsibility was his to bear for Ronald's current unhappiness. Maybe he ought to have transferred the title sooner, but he had never trusted the boy's judgment. Events appeared to have confirmed his suspicions. Ronald had his own farm now, a wedding present. A married man needed land, so his father gave him the farm that the MacLeans had always called the "home place." It gave Gil satisfaction to see it pass from father to son and he thought it might bring Ronald luck.

The home place consisted of the original quarter Gil's father had homesteaded, the pre-emption, and another 320 acres picked up cheap from a Finnish immigrant who went to pieces when his wife ran off on him. Over the years the MacLean family acquired other holdings but the home place was special. Situated in a valley, it was a mix of rich bottom land and steep, wooded hills. In the spring, down by the river, blizzards of gulls floated in the wake of tractor and disker, pursuing easy pickings, while hawks rode the air high above the lean hills and, shrieking, fell to plunder these lazy storms of white birds. To Gil it had all been beautiful. It was all he had ever wanted, to possess that place and those sights. A day spent away from the farm made him restless, cranky. Returning to it, even after the briefest absence, he acted oddly, dodging through the wires of a fence in his city clothes to wade about in his crop, hands running back and forth lightly over the bearded heads the way another man might absent-mindedly stroke a cat. Or he might suddenly strike off for the hills with all the energy and purpose of someone hurrying off to keep an appointment, tie flying over his shoulder.

His wife used to say: "Gil's gone off to satisfy himself that nobody so much as shifted a cup of dirt on this place when he was away."

What Gil never confided to his wife was that he felt more present in the land than he did in his own flesh, his own body. Apart from it he had no real existence. When he looked in a mirror he stood at a great distance from what he regarded, but with the land it was different. All that he had emptied of himself into it, he recognized.

The road to the home place ran due east without deviating a hair, rising and falling regularly as a sleeper's breath as it made its way over a succession of bare hills. The emerging sun drew his eyes into a squint when he topped a rise; the blue shadows in the hollows forced them wide again. In the back of the truck the slither and clatter of iron shoes was unremitting. The colt was either highly strung or lacked balance. If it lost its footing and fell it would be a task to get on its feet again; the box was narrow and there was little room for manoeuvring. He'd have to go back and get Ronald out of bed to help him.

Turning Ronald out of bed was not an easy job. Despite his son's difficulties falling asleep, once he was gone he wasn't likely to stir. Often he didn't wake before noon. Gil, on the other hand, roused to the slightest sound. That first night the gritty scraping of the shoes on the stairs had been enough to jerk him out of a dreamless sleep. He'd never been one to lock doors, he had only himself to thank that a night intruder was climbing up to him. It was like the television and its stories of grinning madmen invading houses and arming themselves with drapery cords and butcher knives to strangle and stab. The old man bunched up his pillow and held it out before him, ready to parry the first knife thrust. The footsteps, however, went on past his door. Only when the toilet flushed did he realize it had to be Ronald.

He simply shook in bed for several minutes, too angry and too relieved to ask himself what his son might be up to. Finally he grew calm and curiosity prodded him out into the hallway to investigate. The light was on in Ronald's old bedroom and the door stood ajar.

Ronald was lying flat on his back on the bed, staring up at his model airplanes. As a teenager, even as a young man, he had exhibited little interest in anything other than building models of airplanes from kits, squeezing tubes of glue, pasting on decals, and painting engine cowlings with brushes whose tips he sucked into needle points. The models had never been removed. Forty or more of them hung suspended from the ceiling on fine wires; his room was almost exactly as he had left it when he chose Darlene. Flying Fortresses, Mustangs, Zeros, Spitfires, Messerschmitts, a whole catalogue of war planes dangled there. The light in the bedroom was also as harsh, pitiless, and glaring as it had ever been. When Ronald was fourteen he had unscrewed the bulb in the ceiling fixture and replaced it with a more powerful one. He also dispensed with the shade because he wanted the models hanging beneath the light bulb to cast their shadows on his bedspread and linoleum in the way fighter planes and bombers passing between sun and earth print their images on country lanes and city squares. These shadows were repeated everywhere about the room, and in their midst lay Ronald, gazing up into the strong light, gazing up at undercarriages and silhouettes.

"What's all this, Ronald?" his father said. "This is a hell of a time to pay a visit. It's past two."

Ronald said: "I can't stand it. I can't sleep there no longer." He kept his eyes fixed on the planes as he spoke.

Gil knew there was talk going around town about his son and his daughter-in-law, all of it unfortunate. Darlene had come stamped with the word trouble; he'd seen it from day one. The old man sighed and took a seat on the straight-back chair beside the dresser. Ronald was not exactly the forthcoming type, he was prepared to wait him out.

After a considerable stretch of silence his son said: "I should never have left." Gil knew what he meant. Ronald wasn't saying he ought not to have left Darlene; he was saying he should not have abandoned this room and the comfort and solace of those planes that could not fly.

It was strange that, given all the worrying he had done about Ronald and Darlene, Gil had never seen the real danger. Now he did. The realization of what might lie ahead was like an attack of some kind. Before he could proceed it was necessary to relieve the pressure prodding his breastbone and robbing him of breath. He arched his back and squeezed his eyes tight until it eased and he could speak. And speak he did, urgently, for a solid hour without interruption and with a drying mouth. He said it was the government and the courts. They'd gone and changed the marriage property laws so that the women ended up with half of everything these days. Did Ronald know what that meant? Darlene could lay claim to a half share of the home place. "No divorce, Ronald," he repeated. "No divorce. Don't let that bitch break up the home place. Don't you give her that satisfaction." Only when he had wrung this promise out of Ronald did he cease arguing. For a moment he was overcome by his son's loyalty. He patted the back of his hand and murmured: "Thank you. Thank you."

In a month, however, Ronald came creeping back up the stairs. In baffled rage and fear of the future, Gil shouted through his bedroom door: "Don't expect any sympathy from me if you won't try to adjust!"

Ronald explained that he had a problem going to sleep in the same room, the same house as Darlene. That's the reason he came home every once in a while, to relax and catch up on his sleep. Not that it was easy for him to get to sleep in his old room either, but there he could manage it. What he did was stare up at the glowing bulb and planes until the moment arrived when he could feel the sun hot on his back and suddenly he was winged and soaring, flying into sleep, released, sometimes for twelve hours at a time.

Ronald had been paying his visits to his father's to sleep for a year. About the time they started he commenced on improvements to the home place. This meant pushing bush and clearing land up top, above the valley, in the hills. Gil had pointed out this was nothing but sheer craziness. Marginal land like that was suitable only for pasture, cropping it would never repay the cost of breaking and if the hillsides were stripped of cover they would erode. But Ronald, who was usually willing to be advised, wouldn't listen to his father. A cunning, stubborn look stole over his face when he said: "We'll see. I hired another dozer. Pretty soon the brush piles will be dry and ready to burn."

All spring Ronald fired his huge, gasoline-laced bonfires of scrub oak and poplar. The gusty roar of flames was like constant static in his ears, heat crumpled the air around him and stained it a watery yellow, greasy black clouds mounted indolently into the purity of blue skies. The scars of the dozer blades fresh on the earth made the old man indignant. In places the soil had been cut so deep that streaks of rubbly gravel were exposed.

"You won't grow wheat in that," Gil MacLean shouted. "So what'll it be? Carrots?"

Smiling oddly, Ronald said: "I'm not growing nothing. I'll open a pit and peddle gravel to the Department of Highways by the yard."

"That's not farming," his father returned, disgusted. "That's mining."

It was all Ronald had any interest in at present, pushing bush, clawing up roots, burning. His face appeared hot, scorched. His eyes were forever weepy and red, their lids puffy and swollen, lashes singed away. The ends of his hair had crinkled, crisped, and gone white in the furnace-heat. Everything else Ronald neglected. He hadn't yet done his summer fallow and his cattle were continually straying. This morning Gil was determined to mend Ronald's fences because he was ashamed of what the neighbours would think with his son's cows belly-deep in their crops.

The old man crested the last rise and the valley spread itself out at his feet. There were days when he would pull his truck over to the shoulder of the road and look with deep satisfaction at the slow river and the sombre quilt of green and black fields, look until he had his fill. From such a height the home place looked fatter and richer than with your nose shoved in it. Up close dirt was dirt. There was no time for stopping and admiring this morning though. He was in a hurry.

Gil entered his son's property by a little-used side gate because he didn't want Darlene spying his truck and reporting his doings to Ronald. He parked, unloaded the horse, and slung a duffel bag of tools and a coil of barbed wire on the saddle. Within minutes he was riding down an old trail they had hauled hay on in summer and wood in winter in his father's time. Neither of those things would be possible now, encroaching wild rose and chokecherry bushes had narrowed it so a loaded wagon couldn't pass. The occasional sapling had taken root between the old ruts. Sunlight and sparrows strayed amid the poplar leaves overhead. Ronald's dozers hadn't reached this far yet, hadn't peeled all this back. Maybe his money would run out before they could, that was Gil's fervent hope.

It was eight o'clock before Gil located the first break in the fence. The wires were rotten with rust and would have to be replaced. He set to work. The old man ought not to have been taken by surprise. He knew the very nature of a young horse was unpredictability. It happened when he was playing out sixty yards of wire, lazy-man style, one end of the coil dallied round the horn, the horse walking it out. It could have been the sound the wire made hissing and writhing after them through the grass and weeds. It could have been that a barb nicked the gelding's hocks. Suddenly the colt froze in its tracks, laid back its ears, and trembled all over like a leaf.

Gil had been a horseman all his life, nearly all of his seventy years. He knew what was coming and he fought with all his strength to keep the gelding from pulling its head down between its forelegs. If the colt managed to get its head down it would be able to buck. It managed. An old man's strength was not sufficient. The horse squealed, wriggled, snapped out its hind legs. Gil's lower plate popped out of his mouth. The sky tilted. He fell.

It was bad luck to get snarled in the wire. The colt dragged him several hundred yards, the old man skipping and bounding and tumbling along behind like a downed water skier without the presence of mind to relinquish his grip on the tow rope.

When it had winded itself the horse came to a halt, stood rolling its eyes and snorting. The old man began to paw himself feebly, searching his pockets for a pair of fencing pliers with which to cut himself out of the jumble of wire. Using the pliers, he had to move cautiously and deliberately so as not to excite the skittish colt. Nevertheless, when the final strand of wire parted with a twang the colt kicked him twice in a convulsion of fear before trotting off a stone's throw away. There it circled about anxiously, stepping on the ends of the dragging reins and bruising its mouth.

The old man lay still, taking stock. There seemed to be a lot of blood, the wire had cut him in many places. He sat up and the blood gushed out of his nose and mouth and spilled down his jacket front. He peered about him, dazed. The colt had dragged him to a desolate place. Ronald's dozers had been at work. Here there was nothing but bare, black earth engraved by caterpillar treads, piles of stones, and the remains of bonfires, charred tree trunks furred in white powdery ash.

While he sat up the blood continued to pour from his mouth and nose. It was better to lie back down. He was feeling weak but he told himself that was because he had taken nothing that morning but a cup of instant coffee. "I'll rest and my strength will come back," he told himself.

Gil closed his eyes and became aware of the powerful scents of sage, milkweed, grass. How was this possible in a place scoured clean? Then he realized they were coming from his clothes, had been ground into them by the dragging.

During the next three hours he tried a number of times to sit himself up, but the blood always ran so freely from his mouth he resigned the attempt. "Not yet," he muttered to himself. "In a while." He had little sense of passing time. There was only thirst and the stiff, scratchy ache of the wounds on his face, hands, legs.

When the sun shone directly down into his face he realized it was noon. The bright light in his eyes and the time of day made him think of Ronald. He would be waking now, looking up at his airplanes.

He had asked Ronald: "What is it with you? Why do you stare up at those planes?" And Ronald had said: "I like to pretend I'm up there, high enough to look down on something or somebody for once in my life."

Gil had laughed as if it were a joke, but it was an uneasy laugh.

Suddenly the old man was seized by a strange panic.

Making a great effort, he sat himself up. It was as if he hoped the force of gravity would pull everything he just now thought and saw down out of his head, drain it away. What he saw was Ronald's lashless eyes, singed hair, red burning face. What he thought was that such a face belonged to a man who wished to look down from a great height on fire, on ruin, on devastation, on dismay.

When the old man collapsed back into the wire he saw that face hovering above, looking down on him.

"You've got no right to look down on me," he said to the burning sky. "I came to fix your fences. I gave you the home place and showed you how to keep it."

His vehement voice filled the clearing and argued away the afternoon. It became harsher and louder when the sun passed out of Gil's vision and he could not raise himself to follow its course. The horse grew so accustomed to this steady shouting and calling out that only when it suddenly stopped did the gelding prick its ears, swing its head, and stare.

*—1992*

*Diane Schoemperlen (b. 1954) is from Thunder Bay, Ontario. She is noted for challenging the conventions of realistic fiction with unconventional structures, points of view, premises, and plots, but beneath the playful use of imagery and language are deeper explorations of the human condition. In her novels, including* In the Language of Love *(1994) and* Our Lady of the Lost and Found *(2001), and in several collections of short fiction, including the Governor General's Award–winning* Forms of Devotion *(1998), she widens our notion of what constitutes a story, finding epiphany in unexpected places.*

## Diane Schoemperlen
# Forms of Devotion

Strangely enough we are all seeking a form of devotion which fits our sense of wonder.

—J. Marks, *Transition*

### I. FAITH

The faithful are everywhere. They climb into their cars each morning and drive undaunted into the day. They sail off to work, perfectly confident that they will indeed get there: on time, intact. It does not occur to them that they could just as well be broadsided by a Coca-Cola delivery truck running the red light at the corner of Johnson and Main. They do not imagine the bottles exploding, the windshield shattering, their chests collapsing, the blood spurting out of their ears. They just drive. The same route every day, stop and go, back and forth, and yes, they get there: safe and sound. In the same unremarkable manner, they get home again too. Then they start supper without ever once marvelling at the fact that they have survived. It does not occur to them that the can of tuna they are using in the casserole might be tainted and they could all be dead of botulism by midnight.

They are armed with faith. They trust, if not in God exactly, then in the steadfast notion of everyday life. They do not expect to live forever of course, but they would not be entirely surprised if they did. On a daily basis, death strikes them mostly as a calamity which befalls other people, people who are probably evil, careless, or unlucky: just in the wrong place at the wrong time.

On weekend mornings, the faithful take their children to the park and assume they will not be abducted or fondled behind the climber by a pervert in a trench coat. In the afternoons, they work in their gardens, quite confident that those tiny seeds will eventually produce more tomatoes, zucchini, and green beans than they will know what to do with. They dig in the dirt and believe in the future. They put up preserves, save for retirement, and look forward to being grandparents. After they retire, they plan to buy a motorhome and travel.

When they go to bed at night, they assume that their white houses will stay standing, their green gardens will keep growing, their pink babies will keep breathing, and the yellow sun will rise in the morning just as it always does. Many of the faithful are women, giving birth being, after all, the ultimate act of pure faith. When their sons and daughters (whose as yet embryonic faith may temporarily fail them) wake sobbing from nightmares and wail, "Mommy, I dreamed you were dead. You won't die, will you?" these faithful mothers say, in all honesty, "Don't worry, I won't." The faithful sleep soundly.

If ever they find themselves feeling unhappy or afraid (as sometimes they do because, although faithful, they are also still human), they assume this too shall pass. They expect to be safe. They expect to be saved in the long run. They are devoted to the discharge of their daily lives. It does not occur to them that the meaning of life may be open to question.

## II. MEMORY

Remember to put out the garbage, pick up the dry cleaning, defrost the pork chops (the ground beef, the chicken thighs, the fillet of sole). Remember to feed the dog (the cat, the hamster, the goldfish, the canary). Remember the first smile, the first step, the first crush, the first kiss. Remember the bright morning, the long hot afternoon, the quiet evening, the soft bed, gentle rain in the night. Also remember the pain, the disappointments, the humiliations, the broken hearts, and an eclectic assortment of other sorrows. Take these tragedies in stride and with dignity. Do not tear your hair out. Forgive and forget and get on with it. The faithful look back fondly.

They are only passingly familiar with shame, guilt, torment, chaos, existentialism, and metaphysics. The consciences of the faithful are clear. They are not the ones spending millions of dollars on self-help books and exercise videos. They know they've done the best they could. If and when the faithful make mistakes, they know how to forgive themselves without requiring years of expensive therapy in the process.

In the summer, remember the winter: snow sparkling in clear sunlight, children in puffy snowsuits building snowmen and sucking icicles. Remember hockey rinks, rosy cheeks, Christmas carols, wool socks, and hot chocolate with marshmallows. In the winter, remember the summer: tidy green grass beneath big blue sky, long-limbed children playing hide-and-go-seek and running through sprinklers. Remember barbecues, sailboats, flowers, strawberries, and pink lemonade. The faithful can always find something to look forward to. The faithful never confuse the future with the past.

### III. KNOWLEDGE

The knowledge of the faithful is vast. They know how to change a tire on a deserted highway in the middle of the night without getting dirty or killed. They know how to bake a birthday cake in the shape of a bunny rabbit with gumdrop eyes and a pink peppermint nose. They know how to unplug a clogged drain with baking soda and vinegar.

They know how to paint the hallway, refinish the hardwood floors, wallpaper the bedroom, insulate the attic, reshingle the roof, and install a new toilet. They know how to build a campfire and pitch a tent singlehandedly. They know how to tune up the car, repair the furnace, and seal the storm windows to prevent those nasty and expensive winter drafts.

They know how to prepare dinner for eight in an hour and a half for less than twenty dollars. They know how to sew, knit, crochet, and cut hair. They know how to keep themselves, their houses, their cars, and their children clean, very clean. They do not resent having to perform the domestic duties of family life. They may even enjoy doing the laundry, washing the walls, cleaning the oven, and grocery shopping.

They know how to make love to the same person for twenty years without either of them getting bored. They know how to administer CPR and the Heimlich manoeuvre. They know how and when to have fun.

The faithful know exactly what to say at funerals, weddings, and cocktail parties. They know when to laugh and when to cry and they never get these two expressions of emotion mixed up. The faithful know they are normal and they're damn proud of it. What they don't know won't hurt them.

## IV. INNOCENCE

The faithful are so innocent. Despite all evidence to the contrary, they believe that deep down everybody is just like them, or could be. They believe in benevolence, their own and other people's. They think that, given half a chance, even hardened criminals and manic-depressives can change. They are willing to give everyone a second chance. For the faithful, shaking off doubt is as easy as shaking a rug.

The faithful believe in law and order. They still look up to policemen, lawyers, teachers, doctors, and priests. They believe every word these people say. They even believe what the radio weatherman says in the forecast right after the morning news. It does not occur to them that these authority figures could be wrong, corrupt, or just plain stupid. Mind you, even the faithful are beginning to have serious reservations about politicians.

The faithful take many miraculous things for granted. Things like skin, electricity, trees, water, fidelity, the dogged revolution of the earth around the sun. They believe in beauty as a birthright and surround themselves with it whenever they can. They believe in interior decorating and makeup. They never underestimate the degree of happiness to be engendered by renovating the kitchen, placing fresh-cut flowers on the table, purchasing a set of fine silver, a mink coat, a minivan, or miscellaneous precious jewels. The faithful still believe you get what you pay for.

The faithful take things at face value. They do not search for hidden meanings or agendas. They are not skeptical, cynical, or suspicious. They are not often ironic. The faithful are the angels among us.

## V. STRENGTH

The faithless say the faithful are fools. Obviously it must be getting more and more difficult to keep the faith these days. Read the paper. Watch the news. Wonder what the world is coming to. All things considered, it has become harder to believe than to despair.

The faithless say the faithful are missing the point. But secretly the faithless must admit that if indeed, as they allege, there is no point (no purpose, no reason, no hope), then the faithful aren't missing a thing.

The faithless say the faithful are living minor lives, trivial, mundane, frivolous, blind. But secretly the faithless must envy the faithful, wondering if they themselves are simply too faint-hearted for faith.

While the faithless gaze into the abyss, fretting, moaning, and brooding, the faithful are busy getting on with their lives: labouring, rejoicing, carving Hallowe'en pumpkins, roasting Christmas and Thanksgiving turkeys, blowing out birthday candles year after year, and kissing each other wetly at midnight on New Year's Eve.

No matter what, the faithful know how to persevere. They are masters of the rituals that protect them. To the faithful, despair is a foreign language which they have neither the time nor the inclination to learn. The faithful frequently sing in the shower.

The faithful understand the value of fortitude. They carry always with them the courage of their convictions. They do not go to extremes but they could perform miracles if they had to. The faithful will not be crushed by the weight of the world. The faithful are sturdy and brave.

## VI. IMAGINATION

The faithful have their imaginations well in hand. They do not lie awake at night imagining earthquakes, tornadoes, flash floods, or nuclear war. They do not deal in cataclysms. They do not entertain the possibility of being axed to death in their beds by a psychokiller on the loose from the psychiatric hospital on the eastern edge of town. They do not lie there wide-eyed for hours picturing malignant cells galloping through their uteruses, their intestines, their prostate glands, or their brains. To the faithful, a headache is a headache, not a brain tumour. They do not imagine themselves rotting away from the inside out. They do not have detailed sexual fantasies about the mailman, the aerobics instructor, or their children's Grade Two teacher. The nights of the faithful are peaceful. Even their nightmares have happy endings. The faithful wake up smiling. Their subconsciouses are clear.

Imagine perfect health, financial security, your mortgage paid off, a new car every second year. Imagine mowing the lawn on Sunday afternoon and enjoying it. Imagine raking leaves in the fall without having to contemplate the futility of daily life. Imagine your grandchildren sitting at your knee while you tell them the story of your life.

The faithful are seldom haunted by a pesky sense of impending doom. They imagine that their lives are unfolding as they were meant to. They imagine that they are free. They imagine finding their feet planted squarely on the road to heaven. The faithful are prepared to live happily ever after.

Imagine laughing in the face of the future.

Imagine belonging to the fine fierce tribe of the faithful.

## VII. PRAYER

Pray for sunshine, pray for rain. Pray for peace. Pray for an end to the suffering of the unfortunate. Pray silently in a language simple enough for a child to understand. It is not necessary to get down on your knees with your eyes closed, your hands clasped. It is not necessary to hold your breath. Pray while you are cooking dinner, doing the dishes, washing the floor, holding your sleeping child in your arms. Pray with your heart, not just your mouth.

The faithful know how to pray to whatever gods they may worship. The faithful are praying all the time, every step of the way. Their prayers are not the sort that begin with the word *Please*. They do not bargain with their gods for personal favours. They do not make promises they can't keep, to their gods or anyone else. They do not beg for money, power, easy answers, or a yellow Porsche. They do not beseech, petition, implore, solicit, entreat, adjure, or snivel. They do not throw themselves upon the unreliable mercy of the pantheon. They are not dramatic zealots. The faithful are dignified, stalwart, and patient. All things come to them who will but wait. They are committed to simply enduring in a perpetual state of grace. Their faith itself is a never-ending benediction. The faithful may or may not go to church on Sunday. Their faith is their business.

The prayers of the faithful are mostly wordless forms of devotion. Actions speak louder than language. The faithful are reverent, humble, blessed. They are always busy having a religious experience. The faithful are seldom alarmed or afraid. The faithful barely have time to notice that all their prayers have been answered.

## VIII. ABUNDANCE

The faithful have more than enough of everything. They are never stingy. They believe in abundance and they know how to share the wealth. They give regularly to local and international charities and to most panhandlers. They give their old clothes and toys to the poor. The faithful are always generous. Of course they can afford to be. Of course there's more where that came from.

Every evening at dinner the faithful cry, "More, more, let's have some more!" The table is completely covered with heavy oval platters of meat and giant bowls of mashed potatoes and garden salad. They always have dessert. They prefer their children soft and plump. The faithful never bite off more than they can chew.

The days of the faithful are as full as their stomachs. They have energy to burn. They never whine about having too much to do. They like to be busy. They do not need time to think. Their bounty abounds. Their homes and their hearts are always full. Full of exuberance or solemnity, whichever current circumstances may require. The cups of the faithful frequently runneth over.

The arms of the faithful are always open. They have time for everyone. The faithful know how to share both the triumphs and the sorrows of others. They've always got the coffee on, blueberry muffins in the oven, a box of Kleenex handy just in case. The faithful know how to listen and they only offer advice when they're asked.

The faithful know how to count their blessings, even if it takes all day. They have all the time in the world. They know when to thank their lucky stars. The faithful are privileged but they are not smug.

### IX. WISDOM

The faithful are uncommonly wise. They are indefatigably glad to be alive. To the faithful everything matters. It does not occur to them that their whole lives may well end up having been nothing but a waste of time. The faithful are always paying attention. They know how to revel in the remarkable treasures of the everyday: a pink rose blooming below the window, a ham and cheese omelette steaming on the plate, a white cat washing her face in the sun, a new baby with eyes the colour of sand, a double rainbow in the western sky after a long hard rain. The faithful love rainbows and pots of gold. They know how to take pleasure wherever they can find it. The faithful are always exclaiming, "Look, look, look at that!" To the faithful nothing is mundane.

The faithful are everywhere. See if you can spot them: in the bank lineup on Friday afternoon, at McDonald's having hamburgers and chocolate milkshakes with their children, in the park walking the dog at seven o'clock on a January morning, at the hardware store shopping for a socket wrench and a rake. The faithful may be right in your own backyard.

The faithful are thankful for small pleasures and small mercies.

The faithful are earnest.

The faithful are easily amused.

The faithful do or do not know how lucky they are.

The faithful frequently cry at parades.

The faithful are not afraid of the dark because they have seen the light. Nothing is lost on the faithful. As far as they are concerned, wonders will never cease. The faithful are convinced that the best is yet to come.

## X. HOPE

The hope of the faithful is a tonic. Their eyes are bright, their skin is clear, their hair is shiny, and their blood flows vigorously through all of their veins. Even in times of adversity, the faithful know how to take heart. At the tiniest tingle of possibility, the faithful are not afraid to get their hopes up. They believe in divine providence. It all depends on how you define *divine*. The faithful are not fools. Although the faithless would dispute this, the faithful live in the real world just as much as anyone. They know all about hoping against hope. But they are not troubled by paradox. They are immune to those fits of despair which can cripple and dumbfound.

Concerning matters both big and small, the faithful have always got hope. Their whole lives are forms of perpetual devotion to the promise which hope extends. The faithful breathe hope like air, drink it like water, eat it like popcorn. Once they start, they can't stop.

Hope for world peace. Hope for a drop in the crime rate, shelter for the homeless, food for the hungry, rehabilitation for the deranged. Hope your son does well on his spelling test. Hope your team wins the World Series. Hope your mother does not have cancer. Hope the pork chops are not undercooked. Hope your best friend's husband is not having an affair with his secretary. Hope you win the lottery. Hope the rain stops tomorrow. Hope this story has a happy ending.

The hope of the faithful is infinite, ever expanding to fill the space available. Faith begets hope. Hope begets faith. Faith and hope beget power.

The faithful lean steadily into the wind.

*—1994*

Michael Winter (b. 1965) *was born in England but moved to Newfoundland at the age of ten, a dual heritage reflected in the name of his narrator Gabriel English. Winter grew up in Corner Brook, though he now divides his time between St. John's and Toronto. Part of the new wave of Newfoundland fiction, Winter's works include* Creaking in Their Skins *(1994),* One Last Good Look *(1999), and* The Big Why *(2004). "Archibald the Arctic" is the title of a book written by Archibald Fleming (1883–1953), an Anglican missionary to the Inuit.*

## *Michael Winter*
# Archibald the Arctic

Early on New Year's Day my mother woke me to say, calmly, that two police officers were at the door. She said this in the same way she'd say there's a fried egg sandwich in the oven. I was seventeen, home for Christmas, staying in Junior's room, in his bed in fact. I had been out with Geoff Doyle and Skizicks the night before, we ended up on Crow Hill throwing our empties down on the tracks, enjoying the wet distant crumple they made, waiting for the fireworks to sputter into the cold dark air. I remember Skizicks, who is a year older and knew we were virgins, saying he'd screwed Heidi Miller against the wall in behind Tim Horton's. Over the course of two long minutes we counted the reports of eleven shotguns, sounding small, disorganized and lonely.

I walked to the porch in my cold jeans, barefoot. I was hungry and my head hurt. I worked my mouth. The police officers were still outside. I opened the screen door. The white metal handle was frosty. Snow was drifting lightly onto their new fur hats, their epaulets, sliding off the waxed cruiser which hummed quietly in behind my father's car. There were no lights flashing. The driveway needed to be shovelled. Doyle would be up in his window, if he was up. The officers were facing each other, conversing. Their footprints were the first to our door in the new year. They looked fit and very awake.

Are you Gabriel English?

Yes.

We have a warrant for your arrest, son.

I knew there was something you could say here. I searched for the proper wording.

Can I ask what the charge is?

We'll discuss that at the station.

Am I under arrest?

This is what my father had taught us. When the law wants you, ask if you're under arrest. I was glad I could remember it.

We'd prefer to formally charge you down at the station, son, after we've cleared a few things up.

My father, who had been in the bathroom shaving, came to the door. He was still in his undervest, mopping his neck and chin with a white towel. He wasn't wearing his glasses, which gave him a relaxed look. He said, Would it be all right, fellas, if the boy had some breakfast? I'll bring him down right after.

The way he dried himself with the towel showed off his massive, pale biceps, his thick wrists. The thickness was well-earned. There was a beat and then the older officer said that would be fine. He decided to look at my father for a moment and then they turned and made new footprints back to the cruiser.

My father turned to me and said, Well what a way to start the new year. He said this in a way that reassured me. He knew already that I hadn't done anything, that I wasn't capable of doing a bad thing. He was confident about this, all he knew about me was good things. I was the good son. His impression reinforced a faith in my own innocence. It made me realize what must have happened and suddenly I got upset.

It's Junior, isn't it, he said.

I suspect it's Junior, Dad.

And why do you suspect him.

He knew that I must be in league with Junior, had information that we'd kept from him. Over breakfast I told him what I knew. He listened as if, while the particulars of the event were new to him, they fit into the larger maze which was the interlaced lives of his sons. He said, They're going to begin with a presumption. That you've been driving. And you haven't. Be flat out with that and the rest hold to your chin. He said, People in charge like to figure things out. They don't appreciate confessions.

We drove to the police station, which was a bunker below the Sir Richard Squires building. The building housed the first elevator in Newfoundland.

I liked the Up and Down arrows by the elevator buttons. That was my earliest appreciation of technology's ability to appear prescient.

I thought it was a considerate touch by the makers. The elevator was the avenue to Corner Brook's public library, which my father had introduced to me before I could read. I would pick up books Junior had chosen, like *Archibald the Arctic* and stare at the riddle of print. Junior loved the northern explorers—of men eating their dogs, and then each other.

The lobby was glass on three sides, with nine storeys of brick pressing down on it. My father took me to the sixth floor once, to a government office where he had some tax business. I could see the Bowater mill, the neck of the bay twisting around the town of Curling, the swans (the whitest things in town) drifting below in the reservoir which cooled the mill's furnaces, the secondary schools on the landscaped hill to the east. I was uneasy in the building. I was convinced the glass footing would topple. I worried for the commissionaire stationed at his desk by the fountain.

The fountain stood in the centre of the lobby behind an iron railing. It drizzled water over its scalloped and flared glass edges.

A boy was carefully tossing a penny in. The fountain was a silent, enormous presence, a wordless example of grander things one could value and live for. I loved the fountain even when no one and nothing told me it was worthy of love.

My father leaned against the rail. He said if he had guts, he'd sell everything and help the poor in Calcutta. That was his base belief about what was right. His weakness drove him to self-interest, to preserving family and constantly bettering our material position. He could appreciate decorative flourishes, but never allowed himself to get carried away.

My mother would say I have these thoughts because we emigrated from England. My mother has given a lot of time to such considerations. She cultivates hindsight, and researches the repercussions of certain acts. Perhaps if I had grown up where I was born, had not felt strange in my own skin, I wouldn't be so sensitive in the world. In the house I spoke with an English accent, outside I pronounced words the way Doyle and Skizicks said them. I said brakfest, chimley, sove you a seat. I was aware of the boundary between blood bond and friends, between house and world. Junior was different. He managed to be pure Newfoundlander.

My father and I walked down to the police station and I began my brief story of never having driven a Japanese car in Alberta and the officer nodded as if he knew the truth of the matter only too well, that my arrest was a technicality, that a million brothers a month pretend to be younger brothers and he was going to add this latest infraction to the pile. I was free to go.

The station, below the library, was a place I had been to only once before, when Doyle and Skizicks and I were accused of breaking a window. We were kicking stones down Valley Road and a neighbour's window crashed in. We ran. We ran home. Junior said, When you're in trouble, where do you run?

Home.

No Gabe, always run away from home.

I found the station small and casual. It didn't look hard to break out of. There were three cells in the back that I could only hear.

I never spoke to Junior about this arrest. He had left to go back to Alberta on Boxing Day. He was plugging dynamite holes in Fort MacMurray.

My father has cried twice—once when a German shepherd we had ran from his knee and was crushed by a snow plough, the other when Junior left to work in the tar sands. It doesn't hurt me to think of him crying for Junior and not for my departure, or even crying for a dog we rescued from the pound, a thin, shivering creature who knew who to thank for fattening him up. He became too fierce in protecting us. Crying is an irrational act and should never be resented. I know Junior's life is a riskier thing. I know that my parents trust my good senses (I am named executor of their wills). There will be greater love attached to wilder men.

Before Christmas I went out with Junior to a cabin belonging to one of the Brads. Junior knew three men named Brad, and my mother had begun to disbelieve him. That the Brads had other names. She would answer the phone and say, No, he's off somewhere with one of the Brads. As if that was a joke and she wasn't to be fooled. But I believe they were all called Brad. I think perhaps naming someone Brad is not a good idea.

Brad picked us up in his black and gold Trans Am and tried his best to charm our mother who appreciated the gesture but still kept her opinion. I sat in the back and we detoured down Mountbatten Road. We stopped at a house with blue aluminum siding. Brad honked his horn and a screen door opened with two women waving and smiling and pointing a finger to indicate one moment. Brad popped the trunk from inside and waited.

Me: Who are they.

Junior: Our wool blankets.

The girls climbed in the back and I remembered Linda from a party Junior had at the house. She had come into my bedroom, sat on the floor with a beer, and told me how she loved Junior to bits.

They nudged me with their hips to get their seat belts on. I was in the middle. Then Linda smiled: You're gonna be our chaperon, Gabe. Danielle leaned forward and pulled on Brad's hair and kissed him on the ear and I could see the perfect contour of her breast.

Brad Pynn had a cabin up in Pynn's Brook. Junior liked to go snow-mobiling and drinking up there over the holidays. He'd flown into town, gotten his presents giftwrapped by Linda at the hardware store he used to work at, and invited her to Brad's.

Brad and Junior had an old plan to rob the small bank above Co-op grocery on Main Street. I don't mind revealing this because, to my know-ledge, they never pulled the heist and now, I believe, the bank is closed. It was a small bank, used by members of the Co-op. It was less formal than other banks. There were just desks, rather than counters with glass. You could walk right into the safe if you were quick. Junior was convinced you could pull off that job. The only problem was, everyone knew him. And if you did it with someone like a Brad Pynn, you could never be sure if he'd blow too much money one night, or brag, or betray you.

This bank scheme was something that always came up after a few beers, or during a vial of oil and a sewing needle, which Junior had out in the front seat, spreading the green oil over a cigarette paper on his knee. The joint was passed and I had to take it from Danielle, smoke, and hand it to Linda. Danielle kept pressing my knee saying, Look at that, if she saw a cute house, or a crow on the melted road that refused to lift. She'd press my knee then slide her hand a little up my thigh, as though she'd forgotten it was my thigh. Linda put her arm along the back window to make more shoulder room. They were quite relaxed.

Junior had a sawed-off shotgun between his legs which I watched him load with a red number four shell. He asked Brad to roll down his window. Cold air pummelled into the car. Junior clicked the chamber closed. He lifted the barrel up to Brad's windowsill, pushed off the safety, stared back at us and said, Watch this.

He saw Danielle's hand on my thigh and Linda's arm around my neck and paused.

There were three black objects ahead standing in the snow on Brad's side of the highway. Brad kept the speedometer at the limit. Junior didn't aim, just pointed at the grade and estimated the distance. He fired and the crows flew up alertly. Brad swerved.

Jesus, June.

He slipped off the road, hit bare ice, fishtailed, adjusted for the swing, pumped the brakes a little, and straightened up. The blast echoed inside the car. Junior was laughing until he saw that Linda and Danielle were horrified. We all saw, through a thin veil of trees, a line of cabins.

Oh, honey. Sorry about that.

Linda clenched her jaw and stared out her window. Her arms crossed and flexed.

Brad owned a Gold Wing which he parked and chained into the cabin over winter, and this bike he straddled and drank beer from and turned on the stereo embedded in the ruby fibreglass windjammer and would have started it up if Junior hadn't, at Brad's request, drained the cylinders and cleaned his valves and left the engine to hibernate in drenched oil.

Brad and June took the purple Arctic Cat for a bomb down the lake to ice fish and to hunt with the sawed-off. They carried a small auger and they had slugs in case of a moose. The girls and I played Scrabble and drank rum mixed with Tang crystals. I missed touching their arms and hips. They were about twenty, both attending the Career Academy and slowly becoming disappointed. But that winter they were still bright, talkative Newfoundland women who wore friendship rings and small twinkling earrings and could imagine ways to have fun and succeed. They'd spent summers working in the fish plant in Curling and winters wearing white skates on ponds like Little Rapids. I could tell they enjoyed me and while each on her own might have been bored with my company, together they shared a glee in flirting, in egging me on. In their eyes I was a man in the making, and I accepted this. Women like a confidence no matter what the confidence is.

Linda said, You're going to be something, aren't you. You're like your brother, but you're smarter and gentle.

Ah Linda he's shy, boy.

And Danielle put her arm around my neck and felt my ear. Her collarbone lifted a white bra strap. Shy? Why you got nothing to be shy about.

She slipped her hand down to my waist.

Have you ever done the dirty? she said.

I didn't have to answer and they laughed and loved the fact that now they were getting into this.

You know something me and Linda have wanted to do?

Linda felt my crotch. She put a hand in my jeans pocket.

Wow. Danielle. Guess what he's not wearing.

Go way.

Danielle slipped her hand in my other pocket. This pocket had the lining torn and her warm, probing hand clasped directly and gently.

Oh Linda we've got a fine young man on our hands.

A growing boy.

Linda unbuttoned my jeans. I shifted in my chair and prayed that the skidoo would be loud. I tried to recall the sound it made as it buzzed up the lake. But as it was, even if Brad and Junior came in the door, nothing could be seen above the table. Nothing except an astonished boy and two eager, laughing women leaning in to him.

Last fall Junior hit a moose. This was six days after the mandatory seat belt law had been established, and it was this law which had saved his life. Dad and I found him unconscious, pinned behind the wheel of his orange-and-chrome VW Bug. Eight hundred pounds of moose had rolled over the bonnet, crumpled the windshield, bent the doorframes and lay bleeding in his lap. The ambulance service had to wait for the jaws of life to free him. He'd loved the Bug, it had lived its previous life in salt-free Florida. Investigators measured skid marks, the animal was towed off with two canvas cables, its injuries charted, witnesses signed statements and it was declared that Junior had been driving with abandon under severe winter conditions.

He bought a Rabbit then, and two weeks later he rammed into the back of an eighteen-wheeler; the Rabbit was dragged four hundred metres before the semi braked. The trucker was furious, he hadn't even seen Junior he was that far up his ass. Up your wind tunnel, Junior said, looking for an opportunity to pass. The trucker wanted to smack him. He would have if my father hadn't stretched his big hands in an obvious way.

Junior began giving up on a Datsun, an old, whipped car. He was motoring around town, scouting for other drivers' infractions. Someone running a red light. If he saw anything, he drove into it. He was making money, he said, from other people's insurance.

When the Datsun had built up a nest egg he asked if I wanted to go for a ride. This was after supper, in early December. He'd decided, he said, to retire the vehicle. The insurance company had declared it a liability and he had to write it off before the calendar year.

We drove to the empty, carefully ploughed parking lot behind the school my father taught at. The street lamps were just flickering on. It was terminally ill, Junior said, and we had to put it out of its misery.

He revved up the motor, spun on the slightly icy pavement, and swaggered the car towards a ploughed mound of snow at the edge of the lot.

Hold on, Gabe.

The headlights lurched, grew in concentration against the bank as we accelerated and approached. The car exploded into compact snow, driving in a few feet, snow smacking against the windshield, the hill absorbed our blow. The motor muffled, hummed, still ran happily. If it had a tail it would be wagging.

Junior shifted into reverse, hit the wipers, spun wide, and galloped for the opposite end of the lot, dipsy doodling around a street-light pole on the way, swinging on the ice and slamming sideways into the far bank of snow.

I had to get out and push this time. The exhaust was clogged with snow. I watched as Junior aimed for a sturdier bank pressed against the school. The car whined horribly. There was no give in the snow. The seat belt cut against his chest as he came up hard on a hidden concrete post. A crease formed in the hood of the car, the grill burst open and jets of water spouted up, dousing the windshield and melting then freezing the snow on the hood. The motor kept running as if nothing had happened. I ran to him.

Can't kill a fucking Datsun, man.

Junior got out to reconsider his approach. I reminded him that if he went through with this demolition we'd have to walk home. He popped the hood (it opened at the windshield) and cranked up the heat to transfer valuable degrees over from the engine. Then he said, Come look at this.

We stood on the front bumper and stared into the dark classroom. On the board were the yellow chalk drawings our father made of various projects: tables, lamps, chairs. There were angles and choice of wood screw and the correct use of a plane and a clamp. The work tables were cleared, the tools all hanging in their racks, the cement floor swept with sawdust and water. Everything in order.

We drove home with the broken radiator, my eyes fixed to the temperature gauge, which hovered past the orange bar.

It was then Junior asked me for a favour. We were parked, the lights shut off, the engine ticking to the cold. He said his insurance was sky-high. What we'd do, he said, is insure his next car in my name and he'd be a second driver. It would save him a hell of a lot of cash.

At the time I wasn't driving anything and when you're not using something, it's hard to feel the importance of giving it away. There was a mature air about Junior needing my help in the adult world. But a warning hunch spread through my body. I knew there would be repercussions, though I could not articulate them. It all seemed reasonable, he just needed to borrow my driver's license for an hour.

It wasn't just the insurance, the police told me. The car was registered in my name too. I had an overdrawn bank account. There was a bad prairie loan. A lien on a leased Ford pickup. In Alberta, his entire life had become my life. He was living under the name Gabriel English. It was as if he never expected me to live a life, so he'd better do it for me.

*—1999*

*Jhumpa Lahiri (b. 1967) was born in London, England, to Bengali parents but has lived most of her life in the United States. The sense of exile created by being connected to but not fully belonging to three different continents is a theme of much of her work, including her debut short-story collection,* The Interpreter of Maladies *(2000), which won the Pulitzer Prize, and her novel* The Namesake *(2003), which was made into a film in 2006.*

## Jhumpa Lahiri
# Interpreter of Maladies

At the tea stall Mr. and Mrs. Das bickered about who should take Tina to the toilet. Eventually Mrs. Das relented when Mr. Das pointed out that he had given the girl her bath the night before. In the rearview mirror Mr. Kapasi watched as Mrs. Das emerged slowly from his bulky white Ambassador, dragging her shaved, largely bare legs across the back seat. She did not hold the little girl's hand as they walked to the rest room.

They were on their way to see the Sun Temple at Konarak.[1] It was a dry, bright Saturday, the mid-July heat tempered by a steady ocean breeze, ideal weather for sightseeing. Ordinarily Mr. Kapasi would not have stopped so soon along the way, but less than five minutes after he'd picked up the family that morning in front of Hotel Sandy Villa, the little girl had complained. The first thing Mr. Kapasi had noticed when he saw Mr. and Mrs. Das, standing with their children under the portico of the hotel, was that they were very young, perhaps not even thirty. In addition to Tina they had two boys, Ronny and Bobby, who appeared very close in age and had teeth covered in a network of flashing silver wires. The family looked Indian but dressed as foreigners did, the children in stiff, brightly colored clothing and caps with translucent visors. Mr. Kapasi was accustomed to foreign tourists; he was assigned to them regularly because he could speak English. Yesterday he had driven an elderly couple from Scotland, both with spotted faces and fluffy white hair so thin it exposed their sunburnt scalps. In comparison, the tanned, youthful faces of Mr. and Mrs. Das were all the more striking. When he'd introduced himself, Mr. Kapasi

---

[1]*Konarak:* village in Orissa state, eastern India.

had pressed his palms together in greeting, but Mr. Das squeezed hands like an American so that Mr. Kapasi felt it in his elbow. Mrs. Das, for her part, had flexed one side of her mouth, smiling dutifully at Mr. Kapasi, without displaying any interest in him.

As they waited at the tea stall, Ronny, who looked like the older of the two boys, clambered suddenly out of the back seat, intrigued by a goat tied to a stake in the ground.

"Don't touch it," Mr. Das said. He glanced up from his paperback tour book, which said "INDIA" in yellow letters and looked as if it had been published abroad. His voice, somehow tentative and a little shrill, sounded as though it had not yet settled into maturity.

"I want to give it a piece of gum," the boy called back as he trotted ahead.

Mr. Das stepped out of the car and stretched his legs by squatting briefly to the ground. A clean-shaven man, he looked exactly like a magnified version of Ronny. He had a sapphire blue visor, and was dressed in shorts, sneakers, and a T-shirt. The camera slung around his neck, with an impressive telephoto lens and numerous buttons and markings, was the only complicated thing he wore. He frowned, watching as Ronny rushed toward the goat, but appeared to have no intention of intervening. "Bobby, make sure that your brother doesn't do anything stupid."

"I don't feel like it," Bobby said, not moving. He was sitting in the front seat beside Mr. Kapasi, studying a picture of the elephant god taped to the glove compartment.

"No need to worry," Mr. Kapasi said. "They are quite tame." Mr. Kapasi was forty-six years old, with receding hair that had gone completely silver, but his butterscotch complexion and his unlined brow, which he treated in spare moments to dabs of lotus-oil balm, made it easy to imagine what he must have looked like at an earlier age. He wore gray trousers and a matching jacket-style shirt, tapered at the waist, with short sleeves and a large pointed collar, made of a thin but durable synthetic material. He had specified both the cut and the fabric to his tailor—it was his preferred uniform for giving tours because it did not get crushed during his long hours behind the wheel. Through the windshield he watched as Ronny circled around the goat, touched it quickly on its side, then trotted back to the car.

"You left India as a child?" Mr. Kapasi asked when Mr. Das had settled once again into the passenger seat.

"Oh, Mina and I were both born in America," Mr. Das announced with an air of sudden confidence. "Born and raised. Our parents live here now, in Assansol. They retired. We visit them every couple years." He turned to watch as the little girl ran toward the car, the wide purple bows of her sundress flopping on her narrow brown shoulders. She was holding to her chest a doll with yellow hair that looked as if it had been chopped, as a punitive measure, with a pair of dull scissors. "This is Tina's first trip to India, isn't it, Tina?"

"I don't have to go to the bathroom anymore," Tina announced.

"Where's Mina?" Mr. Das asked.

Mr. Kapasi found it strange that Mr. Das should refer to his wife by her first name when speaking to the little girl. Tina pointed to where Mrs. Das was purchasing something from one of the shirtless men who worked at the tea stall. Mr. Kapasi heard one of the shirtless men sing a phrase from a popular Hindi love song as Mrs. Das walked back to the car, but she did not appear to understand the words of the song, for she did not express irritation, or embarrassment, or react in any other way to the man's declarations.

He observed her. She wore a red-and-white-checkered skirt that stopped above her knees, slip-on shoes with a square wooden heel, and a close-fitting blouse styled like a man's undershirt. The blouse was decorated at chest-level with a calico appliqué in the shape of a straw-berry. She was a short woman with small hands like paws, her frosty pink fingernails painted to match her lips, and was slightly plump in her figure. Her hair, shorn only a little longer than her husband's, was parted far to one side. She was wearing large dark brown sunglasses with a pinkish tint to them, and carried a big straw bag, almost as big as her torso, shaped like a bowl, with a water bottle poking out of it. She walked slowly, carrying some puffed rice tossed with peanuts and chili peppers in a large packet made from newspapers. Mr. Kapasi turned to Mr. Das.

"Where in America do you live?"

"New Brunswick, New Jersey."

"Next to New York?"

"Exactly. I teach middle school there."

"What subject?"

"Science. In fact, every year I take my students on a trip to the Museum of Natural History in New York City. In a way we have a lot in common, you could say, you and I. How long have you been a tour guide, Mr. Kapasi?"

"Five years."

Mrs. Das reached the car. "How long's the trip?" she asked, shutting the door.

"About two and a half hours," Mr. Kapasi replied.

At this Mrs. Das gave an impatient sigh, as if she had been traveling her whole life without pause. She fanned herself with a folded Bombay film magazine written in English.

"I thought that the Sun Temple is only eighteen miles north of Puri," Mr. Das said, tapping on the tour book.

"The roads to Konarak are poor. Actually it is a distance of fifty-two miles," Mr. Kapasi explained.

Mr. Das nodded, readjusting the camera strap where it had begun to chafe the back of his neck.

Before starting the ignition, Mr. Kapasi reached back to make sure the cranklike locks on the inside of each of the back doors were secured. As soon as the car began to move the little girl began to play with the lock on her side, clicking it with some effort forward and backward, but Mrs. Das said nothing to stop her. She sat a bit slouched at one end of the back seat, not offering her puffed rice to anyone. Ronny and Tina sat on either side of her, both snapping bright green gum.

"Look," Bobby said as the car began to gather speed. He pointed with his finger to the tall trees that lined the road. "Look."

"Monkeys!" Ronny shrieked. "Wow!"

They were seated in groups along the branches, with shining black faces, silver bodies, horizontal eyebrows, and crested heads. Their long gray tails dangled like a series of ropes among the leaves. A few scratched themselves with black leathery hands, or swung their feet, staring as the car passed.

"We call them the hanuman," Mr. Kapasi said. "They are quite common in the area."

As soon as he spoke, one of the monkeys leaped into the middle of the road, causing Mr. Kapasi to brake suddenly. Another bounced onto the hood of the car, then sprang away. Mr. Kapasi beeped his horn. The children began to get excited, sucking in their breath and covering their faces partly with their hands. They had never seen monkeys outside of a zoo, Mr. Das explained. He asked Mr. Kapasi to stop the car so that he could take a picture.

While Mr. Das adjusted his telephoto lens, Mrs. Das reached into her straw bag and pulled out a bottle of colorless nail polish, which she proceeded to stroke on the tip of her index finger.

The little girl stuck out a hand. "Mine too. Mommy, do mine too."

"Leave me alone," Mrs. Das said, blowing on her nail and turning her body slightly. "You're making me mess up."

The little girl occupied herself by buttoning and unbuttoning a pinafore on the doll's plastic body.

"All set," Mr. Das said, replacing the lens cap.

The car rattled considerably as it raced along the dusty road, causing them all to pop up from their seats every now and then, but Mrs. Das continued to polish her nails. Mr. Kapasi eased up on the accelerator, hoping to produce a smoother ride. When he reached for the gearshift the boy in front accommodated him by swinging his hairless knees out of the way. Mr. Kapasi noted that this boy was slightly paler than the other children. "Daddy, why is the driver sitting on the wrong side in this car, too?" the boy asked.

"They all do that here, dummy," Ronny said.

"Don't call your brother a dummy," Mr. Das said. He turned to Mr. Kapasi. "In America, you know . . . it confuses them."

"Oh yes, I am well aware," Mr. Kapasi said. As delicately as he could, he shifted gears again, accelerating as they approached a hill in the road. "I see it on *Dallas*, the steering wheels are on the left-hand side."

"What's *Dallas*?" Tina asked, banging her now naked doll on the seat behind Mr. Kapasi.

"It went off the air," Mr. Das explained. "It's a television show."

They were all like siblings, Mr. Kapasi thought as they passed a row of date trees. Mr. and Mrs. Das behaved like an older brother and sister, not parents. It seemed that they were in charge of the children only for the day; it was hard to believe they were regularly responsible for anything other than themselves. Mr. Das tapped on his lens cap, and his tour book, dragging his thumbnail occasionally across the pages so that they made a scraping sound. Mrs. Das continued to polish her nails. She had still not removed her sunglasses. Every now and then Tina renewed her plea that she wanted her nails done, too, and so at one point

Mrs. Das flicked a drop of polish on the little girl's finger before depositing the bottle back inside her straw bag.

"Isn't this an air-conditioned car?" she asked, still blowing on her hand. The window on Tina's side was broken and could not be rolled down.

"Quit complaining," Mr. Das said. "It isn't so hot."

"I told you to get a car with air-conditioning," Mrs. Das continued. "Why do you do this, Raj, just to save a few stupid rupees. What are you saving us, fifty cents?"

Their accents sounded just like the ones Mr. Kapasi heard on American television programs, though not like the ones on *Dallas*.

"Doesn't it get tiresome, Mr. Kapasi, showing people the same thing every day?" Mr. Das asked, rolling down his own window all the way. "Hey, do you mind stopping the car. I just want to get a shot of this guy."

Mr. Kapasi pulled over to the side of the road as Mr. Das took a picture of a barefoot man, his head wrapped in a dirty turban, seated on top of a cart of grain sacks pulled by a pair of bullocks. Both the man and the bullocks were emaciated. In the back seat Mrs. Das gazed out another window, at the sky, where nearly transparent clouds passed quickly in front of one another.

"I look forward to it, actually," Mr. Kapasi said as they continued on their way. "The Sun Temple is one of my favorite places. In that way it is a reward for me. I give tours on Fridays and Saturdays only. I have another job during the week."

"Oh? Where?" Mr. Das asked.

"I work in a doctor's office."

"You're a doctor?"

"I am not a doctor. I work with one. As an interpreter."

"What does a doctor need an interpreter for?"

"He has a number of Gujarati patients. My father was Gujarati, but many people do not speak Gujarati in this area, including the doctor. And so the doctor asked me to work in his office, interpreting what the patients say."

"Interesting. I've never heard of anything like that," Mr. Das said. Mr. Kapasi shrugged. "It is a job like any other."

"But so romantic," Mrs. Das said dreamily, breaking her extended silence. She lifted her pinkish brown sunglasses and arranged them on top of her head like a tiara. For the first time, her eyes met Mr. Kapasi's in the rearview mirror: pale, a bit small, their gaze fixed but drowsy.

Mr. Das craned to look at her. "What's so romantic about it?"

"I don't know. Something." She shrugged, knitting her brows together for an instant. "Would you like a piece of gum, Mr. Kapasi?" she asked brightly. She reached into her straw bag and handed him a small square wrapped in green-and-white-striped paper. As soon as Mr. Kapasi put the gum in his mouth a thick sweet liquid burst onto his tongue.

"Tell us more about your job, Mr. Kapasi," Mrs. Das said.

"What would you like to know, madame?"

"I don't know," she shrugged, munching on some puffed rice and licking the mustard oil from the corners of her mouth. "Tell us a typical situation." She settled back in her seat, her head tilted in a patch of sun, and closed her eyes. "I want to picture what happens."

"Very well. The other day a man came in with a pain in his throat."

"Did he smoke cigarettes?"

"No. It was very curious. He complained that he felt as if there were long pieces of straw stuck in his throat. When I told the doctor he was able to prescribe the proper medication."

"That's so neat."

"Yes," Mr. Kapasi agreed after some hesitation.

"So these patients are totally dependent on you," Mrs. Das said. She spoke slowly, as if she were thinking aloud. "In a way, more dependent on you than the doctor."

"How do you mean? How could it be?"

"Well, for example, you could tell the doctor that the pain felt like a burning, not straw. The patient would never know what you had told the doctor, and the doctor wouldn't know that you had told the wrong thing. It's a big responsibility."

"Yes, a big responsibility you have there, Mr. Kapasi," Mr. Das agreed.

Mr. Kapasi had never thought of his job in such complimentary terms. To him it was a thankless occupation. He found nothing noble in interpreting people's maladies, assiduously translating the symptoms of so many swollen bones, countless cramps of bellies and bowels, spots on people's palms that changed color, shape, or size. The doctor, nearly half his age, had an affinity for bell-bottom trousers and made humorless jokes about the Congress party. Together they worked in a stale little infirmary where Mr. Kapasi's smartly tailored clothes clung to him in the heat, in spite of the blackened blades of a ceiling fan churning over their heads.

The job was a sign of his failings. In his youth he'd been a devoted scholar of foreign languages, the owner of an impressive collection of dictionaries. He had dreamed of being an interpreter for diplomats and dignitaries, resolving conflicts between people and nations, settling disputes of which he alone could understand both sides. He was a self-educated man. In a series of notebooks, in the evenings before his parents settled his marriage, he had listed the common etymologies of words, and at one point in his life he was confident that he could converse, if given the opportunity, in English, French, Russian, Portuguese, and Italian, not to mention Hindi, Bengali, Orissi, and Gujarati. Now only a handful of European phrases remained in his memory, scattered words for things like saucers and chairs. English was the only non-Indian language he spoke fluently anymore. Mr. Kapasi knew it was not a remarkable talent. Sometimes he feared that his children knew better English than he did, just from watching television. Still, it came in handy for the tours.

He had taken the job as an interpreter after his first son, at the age of seven, contracted typhoid—that was how he had first made the acquaintance of the doctor. At the time Mr. Kapasi had been teaching English in a grammar school, and he bartered his skills as an interpreter to pay the increasingly exorbitant medical bills. In the end the boy had died one evening in his mother's arms, his limbs burning with fever, but then there was the funeral to pay for, and the other children who were born soon enough, and the newer, bigger house, and the good schools and tutors, and the fine shoes and the television, and the countless other ways he tried to console his wife and to keep her from crying in her sleep, and so when the doctor offered to pay him twice as much as he earned at the grammar school, he accepted. Mr. Kapasi knew that his wife had little regard for his career as an interpreter. He knew it reminded her of the son she'd lost, and that she resented the other lives he helped, in his own small way, to save. If ever she referred to his position, she used the phrase "doctor's assistant," as if the process of interpretation were equal to taking someone's temperature, or changing a bedpan. She never asked him about the patients who came to the doctor's office, or said that his job was a big responsibility.

For this reason it flattered Mr. Kapasi that Mrs. Das was so intrigued by his job. Unlike his wife, she had reminded him of its intellectual challenges. She had also used the word "romantic." She did not behave in a romantic way toward her husband, and yet she had used the word to describe him. He wondered if Mr. and Mrs. Das were a bad match, just as he and his wife were. Perhaps they, too, had little in common apart from three children and a decade of their lives. The signs he recognized from his own marriage were there—the bickering, the indifference, the protracted silences. Her sudden interest in him, an interest she did not express in either her husband or her children, was mildly intoxicating. When Mr. Kapasi thought once again about how she had said "romantic," the feeling of intoxication grew.

He began to check his reflection in the rearview mirror as he drove, feeling grateful that he had chosen the gray suit that morning and not the brown one, which tended to sag a little in the knees. From time to time he glanced through the mirror at Mrs. Das. In addition to glancing at her face he glanced at the strawberry between her breasts, and the golden brown hollow in her throat. He decided to tell Mrs. Das about another patient, and another: the young woman who had complained of a sensation of raindrops in her spine, the gentleman whose birthmark had begun to sprout hairs. Mrs. Das listened attentively, stroking her hair with a small plastic brush that resembled an oval bed of nails, asking more questions, for yet another example. The children were quiet, intent on spotting more monkeys in the trees, and Mr. Das was absorbed by his tour book, so it seemed like a private conversation between Mr. Kapasi and Mrs. Das. In this manner the next half hour passed, and when they stopped for lunch at a roadside restaurant that sold fritters and omelette sandwiches, usually something Mr. Kapasi looked forward to on his tours so that he could sit in peace and enjoy some hot tea, he was disappointed. As the Das family settled together under a magenta umbrella fringed with white and orange tassels, and placed their orders with one of the waiters who marched about in tricornered caps, Mr. Kapasi reluctantly headed toward a neighboring table.

"Mr. Kapasi, wait. There's room here," Mrs. Das called out. She gathered Tina onto her lap, insisting that he accompany them. And so, together, they had bottled mango juice and sandwiches and plates of onions and potatoes deep-fried in graham-flour batter. After finishing two omelette sandwiches Mr. Das took more pictures of the group as they ate.

"How much longer?" he asked Mr. Kapasi as he paused to load a new roll of film in the camera.

"About half an hour more."

By now the children had gotten up from the table to look at more monkeys perched in a nearby tree, so there was a considerable space between Mrs. Das and Mr. Kapasi. Mr. Das placed the camera to his face and squeezed one eye shut, his tongue exposed at one corner of his mouth. "This looks funny. Mina, you need to lean in closer to Mr. Kapasi."

She did. He could smell a scent on her skin, like a mixture of whiskey and rosewater. He worried suddenly that she could smell his perspiration, which he knew had collected beneath the synthetic material of his shirt. He polished off his mango juice in one gulp and smoothed his silver hair with his hands. A bit of the juice dripped onto his chin. He wondered if Mrs. Das had noticed.

She had not. "What's your address, Mr. Kapasi?" she inquired, fishing for something inside her straw bag.

"You would like my address?"

"So we can send you copies," she said. "Of the pictures." She handed him a scrap of paper which she had hastily ripped from a page of her film magazine. The blank portion was limited, for the narrow strip was crowded by lines of text and a tiny picture of a hero and heroine embracing under a eucalyptus tree.

The paper curled as Mr. Kapasi wrote his address in clear, careful letters. She would write to him, asking about his days interpreting at the doctor's office, and he would respond eloquently, choosing only the most entertaining anecdotes, ones that would make her laugh out loud as she read them in her house in New Jersey. In time she would reveal the disappointment of her marriage, and he his. In this way their friendship would grow, and flourish. He would possess a picture of the two of them, eating fried onions under a magenta umbrella, which he would keep, he decided, safely tucked between the pages of his Russian grammar. As his mind raced, Mr. Kapasi experienced a mild and pleasant shock. It was similar to a feeling he used to experience long ago when, after months of translating with the aid of a dictionary, he would finally read a passage from a French novel, or an Italian sonnet, and understand the words, one after another, unencumbered by his own efforts. In those moments Mr. Kapasi used to believe that all was right with the world, that all struggles were rewarded, that all of life's mistakes made sense in the end. The promise that he would hear from Mrs. Das now filled him with the same belief.

When he finished writing his address Mr. Kapasi handed her the paper, but as soon as he did so he worried that he had either misspelled his name, or accidentally reversed the numbers of his postal code. He dreaded the possibility of a lost letter, the photograph never reaching him, hovering somewhere in Orissa, close but ultimately unattainable. He thought of asking for the slip of paper again, just to make sure he had written his address accurately, but Mrs. Das had already dropped it into the jumble of her bag.

They reached Konarak at two-thirty. The temple, made of sandstone, was a massive pyramid-like structure in the shape of a chariot. It was dedicated to the great master of life, the sun, which struck three sides of the edifice as it made its journey each day across the sky. Twenty-four giant wheels were carved on the north and south sides of the plinth. The whole thing was drawn by a team of seven horses, speeding as if through the heavens. As they approached, Mr. Kapasi explained that the temple had been built between A.D. 1243 and 1255, with the efforts of twelve hundred artisans, by the great ruler of the Ganga dynasty, King Narasimhadeva the First, to commemorate his victory against the Muslim army.

"It says the temple occupies about a hundred and seventy acres of land," Mr. Das said, reading from his book.

"It's like a desert," Ronny said, his eyes wandering across the sand that stretched on all sides beyond the temple.

"The Chandrabhaga River once flowed one mile north of here. It is dry now," Mr. Kapasi said, turning off the engine.

They got out and walked toward the temple, posing first for pictures by the pair of lions that flanked the steps. Mr. Kapasi led them next to one of the wheels of the chariot, higher than any human being, nine feet in diameter.

"'The wheels are supposed to symbolize the wheel of life,'" Mr. Das read. "'They depict the cycle of creation, preservation, and achievement of realization.' Cool." He turned the page of his book. "'Each wheel is divided into eight thick and thin spokes, dividing the day into eight equal parts. The rims are carved with designs of birds and animals, whereas the medallions in the spokes are carved with women in luxurious poses, largely erotic in nature.'"

What he referred to were the countless friezes of entwined naked bodies, making love in various positions, women clinging to the necks of men, their knees wrapped eternally around their lovers' thighs. In addition to these were assorted scenes from daily life, of hunting and trading, of deer being killed with bows and arrows and marching warriors holding swords in their hands.

It was no longer possible to enter the temple, for it had filled with rubble years ago, but they admired the exterior, as did all the tourists Mr. Kapasi brought there, slowly strolling along each of its sides. Mr. Das trailed behind, taking pictures. The children ran ahead, pointing to figures of naked people, intrigued in particular by the Nagamithunas, the half-human, half serpentine couples who were said, Mr. Kapasi told them, to live in the deepest waters of the sea. Mr. Kapasi was pleased that they liked the temple, pleased especially that it appealed to Mrs. Das. She stopped every three or four paces, staring silently at the carved lovers, and the processions of elephants, and the topless female musicians beating on two-sided drums.

Though Mr. Kapasi had been to the temple countless times, it occurred to him, as he, too, gazed at the topless women, that he had never seen his own wife fully naked. Even when they had made love she kept the panels of her blouse hooked together, the string of her petticoat knotted around her waist. He had never admired the backs of his wife's legs the way he now admired those of Mrs. Das, walking as if for his benefit alone. He had, of course, seen plenty of bare limbs before, belonging to the American and European ladies who took his tours. But Mrs. Das was different. Unlike the other women, who had an interest only in the temple, and kept their noses buried in a guidebook, or their eyes behind the lens of a camera, Mrs. Das had taken an interest in him.

Mr. Kapasi was anxious to be alone with her, to continue their private conversation, yet he felt nervous to walk at her side. She was lost behind her sunglasses, ignoring her husband's requests that she pose for another picture, walking past her children as if they were strangers. Worried that he might disturb her, Mr. Kapasi walked ahead, to admire, as he always did, the three life-sized bronze avatars of Surya, the sun god, each emerging from its own niche on the temple facade to greet the sun at dawn, noon, and evening. They wore elaborate headdresses, their languid, elongated eyes closed, their bare chests draped with carved chains and amulets. Hibiscus petals, offerings from previous visitors, were strewn at their gray-green feet. The last statue, on the northern wall of the temple, was Mr. Kapasi's favorite. This Surya had a tired expression, weary after a hard day of work, sitting astride a horse with folded legs. Even his horse's eyes were drowsy. Around his body were smaller sculptures of women in pairs, their hips thrust to one side.

"Who's that?" Mrs. Das asked. He was startled to see that she was standing beside him.

"He is the Astachala-Surya," Mr. Kapasi said. "The setting sun."

"So in a couple of hours the sun will set right here?" She slipped a foot out of one of her square-heeled shoes, rubbed her toes on the back of her other leg.

"That is correct."

She raised her sunglasses for a moment, then put them back on again. "Neat."

Mr. Kapasi was not certain exactly what the word suggested, but he had a feeling it was a favorable response. He hoped that Mrs. Das had understood Surya's beauty, his power. Perhaps they would discuss it further in their letters. He would explain things to her, things about India, and she would explain things to him about America. In its own way this correspondence would fulfill his dream, of serving as an interpreter between nations. He looked at her straw bag, delighted that his address lay nestled among its contents. When he pictured her so many thousands of miles away he plummeted, so much so that he had an overwhelming urge to wrap his arms around her, to freeze with her, even for an instant, in an embrace witnessed by his favorite Surya. But Mrs. Das had already started walking.

"When do you return to America?" he asked, trying to sound placid.

"In ten days."

He calculated: A week to settle in, a week to develop the pictures, a few days to compose her letter, two weeks to get to India by air. According to his schedule, allowing room for delays, he would hear from Mrs. Das in approximately six weeks' time.

The family was silent as Mr. Kapasi drove them back, a little past four-thirty, to Hotel Sandy Villa. The children had bought miniature granite versions of the chariot's wheels at a souvenir stand, and they turned them round in their hands. Mr. Das continued to read his book. Mrs. Das untangled Tina's hair with her brush and divided it into two little ponytails.

Mr. Kapasi was beginning to dread the thought of dropping them off. He was not prepared to begin his six-week wait to hear from Mrs. Das. As he stole glances at her in the rearview mirror, wrapping elastic bands around Tina's hair, he wondered how he might make the tour last a little longer. Ordinarily he sped back to Puri using a shortcut, eager to return home, scrub his feet and hands with sandalwood soap, and enjoy the evening newspaper and a cup of tea that his wife would serve him in silence. The thought of that silence, something to which he'd long been resigned, now oppressed him. It was then that he suggested visiting the hills at Udayagiri and Khandagiri, where a number of monastic dwellings were hewn out of the ground, facing one another across a defile. It was some miles away, but well worth seeing, Mr. Kapasi told them.

"Oh yeah, there's something mentioned about it in this book," Mr. Das said. "Built by a Jain king, or something."

"Shall we go then?" Mr. Kapasi asked. He paused at a turn in the road. "It's to the left."

Mr. Das turned to look at Mrs. Das. Both of them shrugged.

"Left, left," the children chanted.

Mr. Kapasi turned the wheel, almost delirious with relief. He did not know what he would do or say to Mrs. Das once they arrived at the hills. Perhaps he would tell her what a pleasing smile she had. Perhaps he would compliment her strawberry shirt, which he found irresistibly becoming. Perhaps, when Mr. Das was busy taking a picture, he would take her hand.

He did not have to worry. When they got to the hills, divided by a steep path thick with trees, Mrs. Das refused to get out of the car. All along the path, dozens of monkeys were seated on stones, as well as on the branches of the trees. Their hind legs were stretched out in front and raised to shoulder level, their arms resting on their knees.

"My legs are tired," she said, sinking low in her seat. "I'll stay here."

"Why did you have to wear those stupid shoes?" Mr. Das said. "You won't be in the pictures."

"Pretend I'm there."

"But we could use one of these pictures for our Christmas card this year. We didn't get one of all five of us at the Sun Temple. Mr. Kapasi could take it."

"I'm not coming. Anyway, those monkeys give me the creeps."

"But they're harmless," Mr. Das said. He turned to Mr. Kapasi. "Aren't they?"

"They are more hungry than dangerous," Mr. Kapasi said. "Do not provoke them with food, and they will not bother you."

Mr. Das headed up the defile with the children, the boys at his side, the little girl on his shoulders. Mr. Kapasi watched as they crossed paths with a Japanese man and woman, the only other tourists there, who paused for a final photograph, then stepped into a nearby car and drove away. As the car disappeared out of view some of the monkeys called out, emitting soft whooping sounds, and then walked on their flat black hands and feet up the path. At one point a group of them formed a little ring around Mr. Das and the children. Tina screamed in delight. Ronny ran in circles around his father. Bobby bent down and picked up a fat stick on the ground. When he extended it, one of the monkeys approached him and snatched it, then briefly beat the ground.

"I'll join them," Mr. Kapasi said, unlocking the door on his side. "There is much to explain about the caves."

"No. Stay a minute," Mrs. Das said. She got out of the back seat and slipped in beside Mr. Kapasi. "Raj has his dumb book anyway." Together, through the windshield, Mrs. Das and Mr. Kapasi watched as Bobby and the monkey passed the stick back and forth between them.

"A brave little boy," Mr. Kapasi commented.

"It's not so surprising," Mrs. Das said.

"No?"

"He's not his."

"I beg your pardon?"

"Raj's. He's not Raj's son."

Mr. Kapasi felt a prickle on his skin. He reached into his shirt pocket for the small tin of lotus-oil balm he carried with him at all times, and applied it to three spots on his forehead. He knew that Mrs. Das was watching him, but he did not turn to face her. Instead he watched as the figures of Mr. Das and the children grew smaller, climbing up the steep path, pausing every now and then for a picture, surrounded by a growing number of monkeys.

"Are you surprised?" The way she put it made him choose his words with care.

"It's not the type of thing one assumes," Mr. Kapasi replied slowly. He put the tin of lotus-oil balm back in his pocket.

"No, of course not. And no one knows, of course. No one at all. I've kept it a secret for eight whole years." She looked at Mr. Kapasi, tilting her chin as if to gain a fresh perspective. "But now I've told you."

Mr. Kapasi nodded. He felt suddenly parched, and his forehead was warm and slightly numb from the balm. He considered asking Mrs. Das for a sip of water, then decided against it.

"We met when we were very young," she said. She reached into her straw bag in search of something, then pulled out a packet of puffed rice. "Want some?"

"No, thank you."

She put a fistful in her mouth, sank into the seat a little, and looked away from Mr. Kapasi, out the window on her side of the car. "We married when we were still in college. We were in high school when he proposed. We went to the same college, of course. Back then we couldn't stand the thought of being separated, not for a day, not for a minute. Our parents were best friends who lived in the same town. My entire life I saw him every weekend, either at our house or theirs. We were sent upstairs to play together while our parents joked about our marriage. Imagine! They never caught us at anything, though in a way I think it was all more or less a setup. The things we did those Friday and Saturday nights, while our parents sat downstairs drinking tea . . . I could tell you stories, Mr. Kapasi."

As a result of spending all her time in college with Raj, she continued, she did not make many close friends. There was no one to confide in about him at the end of a difficult day, or to share a passing thought or a worry. Her parents now lived on the other side of the world, but she had never been very close to them, anyway. After marrying so young she was overwhelmed by it all, having a child so quickly, and nursing, and warming up bottles of milk and testing their temperature against her wrist while Raj was at work, dressed in sweaters and corduroy pants, teaching his students about rocks and dinosaurs. Raj never looked cross or harried, or plump as she had become after the first baby.

Always tired, she declined invitations from her one or two college girlfriends, to have lunch or shop in Manhattan. Eventually the friends stopped calling her, so that she was left at home all day with the baby, surrounded by toys that made her trip when she walked or wince when she sat, always cross and tired. Only occasionally did they go out after Ronny was born, and even more rarely did they entertain. Raj didn't mind; he looked forward to coming home from teaching and watching television and bouncing Ronny on his knee. She had been outraged when Raj told her that a Punjabi friend, someone whom she had once met but did not remember, would be staying with them for a week for some job interviews in the New Brunswick area.

Bobby was conceived in the afternoon, on a sofa littered with rubber teething toys, after the friend learned that a London pharmaceutical company had hired him, while Ronny cried to be freed from his playpen. She made no protest when the friend touched the small of her back as she was about to make a pot of coffee, then pulled her against his crisp navy suit. He made love to her swiftly, in silence, with an expertise she had never known, without the meaningful expressions and smiles Raj always insisted on afterward. The next day Raj drove the friend to JFK. He was married now, to a Punjabi girl, and they lived in London still, and every year they exchanged Christmas cards with Raj and Mina, each couple tucking photos of their families into the envelopes. He did not know that he was Bobby's father. He never would.

"I beg your pardon, Mrs. Das, but why have you told me this information?" Mr. Kapasi asked when she had finally finished speaking, and had turned to face him once again.

"For God's sake, stop calling me Mrs. Das. I'm twenty-eight. You probably have children my age."

"Not quite." It disturbed Mr. Kapasi to learn that she thought of him as a parent. The feeling he had had toward her, that had made him check his reflection in the rearview mirror as they drove, evaporated a little.

"I told you because of your talents." She put the packet of puffed rice back into her bag without folding over the top.

"I don't understand," Mr. Kapasi said.

"Don't you see? For eight years I haven't been able to express this to anybody, not to friends, certainly not to Raj. He doesn't even suspect it. He thinks I'm still in love with him. Well, don't you have anything to say?"

"About what?"

"About what I've just told you. About my secret, and about how terrible it makes me feel. I feel terrible looking at my children, and at

Raj, always terrible. I have terrible urges, Mr. Kapasi, to throw things away. One day I had the urge to throw everything I own out the window, the television, the children, everything. Don't you think it's unhealthy?"

He was silent.

"Mr. Kapasi, don't you have anything to say? I thought that was your job."

"My job is to give tours, Mrs. Das."

"Not that. Your other job. As an interpreter."

"But we do not face a language barrier. What need is there for an interpreter?"

"That's not what I mean. I would never have told you otherwise. Don't you realize what it means for me to tell you?"

"What does it mean?"

"It means that I'm tired of feeling so terrible all the time. Eight years, Mr. Kapasi, I've been in pain eight years. I was hoping you could help me feel better, say the right thing. Suggest some kind of remedy."

He looked at her, in her red plaid skirt and strawberry T-shirt, a woman not yet thirty, who loved neither her husband nor her children, who had already fallen out of love with life. Her confession depressed him, depressed him all the more when he thought of Mr. Das at the top of the path, Tina clinging to his shoulders, taking pictures of ancient monastic cells cut into the hills to show his students in America, unsuspecting and unaware that one of his sons was not his own. Mr. Kapasi felt insulted that Mrs. Das should ask him to interpret her common, trivial little secret. She did not resemble the patients in the doctor's office, those who came glassy-eyed and desperate, unable to sleep or breathe or urinate with ease, unable, above all, to give words to their pains. Still, Mr. Kapasi believed it was his duty to assist Mrs. Das. Perhaps he ought to tell her to confess the truth to Mr. Das. He would explain that honesty was the best policy. Honesty, surely, would help her feel better, as she'd put it. Perhaps he would offer to preside over the discussion, as a mediator. He decided to begin with the most obvious question, to get to the heart of the matter, and so he asked, "Is it really pain you feel, Mrs. Das, or is it guilt?"

She turned to him and glared, mustard oil thick on her frosty pink lips. She opened her mouth to say something, but as she glared at Mr. Kapasi some certain knowledge seemed to pass before her eyes, and she stopped. It crushed him; he knew at that moment that he was not even important enough to be properly insulted. She opened the car door and began walking up the path, wobbling a little on her square wooden heels, reaching into her straw bag to eat handfuls of puffed rice. It fell through her fingers, leaving a zigzagging trail, causing a monkey to leap down from a tree and devour the little white grains. In search of more, the monkey began to follow Mrs. Das. Others joined him, so that she was soon being followed by about half a dozen of them, their velvety tails dragging behind.

Mr. Kapasi stepped out of the car. He wanted to holler, to alert her in some way, but he worried that if she knew they were behind her, she would grow nervous. Perhaps she would lose her balance. Perhaps they would pull at her bag or her hair. He began to jog up the path, taking a fallen branch in his hand to scare away the monkeys. Mrs. Das continued walking, oblivious, trailing grains of puffed rice. Near the top of the incline, before a group of cells fronted by a row of squat stone pillars, Mr. Das was kneeling on the ground, focusing the lens of his camera. The children stood under the arcade, now hiding, now emerging from view.

"Wait for me," Mrs. Das called out. "I'm coming."

Tina jumped up and down. "Here comes Mommy!"

"Great," Mr. Das said without looking up. "Just in time. We'll get Mr. Kapasi to take a picture of the five of us."

Mr. Kapasi quickened his pace, waving his branch so that the monkeys scampered away, distracted, in another direction.

"Where's Bobby?" Mrs. Das asked when she stopped.

Mr. Das looked up from the camera. "I don't know. Ronny, where's Bobby?"

Ronny shrugged. "I thought he was right here."

"Where is he?" Mrs. Das repeated sharply. "What's wrong with all of you?"

They began calling his name, wandering up and down the path a bit. Because they were calling, they did not initially hear the boy's screams. When they found him, a little farther down the path under a tree, he was surrounded by a group of monkeys, over a dozen of them, pulling at his T-shirt with their long black fingers. The puffed rice Mrs. Das had spilled was scattered at his feet, raked over by the monkeys' hands. The boy was silent, his body frozen, swift tears running down his startled face. His bare legs were dusty and red with welts from where one of the monkeys struck him repeatedly with the stick he had given to it earlier.

"Daddy, the monkey's hurting Bobby," Tina said.

Mr. Das wiped his palms on the front of his shorts. In his nervousness he accidentally pressed the shutter on his camera; the whirring noise of the advancing film excited the monkeys, and the one with the stick began to beat Bobby more intently. "What are we supposed to do? What if they start attacking?"

"Mr. Kapasi," Mrs. Das shrieked, noticing him standing to one side. "Do something, for God's sake, do something!"

Mr. Kapasi took his branch and shooed them away, hissing at the ones that remained, stomping his feet to scare them. The animals retreated slowly, with a measured gait, obedient but unintimidated. Mr. Kapasi gathered Bobby in his arms and brought him back to where his parents and siblings were standing. As he carried him he was tempted to whisper a secret into the boy's ear. But Bobby was stunned, and shivering with fright, his legs bleeding slightly where the stick had broken the skin. When Mr. Kapasi delivered him to his parents, Mr. Das brushed some dirt off the boy's T-shirt and put the visor on him the right way. Mrs. Das reached into her straw bag to find a bandage which she taped over the cut on his knee. Ronny offered his brother a fresh piece of gum. "He's fine. Just a little scared, right, Bobby?" Mr. Das said, patting the top of his head.

"God, let's get out of here," Mrs. Das said. She folded her arms across the strawberry on her chest. "This place gives me the creeps."

"Yeah. Back to the hotel, definitely," Mr. Das agreed.

"Poor Bobby," Mrs. Das said. "Come here a second. Let Mommy fix your hair." Again she reached into her straw bag, this time for her hairbrush, and began to run it around the edges of the translucent visor. When she whipped out the hairbrush, the slip of paper with Mr. Kapasi's address on it fluttered away in the wind. No one but Mr. Kapasi noticed. He watched as it rose, carried higher and higher by the breeze, into the trees where the monkeys now sat, solemnly observing the scene below. Mr. Kapasi observed it too, knowing that this was the picture of the Das family he would preserve forever in his mind.

*—2000*

*Richard Van Camp (b. 1971) is a member of the Dogrib First Nation from Fort Smith, Northwest Territories. He has written a novel,* The Lesser Blessed *(1996), a collection of short stories,* Angel Wing Splash Pattern *(2002), and books for children in collaboration with Cree artist George Littlechild. Of his work, which has been widely anthologized and adapted for radio, he says, "I braid the oral tradition I grew up with and combine it with what I see today."*

## Richard Van Camp

# the uranium leaking from port radium and rayrock mines is killing us

and the girl with sharp knees sits in her underwear. She is shivering. The bus is cold. The man at the gun store has seagull eyes. Freckles grow on the wrong side of his face. This town has the biggest Canadian flag anywhere. It is always tangled and never waves. For grass this playground has human hair. It never grows on Sundays. The kids that play here are cold and wet. They are playing in their underwear. They are singing with cold tongues. They have only seven fingers to hide with.

Those are rotting clouds. This is the other side of rain. The band plays but there is no sound. I snap my finger but there is no sound.

There is someone running on the highway. There is no one in the field. Nobody knows the cats here. No one knows their names.

They are letting the librarian's right eye fuse shut. There is a pencil stabbed thru her bun. She can read "I didn't pop my balloon the grass did" in my library book. She looks into me. One eye is pink. The other is blue.

My father said take the bus. There is yellow tape around my house. A finger is caught in the engine but they only rev it harder. There are cold hands against my back. I want to kiss Pocahontas before she dies at age 21. Someone is stealing the dogs of this town while doctors hold babies high in black bags. My mother's voice is a dull marble rolling down her mouth, stolen to her lap, not even bouncing, not even once. She has sprayed metal into her hair. I am sitting on a red seat. My hands open with rawhide.

This is the ear I bled from. There is a child walking in the field. He is walking with a black gun.

In my girlfriend's fist is a promise. She does not raise herself to meet me. Her socks are always dirty. She is selling me a broken bed so she can lie on plywood. Her feet are always cold. The coffee we drink is cold. The bus driver does not wave goodbye. Why are there only children on this bus? Why are we wet and cold? Why are we only in our underwear?

I want to run but I have no legs. The tongue that slides from my mouth is blue.

Friday is the loneliest day of the week she says. The blanket she knitted this winter is torn upon us. She laughs at me with blue eyes. She says if you walk in the rain no one can tell you're crying. The soup we drink after is cold. The popcorn we eat after is cold. Someone is crying in the basement. Someone is crying next door.

The dream we have is something running on four legs, running on pavement towards us. It is running from the highway. It is a dead caribou running on dead legs. I meet its eyes but there are only antlers. In between the antlers is an eye. It too is cold and watching. Its eye is the color of blue.

The plants here have no flowers. The trees themselves are black. The fish are rolling sideways. Rain has started to fall.

The child with the black gun sees my house. He is walking back wards towards me. He swings his head. His eyes are blue. *Can you please sing with me?*

The bus driver does not wave goodbye.

The band is playing but all I hear is galloping.

I snap my finger.

My eyes are blue.

All I can hear is galloping . . .

*—1996*

**Author's Note:**

For those of you who don't know, the Northwest Territories was home to the world's first uranium mine: Port Radium (1932–1960), located in Sahtu Dene territory. The uranium that was used by the US Government to develop the World War II Atom Bomb technology and ferocity behind the detonation over Hiroshima and Nagasaki came from a number of places: American and African mines and Port Radium. The US Government ordered 918 tonnes of uranium from Port Radium. Later, Uranium 2308 was harvested from Rayrock mines (1955–1957) in Dogrib territory in the NWT and was sold to Atomic Research of

Canada. Despite the Canadian government's knowledge in 1931 and 1932 of the serious health hazards associated with exposure to the dust from high-grade radioactive ores, Dene men, referred to as "coolies," were used to transport the radioactive ore along the 2,100-kilometre route called the "Highway of the Atom" without warnings. Many of the Dene later developed cancer. Additionally, 1.7 million tons of radioactive tailings were dumped into the Sahtu (Great Bear Lake)—the ninth largest lake in the world and home to the world's largest trout fishing.

---

**Madeleine Thien (b. 1974)** *is the Vancouver-born daughter of Chinese-Malaysian immigrants, who cites Alice Munro, Michael Ondaatje, and Michael Ignatieff as important literary influences. Her first collection of stories, the award-winning* Simple Recipes *(2001), explores the complexity of relationships, often from a child's perspective. Her debut novel,* Certainty *(2006), takes readers to wartorn Asia in search of answers. Thien, whose fiction illustrates her belief that humans "can understand each other," has also written for children and now makes her home in Quebec City.*

## *Madeleine Thien*
# Simple Recipes

There is a simple recipe for making rice. My father taught it to me when I was a child. Back then, I used to sit up on the kitchen counter watching him, how he sifted the grains in his hands, sure and quick, removing pieces of dirt or sand, tiny imperfections. He swirled his hands through the water and it turned cloudy. When he scrubbed the grains clean, the sound was as big as a field of insects. Over and over, my father rinsed the rice, drained the water, then filled the pot again.

The instructions are simple. Once the washing is done, you measure the water this way—by resting the tip of your index finger on the surface of the rice. The water should reach the bend of your first knuckle. My father did not need instructions or measuring cups. He closed his eyes and felt for the waterline.

Sometimes I still dream my father, his bare feet flat against the floor, standing in the middle of the kitchen. He wears old buttoned shirts and faded sweatpants drawn at the waist. Surrounded by the gloss of the kitchen counters, the sharp angles of the stove, the fridge, the shiny sink, he looks out of place. This memory of him is so strong, sometimes it stuns me, the detail with which I can see it.

Every night before dinner, my father would perform this ritual—rinsing and draining, then setting the pot in the cooker. When I was older, he passed this task on to me but I never did it with the same care. I went through the motions, splashing the water around, jabbing my finger down to measure the water level. Some nights the rice was a mushy gruel. I worried that I could not do so simple a task right. "Sorry," I would say to the table, my voice soft and embarrassed. In answer, my father would keep eating, pushing the rice into his mouth as if he never expected anything different, as if he noticed no difference between what he did so well and I so poorly. He would eat every last mouthful, his chopsticks walking quickly across the plate. Then he would rise, whistling, and clear the table, every motion so clean and sure, I would be convinced by him that all was well in the world.

My father is standing in the middle of the kitchen. In his right hand he holds a plastic bag filled with water. Caught inside the bag is a live fish.

The fish is barely breathing, though its mouth opens and closes. I reach up and touch it through the plastic bag, trailing my fingers along the gills, the soft, muscled body, pushing my finger overtop the eyeball. The fish looks straight at me, flopping sluggishly from side to side.

My father fills the kitchen sink. In one swift motion he overturns the bag and the fish comes sailing out with the water. It curls and jumps. We watch it closely, me on my tiptoes, chin propped up on the counter. The fish is the length of my arm from wrist to elbow. It floats in place, brushing up against the sides of the sink.

I keep watch over the fish while my father begins the preparations for dinner. The fish folds its body, trying to turn or swim, the water nudging overtop. Though I ripple tiny circles around it with my fingers, the fish stays still, bobbing side-to-side in the cold water.

For many hours at a time, it was just the two of us. While my mother worked and my older brother played outside, my father and I sat on the couch, flipping channels. He loved cooking shows. We watched *Wok with Yan*, my father passing judgement on Yan's methods. I was enthralled when Yan transformed orange peels into swans. My father sniffed. "I can do that," he said. "You don't have to be a genius to do that." He placed a sprig of green onion in water and showed me how it bloomed like a flower. "I know many tricks like this," he said. "Much more than Yan."

Still, my father made careful notes when Yan demonstrated Peking Duck. He chuckled heartily at Yan's punning. "Take a wok on the wild side!" Yan said, pointing his spatula at the camera.

"Ha ha!" my father laughed, his shoulders shaking. "*Wok* on the wild side!"

In the mornings, my father took me to school. At three o'clock, when we came home again, I would rattle off everything I learned that day. "The brachiosaurus," I informed him, "eats only soft vegetables."

My father nodded. "That is like me. Let me see your forehead." We stopped and faced each other in the road. "You have a high forehead," he said, leaning down to take a closer look. "All smart people do."

I walked proudly, stretching my legs to match his steps. I was over-joyed when my feet kept time with his, right, then left, then right, and we walked like a single unit. My father was the man of tricks, who sat for an hour mining a watermelon with a circular spoon, who carved the rind into a castle.

My father was born in Malaysia and he and my mother immigrated to Canada several years before I was born, first settling in Montreal, then finally in Vancouver. While I was born into the persistence of the Vancouver rain, my father was born in the wash of a monsoon country. When I was young, my parents tried to teach me their language but it never came easily to me. My father ran his thumb gently over my mouth, his face kind, as if trying to see what it was that made me different.

My brother was born in Malaysia but when he immigrated with my parents to Canada the language left him. Or he forgot it, or he refused it, which is also common, and this made my father angry. "How can a child forget a language?" he would ask my mother. "It is because the child is lazy. Because the child chooses not to remember." When he was twelve years old, my brother stayed away in the afternoons. He drummed the soccer ball up and down the back alley, returning home only at dinner time. During the day, my mother worked as a sales clerk at the Woodward's store downtown, in the building with the red revolv-ing W on top.

In our house, the ceilings were yellowed with grease. Even the air was heavy with it. I remember that I loved the weight of it, the air that was dense with the smell of countless meals cooked in a tiny kitchen, all those good smells jostling for space.

The fish in the sink is dying slowly. It has a glossy sheen to it, as if its skin is made of shining minerals. I want to prod it with both hands, its body tense against the pressure of my fingers. If I hold it tightly, I imagine I will be able to feel its fluttering heart. Instead, I lock eyes with the fish. *You're feeling verrrry sleepy*, I tell it. *You're getting verrrry tired.*

Beside me, my father chops green onions quickly. He uses a cleaver that he says is older than I am by many years. The blade of the knife rolls forward and backward, loops of green onion gathering in a pyramid beside my father's wrist. When he is done, he rolls his sleeve back from his right hand, reaches in through the water and pulls the plug.

The fish in the sink floats and we watch it in silence. The water level falls beneath its gills, beneath its belly. It drains and leaves the sink dry. The fish is lying on its side, mouth open and its body heaving. It leaps sideways and hits the sink. Then up again. It curls and snaps, lunging for its own tail. The fish sails into the air, dropping hard. It twitches violently.

My father reaches in with his bare hands. He lifts the fish out by the tail and lays it gently on the counter.

While holding it steady with one hand, he hits the head with the flat of the cleaver. The fish falls still and he begins to clean it.

In my apartment, I keep the walls scrubbed clean. I open the windows and turn the fan on whenever I prepare a meal. My father bought me a rice cooker when I first moved into my own apartment, but I use it so rarely it stays in the back of the cupboard, the cord wrapped neatly around its belly. I have no longing for the meals themselves, but I miss the way we sat down together, our bodies leaning hungrily forward while my father, the magician, unveiled plate after plate. We laughed and ate, white steam fogging my mother's glasses until she had to take them off and lay them on the table. Eyes closed, she would eat, crunchy vegetables gripped in her chopsticks, the most vivid green.

My brother comes into the kitchen and his body is covered with dirt. He leaves a thin trail of it behind as he walks. The soccer ball, muddy from outside, is encircled in one arm. Brushing past my father, his face is tense.

Beside me, my mother sprinkles garlic onto the fish. She lets me slide one hand underneath the fish's head, cradling it, then bending it backwards so that she can fill the fish's insides with ginger. Very carefully, I turn the fish over. It is firm and slippery, and beaded with tiny, sharp scales.

At the stove, my father picks up an old teapot. It is full of oil and he pours the oil into the wok. It falls in a thin ribbon. After a moment, when the oil begins crackling, he lifts the fish up and drops it down into the wok. He adds water and the smoke billows up. The sound of the fish frying is like tires on gravel, a sound so loud it drowns out all other noises. Then my father steps out from the smoke. "Spoon out the rice," he says as he lifts me down from the counter.

My brother comes back into the room, his hands muddy and his knees the colour of dusty brick. His soccer shorts flutter against the backs of his legs. Sitting down, he makes an angry face. My father ignores him.

Inside the cooker, the rice is flat like a pie. I push the spoon in, turning the rice over, and the steam shoots up in a hot mist and condenses on my skin. While my father moves his arms delicately over the stove, I begin dishing the rice out: first for my father, then my mother, then my brother, then myself. Behind me the fish is cooking quickly. In a crockery pot, my father steams cauliflower, stirring it round and round.

My brother kicks at a table leg.

"What's the matter?" my father asks.

He is quiet for a moment, then he says, "Why do we have to eat fish?"

"You don't like it?"

My brother crosses his arms against his chest. I see the dirt lining his arms, dark and hardened. I imagine chipping it off his body with a small spoon.

"I don't like the eyeball there. It looks sick."

My mother tuts. Her nametag is still clipped to her blouse. It says *Woodward's*, and then, *Sales Clerk*. "Enough," she says, hanging her purse on the back of the chair. "Go wash your hands and get ready for supper."

My brother glares, just for a moment. Then he begins picking at the dirt on his arms. I bring plates of rice to the table. The dirt flies off his skin, speckling the tablecloth. "Stop it," I say crossly.

"*Stop it,*" he says, mimicking me.

"Hey!" My father hits his spoon against the counter. It *pings*, high-pitched. He points at my brother. "No fighting in this house."

My brother looks at the floor, mumbles something, and then shuffles away from the table. As he moves farther away, he begins to stamp his feet.

Shaking her head, my mother takes her jacket off. It slides from her shoulders. She says something to my father in the language I can't understand. He merely shrugs his shoulders. And then he replies, and I think his words are so familiar, as if they are words I should know, as if maybe I did know them once but then I forgot them. The language that they speak is full of soft vowels, words running together so that I can't make out the gaps where they pause for breath.

My mother told me once about guilt. Her own guilt she held in the palm of her hands, like an offering. But your guilt is different, she said. You do not need to hold on to it. Imagine this, she said, her hands running along my forehead, then up into my hair. Imagine, she said. Picture it, and what do you see?

A bruise on the skin, wide and black.

A bruise, she said. Concentrate on it. Right now, it's a bruise. But if you concentrate, you can shrink it, compress it to the size of a pinpoint. And then, if you want to, if you see it, you can blow it off your body like a speck of dirt.

She moved her hands along my forehead.

I tried to picture what she said. I pictured blowing it away like so much nothing, just these little pieces that didn't mean anything, this complicity that I could magically walk away from. She made me believe in the strength of my own thoughts, as if I could make appear what had never existed. Or turn it around. Flip it over so many times you just lose sight of it, you lose the tail end and the whole thing disappears into smoke.

My father pushes at the fish with the edge of his spoon. Underneath, the meat is white and the juice runs down along the side. He lifts a piece and lowers it carefully onto my plate.

Once more, his spoon breaks skin. Gingerly, my father lifts another piece and moves it towards my brother.

"I don't want it," my brother says.

My father's hand wavers. "Try it," he says, smiling. "Take a wok on the wild side."

"No."

My father sighs and places the piece on my mother's plate. We eat in silence, scraping our spoons across the dishes. My parents use chopsticks, lifting their bowls and motioning the food into their mouths. The smell of food fills the room.

Savouring each mouthful, my father eats slowly, head tuned to the flavours in his mouth. My mother takes her glasses off, the lenses fogged, and lays them on the table. She eats with her head bowed down, as if in prayer.

Lifting a stem of cauliflower to his lips, my brother sighs deeply. He chews, and then his face changes. I have a sudden picture of him drowning, his hair waving like grass. He coughs, spitting the mouthful back onto his plate. Another cough. He reaches for his throat, choking.

My father slams his chopsticks down on the table. In a single movement, he reaches across, grabbing my brother by the shoulder. "I have tried," he is saying. "I don't know what kind of son you are. To be so ungrateful." His other hand sweeps by me and bruises into my brother's face.

My mother flinches. My brother's face is red and his mouth is open. His eyes are wet.

Still coughing, he grabs a fork, tines aimed at my father, and then in an unthinking moment, he heaves it at him. It strikes my father in the chest and drops.

"I hate you! You're just an asshole, you're just a fucking asshole chink!" My brother holds his plate in his hands. He smashes it down and his food scatters across the table. He is coughing and spitting. "I wish you weren't my father! I wish you were dead."

My father's hand falls again. This time pounding downwards. I close my eyes. All I can hear is someone screaming. There is a loud voice. I stand awkwardly, my hands covering my eyes.

"Go to your room," my father says, his voice shaking.

And I think he is talking to me so I remove my hands.

But he is looking at my brother. And my brother is looking at him, his small chest heaving.

A few minutes later, my mother begins clearing the table, face weary as she scrapes the dishes one by one over the garbage.

I move away from my chair, past my mother, onto the carpet and up the stairs.

Outside my brother's bedroom, I crouch against the wall. When I step forward and look, I see my father holding the bamboo pole between his hands. The pole is smooth. The long grains, fine as hair, are pulled together, at intervals, jointed. My brother is lying on the floor, as if thrown down and dragged there. My father raises the pole into the air.

I want to cry out. I want to move into the room between them, but I can't.

It is like a tree falling, beginning to move, a slow arc through the air.

The bamboo drops silently. It rips the skin on my brother's back. I cannot hear any sound. A line of blood edges quickly across his body.

The pole rises and again comes down. I am afraid of bones breaking.

My father lifts his arms once more.

On the floor, my brother cries into the carpet, pawing at the ground. His knees folded into his chest, the crown of his head burrowing down. His back is hunched over and I can see his spine, little bumps on his skin.

The bamboo smashes into bone and the scene in my mind bursts into a million white pieces.

My mother picks me up off the floor, pulling me across the hall, into my bedroom, into bed. Everything is wet, the sheets, my hands, her body, my face, and she soothes me with words I cannot understand because all I can hear is screaming. She rubs her cool hands against my forehead. "Stop," she says. "Please stop," but I feel loose, deranged, as if everything in the known world is ending right here.

In the morning, I wake up to the sound of oil in the pan and the smell of French toast. I can hear my mother bustling around, putting dishes in the cupboards.

No one says anything when my brother doesn't come down for breakfast. My father piles French toast and syrup onto a plate and my mother pours a glass of milk. She takes everything upstairs to my brother's bedroom.

As always, I follow my father around the kitchen. I track his footprints, follow behind him and hide in the shadow of his body. Every so often, he reaches down and ruffles my hair with his hands. We cast a spell, I think. The way we move in circles, how he cooks without thinking because this is the task that comes to him effortlessly. He smiles down at me, but when he does this, it somehow breaks the spell. My father stands in place, hands dropping to his sides as if he has forgotten what he was doing mid-motion. On the walls, the paint is peeling and the floor, unswept in days, leaves little pieces of dirt stuck to our feet.

My persistence, I think, my unadulterated love, confuse him. With each passing day, he knows I will find it harder to ignore what I can't comprehend, that I will be unable to separate one part of him from another. The unconditional quality of my love for him will not last forever, just as my brother's did not. My father stands in the middle of the kitchen, unsure. Eventually, my mother comes downstairs again and puts her arms around him and holds him, whispering something to him, words that to me are meaningless and incomprehensible. But she offers them to him, sound after sound, in a language that was stolen from some other place, until he drops his head and remembers where he is.

Later on, I lean against the door frame upstairs and listen to the sound of a metal fork scraping against a dish. My mother is already there, her voice rising and falling. She is moving the fork across the plate, offering my brother pieces of French toast.

I move towards the bed, the carpet scratchy, until I can touch the wooden bed-frame with my hands.

My mother is seated there, and I go to her, reaching my fingers out to the buttons on her cuff and twisting them over to catch the light.

"Are you eating?" I ask my brother.

He starts to cry. I look at him, his face half hidden in the blankets.

"Try and eat," my mother says softly.

He only cries harder but there isn't any sound. The pattern of sunlight on his blanket moves with his body. His hair is pasted down with sweat and his head moves forward and backward like an old man's.

At some point I know my father is standing at the entrance of the room but I cannot turn to look at him. I want to stay where I am, facing the wall. I'm afraid that if I turn around and go to him, I will be complicit, accepting a portion of guilt, no matter how small that piece. I do not know how to prevent this from happening again, though now I know, in the end, it will break us apart. This violence will turn all my love to shame and grief. So I stand there, not looking at him or my brother.

Even my father, the magician, who can make something beautiful out of nothing, he just stands and watches.

A face changes over time, it becomes clearer. In my father's face, I have seen everything pass. Anger that has stripped it of anything recognizable, so that it is only a face of bones and skin. And then, at other times, so much pain that it is unbearable, his face so full of grief it might dissolve. How to reconcile all that I know of him and still love him? For a long time, I thought it was not possible. When I was a child, I did not love my father because he was complicated, because he was human, because he needed me to. A child does not know yet how to love a person that way.

How simple it should be. Warm water running over, the feel of the grains between my hands, the sound of it like stones running along the pavement. My father would rinse the rice over and over, sifting it between his fingertips, searching for the impurities, pulling them out. A speck, barely visible, resting on the tip of his finger.

If there were some recourse, I would take it. A cupful of grains in my open hand, a smoothing out, finding the impurities, then removing them piece by piece. And then, to be satisfied with what remains.

Somewhere in my memory, a fish in the sink is dying slowly. My father and I watch as the water runs down.

*—2001*

# Credits

# Index of Critical Terms